THIS STRANGE

EVENTFUL

HISTORY

THIS STRANGE
EVENTFUL
HISTORY

A NOVEL

CLAIRE MESSUD

W. W. NORTON & COMPANY

Independent Publishers Since 1923

Excerpt from *The Way of Abū Madyan* compiled and translated by Vincent J. Cornell.
© 1996 The Islamic Texts Society. Used with the publisher's permission.

For information about permission to reproduce selections from this book, write to
Permissions, W. W. Norton & Company, Inc., 500 Fifth Avenue, New York, NY 10110

For information about special discounts for bulk purchases, please contact
W. W. Norton Special Sales at specialsales@wwnorton.com or 800-233-4830

Manufacturing by Lakeside Book Company
Book design by Chris Welch
Production manager: Anna Oler

ISBN 978-0-393-63504-1

W. W. Norton & Company, Inc., 500 Fifth Avenue, New York, N.Y. 10110
www.wwnorton.com

W. W. Norton & Company Ltd., 15 Carlisle Street, London W1D 3BS

1 2 3 4 5 6 7 8 9 0

For my family

And one man in his time plays many parts,
His acts being seven ages.

—WILLIAM SHAKESPEARE, *As You Like It*

His life, in which nothing, absolutely nothing, happened. He embarked on no adventures, he was in no war. He was never in prison, he never killed anyone. He neither won nor lost a fortune. All he ever did was live in this century. But that alone was enough to give his life *dimension*, both of feeling and of thought.

—ELIAS CANETTI, *Notes from Hampstead*

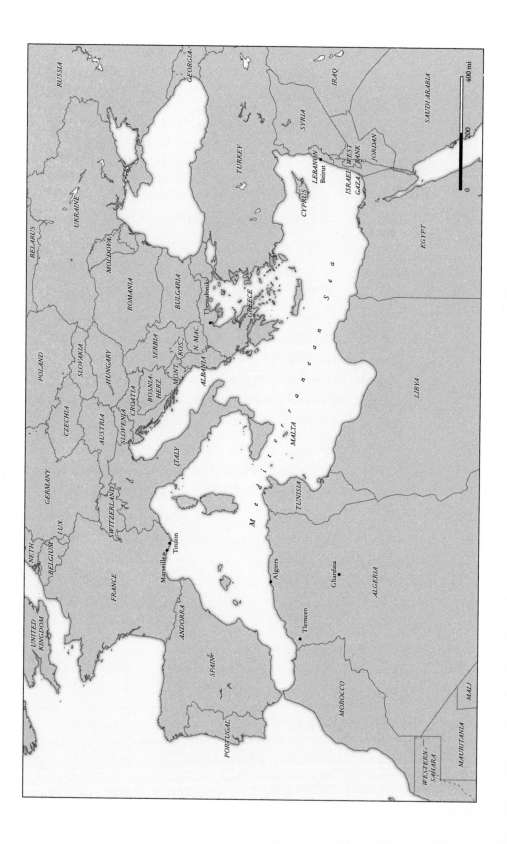

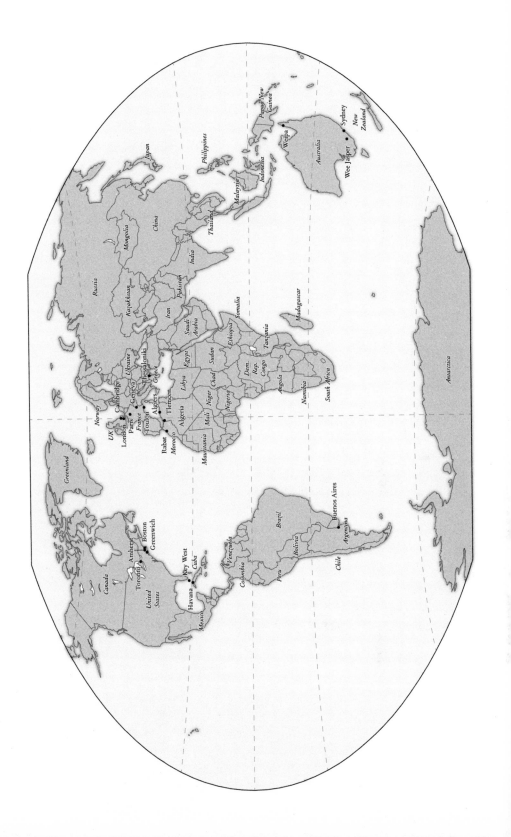

THIS STRANGE

EVENTFUL

HISTORY

PROLOGUE

I'm a writer; I tell stories. Of course, really, I want to save lives. Or simply: I want to save life.

Seven years, the clairvoyant said, that summer afternoon already long ago. Seven years in the Valley of the Shadow. The sunlight through the window behind her head transformed her rusty curls into a golden nimbus. We sat opposite each other over a card table in the front room of her chintzy saltbox, a mile from the waterfront in a seaside New England holiday town. Like most of her clients, I was just passing through. Though I told her I was a writer, she insisted that I was a healer; once she said it, I willed it to be true. Or: I realized I had always willed it to be true, though we're told that poetry makes nothing happen. My desire, as old as humanity, to make words signify.

Seven years' journey in the shadow of Death: at the time of her prophecy, I was almost halfway through, if one counted from the family trip to my late grandparents' home in Toulon, France, to celebrate my father's seventy-fifth—a work, as was said, of colossal administration, a gathering that was also an unraveling: my father in physical collapse, my mother, gaunt, in mental disarray, my aunt dancing in ever tighter circles around her bottle of whiskey, our children, still small, antic in the Mediterranean sun. But the count could have started sooner—from the time my mother could no longer manage to prepare a full meal; or the time, well before, when she could no longer keep track of the kids' birthdays; or, before that still, when she couldn't, for even an hour, manage the kids themselves. . . . But if I start at the end and count backward—*the end* being the last death, my aunt's death, fast on the heels of my mother's, neither death long after my father's—then the Cape clairvoyant held my trembling hand in hers truly at the midpoint.

I'm a writer; I tell stories. I want to tell the stories of their lives. It doesn't really matter where I start. We're always in the middle; wherever we stand, we see only partially. I know also that everything is connected, the constellations of our lives moving together in harmony and disharmony. The past swirls along with and inside the present, and all time exists at once, around us. The ebb and flow, the harmonies and dissonance—the music happens, whether or not we describe it. A story is not a line; it is a richer thing, one that circles and eddies, rises and falls, repeats upon itself.

And so this story—the story of my family—has many possible beginnings, or none: Mare Nostrum, Saint Augustine, Abd el-Kader, Charles de Gaulle, my grandparents, L'Arba, my father, my aunt, Zohra Drif, my mother, Albert Camus, Toronto, Cambridge, Toulon, Tlemcen, oh, Tlemcen: all and each a part of the vast and intricate web. Any version only partial.

Or I could begin with my birth, or my father's birth or his father's birth, or my mother's or grandmother's. I could begin with the secrets and shame, the ineffable shame that in telling their story I would wish at last to heal. The shame of the family history, of the history into which we were born. (How to forget that after attending the birth of his first grandson, my father, elderly then, tripped on the curb and fell in the street, a toppled mountain, and as he lay with the white down of his near-bald head in the gutter's muck he muttered not "Help me" but "I'm sorry, I'm sorry, I'm sorry"?) I could begin, of course, with the aloneness.

Or I could begin with the fact that the owner of our local pizzeria and our former next-door neighbor is an Algerian man whose surname is also the name of the provincial Algerian town of his ancestors, the same town in which my *pied-noir* grandmother taught at the girls' school in her youth, in the years before she married—years that were, in her case, numerous, because she didn't marry until her mid-thirties, then an age by which women were deemed unmarriageable. She might even have taught my neighbor's grandmother or great-grandmother. Or I could begin with the fact that the beloved Lebanese friends of my grandfather's prewar posting in Beirut include the great-uncle of a dear friend of mine in this American life almost a century later, whose daughter played with our son from the time they were round-limbed toddlers. Or I could begin with the angels on my father's last journey to death, the witnesses to his many lives who appeared, sentinels and guides, along that final path, to guide him, the ultimately homeless, to his eternal home . . .

It doesn't matter so much where this story begins as *that it begins.* And if, as I've come to understand, the story is infinitely expanding, rather than a line or thread, then wherever I start is merely that—not *the beginning* but a mere moment, *a way of happening, a mouth* . . .

PART I

✣

L'ARBA, ALGERIA

François, writing a letter to his father, who was far away, decided
to print instead of using cursive: just in case Papa had not heard
the news—he was in Greece, after all, and not in France—François
would tell him. He wrote very carefully in all caps: THE GERMANS HAVE
CROSSED THE GATES OF PARIS. THIS IS THE NEWS WITH WHICH MAMAN
WOKE ME THIS MORNING.

François knew that Paris was the heart of their glorious nation,
though he'd never been there of course. Not quite nine years old, he
had only recently returned with his mother, his aunt Tata Jeanne, and
his little sister, Denise, known as Poupette, to stay with their extended
family in Algeria—the place Maman and Papa called "home"!—from
Salonica, where his father was the naval attaché at the French consulate.
The boy had seen photos of Paris—the Champs-Élysées, the Tour Eif-
fel, Notre Dame—and when Maman had spoken of the "gates" of that
city, he'd pictured the Arc de Triomphe. But then it occurred to him
that in this case the arch of triumph was an arch of defeat; or, rather, it
was an arch of Hitler's triumph, which was very, very unspeakably bad.
He would not draw the Arc de Triomphe in the letter for Papa, because
that would make everyone sad, including Papa. And Maman had said
they all needed only to be happy for Papa, to be *la famille du sourire*,
because he would be worrying so much about them, being so far away,

especially when, because of the war, they could not contact him by telephone or telegram. He would need to know they were doing very well, sending love and kisses—and photos. Maman had asked Tata Paulette, Papa's brother's wife, to take their photo, Maman, Poupette, and him, so they could send it to Papa. In one version they all looked serious and in another they smiled and made silly faces, but in both photos François's ears stuck out madly like jug handles and he was embarrassed by that.

Should he not write about the Germans? That wasn't cheerful news, not *la famille du sourire*; but it was true, wasn't it, and wasn't that the most important thing? Never lie, he had always been taught. But what if *la famille du sourire* wasn't happy, actually? What if Maman was sick and always tired and there didn't seem to be room for them anywhere to live and no money and sometimes not enough to eat? Were they supposed to pretend to Papa that it was nice in L'Arba and that they were enjoying themselves?

Before they had to leave, they'd been living as a family almost a year in Salonica; but France was in danger from the Germans, advancing so quickly across Europe, and when Papa hurried them onto the train in Salonica, Mussolini's Italy was on the verge of entering the war on the Nazi side. Their train had had to cross Italy—hurry, hurry, before they were officially the enemy—and then they traveled through France to Marseille, where they caught the boat home to Algiers.

"Home"! Maman and Papa had always talked about how much they loved Algiers, how much a part of them it was, how he and Denise would love it too, the most beautiful city on earth, its shining white buildings rising in a crescent around the glittering Mediterranean. But when they got there, he'd hardly noticed what it looked like, just that it was very hot. None of their relatives wanted to keep them, which was why they'd ended up kilometers away in the dusty little town of L'Arba, staying with Tata Baudry, who was his father's aunt or his mother's aunt or maybe his dead grandmother's aunt, but mostly very old indeed. At least she was kind.

On the back of the piece of paper, François drew for his father a picture of the trench they'd dug the previous day in the garden. He couldn't draw the mud, how it had rained overnight and filled the bottom of the trench with water, so he just drew it plain and used a lot of brown pencil to color it in. When they had dug it—he and Maman, really, because Tata Baudry was too old and Tata Jeanne too unwell and Poupette uselessly too young; and he mostly of course, because Maman quickly got one of her headaches and had to go inside to lie down—it had seemed enormous, absolutely big enough for all of them to hide in if the planes came. But the next morning, after the rain, it was as if it had shrunk, and he could see that it was only a fraction of the size they'd need. Maybe even too small for Poupette and him. He felt discouraged, and cross; but then Maman told him it was still wonderful, a good contribution to the war effort, and please could he sit at the table and write to Papa to tell him, because Papa, far away in Salonica, defending France, would want to know everything.

Maman made Poupette sit next to him, and told her to write something too, which was ridiculous because she could barely write her own name—she did half the letters backward anyway—and of course now she'd ended up drawing a picture of the cats, who weren't even Tata Baudry's cats; they belonged to the lady upstairs with the enormous white jelly arms who yelled at them out her window almost every time they played in the garden. One cat was black and white; the other was tortoiseshell, which was hard to draw, and Poupette drew that cat, Nanette, as orange. Which was wrong. He simply pointed this out to her and she burst into tears, her eyes enormous and her lashes wet and sticky behind her glasses.

"Cut the waterworks," he said under his breath, not wanting to bother Maman, who was again lying down in Tata Baudry's bedroom; but that only prompted Poupette to wail.

"Did you know," he said in his nicest big brother voice, trying to distract her, "that Nanette has to be a girl cat because tortoiseshell cats are only ever girl cats."

Poupette made as if to scrunch up the paper. "You told me she's all wrong. Why can't she be an orange cat? She could be an orange cat."

He put the flat of his hand on top of her drawing. "Your drawing is beautiful. Papa will love it. We don't want to wake up Maman and there isn't any more paper, so please, please don't ruin it. You don't want to ruin your present for Papa, do you?"

Poupette shook her head and slipped her grubby thumb into her mouth. With her other hand she fingered the end of her blond braid, then twirled the braid slowly, stroking the strands. By this he knew the storm had been averted. Looking again at his drawing of the trench, he sighed: just as the trench itself in the morning light had seemed inadequate, so too the picture now just looked like a brown box, rather than a trench. He wondered whether to draw grass around it; but that wouldn't actually be accurate, as the garden was really mostly dirt, reddish dirt, with a few weeds, and in the corner a raised bed for vegetables and at the bottom by the fence the coop for the three chickens. None of that could he draw, certainly not on the same paper on which he was also writing his letter. If he drew grass, just to show how the trench was different from what surrounded it, he would be guilty of the same falsehood as Poupette when she drew the cat as orange.

Did Papa need to know everything exactly? Would it be dishonest, like a lie, to draw something that wasn't there? He decided to leave the trench alone in the middle of the page and instead to explain it in words. "*Voilà*," he wrote, "this is our trench that we dug, mostly me. But then the rain came and now the whole thing is in a mess. We may not fit." He paused, sucked his pen. His sister had slipped off her chair and crept over to the sofa, where she curled up with her head against Tata Baudry's black serge side, and continued to suck her thumb and twirl her braid, thoughtfully. François could tell that she was annoying Tata Baudry, who had been knitting but now could not, because her needle would have poked at Poupette and besides, Poupette's head was weighing on Tata Baudry's arm.

François was hungry. He knew that in the bread bin there was still the nub of the baguette from lunch; and he knew exactly how much honey remained in the jar in the cupboard. But this was not Salonica or Beirut, where they'd lived for years before Greece, and where his friends and his happy memories were. There, when he got home from school each day, the housekeeper Monica or his Tata Jeanne, his mother's invalid sister who lived with them, would slather slabs of toast with butter and jam for *goûter* and urge him to have another piece if he felt like it, because he was a growing boy. If he closed his eyes he could imagine himself back in the kitchen in Beirut—Beirut was his dream, much better than Salonica— with Guy and Jérémy, his best pals from school, all stuffing their faces and laughing, talking about going swimming at the club or maybe him even boasting about the officers' families' summer camp in the mountains, where he could waken at dawn and from the window gaze out over the valley to the city and the sea beyond, the fresh, dry breeze kissing his cheeks and his forearms before the sun rose hot in the sky. Those summer days, long and so free, all the navy kids playing, exploring, building their forts and staging battles, pausing only for lunch, everyone together, adults and children, at long tables in the refectory, waited on by the sailors in their whites, bearing large round trays above their shoulders as if service were an elegant, choreographed dance, their wide trousers swishing . . . and the lemon squash he so loved, just the right amount of sugar, not too pulpy—it was never as good anywhere else. His mouth watered at the memory; but of course it was just a memory. Here there were lemons but no sugar, and the honey too precious, Maman explained, to waste on sweet drinks.

"Here" was France—Algeria of course, but Algeria *was* France—and this was home, apparently, and François was supposed to feel happy and safe, or as safe as anyone could feel right now, Maman said, referring, he knew, to the war. This was where his family belonged, and where they had been from for a hundred years, Maman told him, and Papa had written a letter expressly and only to him to say how much he hoped François would like Algiers and feel at home there, because it was their place, he'd said, the part of France where they belonged, that they were still building and perfecting. So far he couldn't see a single good thing about it.

Since they'd left Papa and Salonica, life had been nothing but effort and fear and trying to pretend he didn't mind, and pretending to Maman and Poupette that he was okay, really. He could tell that Maman was pretending too, and then what were they pretending *for*? Poupette, he supposed, who was such a scaredy-cat and so easily upset that all he had to do was frown at her particularly hard and she would start to cry. Sometimes he couldn't help doing it, though afterward he felt guilty. He wished she were more fun to play with; too small, too timid, she never had good ideas and even though mostly she did what he told her ("I'll be the general, and you be my soldier, okay?"), she wouldn't attempt anything brave or hard, like climbing a wall or a tree or jumping down from it, or properly building a fort with anything but cushions indoors, and here at Tata Baudry's, there wasn't even room to do that, or enough cushions, for that matter. And the apartment was so small, just two rooms, and so full of *things*—boxes in piles and broken chairs in addition to regular chairs—at least three broken chairs, not counting the armchair by the window, whose seat you fell through if you weren't especially careful when you sat down—and more tables than was sensible, like it was a warehouse, not an apartment—and it smelled bad, of dust and old lady, slightly fishy. Maman whispered that it was filthy and they must clean it from top to bottom, but every time she tried to move or tidy or wash in the flat, Tata Baudry would flap her black-clad arms as if she were a chicken and they were wings, and would fuss: "*Mais non, mais non*—you are my guests!" which officially meant "You shouldn't be working when you're staying with me" but actually meant "Please leave my things alone."

Nonetheless Maman had on the first day locked herself in the water closet—a cold-water tap, a Turkish toilet, a tiled floor, a dirty window— and had cleaned it furiously, so that at least Poupette wasn't afraid to go inside. The spaces between the tiles hadn't really got less black but the tiles themselves were now quite white and the room smelled of bleach and that was definitely better.

Tata Baudry, soon to celebrate her eighty-fifth birthday, was very small, not really taller than François himself, her sparse, iron-gray hair combed back tightly in a bun. Because she didn't have many teeth left, and wore her false set only for special occasions, her mouth crumpled easily, disappearing her lips, and her chin tucked up toward her nose. Her skin was very brown, brown as a Bedouin's, and wrinkled, her stout little sausage fingers knobbly and twisted by arthritis. When she laughed, it sounded as though she had no voice at all, and instead just a black space in her throat. She always wore a long black skirt and a black blouse with leg-o'-mutton sleeves, the cuffs and collar of which were a rusty brown with age. Even in the great heat she wore this dress, or these dresses, which, if they were multiple, all looked the same. Her feet, rarely glimpsed in their weathered black boots, were minute, the size of Poupette's feet. Tata Baudry was like a fairy—or a witch—a storybook character. She was so old François couldn't really understand it: surely she'd always been old. Until now he'd thought of Tata Jeanne as old, Maman's older sister, but he could see that Tata Jeanne looked almost like a girl next to Tata Baudry, her hair abundant, her cheeks fleshy, her mouth wet. Getting old, he'd decided, was about drying out, like the leaves in autumn or the flowers pressed in Maman's Bible. Tata Baudry had no moisture in her.

L'Arba was boring, the tiny apartment full of things like a cage. No school, no activities, no soccer games. Sometimes he and Poupette sat on the back steps racing ants or beetles: he set up a course with two lanes made of twigs and pebbles and they each claimed an insect and set it loose. Out in town for the shopping, he caught sight of kids their own age, mostly indigenous kids but in recent days French kids too, like him and his sister, but they moved on the streets as if behind a screen and he had no way to speak to or touch them. Once or twice a boy stared back, even once a pretty girl with chestnut pigtails and a blue Peter Pan collar on her checkered dress, but it seemed all the kids, him too, were pulled along by their mothers like dogs on leashes. As if there was somewhere to be. As if they'd contaminate each other if they stopped and spoke.

They'd come to L'Arba for a bunch of reasons. One of them was the anxiety about bombardments in the city—this was why more and more mothers and kids appeared each day in the little town, escaping the possibility of something that hadn't yet happened. The Italian planes had flown over Algiers, as if preparing to attack; but now that Hitler was in Paris, maybe it would be the British. Maman had explained that the British, all this time their allies, would now be on the other side. This made little sense to François. She said the Germans were still the enemy—of course they were: *les Boches* had been the villains not only in history lessons and in real life but in every game he'd ever played, except when he and Jérémy and Guy played Cowboys and Indians of course. You couldn't suddenly change the facts. The British were annoying and sometimes needed to be put in their place—they didn't understand *Liberté, Égalité, Fraternité*, because they'd never had a revolution. But basically, fundamentally, they knew which side was up, as Papa put it, and they knew right from wrong. So why would they bomb Algiers? And what would bombing be like? With his cousin Jacky, François had played Air Force—they'd run swooping through the park in great arcs, shouting "rat-tat-tat-tat" for the guns and making the shrieking noises of bombs dropping. But they hadn't ever heard an actual bomb. He was a little curious, although he wouldn't have acknowledged it, because when anyone said the word "bomb" in front of Poupette her eyes grew enormous behind her glasses and her lip started to tremble. She was a jelly.

They'd also left Algiers of course most of all because there was nowhere for them to stay. It was as if nobody had been expecting them when they arrived, exhausted, minus Poupette's suitcase, at the port and lumbered off the ferry, which had bucked so badly he'd vomited three times during the overnight crossing. (Poupette had vomited five times, so.) The journey was a blur. He'd been frightened in the station in Milan, when they got there from Salonica, because he could see that Maman was frightened, and that even bleary, oblivious Tata Jeanne was alert with anxiety, in the train station full of fascists—who looked just like regular people; you couldn't see by looking that they were evil—when the man behind the ticket counter told her their tickets were invalid, that there were no more trains to France and that the border was shut. He'd worn a look of mocking triumphal scorn. As for Maman, she'd had an expression then on her face that François hadn't seen before, an animal look, hunted. That had frightened him and he had resolved to be only stronger, and had held her hand. Then the skinny little porter had sidled over with his trolley, and had said something in Italian, and Maman had shaken her head, and the porter had whispered in a singsong French, like the spaghetti-maker at the Italian café in Beirut. He'd loaded their bags and whisked them silently through the crowds in the cavernous hall, to one of the farthest platforms. He'd not left them until they were safely installed in their carriage, and had smiled and waved through the window when he departed. "I couldn't even give him a *centime*," Maman had lamented, "because it's forbidden to change francs to lire here now."

François had been very hungry but had said nothing. He'd needed to pee so badly, but didn't go to the toilet until the train was underway, because he knew it would worry Maman if they weren't all together. He'd played endless rounds of rock, paper, scissors with Poupette and then read her from the *Fables de La Fontaine* until she fell asleep, her thumb slipping spittily out of her newly opened mouth. At Marseille, he'd helped by carrying Poupette piggyback to the taxi—he'd let her pull his ears to direct him left and right and this had made her laugh—but in the hubbub at the curb—so many people wanting taxis, and they'd needed an especially large one for all four plus their luggage—someone had made off with Poupette's suitcase, which they'd discovered almost at once, and Poupette had instead begun to sob—her special doll, Henriette, with a porcelain face and hands and real hair and a damask dress, had been neatly packed inside the case among her knickers and nightgowns—which seemingly had gone on for hours.

All four of them in one room at the Select, and the toilet down the hall. Again he'd inconveniently needed to pee in the middle of the night and had bravely ventured out of the room alone without waking Maman. The hallway carpet had been faintly sticky under his bare feet, and the wall lamp very dim and flickery. His heart had thundered in his chest, even more so when he'd pulled the chain and the flushing water roared down from the high cistern. He'd run back to their room holding his breath against murderers, monsters, and bad thoughts. And Maman and Tata Jeanne had both been snoring, out of sync with each other, comical, with Poupette lying between them in the big bed—he could see their forms in the whey-thin light from the open window—and he'd returned to the folding cot set up for him in the corner and had lain still, willing his heart to quiet as dawn spread through the room. So much of his courage was invisible to the world; each day filled with courage.

Once in Algiers, unmet at the train station even though Maman had sent a telegram to Papa's brother, Uncle Charles, the day before, from Marseille—you could still send a telegram within France—they'd again taken a taxi, this time to Charles and Paulette's apartment. The boat had been crammed with people both returning and newly arriving, fleeing France to stay with relatives in Algeria or maybe even without contacts, because everyone had heard already by then how swiftly the Germans were advancing toward Paris. Standing in line at the café on the boat he overheard a woman saying, "I just don't think our army is ready," and her companion shushed her: "Don't even think such thoughts. We have no choice but to defeat them."

"Why are we on this boat then?" the first woman asked.

"Shush," the other said again. "I'm having the fish. And you?"

He'd seen the two women again in the taxi queue, the first lady wielding a large cylindrical hatbox as if going to a wedding. Their substantial bottoms were his last glimpse as they hoisted themselves into the back seat of a large black car.

When they got to the flat, his cousin Jacky opened the door, a boy only a little older than François himself—eighteen months, it turned out—with freckles and a cowlick in his oily black hair. He looked something like a monkey. At first he cracked the door only a little way, as if suspicious, even though he seemed to know who they were.

"Maman," he called back into the apartment without turning his head, "it's the cousins. Papa's cousins."

"Let them in, let them in," they heard from the depths, but the monkey boy stood for a moment looking them up and down, not moving, as if they might be robbers, with a particularly suspicious glare for François. Only when his mother appeared behind him, drying her hands with a tea towel, did he step back and make room for them to enter.

The apartment seemed small in comparison to the villa in Salonica or the apartment in Beirut, the walls close around them, and the floors, of deep red hexagonal tiles instead of light marble, drew the walls in closer still. Tata Paulette led them down a short hall to the living room, where François had the impression of gloom and clutter, dazzlingly interrupted by a strip of light along the floor from the sunshine beyond the balcony. The metal blinds in fact were lowered against the sun, but not quite all the way; hence its exuberant incursion.

Paulette, a dumpling of a woman with thick glasses, briskly kissed them all on the cheeks, including Poupette, who squirmed. She held his little sister's chin for a second. "Who does she look like, this one? The boy is you and his father, of course; but this one?"

"She looks like herself," Maman said with a smile, but François could tell that Maman did not like Tata Paulette. Not much. He was aware that Jacky lurked behind them in the doorway; when he turned to see, Jacky, swinging in the door frame, stared right at him but didn't smile.

"Did my telegram not reach you?" Maman asked, uncertain whether to sit or not. She'd been told in Marseille that the cable would be delivered;

but these days who knew? Tata Jeanne, exhausted, sat without being asked; then Tata Paulette and finally Maman. Poupette scooched over to sit beside her, up close like a puppy. François stood alone in the middle of the room.

"Yes, yes, the telegram came yesterday. We just—we aren't—" Tata Paulette looked up at her smirking son. "Don't just stand there," she snapped. "Go make some coffee for the travelers. Where are your manners?" She turned back to Maman with a false smile. "We're in a bit of turmoil, is all."

"Yes, the news reports—"

"No, it's not that." She looked at François and then at Poupette, who was twirling her braid. "The children could go help Jacky make the coffee," she suggested.

"Of course," said Maman, and shooed them off, even though it was a preposterous suggestion because neither of them knew how to make coffee.

François held his sister's hand, and they followed the sound of the coffee grinder to the narrow kitchen, where Jacky did not seem surprised to see them.

"So you're the fancy navy kids," he said over his shoulder. "Whoop-de-doo."

"Sorry?"

"Where have you come from again?"

"Greece," François replied. "Salonica. It's in Macedonia. Three trains and a boat away." Poupette just stared.

Jacky banged the side of the grinder over the coffeepot, to get out all the grounds. He did this almost vindictively. "And now you've come home just in time for the war?"

"I hope not," François said. "I hope there won't be a war."

"There already *is* a war, dummy. And France is already in it. And we're losing, in case you hadn't heard." Jacky put the pot on the stove and lit the gas, which made a whooshing sound. Poupette flinched. "So much for our precious navy, right?"

François didn't like this boy, any more than his mother liked Jacky's mother. He'd heard Maman refer to Paulette as a *"pièce rapportée,"* meaning she wasn't really of the family, an outside piece brought in. He also understood that she was Uncle Charles's second wife and that Uncle Charles, a schoolteacher, had lost his first wife to something called Pott's disease (the poor man, but such a funny name) and had then married Paulette, years ago before he was born. This was not mentioned, he knew, that she was a *second wife*, but to him the implication was that Uncle Charles had not loved his first wife enough to keep her alive; and how then could he really love his second? And Jacky, this mean boy, was maybe mean because the circumstances of his birth were therefore unfortunate. François knew that Charles had a whole other family before—three or four kids, maybe, grown up now. One of them at least in Paris. François believed he had chosen Paulette over his children, which was almost criminal. Papa and Charles's father had abandoned their family too, when Papa was the age François was now. Charles was Papa's oldest sibling, ten years older, but that didn't excuse anything: he knew what it had done to Grand'-mère and Papa when the father left—his name was never spoken—and therefore he understood that it was a very, very bad thing. Which surely somehow made Jacky and his mother part of an almost crime.

"Are you Catholic?" François asked. He couldn't quite have said why, except that it mattered to his parents.

"I'm a Communist," he said. "Like my dad. We don't believe in religion. It's crap."

François said nothing for a minute, but Poupette gasped. "I'm telling Maman," she said. "That's a terrible thing to say."

"Tell your mother whatever you like." Jacky put coffee cups on a tray, banging them. "Pipsqueak."

THEY'D STAYED ONLY one night with Tata Paulette and Jacky. Uncle Charles wasn't there. François gleaned that Uncle Charles had done something wrong involving a woman—he overheard Tata Paulette refer to "*cette garce*," when she thought he couldn't hear—and now he wasn't allowed to live at home. They were having their own war. After the first night, Maman took them to the Cousines Breloux, three old ladies who were also somehow relatives but so ancient that he couldn't quite grasp the connection—they weren't called "Tata," so they weren't aunts; they were cousins, but antiques! Whose cousins could they be? These three old creatures lived in a much larger flat than Tata Paulette and Jacky, where everything was covered with ironed white lace doilies—the tables, the chairs, the sofa—and the atmosphere quiet as a church. Like a church, it smelled of floor wax. He and Poupette tried very hard to be good, but they'd been there only a week when he was chasing Poupette around the living room, both of them trying hard not to squeal—the sisters were in their bedrooms; it was the end of the endless siesta hour—and she knocked a china lamp off the end table. It broke into a thousand pieces.

Maman rarely yelled at them. Although she did not yell at them that afternoon, she grew very stern as she swept the fragments into the dustpan. "Do you have any idea, children? Do you have any idea what you've done? François, I expect better of you."

Disappointing Maman was the worst thing. They had no word of Papa: Was he still in Salonica? Was he somewhere else? On his way to join them or headed in the opposite direction? And because Papa was elsewhere, François was, as Papa had instructed, the man of the house. It was his job to take care of Maman, and he had failed.

But he hadn't understood what she meant, exactly, until two days later when, under the rueful but firm gaze of the oldest Cousine Breloux, they'd packed up their suitcases all over again, this time to go to the bus station and board the overcrowded bus to L'Arba. He'd had to sit on Tata Jeanne's knee, barely fitting between her lap and the seat in front, crammed against the smeared window with, between them and the aisle, a fat unshaven man whose thighs seemed ready to burst the seams of his trousers, and who smelled so strongly of old sweat that Tata Jeanne draped her hankie, doused in eau de cologne, over half her face, and François breathed through his mouth for the whole journey.

THEY WENT TO L'ARBA because school was canceled for the last month, all over Algeria, so it didn't matter that they weren't in Algiers. Papa had wanted very much for François to finish the school year, and to be promoted in September. In Salonica, he'd been the best in his class, and the teachers at the Mission Laïque had put him up a grade halfway through the term. Papa wanted him to keep this advantage—to be a year younger than his classmates. Because even better than being top of your class was being top of your class and youngest at the same time. Papa had explained that he himself had been the best and the youngest, and that this was what he hoped for from his son. So it was a huge disappointment that when Maman went to speak to the people at the Board of Education in Algiers—before he and Poupette broke the lamp—they told her that not only were there to be no further classes because of the war, but that no pupil under ten was allowed to enroll in the 5e under any circumstances. Which meant that François, turning just nine at the end of June, would not be permitted to do so in September. If they were fortunate enough to have school at all—when Maman reported the conversation she mimicked the man who had said "*IF*," as if it were in capital letters and italics at the same time—then François would be repeating 6e and that was that.

When they arrived at Tata Baudry's, smaller and grimmer by far than Tata Paulette's, and suffused always with the reddish dust that sifted through the air of the village and landed, like cinnamon, on everything, including their skin, Maman had at first the intention of renting a separate place for the three of them, modest, just one bedroom and a sitting room, like Tata Baudry's, and leaving Tata Jeanne to stay with and help the old woman. But it fast became clear that there was nothing left to rent in L'Arba, and that even if there had been, they couldn't have afforded it. Fatherless families from the city had overrun the town; even the sections of the town traditionally inhabited only by Muslim families were sprinkled now with white faces. At the butcher, they told Maman that three hundred children were being housed in the school, sleeping on cots in the classrooms, watched over by schoolteachers sent out also from the city.

With so much uncertainty, Maman's migraines became more frequent, a challenge in the little space. Tata Baudry and Tata Jeanne slept at night in the bedroom, and Maman, Poupette, and François in the sitting room—Maman on the sofa and the children on cushions on the floor—but when Maman was ill, the other women ceded the bedroom for the day and the evening, and they and the children were crammed among the boxes and broken furniture in the hot, still afternoons. Tata Baudry spoke of having the doctor come and apply leeches to help with Maman's ailment, but Maman was against the idea.

FRANÇOIS WAS SO HUNGRY he thought he might faint. He wondered how he might get something to eat without annoying or alarming anyone. He decided simply to ask the old lady.

Tata Baudry's eyes were still clear in her withered face, and she was, he knew, sympathetic to children—a midwife, she still delivered babies in the town or on the farms—and when he asked her if he might eat the end of the baguette, she smiled at him with her eyes, put down her knitting, and pulled a couple of copper coins from the depths of her rusty skirt. "Better than the crust, why don't you go get yourselves a *pain au chocolat*," she suggested. And, pushing a little at Poupette's soft body beside her: "Take this one with you. It'll do you good to get out."

"Isn't it too expensive?"

"My treat. No need to tell your mother. This morning one of the Berber families brought me *khobz* as a thank-you for delivering their son last month, so we've got bread enough for supper and tomorrow. The *pains* will cost the same as tomorrow morning's baguette. The Lord provides. Off you go. Enjoy yourselves."

This last exhortation François took as license to go exploring. Poupette was an annoyance, but she'd do as he told her. The *boulangerie* was only two blocks away, on the ground floor of a small apartment building. The streets were very quiet, siesta quiet, and baking hot. You wouldn't know that it had rained the previous night; even the sidewalks seemed cracked and almost wrinkly from the heat, like Tata Baudry's hands. Poupette trailed behind him, scuffing her shoes with each step.

"Hurry up."

"Why?"

"We're getting a treat, that's why. When did you last have a *pain au chocolat*?"

"I like *pain au raisin* better."

"Beggars can't be choosers, ninny. Let's see what they've got."

They were alone in the shop with the *boulangère* in her white smock and a couple of noisy flies that hissed against the glass. The trays behind the counter were all but empty—a few braided baguettes, overcooked, a lone square slice of pizza, and three sausage rolls. There remained a handful of croissants and a single *pain au chocolat*.

"What do you want?" he asked Poupette.

"They don't have what I want."

He could see the *boulangère* purse her lips.

"What do you want of what they have?" and then: "I'm sorry, madame, she's just little."

"You have to come first thing in the morning if you want a choice," said the woman. "Besides, there's a lot we don't do right now. Usually we'd bake with butter, but it's just lard nowadays." She shrugged.

"We'll take two croissants please, and the *pain au chocolat*."

She wrapped them in a piece of brown paper and deftly twisted both ends to make a little package. Once he'd paid, François still had a coin, and with it he bought a bottle of still mineral water. It came from a shelf and he knew it would be warm, but he also knew the pastries would be dry.

Outside, they walked to the square and sat on the edge of the fountain at its center. A barely discernible trickle of greenish water dribbled from the fountain's spout, like a man asleep drooling, and it made a small wet sound that seemed, at least, to evoke coolness. In the shade of the archway opposite, a lone old man in a white djellaba sat on a wooden chair watching them, fanning himself. François felt conspicuous and foolish, and wished they'd at least worn hats—Would Poupette burn? She was so fair—but he couldn't see anywhere else to sit.

"Croissant?"

"You promised me *pain au chocolat*."

"You said you didn't even like it."

"Not as much as *pain au raisin*. But I didn't say I didn't like it."

François sighed. He placed the bottle of water at his feet and opened the paper packet on his lap. "Look, see, we have two croissants and one *pain au chocolat*. I can tear it in half."

"But I want the *pain au chocolat*."

"Half."

"Without any jam, the croissant is dry," Poupette complained.

"That's why I got the water." François closed his eyes. She was so annoying. He didn't want to disappoint Maman, though. He didn't want her to think he'd been selfish or childish. "What if you start with half the *pain au chocolat*?"

"No! I want it. Give it to me. Please?"

He looked at his little sister, importunate in her greasy eyeglasses. "Okay." He held up the bread. "You can have the whole thing in return for two things. One, I get the two croissants, okay? Both of them." He didn't think this was too much to ask, not even unfair, because she hardly ate anything, and he was ravenous. "And then you'll go with me exploring. Okay?"

She reached for her pastry. "Exploring where?"

"Wherever I say. Okay?"

"Okay," she said doubtfully. And after a bite, her mouth full: "But if I get tired, will you carry me?"

"No guarantees. I'm the general and you're my soldier, right?"

She saluted with her free hand. *"Bien sûr, mon général."*

ONCE THEY WERE done eating and had drunk half the water—"Why can't we finish it? I'm still thirsty." "Because we might need it while we're exploring." "Can't you fill it up from the fountain?" "No, dummy. That's okay for animals, but it would make us sick. Or it could"—they stood and brushed the crumbs off themselves and François pointed to one of the dusty streets that led away from the square. He chose it because in the far distance, in that direction, rose the foothills of the mountains: brave explorers climbed mountains, so this was where they would go. He didn't bother to announce this because Poupette would complain that it was too far, before they'd even set out.

The narrow street was quiet. They could occasionally hear voices or movement from inside the open windows, but they didn't see anyone except two sleeping cats curled into crescents and a little white dog with brown ears, rooting like a pig in some garbage behind a small blue truck. At least the buildings made the street shady. When they came to its end, they were at a much bigger road, and again François chose their direction by finding the mountains at the horizon. Several cars passed them as they walked what began to seem a long way, and when they passed a cluster of Arab men drinking coffee outside a small café, François felt their curious gaze and wondered if he should turn back. But just then Poupette grabbed at his elbow with her sticky fingers and whined, "I'm too hot. Let's go home now," and her weakness, so predictable, annoyed him and he shook his head. "We're on an adventure," he said. "You promised. I gave you the whole pastry and you promised."

"But François—"

"It's *'mon général'* to you."

"You're mean."

"Just wait," he said. "Just a little bit farther. It's going to be amazing." He hoped that he wasn't lying. But they couldn't give up yet. Poupette grumbled and scuffed her shoes again, so he reached out and held her hand, even though they were both hot, their fingers puffy, and a squelchy film of sweat then suctioned them together. "Trust me," he said.

As they came to the edge of town on the Route d'Aumale, the sidewalks ended and the road broadened out. On either side, instead of buildings, stretched long rows of tall plane trees, their branches spreading out to make a vast unbroken umbrella of shade that rustled in the hot wind. Behind the trees on both sides there were green fields, first the vineyards in tidy rows, shiny green as if washed, above the loamy earth, as perfect as a painting, and then, beyond, the tall wheat fields, rippling like dancers. In a distant field they could see farmhands scything, and a truck, too; but all they could hear were the thick cicadas and a deep dog's bark, far away. Without the sun's heat, the air felt bearable, and François turned to smile at his sister. "This is great, right?"

She shook her head and looked at the ground, but he nudged her. "Look up at the trees. And smell the air—it smells green."

At the far end of the second vineyard on the left—the vineyards felt very long even to François—a dirt road branched off the Route d'Aumale. Without hesitating, he turned down it, dragging Poupette behind him.

"Too far," she whined. "I'm so tired."

"Be a good soldier. Not far now."

After a time, they could hear faintly the sound of water, growing louder, and when they came to the end of the vineyard they found its source: a narrow creek, a brook really, running in a stone-filled gully among tree roots and boulders.

"See—we're nearly there!" It was like a dream. They took off their shoes and forded the brook, which, deliciously cool and soft, came up almost to François's knees and seemed to tinkle over the stones like a carillon. He held tight to Poupette's hands, both of them, because the water came of course higher on her—he made her tuck her dress into her underpants first—and because the stones were slippery and uneven underfoot. Clambering up the far bank, they came upon a grove of old olive trees, and in the midst of them, a clearing, a silvery shade, with soft mossy turf underfoot.

There, François threw himself down on his back, chucking his shoes and socks away from him and gesturing for Poupette to do the same. The air was filled with the chittering of the sandgrouse near the water's edge and the shocking pecking song of a red-necked nightjar, hidden somewhere in the olive branches. Above them, the sky had transformed from a burning void to brilliant blue again as the sun dipped, lowering to the west. A trio of puffy white clouds drifted overhead.

"Look, look, it's the white lambs we saw from the train when we left Salonica!" François said, referring to a flock of sheep glimpsed from the window on a similarly arable plain.

"Don't say that." Poupette spoke around her thumb, now firmly planted in her mouth.

"Why not? It's sweet."

"No it's not. Because that would mean the lambs died because of the war and are in heaven now. And that might mean the Germans have killed Papa too."

The nightjar laughed raucously.

"Don't be silly. They aren't really the lambs. It's just a way of speaking." François closed his eyes so she wouldn't see the tears forming in them. He pulled with his fingers at the soft grasses as if holding on, for dear life, to the earth, as if he might fall into the great sky. "Papa is very strong," he told his sister. "No filthy German is going to kill him. Anyway, he's in Greece and there aren't any Germans there. He's probably halfway home to us by now." He paused. "And then Maman won't have any more headaches, and there'll be plenty to eat—you can have *pain au raisin* whenever you want. And we'll get a beautiful new villa all for ourselves in Algiers, where we can see the sea, so we can wave to all our friends in Beirut and Salonica. And we'll all be together, and France will kill all the *Boches*, maybe with the help of England, okay, and then we'll win the war and go back to Beirut and live happily ever after."

The sandgrouse chittered, the nightjar mocked. Poupette's spitty thumb fell from her mouth and her head fell to face him, her cheek against the grass, her water-blue eyes behind their skewed glasses fluttering shut. *Mon général.* He would have to carry her home on his back, all the way, without complaint.

JUNE 1940

⚓

SALONICA, GREECE

On June 14, 1940, a Friday, the day the Germans conquered Paris, Gaston Cassar, the French naval attaché in Salonica, was to attend, with his colleague Monsieur le Consul Clouet, an evening reception at the home of the Romanian consul.

When the invitation had arrived, over a month before, Gaston's family, his wife, Lucienne, and the children, eight-year-old François and little Denise, just six, still lived with him in the rented villa at 175 Rue Reine Olga, along with Lucienne's invalid older sister, Tata Jeanne. On May 21, he'd sent them all away by train—back across Greece, across Italy, across France, to catch the boat to Algeria, on the other side of the Mediterranean in North Africa, where they came from and where they would be *safe*. Since seeing them off at the station, Gaston had heard no word: as the war's chaos seeped into all life, communication across borders collapsed, and no letters or even telegrams had come through. Gaston worried desperately, panicked even; but he was a trained naval officer, and he knew that his duty to his country—poor, beloved France—must come before all else.

PRIOR TO HIS Salonica posting, Gaston Cassar had spent four years as the naval attaché at the consulate in nearby Beirut—no small achievement for an officer from a background as humble as his own. His superiors had sent him from Lebanon to Greece in September '39, after the onset of war, to be their eyes and ears, to spy, in effect: What, they wanted to know, might the fascist Italians be up to in Albania? In the Aegean? What possible spies gathered in the Macedonian port of Salonica, strategically important since ancient times? At first, Gaston had thought that this was, if not a promotion, then at least a significant role for French naval intelligence. Now, though, as his known world collapsed—Germans marching in the streets of Paris!—he felt useless, trapped in this remote and irrelevant backwater, alone without his beloved Lucienne and the children to ground him.

BY THE TIME he'd dressed, on the morning of June 14—Gaston took particular care with his uniform, white, pressed, his buttons polished—the news of France's humiliation was widely known. The two housekeepers of his rented villa treated him with funereal respect, their eyes downcast. He walked the short distance to his office, ashamed—how could he not be?—yet defiant. There had to be a space for resistance, somewhere.

At the consulate, where the high windows stood open to the garden and the profusion of birdsong was louder than the traffic, his assistant Cotigny brought him a double espresso and a glass of water.

"Clouet?" Gaston had noticed that the outer door to the consul's suite was shut.

"Not here, monsieur. Madame Turner"—Clouet's secretary—"telephoned to say that we're officially closed, today."

"Are we?" Gaston almost smiled. "And yet here we are, you and I. We haven't ceased to exist. We haven't ceased to be French. France hasn't vanished from the planet."

"My understanding—I may have made a mistake—but I believe the consul wishes to comprehend where we stand. I mean, as a diplomatic office, as a—where France stands—"

"Yes, quite. The consul wishes for clarity." Of course Clouet was hiding, failing in leadership in this essential moment as he'd amply shown he'd fail in every moment leading up to this one. Just when it was most important to stand up for France, Clouet scuttled off into a dark corner. Gaston wished he could vent his frustration; but not with Cotigny. "What's on the agenda?"

"There was a lunch with monsieur le consul and two French businessmen—in textiles—but that was canceled already three days ago. I believe they stayed in Athens. And there's the cocktail this evening at the Romanian consul's residence."

"That's still happening?"

"As far as we know."

"Clouet won't attend?"

"If the office is shut today, sir, I think it's safe to assume he will not attend."

Gaston drank his coffee in a single swig and wiped his mouth with the white linen napkin that had lain beneath the cup. It had, embroidered upon it, their nation's escutcheon, the famous three words. Someone had sewn the stitches; someone had ironed the linen. So many lives in their hands. "Then I'd better go."

"As you see fit, sir."

"We represent a nation, our nation. She is in crisis. All the more reason to stand up honorably on her behalf."

Cotigny nodded and made as if to withdraw.

"Just check for me that it's still happening, okay? I don't want to show up and interrupt them *en famille*, that odious pair."

GASTON HAD LONG been wary of the Romanian consul and his wife, Radu and Cristina Mazilescu, with whom he'd dined at various soirées over the preceding year. They made a great show of loving France and all things French, but Romania was known to favor the Axis—Gaston would have said that they curried favor with Germany. At earlier cocktail parties, when people had decried in alarm the German advances across

Europe, Mazilescu had said nothing, had stood in sinister silence in the circle of diplomats in his navy double-breasted suit, his cigarette dangling in its ridiculous ebony holder as though he were playing a French count in a Hollywood film. All he lacked was a monocle.

The wife, Cristina, he and Lucienne had liked marginally better. Lucienne, always generous, had described her as warm, but chiefly Gaston thought the woman pretty and vain. Her bleached-blond hair and the cloud of floral scent that always surrounded her made Cristina Mazilescu, for Gaston, a figure simultaneously of desire and of distaste. He mistrusted her. The couple had only one child, a wan blond boy of François's age, glimpsed at school performances and notable for his large, mournful, pale eyes—and this too implied Cristina's lack of substance: she had doubtless preferred to keep her fine figure rather than to give herself over wholly to family.

In normal circumstances, Gaston, though not himself a consul, would have been doing the Romanians a favor by attending their silly party. But on this day—he bathed again in the evening, before going out, and again polished his buttons and his shoes, and pomaded his curls—on this day the significance of his attendance at the Mazilescus' was different. He was going to make a show of favoring them with his French presence. He was going in lieu of Clouet, who refused to shoulder the responsibility. Perhaps there was even a wisdom in having the less senior officer do the honors. But his real role, they would all know, was a form of face-saving, of insisting to the victors who would be there—the German consul would doubtless be of the party—that France was not afraid; that France was not ashamed. That France continued as she had been, in spite of the wounds. The wounds were not mortal.

Yes, Gaston told himself as he climbed the steps and the door to the villa was opened by a liveried footman with brushy mustaches, even as his hands trembled by his sides, yes, he was doing his ghastly duty to the best of his ability. He was convinced that this was right. He wished only that his beloved Lucienne were by his side, her fingers interlaced with his.

"Bonsoir, madame," he said as he bent to kiss his hostess's hand. "While difficult for us, a good day for you, I think?"

Cristina Mazilescu stood alone in the lobby, in black satin with a pink camellia in her white-blond chignon. As he straightened, she clutched his arm and drew him not toward the drawing room, from which the hum of voices emanated, and where he could already glimpse the back of the Italian consul's curly head, but in the opposite direction, into the dim dining room, with its jade damask wallpaper, and from there out onto a stone balcony that overlooked a grassed courtyard with a trickling fountain. The drawing room also gave onto a balcony, its doors open, and the sounds of the party drifted to join them.

"I must just say something." Cristina's red mouth was a thin line; she looked near tears. "I've been waiting for you to come."

"Me?"

"We had word this afternoon that the consul wouldn't attend but that you, Commander, would come in his stead. So yes, for you."

"But, madame, doesn't this appear odd——" If anyone came out onto that balcony for a smoke, the two of them would appear to be in a compromising tête-à-tête.

"We won't be long. But I must speak with you."

Gaston stood as far from her as the balcony allowed, crossing his arms in front of his chest, a minimal defense.

"I know—we both know, Radu and I—what you think. What you must think of us. You know, of course, that we dine with the German consul"—Gaston closed his eyes for a second, in acknowledgment—"and you'll have anticipated, I expect, that he's here."

Of course: she was determined to avoid a scene. This was why she'd taken him aside. He looked again at the neighboring balcony, the yellow light spilling out of the windows.

"But you surely think, then, that this is our desire." She stepped forward, leaned toward him, spoke quietly but with intensity: "This may be my one chance to explain—and it may make no difference to you, but it matters to me, to us. Radu and I met as students in Paris. We fell in love there not just with each other. Your culture, your history, your country—we think of them as ours, too." She paused. "We feel exactly as you do about the Germans, about *him*"—she flung an elegant arm behind her in the direction of the party, and her camellia trembled—"and we are ashamed, *ashamed*. But we are the representatives of our government, Radu is; we are under orders from Bucharest, and our own opinions are irrelevant. We do our jobs, as you do. We uphold the official line, or we resign and face imprisonment, or worse."

Gaston appreciated the dilemma, aware, only dimly, that he might in time face a similar one.

"This tragedy," she went on, "as far as we're concerned, it's not just a tragedy for you and for France, which we love so dearly. It's a tragedy for us—I don't mean the two of us, I mean for Romania. Your triumph, your success—that was our country's one hope. And now?" A tear glimmered on her smooth cheek.

But he could see, behind her head, movement at the drawing room window, and could hear two voices loudening. He stepped back off the balcony, into the shadow of the dining room. "We'll call attention to ourselves, madame. Your absence from the party will be remarked."

"It will." Following him in, she brushed her face, smoothed her dress, and abruptly altered her tone, speaking, as she strode in front of him back into the front hall, in a bright and brittle public voice: "Of course I'll tell my husband you came to pay your respects. Very good of you. We understand that you can't stay. I'm sure you've a great deal to take care of." She all but pushed him out the door, and as the footman closed it gently behind him, Gaston was again aware of the shame, his nation's shame and his own: shut out by the Romanians; imagine! And with a great deal to take care of, no less—when in fact he was headed back to his lonely villa, to eat a hard-boiled egg and a piece of cheese with cold bread at the kitchen table under the dim, sulfurous overhead lamp, writing another letter to Lucienne—a letter into which he would pour his anguish and his dread, his untethered love, the camellia, the tone of Cristina's voice, the smell of cigar smoke, the minutiae of these strange days—a letter he would then send care of his brother, Charles, in Algiers, not knowing whether Lucienne was there to receive it, not knowing whether Lucienne and the children had made it to Algiers at all.

So much he had to take on faith. So much of life he had to live, in this moment, as if, as if it made sense when it could not. He loathed beautiful Salonica that night, and their elegant villa, in which he now found himself alone, and the stylish furniture they'd chosen and bought as if pretending—no, decidedly pretending—that disaster wouldn't find them there. He loathed it all.

GASTON SHOULD NEVER have brought his family from Beirut to Salonica, but he hadn't been able to imagine living without them. Lucienne had seemed unafraid, and together they'd chosen the villa to rent, amazed by the space and amenities they could afford, charmed by their gracious landlord, Monsieur Hernandez, a prosperous Jewish merchant who lived with his wife in a mansion not far away. For months, all through the winter, in spite of the faraway war, Gaston had loved walking home each evening along the broad boulevard, away from the glittering seafront to the house where the children played in the afternoons in the shady, fragrant garden while their aging Tata Jeanne, knitting, kept an eye from the open window.

Daily he'd looked forward, as to gifts, to the monkey-limbed leaping embrace of little Denise, her scrawny legs tucked around his waist when he lifted her, her hot, delicate little hands patting his cheeks between kisses, her fine straw-blond hair escaping from its braids to dance around her skull, catching the light. François hovered always shyly behind his sister, his glances hopeful but uncertain: he so powerfully longed for his father's approval. When he had a good result at school to announce, he drew near, smiling outright, and brushed the dark swath of hair from his eyes. Gaston wanted so much of that boy, for that boy, his son and heir, his own future: already François understood it, and feared disappointing his father; and that fear alone disappointed Gaston. Though even that disappointment was a kind of love.

Gaston loved above all, and looked forward to especially, the moment when he would see Lucienne, his beloved wife, often from behind, either at her desk or standing by the dining table or even at the sink in the kitchen: he would admire the shape of her back, the line of her nape, and would thrill to approach her and rest his hand on the small of her spine, feeling the rise of her buttocks only slightly, the promise of Eros beneath the careful layers of cretonne and silk, the slight swish of the fabric if he moved a finger . . .

But even then, through those months from September to May, he'd felt dread, in waves. A growing sickness of it. News of the wider world, only ever bleaker, penetrated their enclave: not just Germany's relentless advances, but also a growing apprehension of the hopeless unpreparedness of the French command. His superior in Beirut, Cherrière, told him in the early spring that the leadership in Paris spoke frankly of the need to compromise if the Germans continued to advance. Even then, the French army anticipated defeat. Gaston's heart beat even in his fingertips at the memory of Cherrière's scratched voice, of the weariness, almost blurriness, of his usually tough demeanor—before the French war had even begun. By mid-May, when Gaston received the Romanian consul's invitation, the news from points north had grown dire: from the initial attack on Belgium and Holland, the Germans had taken only four days to reach northern France and by May 14, they were entrenched there, their sights on Paris.

From early May onward, Gaston focused his dread and distress on the fate of his family. Why, he kept wondering, had he brought them with him to Salonica, instead of parking them in Algiers with his brother or his aunts? The children as well as Lucienne's invalid sister, Tata Jeanne, who was prone to unforeseeable seizures of daunting severity. He and Lucienne belonged in Algiers; they loved the beautiful city where they'd both grown up, where their parents and grandparents had grown up. They'd been shaped by it, felt it part of them, and though they had nowhere there to live (the navy had kept them on the move since they married), Algiers was the home to which they'd always planned, eventually, to return. If he'd been willing to be separated from his beloved and their children, Gaston could have settled them properly in an apartment there before the world lurched into crisis. But he'd believed he could not live without them—without her, Lucienne. And who could have foreseen, the previous autumn, how quickly the Germans would advance across Europe?

From the first week of May, it was clear that Lucienne, Tata Jeanne, and the children needed to get back to Algeria as quickly as possible, traveling overland by train to France, as far as Marseille, and then boarding the ferry for home. Italy, under Mussolini, prepared to enter the war in alliance with Germany any day; and when that happened, travel between Greece and France would become impossible. The women and children needed to evacuate posthaste.

Gaston, too, wanted to get out of Salonica. Even knowing that France was likely to capitulate, he wanted to be part of the struggle, to fight honorably and, if need be, to die for his country. And at the same time, he wanted nothing more than to board the train with his wife, to feel her body pressed against his side when she tucked her dark head under his chin, and to know that they would be together, inseparable, always.

LUCIENNE, TATA JEANNE, and the children had departed from the train station near the commercial port late on the morning of May 21. The day was hot even before noon, and in the taxi—crossing town past the vast Jewish cemetery, with its white marble headstones glittering, past the White Tower, that stolid cylindrical blockhouse with its crenellated cap, along the seafront of shimmering, endlessly mobile wavelets clamoring at the sea wall, and on the horizon, like the eye of eternity, Mount Olympus, home of the gods, wreathed in a dispassionate haze—even as Gaston kept one eye on all these things, he gazed also at his wife,

Lucienne, trying to memorize her in every detail. She sat quietly beside him, her cheeks flushed, her short forehead beaded from the exertions of departure, her hands in her lap folded around the wrinkled linen hand-kerchief with which she dabbed, periodically, at her temples or at the corners of her eyes. They traveled alone in one taxi; Tata Jeanne and the children were in another, just behind them. Because of this, in spite of the driver, he reached to stroke her hair, her cheek.

"Aïni," he said, almost trembling. And then nothing more. All his emotion in that private name. They both knew this was the moment for their real farewell, rather than in the chaos of the station with the children and their aunt, broad-hipped, thick-calved Jeanne all but blind behind her glasses, almost like a third child.

"Have faith," his wife said, reaching to take his hand between hers upon her lap, an intimacy the driver could not see in his mirror. They both knew that everything from this moment forward was uncertain: when or even whether they would be reunited; where or how a reunion might take place; what might lie in store for them and the children—so young, the children, all promise still. Even their continued existence felt uncertain, and the distance from Salonica to Algiers loomed enormous and perilous, an odyssey.

The station's bustle was in fact a gift, panic manifest in the pushing crowds, the insistent echoing Tannoy, the belch of the trains' engines as they clattered down the platform behind the porter, a fat man with volu-minous mustaches, who wore his cap on the back of his head, brim sky-ward, to jaunty effect. The surrounding madness settled Gaston, made him calmer. This, he knew how to do: to project the necessary ease and confidence that was—he so wanted to teach this to his son—the noble falsehood of a leader. He stood in the doorway of their carriage, once the luggage had been stowed (How could they have so much luggage? How would they manage, changing trains? How would they manage at all?): one by one they hugged and kissed him, Denise and Tata Jeanne tearful; François in the guise of *petit homme*, knowing what his father wanted, shook Gaston's hand and whispered formally, "I'll take care of everyone, I promise."

And Lucienne: those eyes that glittered like the Mediterranean. Her smile was sorrowful and loving, and even when he stood outside the train, on the *quai*, and the children and Lucienne filled the window with their waving, she smiled at him, she smiled for him, the one person who saw him fully and genuinely, to the last she smiled, until he couldn't make them out any longer.

He'd thought, that afternoon in late May, that he might not be able to go on. He had wished to be in that carriage with them—he could see so clearly in his mind's eye the plum velveteen seats, their scuffed, bulbed wooden armrests and once-white antimacassars, the dust motes drifting in the shafts of light from the window, the one sallow Greek matron in a black suit who occupied the carriage with them—in *his* seat, the one that should have been his, had they traveled together as a family as they ought to have done.

He'd walked back to the villa, had pulled the blinds and lain on top of the bed, beneath their crucifix and rosary, not to sleep but to listen and imagine, to travel with them, to hear in his mind the grating chuntering of the train along the rails, to see through the glass first the orchards in the river delta, the burgeoning rows of fruit trees just past their flower, then the rise of the mountains, the darker evergreens, the land falling away outside as they climbed. Now they would proceed to the dining car, Denise's tears dried. Might François hold her hand? He might; he would, surely? Her tears dried now, the moment of parting forgotten; she peering at the menu and moving it farther, then closer, then farther, in her attempt to focus. And Lucienne: Aïni.

He had lain until dusk on his back, in his suit, having removed only his shoes. He could hear as if far away the cook, Maria, preparing his solitary supper, calling out now and then to Eleni, who did the cleaning, in the Greek he could barely understand; and then eventually he heard the front door slam, once, then, shortly after, again, leaving him alone in the house. But he was only half aware of the movements around him, because he was in fact lying in the gloaming, traveling, traveling with his family, along the metal rails and high into the mountains, because he did not want to let them go.

THE THREE WEEKS between their departure on May 21 and the fall of France on June 14 proved all but unendurable. Gaston woke daily soon after dawn to the throaty ticking and rustles of the magpies in the oleander outside the window. Daily he experienced the same sensation of falling: his consciousness surfaced exuberant, then plummeted, like a swimmer bursting up from the depths to gasp for breath, only to discover that above the water's surface hangs a choking smoke. Each morning, his grief and anxiety returned to him. Meticulous always, he had trouble forcing himself to shave, to consider his face in the mirror and comb his hair, to straighten his uniform or shine his shoes. These were his daily habits, performed effortlessly until now; but now he wondered, each time: Why? Why? Why was he here, in this spacious but sepulchral villa, where he caught, in strange moments, the voices of the children in the garden, or glimpsed in the corner at dusk Tata Jeanne, knitting in the brown armchair, her heavy arms barely twitching as her needles clacked, only to rub his eyes and acknowledge there was nothing? What was he doing here? What was the point of anything without Lucienne?

He expressed his uneasiness only in the long letters he wrote nightly to his wife, and put in the diplomatic post not knowing when or whether she might receive them. He wrote to her at the Hotel Select in Marseille, where they were due to spend the night; he wrote to her at his brother Charles's in Algiers; he wrote daily. He heard nothing in return.

In the office, Gaston feigned patience, hoping for orders from his superiors that would pluck him from Salonica and carry him closer to the war, render him useful. He spent his days writing careful analytical reports of the situation on the ground, while Clouet, the consul, seemed chiefly preoccupied with shuffling papers, keeping routines, and minimizing expenditures. Gaston was repelled by the man, in whom he discerned fear and weakness. Clouet, a man of over forty, whose children were practically grown, seemed intent above all on protecting his reputation and career prospects. . . . Gaston, wanting to get away from Clouet's backwater and back to Beirut, sent a memo to his superior there, Cherrière, requesting a transfer. He received no response. A terrible silence. This was the tenor of his days, to feel he'd become worse than useless, invisible, as if he'd been erased from the world or the world had been erased around him.

MEANWHILE, GASTON ATTEMPTED to bolster his spirits by spending time with his local friends, a pair of Greeks—Alexandros Zannas, the director of the Red Cross, and his younger brother, Sotirios—along with the refugee Pole Maliszewski, who officially worked for Alexandros as a translator but who in fact, sub rosa, assisted escaping refugees from his Nazi-occupied homeland. A wise and sympathetic trio, they invited him to join them for drinks, even supper, and to listen to the BBC broadcasts from London.

Gaston held out hope for the wisdom of these friends, to whose opinions he listened carefully. He listened, too, to his elegant landlord, who stopped by the villa for an *apéritif* a few days after Lucienne had left. Monsieur Hernandez was part of the large and thriving Jewish community upon whom Salonica's prosperity depended. Gaston had at least had the presence of mind to ask Maria to prepare hors d'oeuvres without seafood or pork; and he chilled a prized bottle of the Veuve for his guest.

Monsieur Hernandez came alone, and on foot. He and his wife lived in a grander villa less than a kilometer farther down the avenue. They'd entertained Gaston and Lucienne twice, once for an intimate dinner of eight and once, at the new year, for a soirée. Lucienne, who loved beautiful things, had rhapsodized about their elegant taste, the Parisian delicacy of their inlaid end tables and gilded chairs, the glittering perfection of the chandeliers ("Imagine," Lucienne had whispered, "That the maids must polish every crystal droplet!") and the enormous, intricate Oriental rugs—Turkish and Persian both—that all but covered the marble floors. "Like Versailles," Lucienne had said as they walked home.

"Distinguished" was the word that Hernandez brought to Gaston's mind. His head was elegantly formed, his large dark eyes thickly fronded by long lashes. His lips were red against his olive skin. Slim, almost delicate, he wore his clothes beautifully—soft wools with a smooth drape—and yet his hairy hands and shadowed chin, along with his firm manner, conveyed a reassuring manliness. He always wore a patterned cravat rather than a tie, an old-fashioned affectation Gaston found appealing. Mrs. Hernandez, still beautiful in her mid-forties, wore Paris fashions. Gaston, who felt it no crime to look, had admired her elegant ankles above her calfskin pumps, and the sparkling drip of jewels at her cleavage. No, Hernandez aspired not to provincial dominance but to the cosmopolitan. And such culture! Hernandez was fluent in at least five languages, among them a beautiful French, like his cravat somewhat old-fashioned, but so elegant.

"What's the word at the consulate?" Hernandez stood in the window silhouetted by the last shafts of sun, champagne in hand.

"No word today."

"The latest of our ships to arrive reported Italian maneuvers off the Dodecanese."

Gaston nodded. "Nothing new. That's part of what I was sent here to monitor nine months ago."

"Have you kept a close eye?"

"Hard to do, practically speaking. They haven't entered the war yet. Your merchant sailors are in a better position to report than I am."

"Only a matter of time," Hernandez said quietly.

"That's why I sent Lucienne and the kids away."

"Will you be going too?"

"Not for now."

"It doesn't look good for France. But maybe you can reassure me."

"Ah." A silence. "I wish I could."

"Do you know," Hernandez sat, unexpectedly, on the arm of the velveteen sofa, the purchase of which had so delighted Lucienne—could it only have been eight months before?—"that Rosa has a Persian passport?" Rosa was his wife. "Curious, no? She's not an immigrant—her parents, her grandparents, her ancestors for over a century back, for several centuries perhaps, were all born in Salonica. Well, all but one, at three or four generations' remove—he, a great-great, an immigrant from Isfahan . . ."

Gaston rubbed his thumb thoughtlessly around the rim of his champagne flute. The glass, being crystal, sang a high mournful note. He stopped at once, embarrassed.

"You're wondering what my point is. I understand. My point is that Rosa has papers that would enable her—us—to relocate to Persia, even though she's never been there, nor does she have plans to go. She's held on to these papers, to this privilege, if you like, as an insurance policy. In case she should *need* to go—in case we should." Hernandez leaned forward confidentially. "And this, my friend, you'd discover in almost every family in my community. It goes back centuries: Rosa's mother had the papers, and her father before her, and his father before that. I don't have additional papers only because I'm purebred Salonican on both sides, back to a time before nationalities were written down." Hernandez's eyes caught the lamplight; night was falling behind him. "But our people have always understood uncertainty, and have lived with it. We expect it. We live always as though we might have to leave at a moment's notice."

Gaston pictured the front hall of their mansion, its opulent furnishings, the vast chandelier with its glittering droplets. Hernandez seemed to anticipate him: "You think of our properties, the business—six ships, four large warehouses, three hundred and sixty-three employees, the tombstones of our ancestors—you wonder what I'm talking about. But remember, we Jews came here as refugees, expelled from Spain in 1492, resettled at the mercy—and the whim—of the Ottoman sultan. The reason so many of us have Spanish names—yes, I see you know. My point is: five hundred years is not enough to make us forget that we are exiles, that even where we seem most at home we may need to leave—"

"Have you plans to leave now? Would you go to Persia, using your wife's papers?"

Hernandez seemed surprised. "No, no—unless you are saying—"

"I have no news that you don't have. We can still hope, even for France."

"Mussolini isn't Hitler," Hernandez said. "They aren't equivalent. And the Germans aren't interested in this little backwater."

"It's quite a strategic backwater, as you know."

"And a long way from Berlin."

"Indeed."

"If we were in Prague, even—or Budapest—"

"We are a thousand kilometers from Budapest," offered Gaston, who had at one point been called upon to calculate the distance. "For now—"

"Yes, for now. But our Raphael is at boarding school in England for a reason."

"Because all the best French boarding schools were full?" joked Gaston. "Or because the tailors in London are more to your liking?"

"Because Rosa and I have faith in the British."

"Ah." Gaston smiled. "Me too; but you know, I question many of their decisions, especially with regard to this part of the world—the violence—"

"But Balfour," said Hernandez. "And the promise of Palestine."

"Well, yes. I suppose."

"Raphael is in his second year at Winchester. He's got used to it now. We won't have him home this summer."

"He's your only?" Gaston knew he was. Lucienne had explained to him: there'd been a complication at birth, apparently, and no possibility of more children.

"Rosa is undone. But his housemaster has arranged for him to go home with another boy—a minor baronet from Cumberland, apparently."

"The land of Wordsworth," Gaston observed.

"Is that so? Yes, I suppose it is. British poetry has never been my favorite."

"How could it be, compared to French?"

"What do you think of Valéry, then, as a poet?"

Their conversation turned to the glory of *la poésie pure*, to the legacy of Mallarmé and Rimbaud and to whether "La Jeune Parque" was a bridge from one era to the next or a modernist dead end. Gaston preferred the Symbolists; and of the next generation, he preferred Claudel for his faith, and Gide for his worldliness, to Valéry—though Gide, of course, was no poet.

THE DAY AFTER the fall of France, a Saturday, Gaston recalled his conversation with Hernandez. He wondered whether to telephone his landlord—but what would he say? Nothing on the ground in Salonica had changed: Budapest was still a thousand kilometers away, and Paris more than twice as far. The simple fact of telephoning—on the Sabbath, no less—would strike Hernandez as cause for alarm, as though Gaston were tacitly urging him to pack up and flee—a folly. Instead, Gaston rang the Zannas household and went round in the afternoon, after the siesta hour, for a coffee in the garden of Alexandros's large family villa. The brothers were present together: Alexandros, the elder, burly, mustachioed, with his almost musical spastic tremor that occasionally rolled his fine, classical head upon its neck and fluttered his fingers even as his dark eyes, watchful and owlish, remained still; and Sotirios, smaller, darker, thin-chested, never without a cigarette, and his stubby fingers stained yellow, like his crooked teeth, from the nicotine. When Sotirios laughed, a rumbling emanated from deep within him like a coming storm; it always seemed to Gaston that the physical depths implied were greater than the size of the man himself. He laughed often, even in the darkest times, for which Gaston was grateful.

Maliszewski the Pole joined them. He, too, smoked obsessively, curiously holding his cigarettes between his middle and fourth fingers. Gaston was always newly surprised by the plain pleasantness of his features, his broad cheeks and flat, colorless hair, side-parted and sticking out in spikes. His clothes never fit well—his trousers fell off him, he swam in his shirts—and Gaston wondered whether his friend had previously been stout or whether he'd always been thin but, relying on the gifts of others to clothe himself, made do with oversized garments.

Maliszewski, like Gaston, lived in Salonica as in a waiting room. He'd fled Warsaw the previous October, soon after the German invasion, and, traveling largely on foot, had made his way to Macedonia through Romania and Bulgaria. The last stretch over the mountains in winter had been awful—this much he'd implied. A few years younger than Gaston, maybe just past thirty, he had no family of his own. He'd been a civil servant living with his mother, who'd encouraged him to leave because his anti-fascist sentiments were well known. Gaston wondered whether there was more to it—whether he dug with the wrong foot, a man with no family, after all—but he'd never voiced this question even to Lucienne. Maliszewski had somehow, with minimal resources, covered much inhospitable terrain between Poland and Greece and, with the help of an anti-fascist network, had made contact with the Zannases. His ambition, from the start, had been to circle around southern Europe and head northward to join the Polish government in exile in London; but Salonica, like a bramble, had caught him.

The word back from London had been that Maliszewski should stay put for the time being: that he was of greatest service as a conduit. Of course Alexandros Zannas employed him, nominally, as a translator—in addition to Polish he spoke Russian, and his English and French were both very good—and this served as a cover for his more important work. Every week or at the most two, Maliszewski received a radio communication alerting him to the imminent arrival of what he called "a posse." The posse might in fact be a solitary individual; usually it was three people at the most; only once, in March, dangerously, a full family of five, two parents, two children under ten, and a baby, this last so small and with so high and thin a cry that Maliszewski had wondered, to Gaston, whether it had been born en route. These posses were composed of fellow Poles, often of Jewish Poles, certainly of Poles who needed to flee. They arrived, without exception, exhausted and muted, still filled with fear and in some cases despair, and always without papers that would lawfully entitle them to remain. Maliszewski's role was to feed and house them, discreetly, until such time as he had word, forty-eight hours in advance, of the irregular boat from Piraeus to Alexandria; at which point he'd borrow one of the Zannas brothers' cars—for the family, he'd had to borrow Alexandros's large Peugeot—and deliver them to the port outside Athens in the nighttime. He prided himself on the fact that all his charges, from the time of his own arrival in December of '39, had landed safely on British territory. But he desperately wanted, himself, to follow them.

On that fifteenth of June, a Saturday, Maliszewski was to accompany, after nightfall, a young rabbi and his wife from Katowice, as well as an older professor from Krakow. The professor, not Jewish but an outspoken Catholic, had been staying for two weeks with Maliszewski himself; the couple had been housed by one of the prominent Jewish families, friends of Mr. Hernandez's.

"I swear," Maliszewski was saying, as Gaston took his seat in the sunken cane armchair nearest the stand of olives, "the old professor, a historian, only wants to eat books. I have to remind him to look up from his studies and join me for even a bowl of soup. I want to say to him, Look up and look around you, man. *This* is history. . . . But he's been working more than ten years on his magnum opus, something about the libraries of medieval monasteries—"

"The Dark Ages," Sotirios interrupted with a phlegmy laugh.

"Like now," added Alexandros. "The darkest age."

"A book about books," observed Gaston. "About the importance of saving books when all else is burning, or seems lost . . ."

Maliszewski wasn't listening to Gaston. "But do you understand, his suitcase contained only books and papers! Maybe one handkerchief, an extra pair of socks, nothing else."

"More precious than jewels . . ."

"More pointless, too," Maliszewski said. "You know I'm a devotee of learning—but honestly."

"He thinks he'll finish his book in London," suggested Alexandros. "And why not?"

"Inshallah," said Gaston. "Think of it, though: this is his hope, his reason for living. If he'd left Krakow without his manuscript, he probably wouldn't have felt the need to leave at all."

"Madness." Maliszewski shook his head. "Utter madness."

"Each of us finds our purpose in a different way." Gaston, like the professor devoutly Catholic, knew he sounded pious, priggish even, to an atheist like Maliszewski; but he didn't stop there. "Each of us, sooner or later, has to confront the question of what makes life worth living. For some of us—"

"Do you think," Alexandros interrupted, "that today of all days we should ask what it's all for?"

Gaston, chastened, stared out toward the end of the garden, at the hazy golden air beyond that stretched over the sea, then closed his eyes.

"The tragedy is devastating," Maliszewski said. He meant France. A statement of the obvious.

"Could hardly be worse." Sotirios reached for another cigarette. "I'm sorry, Cassar."

"And I know how it feels," said Maliszewski. "We're in the same boat now."

Gaston's immediate reaction was to object: How could anyone see France, a glorious empire and a world power, first daughter of the Roman Catholic Church, as in any way the same as poor Poland, a worn football tossed for centuries between Germany and Russia? But Maliszewski wasn't wrong. Even in the shade, Gaston could feel the sweat pricking in his crevices, a physical panic sprouting in the heat.

"Ouzo?" asked Alexandros. A maid, pretty but swarthy, with thick ankles, tramped down from the veranda bearing a tray upon which sat a bottle and glasses: the move from coffee to cocktails. "After a drink, we'll adjourn to the sitting room." With a swooping dip of his chin, Alexandros checked his watch; he was referring to their nightly BBC radio report. "The timing will be perfect." He clutched his trembling left forearm with his right hand, and moved it from the armrest to his lap as if his limb were an unruly child. "Sotirios, you pour."

LATER, ALONE IN the villa, lying naked in the dark beneath the crucifix, the ceiling fan spinning dully overhead, listening to a sudden downpour smattering the pavement and the waxy leaves outside the window, Gaston again felt the sweat rising cold out of his every pore, and his heart drumming—a sensation of falling, so that he almost cried out; he could hear in his head the echo of his cry but didn't allow it to escape him. He pulled the sheet around his body and curled into a ball, willing the night to end, hideously aware of Lucienne's empty side of the bed. Without Lucienne, each of his days loomed before him like a stretch of desert. She was—or he had made her—the source, for him, of meaning. How could he know what to think or what to say, without Lucienne's patient ear and wise advice? What was she experiencing in these days, hearing the same news he heard—although back in Algiers, she might well be hearing other reports, without access to the BBC—who knew what she heard or didn't?

Who knew even where she was—she'd planned to stay with his brother, Charles, but he might not have had room for the four of them, might have fobbed her off on one of the aunts, Tata Titine or Tata Baudry—and what could she be thinking, how worried she must be about him, about money, too, she wouldn't have much beyond what she'd taken with her, and she might have had to spend most or all of that on bribes or other unforeseen expenses along the route . . . the account at home was all but empty—could Charles afford to feed them? Little Denise? Ravenous François? Would she teach? Was there even school, or would there be? What would happen in Algiers once France had officially fallen to the Germans? Would the British, their allies even today, bomb the city? Were there shelters, or were they busy reinforcing basements? What if something had already happened? What if something had happened even on the journey, and Lucienne, Jeanne, and the children had never made it home? But surely he would have heard by now? Yet why, for more than three weeks now, *nothing*? No word since their departure?

He remembered her that first spring of their love, when they'd traveled together to the Sufi shrine at Tlemcen. Home from university, he'd lied to his mother, told her he was visiting a high school friend who'd moved there, and he instead met Lucienne, an illicit assignation, on the platform at Sidi Bel Abbès. He could relive exactly the moment when he saw her, his head out the window as the train drew into the station, she holding her suitcase before her with both hands, head slightly dipped, squinting in the spring sunshine. The wind on his face as the train pulled in was warm and chill at once, and the horn sounded to him like jubilation. Her yellow silk dress rippled in the breeze around her calves, frothing out from beneath a burgundy coat with large buttons. Her matching cloche hat, tight as a helmet around her plump cheeks, hid her beautiful dark curls, and the thought of them made him long to touch them. Her eyes! He wanted to see her eyes, closed against the glare—oh, the anticipation. He raised his hand and waved, waved, though he was almost with her, and the simple sight of her outline, of her dipped chin, thrilled his whole body, aroused him like a current. He had known, that spring morning, that Lucienne would be his life. She aroused him still, he adored her still, the pale, soft inside of her wrist, threaded with veins, the dip of her clavicle, her scent, of bergamot and sweet sweat—where was her scent? They were animals, destined for each other; why could he not smell her, his beloved Aïni?

His own sweat dried on him like a carapace, and the soft breeze from the fan chilled him. He got up, turned it off, went into the bathroom to splash water on his face. The rain outside was abating. In the dark living room, he stood naked at the window, looking out at the glistening foliage, the glimmer of the wet tarmac beyond the gate. Gaston needed to anchor himself. Lucienne was his anchor, but now he had to rely on himself.

He considered himself strong, but his strength sometimes failed him. What, beyond Lucienne, could serve as his rock? God, of course; of course, God; though sometimes Gaston felt that his faith in God was really a faith in Lucienne and in *her* faith. It occurred to him that he was himself in fact very weak, no more than a blowing blade of grass. He looked down at his naked limbs, his skin pearly in the dark, his hair dark scribbles on his belly and thighs. His hips slim, though not as slim as they'd once been; his penis, dangling uselessly; his strong legs; his wide, flat feet—were they not themselves an anchor? A man is an animal; he, thirty-four years old, an animal in its prime, full of strength, a modicum of wisdom, permeated by the life force—what was he doing trapped here, far from combat, womanish, a eunuch cowering at the sidelines of the war, trussed by the orders from Beirut and Paris, in abeyance. Was he afraid to die? Of course—but more afraid to fail in his duty.

Maybe somehow the navy would be able to keep fighting. Maybe the navy could join the Allies and fight. If he could only get back on a ship. In the morning he would cable Beirut again about a commission—as if they'd be listening, as if they'd have time to answer. France had fallen—but surely he could still anchor himself in his calling, in the navy. Gaston was close to tears. What am I? he asked the empty sitting room, the dripping night: What am I for? And the litany that he and Lucienne had more than once recited together returned to him: I am Mediterranean,

I am Latin, I am Catholic, I am French. These, then, were his anchors; these things, a priori and immutable, defined him, and must determine his actions.

BY SUNDAY AT NOON, in reply to his request, he received at last a cable from Cherrière in Beirut, summoning him back to Lebanon. He could take a couple of days to shut up shop but should secure passage on the boat from Athens as soon as possible. Clouet, he could tell, was envious when Gaston called to tell him: at least Beirut was under French mandate, if not fully France; at least there, whatever came, they would feel connected to the fate of the nation.

The last days in Salonica proved simultaneously hectic and languorous, even rudderless. Chaos emanated from France like a gas; the government had retreated to Bordeaux and endeavored to regroup. The terms for an armistice were under discussion. Late on Sunday came word that the Maréchal Pétain had assumed the role of prime minister, with General Weygand as minister of defense and Admiral Darlan in charge of the navy. Would the government stay in France or retreat to Algiers? Would they find a way to retain some semblance of French autonomy? The conversation in Alexandros Zannas's garden that Sunday evening circled around these uncertainties. Maliszewski, not yet back from his run to Piraeus, didn't join them, which made Gaston anxious. Sotirios, with his wheezing laugh, made a joke about the Greek prime minister, Metaxas, having no time for the Poles, but Gaston couldn't see the humor. Everything was in free fall.

"And the ascendancy of Pétain?" asked Zannas, "What will it mean?"

"Order," Gaston acknowledged, "which is preferable to chaos, especially in defeat. But beyond that—"

"A retreat to Algiers?" asked Sotirios, swirling his milky ouzo in its tumbler. The late shafts of sun fell dappled through the garden, dancing on the bougainvillea, the olive grove, on his face, his glass. Everything was the same; everything was different.

"No, I can't see it. The word is that Weygand has been pushing already for a week for a truce with the Germans."

"I see."

The three men were silent for a minute.

"Any word from home?" asked Sotirios.

Gaston shook his head, Lucienne's absence a constant dull ache. "I'm hoping that when I get to Beirut the communication will be easier."

"Should be. When do you go?"

"This week, I expect. Stuff to sort out. The furniture . . ."

"That beautiful sideboard!"

Gaston winced.

"No, I mean it," Sotirios insisted. "Just because the world is on fire doesn't stop the sideboard from being beautiful. What will you do with it all?"

"Storage, I expect. What boats are traipsing across the Mediterranean now?"

"Well, the boat to Alexandria should have set out before dawn," Alexandros said, reminding them again of Maliszewski.

"Please God the professor and the rabbi will soon be drinking gin and tonics on the other side."

"When is he back, then?"

"He may have a new posse on his hands already," Alexandros said. "We can't know. So much we can't know."

"The trouble is, we don't know anything." Gaston covered his face with his hands.

"The worst is not / So long as we can say 'This is the worst,' " Alexandros offered in English. "That's Shakespeare—*King Lear.* Helps me keep perspective."

"As long as we live and breathe," Sotirios laughed grimly, "even if I don't breathe so well." He lit another cigarette.

"I won't leave without saying good-bye," Gaston said, rising from his cane chair. The air smelled of the jasmine along the wall as dusk came on, and faintly of sea brine. "Don't get up. This is how I like to think of you both, of us: in this lovely garden. These afternoons, our conversations, are what I'll miss the most."

"Don't get maudlin." Sotirios stood. "Look, you've made me get up, you selfish bastard. You're not leaving yet."

"Not yet."

IN THE EVENT, however, Gaston didn't see Sotirios again before his departure. When he'd let Hernandez know of his recall to Beirut, and had sold several less beloved furnishings to the landlord; had given notice and a bonus to Maria and Eleni; had packed up his office and said his formal farewells to Clouet and the office staff; had taken Cotigny for lunch, on the Wednesday; and had arranged for the removal and storage of the rest of the furniture with the nuns at the Mission Laïque; and had prepared and dispatched with his driver the large suitcases in preparation for the transfer to Athens, leaving only an overnight bag—then he rang Alexandros and proposed a drink with him and Maliszewski on the terrace at the Méditerranée Palace, to conclude his Salonica life where it had begun, where the family had stayed during their first fortnight, many months before.

It was Thursday, the twentieth. Gaston was to board his boat for Beirut the next evening. The waiter recognized Gaston and brought him and Alexandros a bottle of Kevala rosé without asking, as though he knew this was the last time. All around them the seafront bustle continued: business, marketing, wives with their shopping. So strange.

"I wanted to ask," Gaston said after they'd toasted each other's good health, "whether you heard the broadcast on Tuesday."

"Your compatriot, you mean?" Alexandros, of course, had heard the speech.

Gaston had been in a café behind the Rotonda by himself when the owner had turned up the radio.

"*Moi, Général de Gaulle,*" they'd heard, in French; and it seemed to Gaston, over and over, "*moi . . . moi . . . moi . . .*"

He'd listened with full attention but could somehow barely grasp what was being said. The voice offended him—its certainty, a pride and almost self-satisfaction, arrogance even. As though this young general—known to Gaston by reputation and not well liked—had suddenly anointed himself, decided to be king.

"I, General de Gaulle . . . invite all French soldiers of the army, the navy, and the air force, I invite the engineers and workers specialized in armaments that are on British soil or could go there, to join me," he said. "I invite the leaders, the soldiers, the sailors, the pilots of the French army, navy, and air force, wherever they may be, to get in touch with me. I invite all the French who want to remain free to listen to me and to follow me."

Gaston could see the need for leadership in this crisis—order, as he'd told his friends, was greatly preferable to chaos, and for order, strong leadership was necessary. But this broadcast, from London—de Gaulle had run away, no? This leadership, he envisioned it as something like the Polish government in exile, was that it? The noble men that Maliszewski so longed to join and serve. But what gave de Gaulle the *right* to stake that claim? Gaston had, listening, wrestled with his hostility—immediate, primitive—to de Gaulle's bombast, his voice, his proposals. As military men, enlisted to serve your nation, how could you run away? Abandon your post? It made no sense. Did he expect the rank and file to scurry across the Channel like rats jumping ship?

But Gaston doubted his impulses too: perhaps de Gaulle was right. Fighting Hitler's Nazis was what mattered. That greater enemy was now within France—and everyone knew that the fascists had their supporters among the French, too. Even people Gaston had known at university, even some in the navy. The great shame of France was to be invaded, as if by a virus, by the Germans and their deadly worldview, contagious as it was; and de Gaulle proposed a way to continue the fight, openly and frankly—wasn't that a good thing?

Back and forth, Gaston had argued all possible permutations in his head in the forty-eight hours since hearing the broadcast. He'd considered the choice before him while walking, while packing, while lunching with Cotigny, though he didn't speak of it to his adjunct. He wished above all that he could speak to Lucienne: in the night he spoke aloud to her untouched pillow, as if she lay beside him, though it smelled only of laundering. How could he know what to do without knowing her mind? He thought of them as joined by an invisible thread, always united, one heart in two bodies. The two halves from Plato's *Symposium*, who had found each other and their life's purpose. As he liked to tell their friends, the only time they'd ever argued was when he'd tried to teach her to drive, in the hills behind Nice, early in their marriage; after the second heated exchange, she'd put her hand on his, her palm cool even in the hot car, and she'd said with that Mona Lisa smile, "*Basta, chéri*. No more. I don't need to drive. I'm clumsy with these gears and I can see that it's going to annoy you, the way it would annoy me if you were trying to whip up a soufflé in my kitchen. Thankfully you don't need to make a soufflé, and I don't need to drive a car. Our harmony is much more important."

It might not have been strictly true—of course, in twelve years of marriage, they'd had differences of opinion, though he didn't believe he'd raised his voice *at her*—but it was the essence of the truth. And without knowing her opinion—had he ever before been in such a situation?—Gaston couldn't fully know his own. He didn't say any of this to Alexandros and Maliszewski: he respected them both so deeply, and he wanted above all to know what they thought.

Alexandros and Gaston went over the substance of de Gaulle's message: that from London he'd exhorted his fellow Frenchmen to come and join him, to form an army of the Free French outside France to fight against Hitler.

"How can one refuse?" asked Alexandros.

"But it's not so simple," Gaston ventured. "For one thing, you're a civilian—but what if you were an officer? A military man—no matter the service—isn't his own master. We don't choose which battles we fight, because we've given our lives to our country. Zannas, what would you do, in my shoes?"

"I've learned that unless I've walked in the shoes, I can't venture to reply. You're far from home, and even your home—Algiers—is far from Paris. You're farther still from London. The fate of your government is still unclear, no?"

"Pétain has formed his cabinet."

"But I mean, might some of the deputies not still retreat to Algiers? Might there not be a government in exile *there*?"

"Each day it seems less likely."

"I see."

"But the navy?"

"No word yet about our fate. The terms of the armistice aren't yet clear."

"But your hope, I think—"

"Yes, my hope is that the navy, or at least those of us who are outside France, a substantial number, that we can continue the fight."

"Isn't that a pipe dream?" Maliszewski asked.

"No more than de Gaulle."

"Perhaps de Gaulle could command the navy?" Alexandros offered. "I'm only half-joking. He needs men to follow him; and perhaps the navy needs a man to lead."

"Not de Gaulle," Gaston said, with more vehemence than he'd intended. "I trust Darlan. I do. He's an exceptional man, honorable, with integrity. He was my commander, on my first ship." He was quiet for a minute. "There's a human component in all this—"

"Of course there is," Alexandros agreed.

"You have to have faith in a leader."

"Absolutely."

"If I could speak with Lucienne——"

"Yes." Alexandros understood: he had a wife, and children. "It's extremely difficult to be apart in such a time."

"Imagine how a telephone call might change things," Gaston said. "But I don't even know where she is. Where they are."

Alexandros put his hand on Gaston's sleeve. "Don't worry, my friend. Or try not to. Think how tenderly Maliszewski cares for his charges. Good people along the way will have offered them comfort."

"Inshallah." But who knew, really?

To take more time to make a decision was, of course, a decision in itself. Gaston understood this, even as he understood that Alexandros would instantly have sided with de Gaulle. But his friend also appreciated all the ways in which Gaston's situation was less than straightforward. He couldn't grasp, practically, what it might mean in this moment to side with de Gaulle—to go AWOL from the navy and make his way in mufti across Europe to England, ultimately crammed onto some dinghy over the Channel in the dead of night, if he ever got that far. The idea seemed preposterous—it was literally unimaginable—and only more so when every cell in his animal body clamored to be reunited with his family, to get to Beirut above all, to be able to contact his beloved, hear her voice, perhaps even be able to foresee a reunion—

In time, maybe there would be a different moment, an opening that realistically he could take. Sitting at the little table with these precious friends, in front of the sea in the shadow of Mount Olympus, in history and irrelevance at one and the same time, Gaston thought properly, as he hadn't before, of what it had meant for the Pole Maliszewski to leave everything familiar, his Warsaw life, his mother and his friends and his identity, and undertake an ineffable and grueling journey, not knowing where he was going, on a given day or in the end, to be here in this dazzling plaza, sunlit and loved for now, but with no certitude about tomorrow. It was an analogy for life itself, of course; Maliszewski's trajectory was only more extreme in its isolation. Gaston understood in his bones, with a sort of fatalism, that he would take the boat to Beirut and continue on the course that presented itself. He could no more run away to England than he could flap his wings and fly.

Years later, after everything was behind him, he would correspond with Alexandros, though they would never again meet. Alexandros and Sotirios joined the Greek Resistance, and Sotirios died of lung disease in an Italian concentration camp, while his older brother returned to help rebuild their homeland after the war. Alexandros was again, in those years, the director of the Red Cross in Greece. Maliszewski, as the Nazis came closer, slipped onto a boat at Piraeus, bound for Alexandria. Alexandros had heard from him after he got there; his next step, he'd explained, was South Africa, beyond the war zone, always with the hope and intention of gaining London and being part of Poland's government-in-exile. Of Monsieur and Madame Hernandez, there was never further news. Of them, after the war, no trace could be found.

Once arrived in Beirut, Gaston received a letter from Cotigny, with whom he hadn't spoken at length about his choice, but who had surmised his direction by his actions—by the fact that he had gone to Beirut at all. Cotigny wrote, on July 1, 1940:

> I can't hide that I'm in a different state of mind. . . . I will follow my first impulse, which was, as you must know, to seek to continue the struggle with our Allies, by any means within my power. . . . You see, in France, we love talk, and I believe the Maréchal Pétain is just a windscreen that hides a host of worthless little politicians. In the end, what does it 'save,' this Pétain government? I'd like to know. . . . Britain is the only light on the horizon, and as long as she holds out, the war is not lost, hope is not dead, and France will live again. We went to war against an oppressive regime that denies individual liberties and, more than that, seeks to destroy our way of thinking. We can't become the passive or consenting allies of this regime. We must fight to the end, and if fate is definitively against us, we'll disappear. But we must never submit. Britain will

do everything to succeed, because she, too, is fighting for her very existence. So I will make my way to London, to de Gaulle.

Gaston read Cotigny's letter at least a dozen times. Knowing that his aide-de-camp was loath to put pen to paper—an excellent draftsman, he loved drawing maps, but he hated to write sentences—Gaston understood what passion drove him. Cotigny was ready to sacrifice his Salonica life for the fight. But no sooner had Gaston arrived in Beirut and made his way to the terrace of the St. Georges than he was surrounded by old friends, so many of them, men like him, lost without their wives and children and greatly reassured to be in like company—Melchi, Durand-Gasselin, Dalet, Princzon, Largent. He was put up at the home of his old pal Imbert, in his sons' room, as Madame and the kids had retreated to the mountains to escape the heat. He wrote to Lucienne—from whom he'd had word at last, a passel of letters that sketched in the intervening weeks—that Beirut had the surprising aspect of a city without women; but it was very animated nonetheless. That liveliness embraced and included him, bolstered him, pushed away his uncertainty and despair. Now his friends in Salonica felt far away, as did the haze of Mount Olympus, and the moment of choice.

PART II

AMHERST, MASSACHUSETTS

They knew instinctively there'd be no saving her, but still, they hoped. Mouret stood grim-faced with François that Tuesday morning in the wadded gray light, the steam of their breath indistinguishable from the smoke of François's cigarette, their bare knuckles and nostrils raw as they watched her chained up to be hauled away.

They'd been back well over a week from their trip—Broussard, their Third Musketeer, had taken the bus back to Williams the morning after their return—and they'd left her parked on Kendrick Place, off the main road, so she'd be sure not to be towed when the snow came. It was true that they'd left her buried a few days after the blizzard. When they came with the shovels borrowed from Theta Delt, Mouret, who had a side interest in the classics, said she resembled an ancient Greek burial mound, a tumulus—as if, when you dug, you'd uncover gilded boxes, platters, shields, and filigree crowns, instead of a lumbering dun jalopy, with her bug-eyed, snub-nosed long square front and her sleek, sloped back and her dented left fender. François had thought, as they excavated her, that indeed she was, in her way, not unlike a tomb filled with treasure, now the repository of fantastical American experiences he could not have imagined.

Mr. Chapin, the mechanic, couldn't come out till first thing on Tuesday, with his chain-rattling tow truck and his lumberjack's plaid coat.

Bandy-legged, he darted busily around the Plymouth, slinging his weighty shackles. The two Frenchmen stood by with resigned funereal respect: she'd emitted loud whistling noises and occasional smoke on the last leg back from the South, up through Pennsylvania and New York, and they knew she had a fan-belt problem in addition to the failed ignition.

When François called the garage two days later from the pay phone in the frat house (located in a graffiti-covered cupboard with a fish-bowl window next to the back stairs), Chapin rattled off a list of under-lying problems that François only barely understood. But he did grasp that quite aside from a dead battery she had a cracked chassis, and this, Chapin was telling him, made her not worth the effort or the money to repair. She was finished.

François replaced the phone gently on its cradle and returned to the living room, where Iklé, Rob, and Kaz were playing Kaz's new The-lonious Monk record, all three bent over the speaker as if it were the Delphic oracle.

"What's up, *mon frère?*" Iklé, who, like an old man, affected a pipe, looked up with a gentle smile.

"Plymouth's dead." François came to join them, though he felt almost like crying.

"Major drag. I'm sorry." Iklé patted his arm.

"She was a good old girl," Kaz offered, lifting the needle off the record. "I guess we won't get to California this spring after all."

"Guess not."

"Maybe Stiff'll loan you his Roadmaster?"

François made a vague, dismissive sound in his throat. Stiff, an econ major with copperplate handwriting and perfectly ironed shirts, wouldn't be loaning his Roadmaster to anyone.

The boys, amiable but preoccupied, turned back to their record. Kaz lowered the needle with perfect precision so it neither jumped nor scratched, and the music of Thelonious's wild fingers bloomed again around them.

FRANÇOIS, LYING ON his bed, eyeing the spreading ice on the inside of the windowpane by his head, recalled the Saturday nights in the winter of '49, similarly freezing, when he and Gardel and Servier had scurried from their dorm to the Caveau de la Huchette to hear Sidney Bechet and his piping soprano sax, the vaulted basement so packed that steam as well as smoke hovered commingling above the mass of bodies—the exhilaration, the languid, visceral thread of the music that had pulled emotion from his chest almost against his will. "America," he'd thought then, in the dark winter of postwar Paris, the trials of boarding at the Lycée Louis-le-Grand so brutal: the rows of metal beds lining the length of that freezing, cavernous room, which smelled, nonetheless, of sweat; the shrieking cats in the alley at night; the constant, gnawing hunger; and his feet always cold, always wet, because the northern damp had seeped on the first day through the thin leather soles of his one pair of shoes and had remained, thereafter, a constant. Above all, in those dark months, he had missed the Mediterranean light, its fierce presence, in the brief, breathless, sullen Paris winter days. Hearing Bechet, he'd thought, "America! *There*, I want to go there."

And now he was there, here, in western Massachusetts, in a ramshackle mottled brick fraternity house a couple of blocks from the village green and the campus, the sounds of a wholly different jazz drifting up the stairwell. One semester into his American life, classes soon to begin again, he felt like a raisin on top of a cake, extraneous. Endlessly fascinated, buoyed on waves of desire, he also felt much alone. With Mouret and Broussard, he shared at least a language and a culture, but even to them he was foreign, he knew, a (mostly) white colonial African from that mysterious terrain across the Mediterranean. And to his American frat brothers? He was completely indecipherable.

He could still see the effects of the southern sun—Miami! Key West! Havana!—on the backs of his hands, a brownness more apparent against his white cuffs . . . was it Stiff or Rosie who'd called out, upon seeing

him, "Hey, rug merchant! Showing your true Ay-rab colors at last?"
He'd laughed, of course, with that same noncommittal scoffing sound
he'd made earlier about the Roadmaster, in the case of "Ay-rab," to suggest that he had the requisite sense of humor to fit in with his new fraternity and, at the same time, that they hadn't the faintest idea what they
were talking about. He trusted that the former impression was to the fore;
only sweet Kaz, who, when it was just the two of them, carefully called
him "François," with his best French accent, rather than the "Frank" on
which the group had settled early on, and which was now, for all intents
and purposes, his name—only Kaz might have had some sense, however
vague, of French colonial North Africa, of the fact that many Algerians
were Berbers, not Arabs, and that François was no more an Algerian
than Stiff Childs was a Navajo.

But he'd come to understand, too, that the theater of his American
fraternity, the hazing as they called it, was conceived to cover each of
the members with shame, to make them mutually vulnerable and so
mutually dependent: Had Stiff chosen his nickname? Obviously not, but
he bore it with a smile, as did Rosie, or mostly—though to be given a
girl's name was somehow a deeper barb, François could see, and more
uneasy because, just as Frank was the frat's lone foreigner, Rosie was
the only Jew. François understood too, by this point in the year, that
before he'd arrived, nobody had wanted him—how many of them, a few
beers in, had clapped him on the shoulder and said, "You're all right,
you know that, Frank? You really are. But you've no idea how much we
worried . . ." And then they'd be off, narrating the story of the new program for foreign students—he was one of seven that year, and Mouret
the other Frenchman—and how the previous May the dean had simply
announced—"Out of the blue, can you believe it?"—that each year the
fraternities would be assigned a foreigner—"Without so much as a by
your leave!"—to live with them.

"You gotta understand, Frank," the story always went, "the whole
point of a fraternity is that we're family, we're brothers for life, but unlike

the family you're born with—or stuck with—this is the family you choose. You dig? So it's just not cool, as a principle, as an idea, to send us someone we didn't choose, right?" Inevitably, the drunk brother would grow a little misty and would squeeze François's shoulder a little, a sign of high emotion. "Thing is, Frank, if we'd been given the choice, we would've chosen you."

What was there, really, to say? At the Christmas party, just before they'd disbanded for the holiday, Rob Turner had told him they'd decided "there's never been and never will be another Frog like our Frank"—and there again, though flattered, François had made that vague noise in his throat, this time to express both self-deprecation ("I'm just a Frog like any other") and appreciation ("Aw, thanks guys"), with emphasis on the latter. It was so simple: these men, these American brothers, were good guys, without irony or malice—if also without worldly perspective or understanding—and they wanted to be appreciated. Like children. And like kids, they were fun to be with, living in the present, free.

It didn't escape his notice, in all this, that he'd been assigned to be Rosie's roommate. As he lay on his bed and looked across the scuffed floorboards, it was Rosie's unmade bed he saw, books piled around it in uneven towers, like the ruins of a fortress. Rosie Rosenstein, brilliant son of a Holyoke shopkeeper, who'd no more wanted the Frog than anyone else—or the Ay-rab, or whatever they thought he was—had got stuck with him. He'd made François feel it, too, that first week in September, when he'd mocked François's accent and his English—prompting François's silent vow to eradicate any trace of a French accent before June 1953 (a vow he would successfully keep, betraying himself in later years only in his trisyllabic pronunciation of "nuisance" or in the light, soft *o* when he said "monk")—and François was still wary of Rosie, "touchy as a girl," according to Stiff, easily irritated by disruption and frivolity. "But Rosie's going to Harvard Law," as the *on dit* of the house had it, "and he'll defend us all in court, and keep us in our old age."

Rosie, Kaz, Stiff, Iklé, Rob, and the others—was he happy among

them? Never bored, for sure. Though he felt, often, like an anthropol-
ogist, trying to absorb the local customs, and to make sense of them.
François sat up, lit another cigarette, and opened the frozen window,
admitting snow-scented gusts: Rosie hated it when he smoked in the
room, had asked him not to, and it was officially against the rules, too.
But he was a Frenchman, wasn't he? It was practically his official job to
smoke—they were all sorry only that he didn't smoke Gitanes.

How would he manage to take Susan to New York without the Plymouth? This strange world of single-sex institutions, with rules instead of
parents. He and Mouret joked about "the local mating rituals"—complex
and arcane, compared to back home, not least because it seemed that
there was, in America, the flickering possible promise of sex. Was there
really? Or was it just an illusion?

Susan, from Albany, New York, was a junior at Smith College, down
the road in Northampton. Before Christmas break, they'd been on a few
dates, two dinners in Northampton, the second with a long kiss at the
end, and then a movie, where she'd let him put his hand up her sweater
and fondle her breasts in the dark. He didn't have much sense of her,
really—she had that arch, jokey tone they all affected, like a walking
New Yorker cartoon—but she was pretty, with big brown eyes, and he
could tell that she liked him. She thought he was cool, simply for being
French—she was a French major, after all. She admired his hair, his
clothes, his accent. She sent him scribbled postcards with drawings of
martinis and cigarettes. She was the one who suggested that they travel
to New York together for the weekend.

The prospect thrilled and terrified in equal measure. François knew he
was nice-looking, but he was awkward. Shy. Untamed, his mother sometimes told him, too intense in his emotions, blunt and needy. His project
of public self-restraint was in part so nobody would discern this, so he'd
never be vulnerable. Only his family could know, and only because they
had to, because they'd seen him disarmed, a child. Men mustn't be weak;
weakness was shameful. He wanted to be what Susan thought he was,

the cool French seducer; he was nervous she'd discover the truth, his intense, maladroit self. He'd never yet had sex, not gone all the way—he'd missed his chance, idiot that he was, in Cuba—and he sensed that Susan would, that maybe she already had. She was so confident; but in the anthropology lessons of America, he was learning that this could also be merely a veneer. That she wanted him to be confident, to take the lead, was certain. And terrifying.

This, then, would be the week's pressing dilemma—whether to go by bus or to borrow another guy's car (not Stiff's) or whether to postpone the plan for a while, or indefinitely, and to renounce both the thrill and the terror. Sexual possibility loomed not in their time in New York itself—Susan was to stay with her aunt and uncle on the Upper East Side, and François had booked a single room (at extra cost) in the YMCA on West Sixty-Third—but in the journey there and back. He had so distinct a sense of her smooth, rounded forearms with their small, delicate hands, of the bowlike curve of her upper lip and her thick, straight hair, shot with gold and curled, at the ends, with tongs. He wanted, chiefly, to touch her pale skin, to feel the soft flesh of those forearms, and to slide her fine gold bracelet around the protruding knob of her wrist bone. He wanted to run his fingers through her hair and trace the line of her neck, where she daubed that sickly-sweet perfume, perhaps even place his lips to her clavicle—he remembered the smooth bare skin of her waist beneath his stroking forefinger, the tight rise of her nipples. . . . But it was pointless to imagine any of this if they were taking the bus, swaddled in their winter coats, squashed into those narrow, bone-crushing seats. . . . At the dinner to which the aunt had invited him—a small dinner party, Susan had said—nothing could be less than formal and he probably wouldn't even kiss her cheek; and if they did manage dinner at a restaurant the other evening, even then there'd be only the late January cold of the avenue in which to linger. The rules of the YMCA were as unbending as those of the aunt and uncle. The Plymouth had let him down.

He felt both despairing and relieved. He'd call Susan's dorm and leave a message, telling her he couldn't go after all. What was the point? He'd have to write to cancel the room; he'd better get the note in the post by five. There'd be another chance—there had to be. He just needed to plan better. What did the Americans say, though? Three strikes and you're out. He stubbed the butt in the dirty hollow of the window frame and flung it outside, where it marred the perfect drift below.

He hated the cold; just then he hated the college, too, and Theta Delt and the mediocre first-semester grades he knew he'd receive in his mailbox at the end of the week in a slim brown envelope, neatly typed on college letterhead and signed by the registrar. He should write to his parents and sister, he thought, aware of the little stack of blue airmail envelopes on the corner of his desk, their Algerian stamps, exotic to the frat brothers, mostly torn out, leaving, like wounds, the white letters themselves partially exposed. He missed his family almost constantly, but didn't want to. He wanted not to need them, to be free—free of their constant, clucking worry, their tedious religiosity, their old-fashionedness. He wanted to be new, part of this reborn, postwar world, part of technology, progress, America's global possibility. But too often, here, he felt adrift, as if he wandered on the moon.

He took comfort from his mother's sweet, wide, frank hand; his father's regular flourish, uneven sometimes now in his current state of health; and his sister's varying script. Denise had bafflingly traded her nickname Poupette for 'Juju,' and she altered from month to month the size and form of her writing. She was at this point in a period of minimum scale, as if trying to fit as many words as humanly possible on each sheet of onionskin. Rosie, ever heartless, had glanced over when François was reading one of her letters and had said, "Hope that one's not a girlfriend. Tiny writing like that means she's seriously insecure."

François had merely nodded slightly, noncommittal as ever, though the accuracy of Rosie's comment infuriated him.

LATER THAT NIGHT, in Mouret's room, he tried to explain about his sister. Mouret of the imperial Gallic conk, who looked freshly combed and pressed even as he stretched the length of his bed, his arms crossed behind his head, his stocking-footed ankles crossed in symmetry, listened with his eyes unnervingly closed. He wasn't asleep, François knew; it was how he listened. He, too, had a younger sister, three of them in fact, outside Avignon, where even now they lay tucked up asleep with their hair in curling papers—rebellious Madeleine, calm Emmanuelle, pious little Marie-Hélène. Mouret had described them all so well, and their devout, burgherly household. François could see it all so clearly that he could almost insert himself into the vision, could hear his footfall on the pea-gravel drive, feel his hand upon the sandstone balustrades of Mouret's *maison de maître*, with its long blue shutters and wide tiled veranda, the orderly foliating vineyards stretching off in rows to the horizon. Yes, all this without ever having actually seen the Vaucluse except at speed from the Mistral train, an understanding of his own Frenchness absorbed, by François, osmotically, from literature and films and schoolbooks, the same as for Camus, who had for so long never seen snow.

But how could Mouret picture François's world, of which he'd seen no photographs and heard no stories? Algeria featured barely more clearly in the French consciousness than did Puerto Rico or Guam for the Americans. Mouret was definitely listening as François described their home, a block from the seafront in Bab el Oued, the shadowy stairwell that smelled of everyone's dinners (fish on Fridays), and the wild burst of light when you entered their top-floor flat, with its terrace hovering above the rooftops, facing the vast, electric ocean, now azure, now slate, now shimmering silver and gold, but always above all the purveyor of great light, a promise, a wealth of itself that required nothing in the bank.

François couldn't articulate this; nor did he trust even good-hearted Mouret to understand. That they'd never considered themselves poor—lacking in money, yes, sometimes painfully so, during the war especially, when Papa was gone for such long stretches and the navy payments came through only erratically: they'd done without heat, though never without food, as Tata Baudry always remembered them with gifts from L'Arba, and the cousins made sure they had Sunday lunch each week. They'd taken in lodgers, one after another, three in the hardest year, through the winter of '41–'42, when François and Denise had moved out of their bedroom for these tenants, university students to a man, and had slept alongside wheezing, gelatinous Tata Jeanne in her high, soft bed that smelled cloyingly of dust and old flowers. Denise, forced into the dip in the middle of the mattress, had sneezed a great deal that winter, from allergies, her pale eyes chronically red-rimmed and damp, and surely that was the year Maman had first taken her to the otorhinolaryngologist about her "*végétations*," so that then, with the prospect of Denise's sinus operation—the first of several—Maman had begun to tutor pupils in the evenings in French and history for extra money, and even Tata Jeanne had taken in mending. Yes, there was no question that they'd lacked money, but how to explain that they'd considered themselves worthy, chosen even, rich—yes, they'd considered themselves rich.

But Denise. François was trying to explain to Mouret how he worried for her, they all did, and felt responsible, and that he could never tell whether their worrying only made her in fact *more* insecure, an unfortunate cycle of negative reinforcement from which it sometimes seemed she might not escape. But as a child she had been frail and skittish, her limbs like twigs, her pale blue eyes enormous, like her ears—he'd called her "elephant" when feeling particularly cruel—her white-blond hair in a braided crown around her skull. Insects, loud noises, the dark, being alone even for a minute—everything frightened her and made her cry, so that all of them, even he, her exasperated older brother, had bent to her will.

Strange that such apparent fragility should have amounted, really, to a determination of iron; but she had shaped the course of their days as fiercely as any patriarch. When she was too ill for school—her ailments often nebulous: asthma, allergies, general physical weakness—Maman kept her home and cosseted her, miraculously procured bones for beef broth and plumped piles of pillows behind her pale head. When she was frightened by the bombings—school was on hiatus then anyway—Maman accompanied her to L'Arba and left her in the care of Tata Baudry for several months, where—how could it have been predicted?—the passage of a plague of locusts created for Denise another ungovernable lifelong trauma: the whir and clatter of their wings, the solidity of their shelled bodies, their uncountable, indivisible, overwhelming number.

When Maman went to spend two winter months of Papa's shore leave in Toulon with him before he embarked on the *Dumont d'Urville*, Denise was dispatched to the Cousines Breloux, sleeping in her very own bedroom in their luxurious apartment downtown, fed on milk puddings and fresh egg omelets, while he, just eleven but deemed too noisy and male for their estrogenic environment, was left alone with old Tata Jeanne, who, enfeebled by her illness, was prone to seizures at any time, so that in truth he took care of her rather than vice versa.

When, later, they were sent in that August near the war's end to the state-run summer camp along the coast—a barbaric, unforgettable month of unsupervised freedom, sleeping beneath the swaying marine pines on cots in long canvas tents that billowed like sails in the ocean breeze, running free in a pack, like dogs, along the sand at dawn, and splashing long hours in the sea under the battering sun, so that by month's end, when he returned home, François was scrawny as a prisoner, his whole skin dark as a bruise, with gaunt hollows beneath his eyes and his hair, shaven against the lice infestation latterly discovered in the bedding, a mere dark nimbus around his skull—yes, of that glorious and inglorious month (Maman had said, when he got home, that she barely recognized him) Denise had seen only four days, of which she later recalled only terror, pure terror—the noises, at night, of the wind in the tents and the boughs of the pines, with the roar of the sea beneath; the other girls, all bigger, deep-voiced, large, a knot of them mean, mocking her slowness at running and her splay-footed duck's gait, and the thick glasses that made her large eyes blurry—and her ears, they'd even made fun, the monsters, of her ears! Just four days, before she trod on a wasp that had her left foot swollen like an aubergine, the skin almost split, and Maman was telephoned from the infirmary, summoned not only to retrieve her daughter but to accompany her to the clinic so that the shocking intensity of Denise's reaction might be further assessed.

"Do you see?" François asked Mouret, both of them sluggish with scotch, François slumped in the plaid armchair by the radiator, Mouret's room warmer in the snowbound Massachusetts January than the flat in Bab el Oued had ever been in the soft Mediterranean winters. "So now, she's started university, and I worry."

"About what, exactly? She won't get stung in the lecture hall, will she?"

François laughed a little, Mouret too, but François felt guilty for laughing and stopped. How to explain that he carried her, that he'd long carried her and felt he would always carry her, that he yearned to be free of the burden and at the same time had years before accepted it as his life's sentence? She was weak and he was strong. As much as she had blubbered and dithered and shied from challenge, he, in return, had made himself the stoic, the strong and indomitable, "Take them by surprise!," "Cave adsum," show no weakness, a wall, a rock, just hold it in, always in. And his mission was to triumph, to be the best at everything he undertook—and to undertake only that at which he might excel—and this, of course, was why the time at boarding school in Paris could not be spoken of, barely even Sidney Bechet could be spoken of, but certainly not those long, destroying, dark months that had all but—no, that *had* defeated him. Aloud, to Mouret, he said, "Who knows? She might get stung. I'm not there, that's the point. I told my best friend to look out for her—she's following in my footsteps, right? She's chosen law."

"It pisses you off, I think?"

"A little. It's like she's in my place. Chasing my friends. Clamoring after my professors. 'Oh, I love this one,' 'Oh, this one's too harsh, but he knows I'm your sister.' . . . But at any moment it can all go wrong. And then it's ruined, maybe for both of us."

"Or maybe it's ruined either way?"

François sat up a little. "How so?"

Mouret opened an intelligent eye, to meet François's. "Maybe it's worse if she loves it, if she fits right in, if she really takes your place . . ."

François, at that, could only emit his familiar snort, as if to say at once "An absurd notion" and "So what if she does?" "I know Servier has blown her off," he said.

"Your friend? He told you so?"

"No—he doesn't write. He's like me—illegible chicken scrawl, better things to do. No, no—she told me. She's furious with him."

"Because she fancies him." Mouret did not pose this as a question.

"How'd you guess?"

"I've got little sisters of my own, *cher ami*. Sometimes I think that's our main purpose, to introduce our sisters to the eligible bachelors from amongst whom they'll select a mate."

François couldn't imagine introducing his little sister, all nerves, as a romantic prospect. "Speaking of which," he said, "I've written to cancel my New York trip with Susan. Without the car—"

Mouret sighed. "I know, I know. That Pamela girl, the one from Skidmore, wants us to go up there for their winter dance in two weeks—you were to squire her roommate, Jane. But without the Plymouth—"

François shrugged, poured them each another—a final, he told himself—thimble of scotch.

"She was our best girlfriend," he said. He knew that Mouret fancied Pamela the way he did Susan: the allure was general, rather than specific, and they'd be as happy to find another. The car, though, they'd adored, and would miss greatly.

"Have we told Broussard?" Mouret asked.

"Have you?"

"He wanted her for Montreal, next month."

"We were going together."

"Yeah, well."

Their plans dissolved in ashes around them. François stood, a little unsteadily, placed his glass—filched from the dining hall—with careful deliberation on Mouret's dresser. He lifted his coat from the hook on the back of the door and pulled his scarf from its sleeve.

"Hurry up please its time," he said in English. They'd both been reading T. S. Eliot. Mouret bestirred himself from supine to sitting upright, his feet on the floor.

"I bet you stay here," François said to Mouret, suddenly certain of this, too, as a gulf between them (and indeed, he was right: his friend would stay, and marry an American, and become a professor of French literature at the University of Chicago, where the winters were, if possible, longer and more harsh than even in western Massachusetts, forsaking forever the soft golden light of Avignon and his three lovely sisters).

"Not you?" Mouret seemed to take it as a given for them both.

"I need the light." In his mind's eye, he saw the gilded flood of sun upon the sea, the sheen of those days, even in winter, which he suddenly missed greatly. His mother, his home. But, he told himself, you mustn't care too much about a place, the way you mustn't care too much for people beyond your family. Loyalties, absolute, must be limited. Triumph was born of continence, and restraint.

ON THE WALK back to Theta Delt through the frigid night, the near-full moon lighting the snowy common like a vast blue lamp, so that the trees cast shadows, François relived his latest unacknowledgeable adventure, a recent failure that it burned him to recall. If he thought of his mother or sister, he could hardly bear it; they would have been horrified. But if instead he pictured Hemingway, or Boris Vian, or even Jean Marais playing *anyone*—then for a moment, just a moment, he could see himself, too, voracious for life experience without rules, or shame.

Havana. He'd barely admitted to his parents that he'd been, only two lines in his long letter home about the Florida trip. The drive down the coast in the Plymouth, with Broussard and Mouret, so long anticipated, the three of them giddy, the weather warming little by little till suddenly it was summer. They wore sunglasses and dangled cigarettes, lit or unlit, from their lips, and François bought a cheap leather jacket, pretending to be Brando in *The Wild One*. America as it flashed by loomed bright and strange, as delicious to them as Buñuel's surrealism: vivid tableaux lodged in his memory like scenes from dreams, unforgettable, alluring, uneasy.

All through the Carolinas it had spat with rain, past metal-roofed houses with rocking chairs on the verandas. Hardly a white face, farmland, a succession of pig farms along the route—he'd made a note in his journal about the pigs, in between the cornfields: Who could have known they came in so many colors? Red, brown, white, striped, pink, black, vast as water barrels, their solid backs slick and shiny with the rain. He'd seen them in hordes, jostling, but through the rain-spattered window, at speed, heard no sound, a porcine dumb show punctuated instead by gusts of shit-stink filtering into the vents of the Plymouth. In laughing disgust, the three of them had lit cigarettes to mask the smell—they were half price in the South, anyhow.

After the corn and pigs came open fields bounded, like ranches, by miles of white fencing, and dotted with old horses standing immobile, like something out of a Russian painting. And in the distance, dark bands of trees draped with ghostly Spanish moss, between which loomed the odd dwelling—a white clapboard church, bright and ready, or a tumbledown shack, its grassy roof patched, a Black man on the porch, stern-faced, smoking.

Even after the rain stopped, the air was saturated with moisture and the verdure abundant, overgrown. For a stretch, the route was lined on both sides by trees at once magnificent and sinister: they drove several miles as if through a tunnel of shade, the great boughs looming over the car like giants' arms. In Charleston, they stopped at a Chinese restaurant where the only other customers were a family of deaf-mutes whose hands fluttered like birds over their steaming soup. The young waiter, his cuffs too short and a mite dirty, delivered their dishes on a battered tray and retreated to the kitchen without a word, the swing door slapping behind him, leaving the room so quiet that the Frenchmen didn't dare speak aloud to one another, the experience wreathed in a mystery almost sacred. Back on the road, they turned the radio to top volume and shouted French curse words out the windows. But before that they'd stopped to use the public toilets in the town square, and François had taken note of the sign on the door, infamous in rumor—*this* was the South—but seen there by him for the first time: "Whites Only."

Once they were over the state line into Florida, the sun became a hot ball, the ghostly moss turned into palm trees, fringing turquoise lagoons. They spent a night in St. Augustine, where, on a little square planted with poppies and decorated with Christmas lights, he bought a Native doll dressed in beaded burlap, complete with papoose, and a set of painted maracas for his sister and parents, who would never come there; and when they took their breakfast of buttered bread and milky coffee at an iron table on the pavement beneath a fluttering red awning, he observed to Mouret and Broussard that they might as well have been in Nice. He felt, in his body, at home for the first time, in America: the light, the warmth, the salt smell of the ocean. But this vast country was also always only ever more unknown, more new.

On the highway, when he wasn't driving, he noted with pleasure in his little book, his scrawl worsened by the car's motion:

All-U-Can

Hi-way

4-Sale

Thru.

This American English thrilled him—its energy, its freedom, its carelessness.

"You're the new de Tocqueville," Mouret joked, his hairy fingers tapping the Plymouth's Bakelite steering wheel. He intended his mockery fondly, but François was stung, and briefly silent.

THEY SPENT CHRISTMAS in Miami, three in the room, sweating. First they swam in the ocean, a few blocks from their pink hotel, and then paid extra for the shower, to be clean for Christmas. Had it been his own idea or Mouret's—surely not Broussard's—to attend the midnight Mass at Gesù downtown? Somehow, even in his willful godlessness, he felt he owed it to his mother: it wasn't Christmas without Mass. They'd imagined going out afterward, somehow drinking rum on the beachfront in the small hours, but the service proved interminable, incense and droning and gilded raiment. The church, like a stage set, seemed freshly painted, and they'd been guided to their seats—trapped from the aisle by two stout aunties wearing black lace veils—by one of a posse of Swiss ushers in white smoking jackets, as though Mass were, indeed, a performance, a Hollywood movie. Only Mouret took Communion, though François felt his mother's disappointment when he stayed resolutely in the pew with his arms crossed. Ultimately he hated himself for all of it, the ritual that was no consolation but a parody of ritual, and their eventual release, exhausted, into a city asleep in readiness for Christmas morning. Back in the room, no screens on the windows so they had to choose between sweltering and mosquitoes, they turned off the light and drank the mickey of scotch saved in the glove compartment since Washington, D.C. They had only one glass between them—found on the edge of the sink in the communal toilet; Mouret had washed it thoroughly in hot water—and François felt sure, each time the glass was passed, that Broussard gulped more than his share. They joked about how strange this Christmas was proving and how they'd remember it always, but it was his first away from home, and secretly he felt a bit miserable.

Their dip in the ocean on Christmas morning roused him from melancholy—the long swath of pale sand was only sparsely peopled, and the sparkling waves delighted. They'd already checked out of their room and had to change into their rumpled clothes, salt- and sand-speckled, behind a wooden shower cabin, before getting back in the car.

Broussard and François dropped Mouret, still damp, at the airport for his flight to New Orleans, where he was to stay with family friends, grand French expatriates, in their mansion. He'd invited them to join him—if they brought dinner jackets, they could escort two beautiful young debutantes to the midwinter cotillion, a full gander at New Orleans society, by all accounts gothic and strange. But Broussard and François had demurred, determined not to be constrained in penguin suits, clamped into small talk at fussy dinner tables. No girls, however pretty, were worth the trouble. They might have gone for Mardi Gras, but in December they wanted Hemingway or Bogart: the sea breeze flapping their shirts and a flask in the pocket of their shorts, the light so fierce they had to squint. So after they dropped Mouret, the two of them headed farther south—"Just two Musketeers now," observed Broussard, the map in his lap while François drove, both of them unshaven in their dark sunglasses, the leather jacket abandoned in the back seat.

"For a few days."

Mouret had promised to rejoin them in Miami before the turn of the year—1953!—and then they'd drive back north. The plan was the Keys and then Cuba, and as they drove ever farther into the sun, François recalled the Paul Bowles novel Iklé had given him at Thanksgiving: an irony surely that in *The Sheltering Sky*, an American ventured into François's Sahara, on a one-way voyage to existential extremity, while here he—and Broussard, in his way, Frenchmen both—ventured similarly into these alien American tropics: heading on, out, south, like a thread unspooling, with ever less certainty of the possibility of return. François wanted to see the world, to devour it. The question was, How far could you go? And what would you find at the end of the road? You'd find yourself, surely: your existential self.

He didn't say this aloud to Broussard, who put his feet up on the dash and fiddled with the radio—stations increasingly hard to catch, the dial filled with static—and stuck his fingers out the open window to feel the salt spray.

The land grew thinner and thinner, the light more intense. Their long spit of land, or sand, was bounded on both sides by green water—truly green, the blue of the southern seas, as François's father had told him, in a letter, recalling his first navy voyage to the Americas in the late 1920s, a lifetime before. On one side, for a while, the rolling green expanse was seeded with tiny islets, a cartoonist's version of desert islands, each a mere hummock rising out of the water, topped with wavering shrubs like fat locks of hair.

When they reached the Seven Mile Bridge at Marathon, François's heart constricted and he struggled against the panicky urge to turn the wheel and fly the Plymouth into the oily green ocean. The bridge, seamed and bumping beneath their tires, went on forever, the water glaring all around them as their thin strip of tarmac proceeded to eternity. They had to stop the car for boats to pass through the open swing span over Moser Channel, and they got out to stretch their legs and smoke, alongside families—thick-waisted dads in short sleeves and their wives in cat-eye glasses with scarves around their hair, corralling hyperactive kids who shrieked into the wind—and fishermen, leathered and warped, hunched alone, squinting disapprovingly at the tourists.

Broussard marveled at the flimsy barrier. "You could fall over it without even meaning to," he said, leaning his lanky torso at a perilous angle. François was enough his parents' child to say, "Don't!" before he thought better of it.

"Think they get a lot of suicides out here?" Broussard asked, hawking a loogie like a jellyfish into the water before he straightened up, as a pouch of gray pelicans soared overhead.

"Hell of a way to come just for that." Though François could feel the allure, like the pull of a magnet. "Let's get back in the car."

By the time they got to Key West, François had had enough of the ocean and the signs for boat charters, live shrimp, bait; enough of the dirty shacks along the water's edge and the ragged jetties, their mooring bollards like dead men's stumpy teeth, a sense of the whole world battered relentlessly by water and light, no longer the promise of his beloved Mediterranean that he'd felt farther north, but something more extreme, almost scary.

He experienced the town—the flat land broadened out to sustain a grid of streets, from many of which you did not see the water—as pure relief. That the houses, tidily trimmed, white or brightly colored, evoked a fairy-tale past was in some ways pleasing, but not the point: like the Swiss ushers in their smoking jackets at the Gesù church, they felt theatrical, a movie set. Someone else's movie. Relieved, he also felt restless, keen to catch his breath and press on, press farther, see more. Still, it was a mercy to be on terra firma, or to have the illusion of it. He'd seen *Key Largo* at the cinema in Paris in the unspeakable year, and recalled vividly the sense of the characters trapped in the hotel while the hurricane raged. What were these Keys but one enormous beach, an expanded version of the sandy islets protruding from the waters along the route? Every trace of humanity felt to him as fragile as the lone wavering shrub upon one of those islets, awaiting destruction by the elements.

Broussard, apparently, experienced nothing like this: after they parked the car, he slung his bony limbs around, jauntier than ever, in a salty little jig on the tarmac.

"We did it," he sang, "we made it! The end of the goddamn earth!" Playful, he slapped François on the shoulder. "Once we've dumped our stuff, I want to see where the Atlantic and the Gulf of Mexico meet. I want to put my foot in one, and then put my foot in the other."

"Sounds like a plan. That'll take about ten minutes."

"Just the beginning, my friend. We're gonna like it here. No suits, no ties—poor Mouret, unlucky prick. *This* is America, right?"

"Right." François took both their duffels from the trunk and threw Broussard's to him more aggressively than was necessary. He missed Mouret. Broussard caught it.

After two days at the Key Wester motel—two stories of flaking pink stucco with green shutters at the windows, the building as long as a train, overlooking a lawn traced in swirls of white stone footpaths and a chemically electric pool, with the soft roar of the sea audible from their room and bright paper parasols in their poolside drinks—François agitated for Cuba. He'd seen *Week-End in Havana*, a lot funnier than *Key Largo*, in repertory at the Majestic in Algiers when he'd skipped his property law lecture on a Thursday afternoon: like the actress in that film, whose cruise unexpectedly ends in Florida, he longed with sudden desperation to see the Paris of the Caribbean.

"It's a forty-minute flight," he wheedled.

Broussard, browning his countable ribs on a pillowed lounger by the pool, seemed barely to hear.

"Another world. Forty minutes away. A whole different culture. Totally different from this. Alive, full of history. Cafés and dancing! Enough of the seagulls, blue sky, and American plastic."

"I *like* American plastic, my friend. If this is American plastic, I'll take it. It's like we're in a movie."

"Haven't you seen enough of this movie? The plan was Havana next. They say the girls are prettiest there—that Latin beauty."

Broussard sat up enough to sip his punch from its tiki glass and nodded discreetly at a bikinied blonde stepping gingerly, toes pointed, into the pool. "Girls look just fine here," he said, then lay back down and closed his eyes. "Go—go if you want. I'm tired. I'm happy here. I don't need some pedagogical Fulbright push, some history lesson complete with cathedral and museums, to feel fulfilled. Everything I want"—he gestured broadly with his arm, but blindly, his eyes still closed—"I've got right here. I am our French ambassador to Key West. I will happily write my cultural report later. You can tell me all about Havana."

AND SO FRANÇOIS found himself, forty-eight hours later, waking alone at noon in a hotel room at the Inglaterra in Havana to car horns and screeching brakes. And less loudly, but not less assertively, to the chambermaid's persistent knocking. The room was dim, dust motes drifting in the shafts of light. The ceiling fan, impossibly high above his head, slapped softly. He grabbed his watch from the nightstand: checkout was, had been, at eleven; his return flight was at three.

One night in Havana and he'd slept away the morning. His head throbbed, of course. His packet of cigarettes was empty, of course. His wallet too, he knew. Thank goodness he'd hidden ten dollars with his passport in the nightstand, between the newsprint-thin pages of the Gideon Bible. He could get back to Broussard and, if he had to, could borrow from Broussard and, when they retrieved him in Miami, from Mouret—Mouret would be good for it, and wouldn't make him feel like shit. Frugal, he'd never had to borrow money before. Thank goodness he had aspirin. He couldn't risk spending more on breakfast, or lunch, or whatever meal it might be. He might throw it up, anyway. Then again, he might puke bile if he didn't eat something—he could feel his stomach griping, its walls constricting in spasms. He needed a shower.

"Ten minutes," he called in English to the chambermaid. He didn't open the door, on which he'd somehow remembered to hang the "Do Not Disturb" sign—"*No Molestar*" in Spanish—because he didn't want to see her reproving face. "Ten minutes, I'll be out of the room."

LITTLE MORE THAN twenty-four hours in Cuba, in the end. Without Broussard to split the bill, the cost of two nights was more than he could manage; and that was before he lost all his spending money. He'd arrived before dawn on the twenty-eighth, and sat at a café as the city unfurled around him into day—singing vendors and hawkers setting up their stalls, including the orange-juice pressers with their carts full of oranges like tennis balls, reminding him intensely of home. Clusters of impressively uniformed policemen and military, bandoliered and armed, more armed men than he'd ever seen, mingled among the growing crowds.

Walking the monumental arcaded Paseo, past statues and cafés, he ogled the exuberant meandering crowds: men and women of all colors and races, Black, brown, tan, white, holding hands or linking arms, laughing, bickering, couples of various races in every combination and their rainbow children, so different from the American South, and from his own homeland. This freedom—purely imaginary to him till this moment—struck him perhaps more than anything else: the vitality, the here-ness, of the crowds, thrilling simply in daily existence, in *being*. Even those with a mess of teeth or rough skin were dressed as if for a party, the women in fluttery sleeves and cinched waists, the men in dress shirts and pressed trousers, their black hair carefully brilliantined and their shoes spit shined.

By noon, in spite of a second coffee, drunk standing up, he was flagging, unshaven and unslept. The Hotel Inglaterra loomed suddenly before him, a touch shabby, and he entered its cavernous tiled lobby to inquire about the cheapest available, with bath down the hall, for which he paid, wisely as it transpired, cash in advance. He slept, until dusk, like the dead: he was there, after all, for the nightlife. Maybe, he hoped, a girl.

The shorter of the evening doormen suggested the finca. "One night only? Casinos are the same in every country, and you can go in Paris to see the girls dance. But this place, this is the real Cuba!" He touched his hand conspiratorially to the lapel of François's rumpled jacket. "And you can put money on the cockfights, if you ask for the fat waiter named Jorge."

The taxi dropped him at the finca, down a gravel road between two darkened fields in which he could make out the odd pale cow. It proved thrillingly atmospheric, a compound of low-slung buildings surrounded by trees, with a large and busy restaurant terrace strung with fairy lights. At one side, with the dark woods behind them, a band played on a raised dais, a dance floor set out at their feet.

The waitress, pretty, olive-skinned, with a sexy mole, perhaps kohled, upon her upper lip and plump, firm cleavage nestled in white cotton ruffles (it struck him like a chef's artful presentation of a delicacy upon a plate), escorted him to a table by the edge of this dance floor, where he could watch matrons puffing to the salsa beat, swung in circles by their balding spouses, alongside younger couples more sensuously entwined. Looking around, he noticed other men alone, mostly older, similarly settled at small tables like his own, some joined by women, all as prettily attired as his waitress, and as young. Of course: he hadn't been wrong to hope; though these women were surely paid. One such couple danced just five feet from him, the man's hands playing over the woman's satin-covered buttocks. Always his mother's son, he hadn't, somehow, imagined paying.

Most of the restaurant tables were long and loud and filled with families, generations together, small children lolling sleepily on their grandmothers' laps while the bigger kids scampered out to the parking lot to play tag between the cars. Large parties were repeatedly served with abundant platters of beef, chicken, pork, and rice, and bottles of beer and wine. The whole restaurant smelled of singed meat.

François ordered pork, rice and beans, a scotch, and a bottle of beer, and another, and eventually another. At first he drank quickly: he felt he needed courage to ask whether a girl might join him. But with each drink, this seemed less possible. At Amherst or in Paris, alcohol helped him bridge the gap between himself and the outside world, but here, alone, in this Havana dream, it had the opposite effect. He felt he retreated further into himself, became less and less visible, almost disembodied. When the waitress placed his espresso cup on the table, he wanted to reach out and stroke her forearm, which hovered, for a moment, before him. Instead, unable to move, he looked up, just halfway, into the frilled platter of her bosom. He was washed with shame for his desire, and shame for his shame.

Eventually, drunk and at a loss, he asked her about Jorge. The families were clearing out, the dance floor thinning, and the edges of his vision had gone blurry, as though a camera lens had tightened its focus.

"You don't want company?" the pretty girl asked directly at last. But her tone and her expression seemed to him pitying. Why didn't you ask sooner, he wanted to say. The answer, this far into his cups, and against the distant throb inside him, had to be no: his mother, for all that, had remained too close in his head. He couldn't do it.

"No company, no thank you. I was told to ask for Jorge."

She nodded, unsmiling, and brought him another beer and another scotch, though he'd already paid his bill. When she leaned over him again, she smelled, he noted wistfully, of lemons.

Jorge, tall as well as fat, had a nose like a carrot. "Of course, amigo, you're here for the game—I wish you'd said earlier. It's three dollars entry"—half again as much as his already expensive meal, which would leave him with less than four dollars—"with a minimum bet of fifty cents per fight. Drinks are on the house."

Having come so far and having failed to claim a woman, François, to save face, had to accept.

The cockfights took place in a large barn behind the kitchens, raked seats around a chicken-wire enclosure with a dirt floor. The space, hazy and hot, reverberated with noise, human and fowl. Rows of men leaned forward on their benches or pressed up against the wire fence, bug-eyed, sweat-slick, wreathed in smoke from the butts that dangled, forgotten, from their lips. As François slid onto the end of a bench, two men entered the ring from opposite sides, each holding a squirming bird—one russet, one predominantly golden, both with their silly crimson combs flopping like failed crowns—upon whose talons lethal gilded spurs had been tied and upon whose beaks a further, razor-sharp proboscis had been securely attached. Each man stroked his bird, lovingly it seemed, and appeared to whisper encouragement.

A long-haired kid in a blue apron full of money tapped François on the arm and took his bet—fifty cents on the russet; it seemed larger—then pushed his way down the row, all but ignored: all eyes, all energy, all focus—all Eros, indeed; or was it Thanatos?—on the moment of stillness in the ring, the quiet before.

A referee's voice called out; the birds dropped to the dust and
darted at each other, nimble but encumbered, screeching and slashing,
while around them the men, too, screeched and chivied and jeered. In
minutes—two? three?—the russet lay eviscerated in the dirt, seeping
quantities of thick, crimson blood. His owner cradled him in his arms in
a blanket, like a baby, even as another kid stepped forward to sprinkle
sawdust over the red pool. It came to François that the stink in his nostrils, strong enough to make him gag, was not just smoke and sweat and
dirt but chiefly blood. He might have chosen the sweet-scented girl with
the smooth flesh, and instead had chosen this.

A shot of dark rum appeared on a tray, alongside other little glasses of
rum, passed along his row like Communion. He'd barely seen what had
happened to the golden victor, not himself unbloodied—would that cock
fight again, on this night or another? After all, how quick the fights were,
how swift the feints and bloody rents, how speedily the birds, doted upon
by their hopeful masters, fell to and were felled. How many times the
aproned boy appeared, palm out for François's fifty cents: a couple of
times he won, and got back a dollar, but even in his drunk fog he knew
the game would not stop, not for him, until the boy—he peered, once,
beyond the thatch of hair and saw only boredom in the kid's eyes, a sort
of deadness—had taken his last coin. Or until he passed out from the
rum, whichever came first.

IN THE SHOWER at noon the next day, he tried to piece together the
rest. He'd reached the point where his pockets were empty, and had, on
his dignity, lurched from the barn. Perhaps, yes, he had vomited in the
parking lot, an amber splatter on the gravel between two cars, and then
smoked his last cigarette—the pack, one from the cartons bought cheap
in the Carolinas, had been full when he'd left the hotel—and wondered
how to get home.

An older man had driven him back. Maybe an employee of the finca—
who knew? François recalled a mustache, a white linen sleeve, the sound

of the wind in the open window. The man didn't speak much English, and had no French for that matter; he didn't expect money, either, and at the Inglaterra had got out of the car to help François to the door and had rung for the night porter.

It made sense, François thought, as he dressed in the clean shirt he was grateful to have brought—the old one smelled of smoke and bile, though it bore no visible stains—that they'd want to get the tourists home safely. You couldn't keep fleecing them if they were discovered stumbling blindly through a cane field at dawn because they hadn't had the cab fare back to town. From the point of view of the restaurant, the ride home was a sunk cost. As for himself, he'd had his chance, and wasted it: he could've paid for sex, but instead had been screwed by Jorge's cockfights. His shame, another that he wouldn't tell the others. Another sunk cost.

THE PHRASE, IN his head, stayed with him, back to the Key Wester, back to Miami with Broussard, all the way back north with Broussard and Mouret, who'd been a hit with his New Orleans debutante and had an open invitation to return. It stayed with him when they stopped among the Mennonites in Pennsylvania; when Chapin took the Plymouth away; as he suffered through the remainder of the bitter winter and longed ever more for the Algiers light, for the smells of the flat Rue Guillaumet, for his mother's hand upon his head like a blessing. The ride home—home, as faint as a mirage—was a sunk cost.

✛

ALGIERS, ALGERIA

D enise should have been studying for her Roman law test—*jus personarum*, incorporating the condition of the slave and the status of the citizen—but how could she focus on that—or on the upcoming oral with Lemosse that would cover the public institutions of Frankish Gaul, as well as the origins of the feudal system—when she wanted to be thinking about her costume for Sunday night's masked ball?

With Maman's help, and in theory at least with Tata Jeanne's, they were sewing the dress out of old navy yachting twill from the steamer trunk in the basement storage, though even after three washings it still smelled musty. The ball's theme was "1900," so a long skirt with flounces, and a frilled décolleté with little cap sleeves. Maman proposed a layer of lace over the bust and a band of lace rosettes around both the neckline and the flounces, in a lighter blue: she'd bought the lace white, machine-made, along with a pair of elbow-length cotton gloves—there wasn't time to make the lace themselves, and both she and Tata Jeanne had lamented that, anyway, their eyes were no longer up to the task— and she'd dyed lace and gloves both in a bucket of indigo on the balcony. Its railings were now festooned with the drying results. Denise could see the bands of lace fluttering ghostly in the dusk through the window, whenever she raised an eye from her textbooks.

Maman insisted that she knew how to make the rosettes, how to drape the fabric so that it would fall elegantly and show Denise's figure to best advantage (so as not, Denise understood, to make her look thick-waisted and fleshy or her arms like hams)—Maman promised all these things with such calm confidence, but was it true? Could she? Yes, she could knit beautifully and even now with her glasses hemmed in stitches so fine you could barely see them, but this required a different talent. Denise was unsure and couldn't stop thinking about it, half in excitement, half in dread. She'd procured silk stockings and a pair of low-heeled navy pumps she thought she could dance in, and her mask would be ready to pick up on Friday afternoon. She'd decided on an eye-and-nose design of navy velvet with sequins and a rising tuft of feathers at one side, held by ribbon rather than elastic.

Anne Marie Marconi, one of Denise's new great friends from the *faculté*, along with Marie José, had invited her to spend the weekend with her family out at Rivet, to go first, on Sunday afternoon, to the ice dancers at Boglioni—their show was all the rage—and later to the ball from their house. Her father was a pulmonologist at the tubercular sanatorium, an eminent man, and they lived in a grand villa set among lush palm gardens that Denise had visited for Sunday lunch in October. The ball would take place downtown, only twenty minutes by bus from the Rue Guillaumet, and in a way it seemed strange to attend from a house in the country, as far away really as Tata Baudry's in L'Arba, but it also felt like Tolstoy, somehow, and of course the fun was in being together, at the ice follies first (in Algiers, imagine!), then getting dressed up together beforehand and coming back to gossip afterward late into the night.

Strangely, Denise considered, this would be her first formal dance at which neither her parents nor her brother were also in attendance: all the others had been her father's X parties or navy parties (like the one in the autumn with the Turkish officers, including Mehmet, who'd surprised her by being blond, and had paid her such attention the whole evening, two hours conversing in English, their only shared language, and had sweetly asked, at the end, if they might correspond). Only once had François taken her with him, the previous June, six weeks before he left for the States, to a dance at the Fac; but he'd parked her with another girl, like her just finished at the lycée, and, like her, brought by an older brother, a stout and dull girl who'd seemed an unfortunate mirror, and she'd hardly seen him again until it was time to go home.

This party would be different. For one thing, she was herself a university student now, a law student, climbing the grand staircase on the Rue Michelet and slipping into the back of the boisterous lecture halls, aware, whether it was disagreeable Madame Bosquet, or lovely Monsieur Breton, or Boulours, who was sometimes disagreeable and sometimes lovely, that she was like her brother's ghost or emissary, hearing the lectures he had heard, that she had, in some way she couldn't quite articulate, stepped for the first time into a life she'd considered mythical, unattainable, the glamorous, adult, real life of her older brother, François. Until now, she'd never liked school—she couldn't ever bring herself to care much about it. What, she'd always wondered, was the point? She wasn't particularly good at it, and she was a girl. She'd always preferred her piano—she could practice for hours at the piano, and she *knew* she was good at that, her fingers faster almost than her eyes could follow, her relation to the instrument bodily, intuitive—that was always what she'd said, that she couldn't *think*, she didn't know what thinking *was*, that she could do things, and understand things, but not analyze them. She'd thought (or had she been taught? Who could be sure?) that this was a distinction between men and women. Not always, of course—there were exceptions, like Marie Curie—but mostly. Except that now, studying law, she found that the words fit in her head in a way nothing at school ever had. She didn't always have the answer as quickly as the brightest boys, but sometimes she did. She would never have raised a hand in the classroom, but on paper, in exams or essays, in the one-on-one orals, she found she could show what she knew. The Fac, like the imminent masked ball, evoked in her equal parts anxiety and excitement.

She could hear Maman moving in the kitchen, preparing supper. Tata Jeanne, knitting in her corner, also heard the water running, the juddering of the pipes, and made as if to stand. She reminded Denise of Uncle Charles's old black spaniel, who, in his last days, would lift his grizzled muzzle and wag his tail but who couldn't, for all his goodwill, raise his carcass from the blanket by the stove on which he lay.

"Stay, Tata," she insisted, folding her pen inside her notebook and moving the pile of textbooks to the side of her father's armchair—he wouldn't be back for another three days—"I'll go."

Tata Jeanne didn't protest, just smiled resignedly over her glasses and looked back to her knitting. They both heard Maman turn on the radio in the kitchen for the news.

"Did you hear any more about the storm?" Tata Jeanne asked.

"Maybe there's a report now." Denise made for the door.

"A hundred-year storm, they called it, no? No, a thousand-year storm."

"Surely not a thousand?"

"Catastrophic."

"Yes, certainly."

The great storm had pounded the coasts of England, the Netherlands, Belgium overnight between the thirty-first of January and the first of February, flooding fields and roads and towns, overflowing the dikes, destroying thousands of homes. Many were missing or dead, maybe thousands. Denise didn't care to think about it—it was more than fifteen hundred kilometers away, after all, and her nerves couldn't take it, she couldn't start worrying about orphaned Dutch children or English grannies the age of Tata Baudry with nothing to eat and nowhere to sleep—once she started worrying, she wouldn't be able to stop. She'd find herself awake at three a.m. with her teeth chattering.

Tata Jeanne, in contrast, reveled in disaster: each plane or bus crash, every earthquake or avalanche, however remote, Tata Jeanne thrilled to the details and kept track of the dead and maimed as tidily as she counted her knitting stitches. She was like Madame Defarge at the guillotine or like one of the Fates, knitting instead of spinning, cheerfully observing life's dramas as though it were all a Saturday matinée. As she left the room Denise heard her aunt say, "If they report a new death toll, be sure to come through and tell me."

In fact, the man on the radio was blathering about the upcoming elections, some speech that Soustelle had given or was going to give, the shifting poll numbers, the possible shape of the council. Without asking Maman, Denise turned it off: she'd found an unsuspected interest in Roman law but she still couldn't stand politics, those boring fat men in suits with their greasy combovers, or the fierce young militants at the university, rallying for Algerian independence.

"Your father will want to know the updates." But Maman didn't turn from the sink, where she stood peeling potatoes. Denise caught the glimmer of her mother's gray roots, a sign of age almost always carefully concealed—"*un an de plus, un soin de plus*," she always said. But Papa had been away ten days, and she must have been saving the housekeeping money, putting off as long as possible the visit to the hairdresser. Denise felt suddenly emotional—it would be on account of the stockings and the lace and the gloves and the mask. Maman was kindness itself, "a lay saint," Papa always said.

"Will you top and tail the beans, dear?" Maman turned and handed her the dented colander. She looked tired, the bags under her eyes more pronounced than usual. "I wondered about baking apples for dessert, but we've only got two. You and I could share one, maybe? And the other a little treat for Tata Jeanne?"

"Sure. I'll core the apples when I've done the beans. Do we have raisins, then?"

"A few. Enough. Maybe a little calvados with the sugar."

Maman and Papa often spoke fretfully behind her back about how little Tata Jeanne had to look forward to, how few pleasures she had, but Denise thought her invalid aunt, given her infirmities, led quite a nice life, warm and fed and well surrounded. She'd come to live with them when Denise was very small, before even Beirut, after her and Maman's oldest sister—long the headmistress of the teachers' college for girls in Constantine—had dropped dead in the bathtub only a few months after her retirement. That aunt, Fée, had been older by eight years than Tata Jeanne, whom she took care of for so long; and Tata Jeanne in turn was twelve years older than Maman. Denise had come to understand that in addition to Marie-Thérèse (never mentioned, who came between Fée and Jeanne and who'd died in France before Denise was born), there'd been miscarriages and dead babies in between the sisters, one a toddler even (diphtheria!), just as she'd come to understand—Tata Jeanne's indiscretion—that even in her own generation there'd been miscarriages, three, before François, and a stillbirth after herself. By which time, Denise had calculated, Maman would have been frankly old, as she'd been forty-one when Denise was born.

But now, firmly in age, Maman, soon to be sixty-one, was still caring for her older sister. As if Tata Jeanne were a child, Papa and Maman kept from her all the worries of the household and of their own health. Maman had confided to her friend Aline that Papa was in a state of nervous exhaustion—she had lowered her voice in the living room, thinking that Denise, in her bedroom, would not hear; but Denise wasn't called elephant ears for nothing. And then Maman herself, all the tests in the last few months, the visits to the neurologist, to try to figure out what was causing her *malaises*, and whether or not they were linked to her terrible migraines. None of this could be revealed to François, at all costs. He was to be free to enjoy his American adventure—he'd earned that, they were all agreed—but he was better now, so much better. This, too, was how you took care of other people, Denise knew already, though she wasn't any good at it: you pretended you were fine, that everything was fine.

Maman's new medication seemed to be helping, at least a little, so that was something: when Denise wrote now to François, she felt less like a liar. But she must have put on seven or eight kilos, which Denise knew dismayed her. Maman always said that it was part of a wife's job to be desirable to her husband, and that meant, among other details like weekly visits to the hairdresser, not getting fat. Which is why of course it was a shame that Denise was fat to begin with. No man would ever look at her as long as she was fat—except perhaps Mehmet: maybe in Turkey the ideas of beauty were different. That was why Servier thought he could cut her dead the way he had.

She topped and tailed the beans, she cored the apples, she stirred the beef in its wine sauce on the stove. She was on the verge, she felt, of doing something about it—her weight, that was. Not in time for the ball, obviously—the dress would be as it would be. But when the weather got a bit warmer—she couldn't stand being cold, and being hungry made her cold—she'd decided to stop eating lunch and maybe breakfast too. Now that she was so often out at the Fac, Maman wouldn't know what she ate or didn't. Denise had recently taken up smoking, though her parents didn't yet know, and Maman surely would disapprove, as she considered women who smoked "fast." Anne Marie was a smoker, so Denise's new habit was logical—and she loved it: the cigarette looked elegant between her fingers, lent her square hands a touch of glamour. It gave her something to focus on, to look forward to, to talk about, or, better still, to bond her to strangers, a way of joining a group or striking up a conversation. It stopped time for a few minutes and opened a little window of possibility, flirtation even. It made her feel less anxious in herself, and cooler in the world, and the burning in her throat soothed her, and changed the way things tasted, and quelled her endless appetite, especially for sweet things, which were her downfall. She loved pastries, croissants, and *pains aux raisins*, and the chocolate cake Maman made for parties and served with crème anglaise, and she loved ice cream in summertime, even when it was cheap and tasted thin, dotted with little chips of ice, still she loved it, biting into the bland, sweet, latticed cone, a little soggy where the ice cream had melted into it—and chocolate, she loved almost all chocolate, she didn't need to choose, like some, between milk or dark. She still recalled her first chocolate bar, late in the war, a gift from an American soldier, spring of '44 probably, she would have been ten, almost eleven, on the street when she was walking home from school with Josiane from two doors down, and the trio of Americans in uniform had stopped them—the girls were nervous—to hand them each a milk chocolate bar wrapped in foil. How it had melted on the tongue! She remembered the soldier's bristled buzz cut, through which shone the slanted afternoon sun, and how his scalp itself shone, and the angry red pattern of pustules across his cheek—it was well before her own struggle with acne, and she'd been repelled. But he'd winked at them, and grinned, and she and Josiane had laughed when he said, "*C'est bon, non?*" because in fact he'd said, "Say bong" and it sounded so funny. Papa, when he found out, had been furious of course. That the girls had taken gifts from strange men, flirtatious Americans.

It occurred to her that Maman suggested that they share a baked apple not only to be kind to Tata Jeanne but to reduce the amount of sweet for both mother and daughter, without depriving themselves altogether. When the weather grew warmer, even just a little, she would renounce sweet things as well as lunch: smoking could fill the gaps. But not tonight.

AFTER DINNER, in her room—the bedroom that she and François had shared as kids, and had vacated for the tenants; the bedroom that she had left again when François reached puberty (what her parents referred to with a rueful smile as "*l'âge ingrat*," the ungrateful age) so that he might sleep alone while she shared with Tata Jeanne; and that she had regained and claimed only the previous August, the week after they returned from seeing him off for America in the tempest at Le Havre. So it was her bedroom even as it was also the ghost of his bedroom, his books still lined up on the shelves and some of his clothes still hanging in the armoire, and when he came back to stay—assuming he did, though she knew Maman was certain he wouldn't, not really, because "sons leave home," she always said, implying thereby that daughters did not—anyway, assuming he returned, she would move back in with Tata Jeanne, and indeed had once joked meanly to Marie José and Anne Marie that she wouldn't really have her own room until Tata Jeanne died.

She'd felt so guilty about this joke that she'd mentioned it in confession, and Père Denelain had told her not only to say Hail Marys but also to do penance by taking special care of her aunt, as a result of which, in a fit of guilt, she'd undertaken a biblical pedicure of Tata Jeanne's leathery horned feet, soaking them in warm salted water and rubbing the soles and heels with a pumice stone, carefully clipping the thick, yellowed nails and trimming the cuticles, before patting them dry and swaddling them in towels like two plump infants. "Just like Christ Himself, with my foot washing," she'd then joked to her friends; though this blasphemy she did not confess to Père Denelain both because it seemed too wicked and because she couldn't face a further penance.

But for now it was her room, and she slept not in the narrow bed next to the window that had been her brother's—that would have felt like a different blasphemy—but in its twin, the bed of her earlier childhood; though as she sat to write him a letter, she chose his bed on which to sit, her back against the spindled headboard, resting her onionskin pad on his second-year maritime law textbook, which in turn rested upon her raised knees. She was writing very small at the moment, in tight, even rows, so that from afar her pages were all ink, and she'd taken to signing her letters "Your Juju," in reference to an old joke about her being his "junior," in English, and since his letter about his Christmas trip she'd been addressing him as "Frank de Floride," which amused her, at least.

What would she tell him? She'd already complained about his friend Servier, and didn't want to mention him again—though just yesterday he'd ignored her one more time when he walked by with his band from the student council, his lock of dark hair flopping over his right eye. If she wrote too much about Servier, François would suspect that she liked him, but really *liked* him, in that way where she knew which lectures he attended and who he hung out with, where she tracked his regular coffee hours at the cafés closest to the campus. François could tease mercilessly, and Servier, of course, would never look at her—until, unless, maybe if she were slim, and if she were slim he might not be the only one. Did the Cousines not always say that she had the most beautiful blond hair, and that her eyes were the most arresting shade of blue? Her eyes might look pale and watery to her, she might long for eyes like her mother's, the color of the Mediterranean on a sunny day; but different traits appealed differently and . . . maybe, if she were thin, who knew? Trust in God, Maman always said, He has a plan for each of us.

She forced her mind back to the task at hand. If not Servier, then what? She could try to tell him about Servier's effort, as senior representative on the student council, to involve that good-looking Muslim boy in the law program, Mohammed—what was his last name? Benyahia, that was it—whom François had known at school; he'd been elected to the Muslim student union, and Servier was trying to get them to join the council, so the Muslims and the French students would work together . . . but now there was resistance from the Communists—most of the Muslim kids were nationalists, nowadays, and had the backing of the Algerian Communist Party. But Benyahia wasn't a Communist—Servier thought he'd have more luck with him. This stuff would interest François, she knew, but she couldn't follow it properly—all she knew was that the Muslims gave impassioned, even angry speeches, at which pretty Anne Marie rolled her eyes and giggled, saying, "The natives are restless."

No, Denise would write instead about something she actually cared about: the plan for the masked ball and her dress (Maman was working even now on the rosettes, while listening to her weekly radio drama in the living room with Tata Jeanne), and the ice follies of course—though just the plans, right now, while in next week's letter she'd be able to tell him what it had all been like. Imagine, time was so strange, and by next Tuesday everything she so looked forward to—the very thought of which set butterflies dancing and almost made her tremble—would be behind her. So yes, she wrote out the plans for the coming days, and that Papa would be back on Thursday night, flying into Maison Blanche from his meetings in Paris, and then leaving on Sunday, even before the ice follies and the ball, for the oil wells in the desert down south, probably taking Madame Dechel with him in the car to spend a few days with her husband. She wrote about the big storm in Britain and Holland—would he have heard about it in Massachusetts? Surely he would, with so many missing and dead, the way in Europe they heard about flooding and famine in Bangalore. How much did Europe matter to the Americans? It was hard to gauge; but surely at least a little, given how much time they, the Europeans, she and her friends for example, spent watching American films or reading American writers or listening to American music. Do they ever think about us? she asked him; but it seemed like she already knew the answer.

She had two things she very much wanted to impart. One had actually happened; the other was in her head, but in her head much of the time, and it felt as though it required courage for her to write about it, but she would, tonight. First, though, the strange incident, on Friday last. If she was going to keep secrets from François about Maman and Papa and their worries, then surely she might in exchange share with him what she had determined to keep secret from them.

Late morning on Friday, she and Marie José and Anne Marie had just come out of Boulours's lecture—a good day, for him; he'd been quite amusing and had made a joke that had the whole hall laughing aloud—and the three of them bounded down the many steps outside the main building and set off for a coffee at the Otomatic before their next lecture. They were leaning into each other as they walked, heads together, conspiratorial, still laughing, with Anne Marie in the middle. She always was, the center of things, the prettiest, with her dark curls that so elegantly framed her face, and her slightly upturned nose. Denise and Marie José were both plumper and plainer than she—sometimes, in the grip of particular self-doubt, Denise wondered whether Anne Marie had chosen them so as to look the prettiest. But the truth was that they all made each other laugh, and that was why they were close friends—they laughed so hard they fell off chairs, or coffee came out of their noses, and Marie José had once confessed to Denise (though not, significantly, to Anne Marie) that she'd laughed so hard she'd wet her pants. Just a tiny bit, but still. Anyway, they were laughing as Anne Marie told them about Leyris, the handsome second-year Leyris with the soulful eyes and gaunt cheeks, always dapper in his trench coat with a cigarette drooping from his lip, hurrying into lectures late or out early as though he had more important places to be, but he'd come up behind her that morning when she was checking the notices on the bulletin board outside Boulours's class, and standing at her shoulder where she could barely see him out of the corner of her eye, so that when he spoke to her she was forced to turn and there he was, his face so close to hers, she couldn't help but stare at him, his long curled eyelashes and those sad eyes like an Italian film star, and he'd said, "Where did we meet?," which was also like a line from an Italian film because they'd *never* met, it was far more mundane than that and he had to have known it—"Oh my God, he was flirting, such a flirt!" squealed Marie José, delighted, leaning in open-mouthed as if Anne Marie's story were manna itself, and Denise was asking at the same time, speaking over Marie José: "What did you say? What did you say?"

But she never heard what Anne Marie said because she was thrown suddenly into the air, her feet vanished beneath her, and she landed hard on her tailbone. She had trouble articulating the experience in words: all the feelings, the sensations, were so vivid, the collapse of time, the confusion—she could say now that it was what she imagined it might be like to be attacked by a shark, a great, sudden brute force devouring you, but in this case of course it was not a shark but a car. And in the same fragmented moments in which she felt the guttering of her coccyx all the way up her spine and then the grit of the sidewalk digging into her palms as she tried to right herself but instead tilted onto her hands and knees and crawled, like an animal, toward the low stone wall along the pavement, in the petrol stink, a cloud of exhaust, while she heard Marie José's squeals turn into screams, "like a stuck pig," they would laugh only a few hours later, but in those first moments, with the combination of Marie José's screams and Anne Marie's eerie calm, Denise wondered if she'd been disfigured or had lost a limb or at least a finger, or what had happened? What had just happened?

In all this intensity, these shards of thoughts and feelings, she saw the car, the car pulling back off the sidewalk and continuing down the road as if nothing had happened, and in the passenger seat, the window down, her head turned back to gawp, amused, yes amused, she could have sworn she saw that girl she knew, she knew her by sight, not just from the Fac, she'd seen her a few times around the university, but—now she'd done her hair differently, but still—wasn't she, so familiar, that girl from the lycée, that boarder, in school she never spoke, so shy and serious—a Berber girl from the provinces, pretty though, and clever—what was her name—was it even her? At first she could have sworn it was, she had the feeling the girl had been first amused and then, when she saw Denise's face, shocked, as though the whole thing had seemed a lark, funny even, and only when she recognized Denise had she been chastened.

That was the story Denise compiled from the fragments, later. That the man and the woman, the girl, really, if it was in fact her classmate— Zohra, yes, Zohra, the name came back to her even as her certainty evaporated; maybe it hadn't been her?—did it matter? Denise wouldn't report it either way, for all Marie José said she ought to, she must! No, Anne Marie demurred, an unfortunate accident, but you're fine, really, a moment's inattention on the driver's part, they were probably canoodling in the car and then—who'd seen enough even to pursue it, they'd been so shocked, all three of them—

But here was the thing, she wrote to her brother: the car attacked her from behind like a shark, a blue Deux Chevaux, it mounted the curb and took a bite, as it were, and then slipped back into the ocean, back onto the road—but *the car wasn't going fast*—it could really have injured her if it had been going fast, right? It was perfectly calibrated—the speed, the silence, the suddenness—as if the driver had planned the whole thing, maybe a joke, but maybe to terrify, or terrorize her, if you'd rather, to make her afraid just to walk down the street laughing with her friends. To make her afraid to be. Why would someone do that? To Denise, who wouldn't hurt a fly? Who was the driver? She had no idea: she'd seen only the back of his head, if even that, an impression of dark hair, but the girl, if it was Zohra, well—

She'd hauled herself onto the retaining wall while Anne Marie picked up her handbag and her satchel, which hadn't been properly closed and had spilled its contents even into the gutter. Denise had the sense of other students milling, murmuring, asking if she was okay—*"C'est pas grave,"* she kept repeating, *"ça va aller, c'est pas grave."* And she meant it—she could see now that she had all her limbs and digits and, as far as she could tell, she wasn't even bleeding. Marie José offered to run down the Rue Michelet and get her a coffee from the Otomatic—they'd been headed there anyway—and while she was gone, before Anne Marie had gathered her books and pens and even the eraser, blue and pink, that had flipped into a puddle—when Denise sat alone on the wall with her tailbone aching, unsure yet how much it hurt, she started to shake, everywhere, all over, her arms and legs and head and shoulders, uncontrollably, like a dry leaf in a great storm, and she could do nothing about it.

Anne Marie, seeing this, rushed to her side and enveloped her, so sweet-smelling, those lovely black curls tickling her cheek, and she held her, you might say quelled her, until Marie José returned with the coffee and the moment had definitively passed. She did not put this in the letter to François—what relief and security she had felt, held in her friend's arms, though they weren't particularly strong arms—but said instead simply that she had trembled all over, uncontrollably.

And of course the story would become properly a story a few years later, when the troubles were fully underway, when Denise was no longer in Algiers—none of them were, by then, François in Paris and she at the hotel school in Lausanne, and Maman and Papa in Morocco, where the troubles found them anyway—but only then, after September '56, when

Zohra Drif bombed the Milk Bar and a few months later, in late January '57, almost exactly four years after the Deux Chevaux knocked Denise off her feet, the bombing of the very Otomatic café to which Marie José had run for her restorative coffee—and the Otomatic at the same time as the Coq Hardi and the Cafeteria, killing in all four and injuring fifty in a single afternoon—only once all these things had happened, like fatal flowers blooming, did Denise go on to insist that she had definitely seen Zohra Drif in the Deux Chevaux that morning, that she had been deliberately attacked, the driver the opposite of inattentive, that it was an early salvo of the insurgency and that she, Denise, was lucky to have escaped with only torn stockings and a constellation of bruises.

Denise would not tell Maman or Papa about this, not when it happened, nor four years later, nor ever. She didn't tell François all of it, either—not, at the time, about Zohra, because who could be sure? She'd been in a state of shock; nor of course about the effect of Anne Marie's embrace. No, she told him about the car coming out of nowhere, about herself upended, about the uncontrollable shaking, about the need for secrecy, which she underlined: "on no account must Maman and Papa learn about this. They have worries enough as it is."

Which, she then fretted, revealed more about them than she ought. But François was himself so secretive that he could not help but understand. She knew only, about his life, that there was a great deal he did not reveal, and that this had been so for years. He'd made himself into a wall, for good or ill.

This led her to the other part of her letter. She wanted to break down that wall. She felt she was old enough now—a university student, at the law faculty, following in his footsteps but also, surely, making, for the first time, her own footsteps—to address the dynamic between them, to try to be as good a sister to him as he was, always, a brother to her. She had in her heart that memory, all those years ago in L'Arba during the war, when they'd only recently arrived from Greece. Had it been a picnic? She didn't recall any food. How had two small children strayed so far from town on their own? It had been hot, she'd been so thirsty, that she remembered, and when she woke from her nap—on moss, beneath bird-filled trees, by a stream—she had wept at the prospect of the endless return. She still sucked her thumb then—it was why her front teeth stuck out now, or so she'd been told—and she remembered the taste of her thumb and the texture of it, spit-soaked. As if he'd been expecting it all along, he had her climb up onto a boulder and from there onto his back, where he held her legs around his hips, her dusty shoes banging at his knees and calves, her arms around his neck, her head resting against his warm nape. He didn't complain, even when he stumbled and almost tipped them both onto the gravel by the side of the road. Before they reached the edge of town, a man in a truck stopped to ask if they wanted a ride, and he shook his head, saying, "No thank you sir," very politely, and he kept on walking, hitching her a little higher against his back.

"I've wanted to say these things for a long time," she wrote, "I can never tell you enough how much I love and admire you, how wonderful it is to have you as an older brother. You got the short end of the stick, though—a little sister isn't very interesting. I wish I could be more than that. I'm not saying I think you don't love me—I don't think that for a second. But you do look down on me. And sometimes, it's seemed to me that you were lonely or unhappy. You overthink things. But I've never dared to say anything to you—you always seemed a bit cold or intimidating. You're much too good for me, is the trouble. You should have had a sister who could follow you in all your worries, all your discussions, a sister you would've wanted to talk to about your life. But I'm incapable of that. Which must pain you. Know, though, that as long as I live, I'm ready to do anything for you. I'm not in the habit of bragging, but I think few sisters love and admire their brothers the way I do you. I so wish I were a remarkable person. Maybe in the next life."

She paused, reread what she'd written, wondered if it was too heartfelt—François made a joke out of everything. She didn't want this to be something he could mock; this was her heart, on paper. She decided to add a joke of her own at the end, to preempt him, to show that she had a sense of humor too, that she could make fun of herself. "Be a good boy," she wrote, "and if you encounter the Black Dog in the coming months, be like Servier with me and don't say hello, just keep on walking." We love you, she wrote, and we think about you all the time. He thought that just because he didn't tell her things she didn't know him; but he was wrong. She could read between the lines. She added a little postscript: "Tomorrow is Candlemas, and we will each make our own crêpe, Tata Jeanne, Maman, and I, holding a coin. Maybe then we will be rich for the whole year."

Later as she lay in bed with the lights out and the curtains drawn, the room as dark as a cupboard, she thought of Mary and Joseph bringing the infant Jesus to the temple in Jerusalem for his purification rite, forty days after his birth, and of how they were too poor to pay for the offering of a lamb and instead gave two turtledoves, the requested donation for those in poverty: as the law was written, "Every firstborn male shall be consecrated to the Lord," and Christ, the firstborn, was presented as a light in the darkness. Where did that leave a little sister, she wondered. What light in the darkness could she be? And she turned her thoughts instead to the lace rosettes Maman had spent the evening making—maybe her dress for the ball would be beautiful after all.

☙

GHARDAÏA, ALGERIA

Wakened at dawn by the call of the muezzin, Gaston dressed in the spartan little room made available to visiting SiF Alger employees in Ghardaïa. It was one of several in the guesthouse, all cold in winter in spite of the Berber carpets on the floors and on the low bed, only slivers in the whitewashed stone for windows, through which the winter sun flashed along the walls; but at least these walls were thick, since his colleague Dechel, the local manager, and his wife were together in the room next door. Gaston had driven down with Madame from Algiers, almost ten hours and she'd hardly shut her mouth. Thank goodness she was pretty to look at.

Madame Dechel was making a special conjugal visit to her husband, who spent weeks at a time on his own in remote Ghardaïa. Dechel answered to Gaston, who was managing director for Algeria; Gaston, in turn, reported to the bosses in Paris. SiF Alger, an upstart in the business, was a small oil concern engaged, like many others just then, in drilling the Sahara for oil. They had only two active sites, the one outside Ghardaïa and another at Guettara, nearly two hundred kilometers away. Lately, things hadn't been going well: Gaston had had to manage a string of disasters, from damaged equipment to a fatal car crash. Fresh from a thrashing by the directors in Paris, he'd made the arduous trek into the desert for what was supposed to be a good turn: a French camera team, keen to trumpet French oil discoveries, was set to film operations at Ghardaïa for the television news. Whether this could salvage his situation was as yet unclear.

As Gaston was dressing, the button came off his trousers, a smooth horn disk between his fingers, trailing thread. How much worse could things get? Tears welled in his eyes, but he didn't let them spill over. He rummaged in his Dopp kit for the little string of safety pins stowed there by Lucienne for just such eventualities: at least his trousers wouldn't fall down in front of the camera crew. Why would the button fall off now? His trousers were hardly tight. He must have lost almost five kilos since before Christmas; he could barely eat anything, everything tasted like sawdust, and he couldn't sleep either, his worries like a drill buzzing in his brain.

Being so much on the road didn't help. He'd had only two nights at home between the week in Paris and this trip. When he was apart from Lucienne, everything felt worse. Simply her presence soothed him: to hear her working calmly in the kitchen, her footfall on the stairs outside the flat, or to lie in bed listening to her breathing in the dark made him feel safe, even when he fretted. She truly believed everything would turn out well; she truly believed he was a man of substance and accomplishment. She considered his failures fleeting, irrelevant. Morning and night, she covered his face with kisses and stroked his hair, as if they were still young lovers. "Aïni," she'd say, "you are my life." But when he was alone—through the bleak, dark night just passed in his little Ghardaïa cell—doubt and dread assailed him with the same ferocity as in his youth. Perhaps, indeed, with even greater ferocity.

You might have thought Aurélie Dechel a welcome distraction, ten years younger than he with her bottle-blond waves rolled into a gentle bun, and that way of looking up through her lashes in the car, the two of them side by side in the back seat with the disgraced driver López at the wheel—that in itself an irony, of course; to entrust their lives to López only weeks after the calamity!—and yet he'd barely been able to listen to her whittering, as if those carefully tinted lips, uninterruptedly exercised, emitted no sound at all. Eventually he'd pleaded fatigue and closed his eyes for a while, but of course, behind his lids, no rest.

This morning there would be breakfast with the Dechels—their local Mozabite hosts made excellent coffee, poured from on high into little cups; and the bread, dates, and olives were always delicious—and then straightaway the drive out to the oil wells. As he understood it, the motors for the Number 2 and Number 3 derricks had been functioning again since the previous Wednesday, and they'd got enough coming on Number 3 to satisfy the newsmen—"OIL FOUND AT LAST IN THE FRENCH SAHARA!" was the headline. He knew, and Dechel knew, and Martinez, the foreman, and his local sidekick, Bourriane, also knew that the supply was, at least so far, a mere trickle; but with the right camera angle it could be made to look like a gush, if not a flood, and this was the story the metropolitan TV journalists so keenly wanted: "FRANCE FINDS OIL ON OUR TERRITORY—THE FUTURE IS SECURE!" They were already fifteen years behind the British in Saudi Arabia, further sidetracked and discouraged by what Hole, the British consul back in Salonica, had later, in Algiers, dubbed, with his particular dry irony, "Your unfortunate war": France needed this.

At this point, Gaston didn't feel too hopeful about this petroleum venture. An understatement. Why had he said yes, two years ago? He'd needed a job—he'd hated the work in insurance—and it had seemed so promising then: not the gold rush but the black-gold rush. An old friend of his from Beirut, Doisneau, on the founding board of SiF, had persuaded him. They went back to before the war; they were friends. But now it was chiefly Doisneau who had lost faith—in him, in Gaston, not in the useless wells. And how was *he*, Gaston, responsible for those, the province of scientists and engineers, himself only ever the businessman, while Doisneau and the others raised money in Paris, hosting long lunch meetings in the private rooms of fine restaurants near the Comédie Française?

Gaston had been at such a lunch only last week, presenting to the assembly as rosy a picture of SiF Alger as he could without lying outright. A dozen investors in tailored wool—mostly dark but one, the dandy, in Prince of Wales houndstooth—had rustled the starched napery and sipped fine Bordeaux from crystal glasses over their *boeuf bourguignon* while he gulped Badoit and cleared his throat obsessively, desperate that his trembling fingers not be seen. He'd spoken of the new dig at Guettara as promising, when in fact, of course, the drill had the previous month failed in the ground—they'd hoped to strike oil at 350 meters and had got almost that deep, 339, when the equipment broke as it was lifted out again. The first disaster, at 310 meters. With great effort and at great expense they'd managed to drag it back as far as 70 meters below the earth's surface with now no obvious way to haul it farther. It had broken into pieces, one of them apparently irretrievably lodged. This lost matériel itself worth five million francs. He'd told the three bosses the day before the lunch; the other two, besides Doisneau, had insisted that these were the hazards of the undertaking and that they still had faith in him. But Doisneau, dapper Doisneau, had grown surly and thin-lipped, his brows drawn in a flat line above his eyes. He'd offered no absolution, no cheer. And, frankly, Gaston agreed with him: Guettara increasingly felt doomed, a morass of miscalculation and bad luck that might potentially sink the company.

If only the broken drill had been the sole catastrophe. But already, in the late fall, there'd been the three drowned replacement motors, driven down by Martinez from Algiers for the three pumps at Ghardaïa, and the fool had neglected to check that they were siphoned of oil before he set out. Over the brutal desert roads, the motors, jounced, flooded irreparably. A smaller loss than at Guettara, but significant; and that one entirely due to human error. When you were the managing director—and that was Gaston's title—you were responsible. You were as much the fool as Martinez, who hadn't even yet been sacked, because they couldn't find anyone with the right experience—too many oil wells being dug at once, all the experienced workers employed elsewhere. Gaston had suggested promoting the local Mozabite guy from Ghardaïa, Bourriane. He didn't have the paper degree, and he insisted perversely on his boubou and white skullcap except on-site, where he wore the same jumpsuit as everyone else, but he knew more about the terrain and its treasures than the rest of them put together. Only Paris management wasn't having it.

All that he could still have dealt with, were it not for the accident. How was it that the driver López was still employed? His wife somehow related to Doisneau's wife's cousin's wife, something like that. There was a reason Gaston had been told López could not be let go, but it looked bad for the company. They'd agreed to pay out—it should have been enough—but Gaston suffered as a matter of conscience: money couldn't make up for a life.

In the second week of December, López had been driving one of the trucks out from Ghardaïa to the site, the biweekly delivery of food supplies for the men in the barracks. There'd been a sandstorm—everyone who'd spent time in the desert knew what that was like. You might ask why he was even on the road; but he was delivering the food, for God's sake. You couldn't ask the men to work—backbreaking work—without eating! And though he'd never concede it, López, with his complacent round face and silly mustache, had probably not been paying close attention, because he'd have assumed—it wasn't insane—there'd be no other vehicles on the road that morning. And they'd established, thankfully, that the oncoming van didn't have its lights on—how could they have been so stupid? Or maybe their lights didn't even work?

Gaston could picture the gray swirl, a fog composed not of air but of sand granules, the whipped, engulfing tumult of it, the windows sealed and the truck vents closed and still the sand seeping in through invisible cracks, a little here and there around his feet, his knees even, López driving with a keffiyeh around his face, all but his eyes, just to be sure he doesn't choke, hastening now as the storm has worsened in the last kilometer, but he's clocked the distance to the turnoff on the odometer, and now he can see the blue sign, its brightness flickering in the monochrome gloom, and he swings the wheel of the truck, it's a big vehicle, after all, and he's geared down so he puts his foot on the accelerator too, almost able to hear the engine's deeper bite under the constant roar of the storm. And the truck turns, mightily and at some speed—

Two men in the small van, unseen. Two Moroccans, employed at the next dig, ten kilometers down the road—another pissy little outfit like their own. The crash threw López into the windscreen, but luckily the glass, though cracked like a spider's web, did not shatter. He had fifteen stitches across his forehead from his scalp to his brow, and he broke his nose and three ribs, which you knew still hurt like hell seven weeks later. His torso had been bandaged like a mummy, still was beneath his shirt, but all he'd say was "*Ça va aller, patron,*" as though the only way to make up for what he'd done was to swallow the physical pain. He'd volunteered to drive up to collect Gaston in Algiers—and Madame Dechel at the same time—and he'd take him on to Guettara and then back up to Algiers again, a monster of driving when his ribs still made him wince at every pothole.

But López was the lucky one. One of the Moroccans lingered five days in a coma in the little clinic at Ghardaïa before dying there; and the other, the younger one, nineteen only, the same age as Denise, had lost his right arm at the elbow and had suffered permanent disfigurement and, worse, bleeding in the brain. The doctors were still cautious about the possible extent of his recovery.

SiF Alger was paying the medical bills, needless to say, and had paid the funeral expenses for the dead man. But Gaston had insisted— Lucienne, his moral guide, adamantine, had insisted that he insist; had Doisneau been annoyed about this too?—that they give each of the families a lump sum. Was it money for the curtailed life or for the ruined one? Money couldn't compensate, but nor could prayer, and at least with money you could eat.

That's what those boys were—one unmarried, the other the deceased, with a wife and a three-year-old son back in Figuig—the livelihoods of their families, the providers, now forever lost. He'd convinced the Paris trio of the need for compensation not by arguing that it was morally right but, instead, by insisting that a failure to do so might lead to lawsuits and bad publicity that could tarnish the company's reputation. The accident and death had been reported, after all, in all the papers. An additional considerable expense, as yet without a final figure—the lawyers were still working on the details—and, above all, the tragedy of it.

BY NINE, he and Dechel were at the site with Martinez and Bourriane— the latter in a proper gray suit at least, which, though pressed, fit poorly, too short in the arms and too wide in the chest—preparing for the camera crew. A dozen workmen, the most physically presentable (those with the most teeth!), had been pulled from their shifts to be introduced to the journalists and had, for the morning, been equipped with motley hard hats, pith helmets really, from the limited store in the back room of Martinez's office. A sort of wooden stage for the visitors, complete with awning from the sun, had been mounted next to Derrick Number 3, the one that brought up the most oil, though that wasn't saying much. Martinez had retained several drums' worth over the preceding days, which could be discreetly fed through a pipe to augment the true flow, at the apt moment, to enhance the impression of abundance. He'd been careful to stockpile enough for multiple "takes," in case the crew needed to film the moment several times over. Faking an oil rush for the cameras took careful planning.

They hadn't hidden this from the crew. They'd discussed it, Gaston and the journalists, when they'd met in Paris. Gaston had explained that the flow was erratic, which might prove challenging for the footage, but that if the journalists wanted— *Yes, yes*, had been the response, almost before he could explain the plan. So the workers had set up the stage, and then, on the other side of the well, out of sight, the stashed drums and the piping that connected them to the main shaft, purely for the purposes of the close-up. It wasn't a lie—he would never have agreed to a lie—but it wasn't quite the truth, either.

The cook and his team were in the mess hall, laying out trays of croissants and *makroud*, the local specialty, little diamonds filled with date paste and dipped in honey and orange-blossom water. The Parisian visitors always delighted in what they experienced as exotic treats and loved to be told that they were Mzab specialties, particular to the desert, when of course most fine grocers in Algiers were Mozabite, and their wives prepared trays of *makroud* for sale almost anywhere in the big cities— even, Gaston knew, in Marseille or Paris.

Gaston looked up to see Dechel emerging from the main office, shaking his head. Even frowning, he had an aspect less mournful than usual after his conjugal night with the fair and garrulous Aurélie. They generally spent only a few nights together out of each month, up in Algiers; she only rarely traveled south.

If this brief newsreel was successful—if the response in France was positive—it was rumored that the French minister of industry might be persuaded to make a formal visit from Paris, as early even as mid-March. That of course would be a mixed blessing for Gaston and the company— the government would almost certainly look to the bigger digs on the other side of Ghardaïa and might not even mention SiF Alger by name. Somehow Doisneau or the others in Paris had persuaded the journalists to come—they had contacts, through a friend of a friend, and, frankly, there too someone might have exaggerated some aspects of the enterprise.

Dechel was shaking his head. He brushed his fine hair back from above his ear. "They should have told us last night. They could have rung through to Ghardaïa, but apparently they only had someone call an hour ago. One of their team broke a tooth yesterday, God knows how, and had to see an emergency dentist in the city. So they set off only at four this morning. They won't be here till noon."

"Noon?" Gaston felt a surge of annoyance. All this, this stupid show, like dancing monkeys for the press, pretending the wells were more viable than they were, pretending they weren't teetering on the edge of insolvency, crippled by debt, misfortune, incompetence. A laughable theater, in which he was shamefully complicit, and they had to hold their poses for an extra three hours? They were taking the piss. The new France, rebuilt and cosmopolitan, all a farce. The same lies, corruption, and incompetence that had bogged the nation down through the '30s and led inexorably to the war. What now?

But outwardly he showed no more than a raised eyebrow—he hadn't been captain of a ship for nothing—and gave a wry smile. "Time, I think, for some of Mohamed's excellent coffee, and a taste of the *makroud*?" He gestured toward the mess hall. "And surely then we can get a decent two and a half hours of labor out of these men, so the day isn't completely wasted."

"Yes, of course." Dechel snapped his fingers at one of the foremen and spoke to him in Arabic; Gaston understood most but not all of what he said. He was telling the men they'd have to change out of their good clothes before working. He was promising there'd be enough pastries for everyone. The men did not smile.

In Paris, the previous week, Gaston had given his presentation and attended his management meetings at SiF Alger, small meetings in which he'd offered three times to step down, but the two directors besides Doisneau had insisted repeatedly, passionately even, that he stay on at least for six months. He'd agreed reluctantly, though he knew that in six months he would walk away, no matter what. In his brief time at home before setting out for Ghardaïa, Lucienne, his wisdom, had agreed that he must; however terrifying it might seem, financially, they'd manage. Trusting in God, they'd always got by somehow.

To that end, discreetly, after the SiF Alger meetings, Gaston had arranged to see an old acquaintance named Rondot. They'd met at dinners in Beirut in the '30s, when Rondot was with the Iraq Petroleum Company. Now he was a senior executive with La Française des Pétroles, the largest French oil company, and Gaston was asking him for a job.

Rondot had cleverly parlayed an academic background notably less impressive than Gaston's into resounding success. He was surely well paid, too. Above all, he was fully involved with the most essential and expanding business of the future. Not for Rondot a shaky little venture; La Française had twenty-four licenses for the Sahara alone.

As they sat over an *apéritif* at the Café de Flore, across the boulevard from his hotel, Gaston frankly envied Rondot, who, fidgeting with a franc coin throughout, making it appear and disappear, like a cheap magician, charmingly made it clear to Gaston that without fluent English, he'd find no place in any of the big companies.

"But I can read it perfectly well—it's just my accent when I speak." Gaston offered a self-deprecating smile, intended to show his underlying confidence.

Rondot shook his head, making Gaston feel craven and pathetic. "My friend, you've no idea—the Brits, the Americans, they're all over this industry, it's in their hands. What was the IPC, after all, all those years ago? Even our Algeria project is in significant partnership with Shell— and what do you know about the Dutch? Have you *ever* met a Dutchman who'll speak French? It's almost a matter of principle for them, solidarity with their Belgian cousins. No, it's the reign of chewing gum and Churchill from here on out." Rondot twirled his infernal coin again. "We lost the war, my friend. It's all very well for de Gaulle to pretend otherwise, and who can blame us for wanting to believe him? But behind the scrim, the facts are as they are: to the victor go the spoils. The future is in oil, and the future is in English."

At that, they both shrugged, almost playfully, and Rondot clapped his shoulder as they parted, but Gaston was overwhelmed with rue. Back in his small hotel room beneath the eaves, he wrote a note to François, reaffirming that the boy was in the right place, studying in America for a year: "The way of the future. It will be indispensable to be fluent in English," he wrote. "You'll have a head start."

For himself, he could feel only despair. Almost fifty years since he'd been born, half a century: he was old. His triumphs—there'd been a few—seemed so distant now. For so long he'd believed they would lead him where he wanted, where he was destined, to go. But the world had transformed around him, and he couldn't seem to adapt. As if he'd learned to play the violin—not just to play it competently but to make the instrument sing—and had suddenly been called upon by the conductor to switch, in the middle of the symphony, to the bassoon.

He'd had to change instruments so many times! From Salonica, back to Beirut in the summer of 1940; Gaston had after some months been sent from there to Istanbul, and then deployed for a year on a ship escorting supply boats, patrolling the passage between Casablanca and Dakar. In early 1943, once the navy and all of France d'Outre-Mer, the French overseas, had joined with the Allies against Germany, he was summoned back to Algiers to help run naval intelligence, overseeing high-risk submarine runs for the infiltration of spies into Marseille and Toulon, and the exfiltration of assets to safe territory in North Africa. *There*, at least, all the French were finally reunited in the common goal of liberating France. But he'd been swiftly aware that the men recently arrived from London or Cairo or Chad mistrusted him, because he'd returned to Beirut in 1940, because he'd stayed under the orders of the French navy after the fateful day of de Gaulle's broadcast, heard in Salonica three years earlier. *Because he hadn't gone with de Gaulle, at the very start. Because he hadn't run off to London.* These others seemed to keep secrets from his team, leaving them out of the loop. Each time Gaston discovered a colleague's "inadvertent oversight," or when he passed a gathering in the local bistro of which he should logically have been a part, he suffered, and he carried his suffering, like salt in a wound.

He'd suffered, then, yes, but had rallied, because in fact in spite of doubt and suspicion they *did* all work together, and they did succeed, first in smaller triumphs and then in a cascade. Reassigned to the naval HQ in Paris in the bitter winter of '44–'45 to work on the postwar peace, he was awash with renewed hope, buoyed and joyful—to work for the admirals, in concert with the Americans! He remembered well the victory parade for de Gaulle—the tricolor bunting and the flags everywhere, on posts and buildings and in people's hands, the boulevards crammed with cheering hordes on the parade route while everywhere else, the little back streets, was quiet as Sunday at dawn, because everyone, everyone, was gathered to see the great savior pass. He'd had the day off work, they all had, and he'd walked the streets alone, weaving through the masses of spectators, three times kissed on both cheeks by exuberant fellow citizens, several times spattered with champagne and beer, deafened by the joyous shouting, by petards and honking horns, feeling that although he'd been wrong, that June day in Salonica in 1940 (though what other decision could he possibly have made, with Lucienne incommunicado in Algiers?), nevertheless, in the great flood of History everything had ultimately turned, as it must under God's watchful eye, to the good, and here he was, they *all* were, once again united and faithful: France would rebuild, and regain her standing, though it might take decades. Inshallah, he would live to see it, and be a part of it, and certainly his brilliant son would be a part of it, and his daughter, sweet, fragile little Denise (in the spring of '45 she was not yet twelve), she might marry a diplomat or a politician or even a captain of industry, who knew, and then she would be part of it too, part of this great renaissance . . .

And each new position in business since he'd left the navy after the war's end (there'd been four of them) looked perhaps to the outside world like advancement, or at least not, he trusted, like failure. Only Lucienne fully knew what these jobs had cost him. He'd bent and twisted himself into unseemly shapes, each time hoping against hope that this new role would carry him forward, open doors, afford opportunities to become part of "the new France," the renascent France—and yet here he was once again, SiF Alger just another leaky ship barely above water; and whatever France was becoming, it seemed—although he'd devoted his whole life to her—she had no place for him. It seemed that the chancers and the swindlers—these journalists, even, on their way now to capture footage that would tell a happy story rather than a true one—were once again to the fore.

For God's sake, he'd wanted to be a writer! He was—he considered himself—an intellectual. He needed to provide for his family, of course (would the burden of Tata Jeanne always be upon him? Would Denise find a husband?): he'd long ago renounced his dreams of grandeur, though he kept his two manuscripts, the novel and the short stories, in the drawer of the night table by his bed. God was teaching him, always, to be less proud. Yet he couldn't help but *be* proud, he the last son of an abandoned elementary school teacher, herself the daughter of illiterate parents. He'd raised a son who was studying in the United States on a Fulbright fellowship at Amherst College—the only one from Algeria. *The only one.* It wasn't nothing. Was he a failure? No, he was proud, still, and his love—their love, his and Lucienne's—that, perhaps, was the great masterwork of his life. *That*, perhaps, which he had not done alone, and could not have done alone, made all this nonsense, this *crap*, worthwhile. What did Lucienne always say? Trust in His plan. He has a plan for each of us. Then again, the riposte: the Lord helps those who help themselves. Indubitably so.

He did not yet know that by the year's end he'd be transformed again, based in Morocco, as an executive for a French phosphate mining company at Ouled Abdoun Basin, near Khouribga, a situation that would bring with it a new set of crises and concerns. By the turn of the year '54, Lucienne would join him in the company house in Rabat, where they'd acquire a black shepherd bitch named Fiamma for company, leaving the kids to complete their studies in Algiers, living still in the family flat on the Rue Guillaumet, while Tata Jeanne went to finish her days with the nuns at the care home, poor thing.

GASTON HAD WANDERED well beyond the derricks in the direction of the road. His polished shoes were grayed by the sand. He could feel against his belly the metal safety pin in his waistband, another hidden flaw. He could hear behind him, as if far away, the rhythmic metallic soughing of the pumps, and occasional shouts between the men. He didn't turn back to see where Dechel had got to—presumably the mess hall, where Gaston would soon join him. The lunar desert landscape unfolded apparently infinite before his eyes, beneath the brilliant sky. The crisp air smelled of—what? He knew the smell so well by now but could compare it to nothing else: mineral, dry, ancient. The air smelled ancient. At the horizon he detected the swirl of dust that bespoke movement: too early for the van with the camera crew; perhaps a vehicle headed to the next dig over, the one he now thought of as the Moroccans'—the dead man's dig. From the other direction, suddenly, over a dune, a Bedouin appeared alone on his camel, with a second, provision-laden camel in tow. The imposing beasts clomped closer, shuddering their long necks and masticating wearily, ancient as the air. The shrouded nomad raised his arm in a wave. Gaston saluted in return and watched for a few moments as the small caravan proceeded down the highway at its eternal, stately pace, toward the approaching truck in its hive of sand. Then he turned to retrace his own vanishing footsteps, to take up the duties of his day.

PART III

☙

TORONTO, CANADA

M other was waiting, in her silver mink no less, in the front hall as Barbara ladled into a thermos the vichyssoise she'd spent the morning preparing. She'd already made a tuna sandwich—on white bread, no crusts, as he preferred it—and had wrapped it in waxed paper. She was almost ready.

"Two minutes," she called to Mother, who didn't reply, doubtless fussing over her hair or chasing a missing glove; but the silence felt to Barbara like criticism. Lenore was nothing if not formidable. Never mind that she stood only five foot two inches and that Barbara towered over her at five foot nine; Mother made daughter feel small.

They were headed, same as every day, to the Toronto General to take Father his lunch—if he'd eat at all, it would be the food they brought him (and even if he ate, no guarantee that he could keep it down)—and today was Barbara's turn to make the soup. But she'd also suggested, over breakfast, that maybe instead of staying at the hospital until eight o'clock she might leave early to go with Charley to Connie's party. Mother hadn't said yes or no, just "Do what you think is best, dear," in a tone as much weary as anything else that Barbara knew contained disappointment and disdain as well as sorrow—and, of course, weariness above all. If she went to the party—as she had gone only a few days earlier to Disey's dinner—Mother would come home alone to an empty house, and eat a scrambled egg alone, and would then lie awake in bed in the dark until Barbara turned the key downstairs and slipped in. All this although Barbara was twenty-nine years old and five and a half years married.

Sometimes Barbara thought that her mother still didn't really believe she, Barbara, was married at all, that she considered that Barbara simply performed a theater of adulthood for the outside world but that at home, behind closed doors, they could drop the pretense and continue as before. This attitude—so patronizing, Barbara had complained to Charley when they went out for drinks together at the King Edward—enraged Barbara; but sometimes as the weeks went by, she also wondered whether Mother wasn't on to something. It had happened last year when she'd left Europe to come home to Toronto for a while, when Daddy was first ill—this progressive sense of detachment from her "real" grown-up life a continent away, over the weeks and then months she'd been at home, far from her husband. It had caused no small trouble in her marriage.

This time, when she'd set off in late September from Geneva, where François had just started at business school, she'd sworn—not just to François but to herself—that she would not let it happen again. Yet here they were. Charley, who was fond of Lenore but behind her back called her "the Sergeant Major," said Barbara's mother infantilized her daughter, albeit out of love: "She's lonely and you're an only, and she just can't bear to let you go," Charley had said, running her finger thoughtfully around the rim of her martini glass, hoping perhaps that it was crystal and would sing; but it was not, and did not.

"She thinks I belong to her, you mean," Barbara had replied, "and she can't bear for me to have my own life." As the jazz trio in the corner started back up and made continued conversation essentially impossible, Barbara had felt that probably they were both right. What difference did it make, really? The result was the same.

Mother drove them downtown in the Jag—Daddy's Jag, as Barbara thought of it, only two years old, with its lovely sealskin brown hood, its cream leather seats, and its burled walnut dashboard. Mother's car had been the Wolseley, until Father had to go back to hospital. Lenore wore her light gray kid gloves, which matched her mink and her silver hair (carefully waved only the day before at the salon at Bloor and Runnymede), and she wore around her neck the navy-bordered Hermès scarf that Barbara and François had given her when she and Daddy had visited Paris last April, held in place by a rhinestone clasp. She might not be beautiful, she might be square and rather heavy now (though she told the story of how when she was young her arms were so skinny Daddy said he was afraid to hold them lest they break), but she looked every bit the wealthy matron: she'd decided this was important, for the hospital, and she dressed up every day so that when she marched into the lobby of the General or swept down the hallway to the nurses' station, or met with Dr. Ogryzlo outside Harold's room, they would know, each one of them, from the security guard to the head nurse to this foreign doctor who held her husband's life in his hands, that she was—that they were—consequential, people of value and standing, that they must be attended to and well taken care of. That his life must be saved.

Barbara, in the car, looked at her mother (her gray-blue eyes fixed on the road, flickering behind their rhinestone-trimmed cat-eye glasses), while she herself held very still, the soup thermos and the tuna sandwich wrapped in waxed paper, along with the linen and china and cutlery, in a straw shopping bag on her knees.

The strangeness, the strangeness of it, sitting next to her mother as they drove the Lake Shore Boulevard to downtown, the snow in sooty piles along the esplanade and beyond, the lake, steaming and groaning in the cold like a witch's cauldron, just as she'd sat next to her mother in the car on this road at fifteen, all angles and bony knees, as if in the interim she'd never been kissed, let alone licked and stroked and filled, filled by the tongue, the hands, the body of another, as if she were the same shy virgin with an overbite rather than the desired and beloved sophisticate, all woman, she'd thought to have become. And Daddy, he couldn't see it either, he couldn't bear to—only she, Barbara, seemed to know it.

Would having a child make this strange disjunction between who she was and how they perceived her better or worse? Could she bear to have a child? For years now she'd said no, she'd insisted that they be supremely careful—François was perpetually a student, for God's sake; they had no money; they still took loans from their parents on both sides that nobody, not even themselves, really believed they would repay. But she'd be thirty within a year—she'd just turned twenty-nine a month ago, her first birthday apart from François since November '56—and you couldn't put it off forever. All around her, the high school gang had been falling like ninepins—first Marnie and Bud (he was the same age as the rest of them but bald as an egg, which made him and their babies look oddly alike), then Eleanor and John, in Brasília no less—obviously Eleanor had come back for the birth, but now she had returned, with squirming infant, to the unimaginable Southern Hemisphere—and then Judy, and Disey, and even Connie, whose party was this evening, and Ellie and Ed, like Marnie and Bud, already on their *second*—and hadn't she heard that Sunny, out in Hamilton, was just about to pop? Only Charley, reliably, still flew the flag for the single life, their cool career girl climbing the ranks at the ballet, cocktails and dancing de rigueur, and sex, very carefully mind you, but full-on sexual intercourse with at least three boyfriends that Barbara knew of, a thoroughly modern woman, though she could still sit for afternoon tea with Mother and talk like an old Tory and butter wouldn't melt in her mouth. But even she, since she'd started going out with Bobby—should she, Barbara, have married Bobby all those years ago when he was so in love with her? She couldn't see him that way then, and it was too late to think about it now, but since Charley had started seeing Bobby, even *she* seemed to find babies, or some of them at least, cute, delicious even, said they weren't all homunculi—what was Liz Taylor's line in *Cat on a Hot Tin Roof*? No-necked monsters; all children were no-necked monsters, they'd joked a few years back—and now look at them all: encumbered, one after another. Like lemmings jumping off the cliff.

Mother pulled into the drive at the hospital, ready to hand the Jag off to the regular attendant. He knew them well by now: he knew that Mrs. Fisk would tip well if he was prompt, which he always was.

"Mind you don't turn over that soup," Mother said as she got out of the car; and then, for the attendant: "Hello, dear Gregory, always nice to see you. Are you managing?"

"Cold's bitter, but I've got my earmuffs, so."

She smiled an indulgent smile, something rarely wasted these days on Barbara. "We could all do with a pair as good as yours. We'll be back, oh, by eight."

"As usual, ma'am. If you have them ring down just ten minutes before—"

But she'd swooped on ahead, leaving Barbara to manage the lunch and to retrieve, from the back seat, the canvas bag of books and glossy magazines that constituted the day's diversion, including the onionskin pad on which she might, but probably wouldn't, write a letter to François. She couldn't really bear the thought of Mother peering over her shoulder or asking off-handedly what she found to tell her husband. When referring to François thus, Mother always made it sound as though there were quotation marks around the word. Barbara's adult life might seem to her parents absurd, sequestered as it was across the ocean, where they largely didn't have to conceive of it (sometimes, in frustration, François would say that they didn't really believe in the existence of anything or anyone outside the bounds of Metro Toronto or, by a great stretch of the imagination, outside Ontario. They didn't even really believe in Quebec, let alone Europe. It was a miracle, he'd say, that they'd ever let her cross the Atlantic—), but it was real to her, and suffused with intense emotion: it, he, they, Geneva was her secret.

From the moment she'd first seen him on the bus in Oxford, that summer of '55, when they were both enrolled there for summer courses, François had thrilled her. Physically. Charley understood—when she met him, she cooed, "Isn't he the sexy one!" That first date—they'd made a double date of it with the glamorous American on her program,

Gloria Steinem, and her Texan beau—they'd spread a checkered blanket between a willow and a hawthorn alongside the Thames, and François had sat so awkwardly on the ground in his fine trousers, with his knees tucked up, while the Texan, cross-legged and limber, had seemed utterly at home. She'd teased him about it. "I hate picnics," François had confided. "I'm only here for you." And he'd run his finger along her forearm like a current. Later, when it started to rain—of course it had—the others had run ahead across the meadow with the blanket over their heads and he'd kissed her under the willow tree. Ah, the particular smell of him that she discovered then and so loved, and the hot green smell of summer grass and rain, the bruised light glistening around them, and when they got back to St. Hilda's—drenched, their clothes plastered to their bodies, their fingers entwined—they were breathless, laughing, changed.

And it had felt that way since, as though when they were together they couldn't ever be apart, a powerful longing that sometimes she felt even when he lay next to her in bed, the way sometimes she wanted a cigarette when she was already smoking a cigarette. But when they were separated, after a time, it grew hard to remember that urgency, that intense yearning; it felt like a dream, like someone else's life. Everything about him was so far from her known Toronto world, and irreconcilable. Which was why her parents had argued so fiercely against the marriage; and why he, in return, had come to mistrust, maybe even dislike them.

And because their relations were quietly adversarial, she felt she had to protect them all from each other, not just him from them but also her parents and their small but contented lives from his sharp tongue. She didn't relay to him her mother's barbs, or almost never did. She didn't tell him that her mother had once called him "good for nothing," when he was a graduate student at Harvard. She had never told him about her mother's horrible letter—letters, really—the month after the wedding, when she, Barbara, had written in such distress about how hard it was to land in France and begin anew, alone. . . . In that impossible first year, Barbara sometimes thought, the only thing that had kept her from turning tail and rushing home was the trauma of that first letter, in which her mother told her she'd made her own bed and would now have to lie in it, that she'd chosen rashly and foolishly in spite of her parents' advice, that they washed their hands of her. She'd reiterated her complaints that François was still a student at over twenty-five, with no visible income or profession, in addition to being thoroughly foreign, French like those squalling Québécois who'd just set up a separatist party, and more than that Catholic, in fact, like the bandy-legged Italian grocer up on Bloor Street. And, stranger still, from *Africa!* With that surname— now hers, Barbara's, her mother once again pointed out—was he even fully white? And they'd never even clapped eyes on his parents—did their letter suggest they were related somehow?—now off doing God knew what in godforsaken South America with not even enough money to attend the wedding. Well, what did Barbara expect? And within a week of her departure, her mother had emptied her bedroom of all her personal effects and had thrown away, *in the garbage,* all her letters and diaries, so as to make room for Luke Whitworth, Barbara's ex-boyfriend whose family had moved to Kitchener and who would be their lodger for the coming year while he continued at the law school. Years later, it still boggled the mind.

Daddy wasn't a schemer; he wouldn't have thought it through; but Mother, when she agreed to that, and when, with the utmost brutality, she jettisoned Barbara's childhood (her only concession was to have kept the photographs from her bedroom in a box in the basement), had known exactly what she was doing and how profoundly she wounded her only child.

In these circumstances, the war declared (to Barbara) and undeclared (to François) had as its goal the destruction of their marriage. Barbara never doubted this: in 1957, Mother had wanted Barbara to come running back home in tears so that Mother might gloatingly say, "I told you so." And Barbara had determined then, and had not since wavered in her determination, not to grant her mother that satisfaction. God knew it was hard, sometimes almost impossible—when François's volatile temper flared, when he was tired or stressed and difficult, or simply when the snootiness of the French seemed unbearable—but Barbara would not cave.

And then last fall, and again this fall, Daddy had brought her home, not out of strength but in his weakness, not by stratagems and schemes but straightforwardly out of need and love. He was so ill. She knew her mother secretly thought her "Daddy's girl," and so she was: he was the one who cherished her, after all, told her she was beautiful and smart, who stood up for her against Mother's endless pecking. And he was the one who knew how to laugh and have fun. Mother doubtless wondered whether Barbara would make similar sacrifices for her (Barbara wondered this too, sometimes). But the point was that she was here, now, had been here for nearly two months, had been at Mother's side every day (or almost), both at home and at the hospital.

Daddy's single faced onto University Avenue; the big plate-glass window filled the room with light, on this winter day a bright white light, with a rim of condensation fogging near the sill. They could hear, faintly, alongside the beeping of his machines, the susurrations of the traffic on the slushy tarmac of the avenue. Daddy was sitting propped up on pillows when they came in, his majestic head turned toward the light outside. She saw, in the instant before he realized they were there and "made" his face, his features slack and hopeless, his lower lip dangling. But Mother's cheerful "Harold darling! We're *here!*" served as a trigger, and his eyebrows rose, along with the corners of his mouth. He twinkled in his old way, or tried to.

"What treats today, my beauties?" His voice emerged hoarse and thin from his throat, no longer the resonant bass Barbara had always known. His once-imposing body, tall and broad as a giant's, now ravaged, lay in jangled hummocks beneath the pale blue sheet, but for his newly skinny arms, bruised and bandaged and threaded, at the elbow, to the hospital's vast machinery—he was literally tied by his IV and monitors to the wall—with their shiny, swollen, mottled hands, and one shiny, bloated foot, its toes purpled, rested like an immortal haggis upon a throne. She could not bear to look at it, and focused her gaze instead upon Daddy's dear face, the skin of his cheeks hanging in leathery folds, his color ashen, his brows askew. Some kind nurse had combed his spiky hair for his wife and daughter, but as usual nobody had offered him a shave: Mother would do it, all gentleness, but only after lunch. As if she were herself the nurse matron, she made sure that he had eaten properly before anything else. For now, the silvered bristles along his jaw shone dully in the light, and Barbara's solid and indomitable father looked more than ever like one of the homeless men who gathered, palms out to the parishioners, on Sundays outside the United Church downtown.

"How has your morning been?" Mother asked, kissing the haggard cheek. "You looked as though you were thinking deep thoughts."

"No thoughts at all, my love. Thoughts only of you both." He paused to clear his throat, effortfully, repeatedly, as if hoping it might restore amplitude to his voice. "That's not quite true. I was thinking about the annual conference in Ottawa, next month."

Mother, busy laying out the pressed linen cloth upon his wheeled bed tray, and the china side plate from home, and the bowl and spoon for the vichyssoise, did not stop her work. "You'll be fine in a month, dear. We'll drive up to Ottawa together."

Barbara, standing near the window watching, trying to stay out of the way, unsure as ever quite what to do with her hands, wondered whether Mother believed what she was saying. When Lenore set her mind, it was hard to tell: the force of her will was considerable. Either she believed it or believed that believing could make it so. What was it that Bobby's younger philosopher friend Ian had been going on about at Disey's dinner? The performative utterance, was it? Saying it makes it so. Some British philosopher's latest idea. Ian was doing a PhD over there, Cambridge was it, and Bobby'd thought they might all get together in Paris or Geneva; but Barbara, though she liked the fellow, knew straightaway he'd set François's teeth on edge. . . . What was the book called? *How to Do Things with Words*—that was it, which had made it sound quite fun. But Bobby said not so much really. J. L. Austin. Oxford, not Cambridge, like Ian. He'd died not long ago, quite young apparently. Ian had said that the book was lectures he'd given at Harvard, before François was a student there. Not that they would necessarily have gone, but they might have, she liked to think. Ian had said also that in British philosophy circles it wasn't done to publish while you were alive—so strange.

Mother had poured the soup into the china bowl and Daddy was making appreciative noises, but he didn't pick up the spoon. She had also unwrapped his sandwich and laid it out on the plate, with its little pink flowers around the rim, like the bowl, as though they were eating lunch in the sunroom overlooking the back garden, instead of in this strange, cold, white place. A couple of nurses walked by in the hallway, chatting, and the older one—Nurse Macintosh, a mild, sober woman they knew well by now, stuck her head in: "Having another little party, Mr. Fisk? Don't let your ladies tire you out too much. I'll be back for your infusion in forty-five, okay?"

"Must we?" His smile was rueful.

"Don't be silly, Harold, it's doing a world of good. We can all tell."

Barbara could not look at his ghastly foot, nor at his hands, for that matter. The nurses had moved on.

"Let's make an effort, dear." Mother lifted the spoon for him and raised a mouthful of cream soup toward his lips, leaning in to blow on it, gently, in case it was hot, though they all knew the thermos kept things warm rather than hot. "Down the hatch," she said, and Daddy opened his mouth obediently, like a child or a baby bird.

Barbara could see his large, white-filmed tongue. He swallowed the soup with some difficulty.

"And another," Mother said. He opened his mouth again, though Barbara could tell he didn't want to. Hopefully he would get through half the bowl before he gave up. Hopefully he might eat a few bites of the sandwich too—it was soft without the crusts and quite bland, but all of it nutritious. Long ago, Mother had wanted to be a nutritionist, back when she'd assumed she'd go to college, before her father had died, leaving only debts, and she'd had to quit school at sixteen to become a secretary. How many times had she told Barbara this, to impress upon her how lucky she was? But she always paid close attention to the healthiness of their meals.

Yesterday Daddy hadn't been able to keep down any of his lunch. The soup—minestrone—had come up almost as soon as he'd eaten it, and he hadn't even attempted the sandwich. It was the new drug that made him nauseous—the drug he'd spend three hours this afternoon, as he'd spent three hours every afternoon for the past nine days, having infused into his poor body through one of the lines stuck into his arm. Nurse Macintosh would hang the bag of clear, viscous liquid from an S hook on a pole by the bed, and would attach the tube to the port already taped at his elbow. Barbara couldn't really bear to watch the steady drip of it, any more than she could look at his hands and feet, and so what they had come to was that when Nurse Macintosh arrived, she and Mother would go out to find their own lunch, and leave him to endure it in private. Mother had said Daddy preferred that anyway, and sometimes he simply slept, and was then more energetic—if that word could really be used— for their second spell with him, from four to seven-thirty. He was already tired, after all, when they arrived at noon, because each morning he spent three hours in the whirlpool bath. The idea was that the warm water would soften his skin, and maybe it did. Maybe, Barbara wondered but did not ever suggest to her mother, it was the only thing that did—how could it not, so much time in the water? She had only to lie ten minutes in the bathtub at home to turn into a prune; and this awful, frightening drug that made him feel so unwell—an experimental drug, they all said so quite frankly—maybe had no benefit at all.

Daddy shook his head, so apologetic. Mother returned the spoonful to the soup bowl.

"Take a little rest then, dear," she said. "We have all the time in the world. Barb made the soup today—it's a good one, isn't it?"

"My favorite." He was trying to twinkle, for her, for them both. "Delicious."

She had to say something—take his mind off things. She'd tell a story, and maybe while she did, Mother could slip him a bite or two of tuna.

"You'll love this, Daddy," she began, stepping forward from the window and only then conscious that it was colder there, that winter seeped, along with the white light, through the plate glass. She rested her hands on the metal bar at the bottom of his bed, aware that the offending foot hovered just beneath her gaze, that the other one, no less alarming, lay right beside it, beneath the covers, both of them swollen by water pooled beneath their hardened and unbreathing skin: the body turning itself into a carapace, a fatal prison.

"I spoke this morning to a Harvard friend of François's, Arthur—he's still there, of course, in Cambridge, and he was calling because he's heading over to France in the new year, and hoped we might—well, anyways, that doesn't matter. He was telling me about another friend of his, a British fellow we met in Cambridge—he's Canadian, actually, from B.C., but grew up really over there mostly, or maybe—"

"Barbara, you're dithering," Mother said. "The story?"

"Oh, but it is a good one—" Mother already knew this, because Barbara had relayed it as soon as she'd hung up. Mother had broken off a little piece of the sandwich and was coaxing it into Daddy's mouth. He'd shown no sign of vomiting yet; Barbara felt she was keeping them all from thinking about him vomiting—a sort of anti-performative utterance. François would've laughed at that. "No, really—so this fellow, Arthur's friend, his name is Hemming, John Hemming, and he decided to go up the Amazon exploring, you know, with two friends—I mean, they're anthropologists. I'm not sure if he's got his PhD already or if this was research for it, but—"

"Barb, the story."

"Yes, so they got quite far away from civilization, up the river, and they were running out of food, you know, the trip was longer than anticipated, and they had a confab and sent John back to get some food and maybe some assistance, and while he was gone some Amazon tribesmen emerged from the jungle and attacked the other two and killed one with a blow dart. Can you imagine?"

"What about the poor guy left living, then? They didn't boil him in a pot for dinner, did they?" Daddy was making a joke.

"Don't be silly. Of course not. He lived to tell the tale. That's how we know what happened. But the point is, they were an undiscovered tribe, you see. Nobody had ever come into contact with them."

"Who's nobody?" Daddy joked again. "Because they'd certainly been in contact with themselves!"

It was wonderful when Daddy made light of things—a glimmer of himself. He chewed a little bit of tuna, but he waved away the vichyssoise: he wouldn't have any more in spite of all her work.

"So now John, John Hemming, is going to write a book about it—"

"But he wasn't even there!" Daddy joked.

"Well, he wasn't there when the tribesmen blew the darts, no. And thank goodness. But he was there just before and after, and he and the other fellow, the one who survived, they've made a really important discovery."

"Which is, don't drop in on the Amazonian tribe without calling first."

"Oh, you are silly." But she was pleased. "Do you ever think, though, how extraordinary it is that I, Barbara, your daughter, born and raised in Toronto, know a man who's been up the Amazon in a canoe? Or that I've walked among the Roman ruins at Volubilis, near Meknes in Morocco, hiding from snipers, when the Cassars lived in Rabat, or that François and I lived in Ankara, Turkey, for months?"

"Of course we think about it. Rather more than we'd wish to, frankly," Mother said with asperity.

"When I was your age, the farthest I'd been was the smelting plant in

Perth Amboy, New Jersey, where I worked three summers during college to pay my tuition after my dad lost his shirt. And by the time I was your age, it was the Great Depression and none of us was going anywhere." It was also true that Daddy was a patent agent and not a real attorney because there hadn't been enough money for law school. His big brother Edward had got to go, though, and was a JD, and they'd worked together all their lives until the bust-up four years ago. Mother blamed Daddy's illness on that rift—"It broke your father, broke him," she'd said bitterly one night as they drove home from the hospital. But now Daddy wanted to reconcile with Uncle Edward, and although they did not discuss it, Barbara knew that Mother worried that this meant Daddy felt he was going to die.

"But it's different now." Barbara wanted them to see it her way. "The world is getting smaller and we're all more international."

"Of course, dear." Mother carried Daddy's plate and bowl to the sink in the curtained bathroom by the door, where Barbara couldn't see her but could hear her rinsing the dishes. "It's a brave new world." Mother emerged drying the plate with a clean hand towel from the stack under the sink. They kept many on hand because of the vomiting,

"It's not just for my generation." Barbara, conscious that she wasn't being helpful, stepped forward and lifted the linen napkin from her father's tray to shake the crumbs over the wastepaper basket. She looked up at her father as she did this and his expression touched her to the core, a look of loving resignation and something like longing, as though he yearned for what she said to be true, yearned to be able to rise from his sickbed and travel the world, though he never would again.

He raised his purple scaly hand to stroke her cheek, and feeling its roughness she closed her eyes. She hoped this looked to him like love, which it was, and not like revulsion, which it was also (to her shame), or like sorrow (which it was most powerfully, a painful pricking behind her eyes).

"I love you, bunny," he said softly, as if Mother couldn't hear, though she was only feet away.

"I love you too, Daddy," she said, and she leaned to kiss his bristled cheek. He smelled of soap and that unscented moisturizer that had its own scent—lanolin, maybe?—and a little of tuna fish. But underneath, just faintly, he had that smell familiar only from these hospital days—sweet, a little sickly—that frightened her in her very bones.

LATER, WHEN THEY got home after eight-thirty, she and Mother walked Nicky around the block. The air was Siberian, breathtaking, freezing their throats and nostrils. The cocker spaniel made chittering noises of distress until he realized they were more than halfway, then set his sights on home and wagged his stump in relief.

"Dr. Ogryzlo still won't say when Dad can come home for Christmas." Mother's voice was quiet but the frigid night still more so. Their boots squeaked on the packed snow. The moon bathed the houses in blue light.

"Did he say when he'll decide?"

Mother shook her head. "They seem to think the drug is helping. But there's organ damage already. His lungs, his heart—"

"He needs to be able to take some exercise." Barbara said this without knowing if she believed it. How could he possibly exercise, a bag of bones on bloated, ruined feet? "He needs to gain some weight," she amended. "He's got awfully thin."

Mother made a thoughtful sound, then said, "It's all a balancing act. They need to get him moving again, but his feet—they need the skin to soften. They need this drug to work."

For a moment they heard only their boots and the clanking of Nicky's tags.

"I think it's working, don't you?" Mother asked.

She turned to look at Barbara, and Barbara knew what her mother needed to hear. "Yes," she said. "Yes, I definitely think so."

WHEN HE'D BEEN in hospital for that long stretch the previous year—at the Western, where he'd also started out this fall—nobody had been able to figure out what was wrong with him. You couldn't mention the Western to Mother. Thank goodness for Ellie's husband, Ed, whose father was a doctor at the General and who got them their first appointment with Dr. Ogryzlo. Even he, the best rheumatologist in Canada, so they said, had taken well over a month to venture a diagnosis. Scleroderma: a sclerosis of the skin. An autoimmune disease. Tremendously rare, and painful. Dr. Ogryzlo was almost fifty years old and he'd never before seen a case, except in textbooks. The skin hardened into a shell, and when enough of it no longer breathed, your body beneath atrophied—the whole system collapsed. Sometimes the hardening happened only in little patches, then stopped. Sometimes it kept spreading, seeping like a rising tide. They needed, for Harold Fisk, both to treat what was already damaged and to try to stop its advance.

Last year, presented with his joint pain and exhaustion and headaches, the doctors at the Western had told him he had arthritis and was suffering from stress. He'd stayed there for two months; they'd given him anti-inflammatories and massages, and they'd all thought— he'd thought!—he was much better by the end. He and Mother had planned and then taken their trip to Paris in April, even. But when they got there, Barbara had known it wasn't all right. He was already thin, and his gait had altered: he walked as though his shoes pinched with every step, and already then his hands had turned a funny rough mauve, though the fingertips were often white. She'd asked Mother one evening when they were doing the washing up in the Avenue Franco-Russe, while Daddy and François smoked over coffee at the table, and Mother's eyes had glittered in warning: "Your father's fine, dear. He works too hard, is all. And a trip like this, well, it's exhausting. What he needs is three weeks in Bermuda, like we had a few years ago—that was a real rest. The Lantana Club," she sighed. "But he was desperate to come see you, and where you're living, so." After which they didn't talk anymore about it.

Barbara and François had only just moved into their flat in Geneva in September, and they were beginning to get to know the other business school families—they'd barely been there a month—when Mother sent the telegram saying that Father was in hospital again. He'd collapsed at the office, and Sheila, Mrs. Carrington, his secretary, had had to call an ambulance. They took him back to the Western because that's where he'd been a patient before; but thanks to Ed he was moved within a week, and when Barbara arrived on the eighth of October (the very day on which, fifty years later, she would herself die; though also the day on which, a mere four years later, she would give birth to her second child), he was already in his spacious single at the General, visited regularly not only by Dr. Ogryzlo and his team of doctors but by eager clutches of residents curious to see this rare medical specimen.

All the attention, however, did not cheer him. Quite the opposite. Not even she, it seemed, could cheer him most days, which was why his jokes about Hemming in the Amazon could be counted a triumph. Most days he remained subdued, except when he asked them about the outside world, like someone stranded on a desert island. With time, even his worldly interests were fading, as if he were leaving them behind. He hadn't even been excited the previous weekend about the drama of the Grey Cup, played that year at the Exhibition between his beloved Hamilton Tiger-Cats and the Winnipeg Blue Bombers and, for the first time in history, suspended in mid-game due to fog. "It's all about what you can't see," the radio commentator had said, and Barbara had thought, "How true."

And François, across the ocean, couldn't seem to understand it at all— why she'd had to go, he'd understood that, he'd encouraged her, but now he seemed to think, like last year, that she was lingering—malingering—in Toronto because she had more fun there than with him. And maybe last year there'd been a whisper of truth in that complaint, but not now. If only she could show him a photograph of Daddy in his hospital bed, or play him a recording of Daddy's hoarse and weakened voice—but even last week he'd written that awful, mean letter from his hotel room in Rotterdam, telling her she didn't know what a marriage was—

But just when her heart was tempted to harden against him, she recalled the letter of the previous fall, the one she felt made her heart literally ache. He'd been replying to one of hers, in which she'd tried to make light of that whisper of truth and had told him he couldn't know what it felt like for her to be at home for a while—simply to love to be at home!—because he didn't *have* a home. Which was true— his parents and sister were living in Buenos Aires, and had been for years, and he'd never even set foot there, neither of them had. The Cassars came to visit them in Paris instead, and because there wasn't room enough for them in the flat on the Avenue Franco-Russe (even though they owned it; but François and Barbara had been living there), they stayed at the Madison Hotel, in Saint-Germain-des-Prés, where Monsieur Cassar had apparently lived for several months near the end of the war, and maybe that was for them the closest thing at that point to home?

But when François had replied, his sadness was a rebuke to her jaunty tone. He said that yes, now it was of course true that he didn't have a home; it no longer existed—by which she understood that he meant French Algeria, already in '61 lost to them forever, though only this last summer, in July'62, did the country finally win its independence, the French and the *harkis* departing in a mass exodus. Then François wrote to her that when they met, in the summer of '55, and when they married, in the summer of '57, he had absolutely had a home, his home since he was a small boy—he meant Algiers, of course, but he also may have meant more specifically the apartment on the Rue Guillaumet in that city she had never been to see, the contents of which were still, six months after Algerian independence, in limbo. At least they'd been packed up and stored somewhere, thanks to the children of a brother of Monsieur

Cassar's, whom she hadn't met, but still, all of their belongings were stuck indefinitely in what was now a foreign country.

François explained that he had readily, deliberately, turned his back on that home to choose her, Barbara, and the life they would make together going forward—obviously she could never have been expected to settle in Algiers; they needed to make their new home together in a new place. That had been his understanding, and yet she seemed to feel she could be away from him for months at a time without any problem. How could they make a home, the home that was their union, unless they made it together?

She'd felt hurt of course and also exasperated—why couldn't he see that fun was important too, and that their life in Paris (or now in Geneva), while fascinating for him because of his work, simply wasn't fun for her the way driving with Bobby and Charley to Disey's for a dinner party was, well, fun—but also she'd felt sad, sad for him, in his loneliness without her, and sad for him that this strange background of his, this weird, provisional home to which he now alluded but which felt to her as chimerical as a mirage in the Sahara, had evaporated and left him rootless.

In a way, he was like her high school friend Adele, an oddball whose family had come to Toronto from Budapest just before the war: Adele wasn't exactly Hungarian anymore, but she certainly wasn't Canadian. She was Jewish, so her family had a community. But she was foreign, she'd always felt foreign, and when Barbara visited Adele's house, Mrs. Herzl prepared unfamiliar heavy stews, the meaty odors of which suffused the dark curtains and ornate carpets; and Adele's mother's accent always made Barbara want to giggle, not so far from the Fisks' cleaning lady's accent—Rosa was a DP from the Ukraine, just as the Herzls were refugees from Hungary, all of it a little overlapping in Barbara's head, just Eastern Europe, behind the Iron Curtain, now.

They had, on the living room wall, a painting of a lady in a bright red Victorian blouse, sitting in front of red-and-yellow flowered wallpaper, a large, colorful painting, but not cheerful: the woman, unsmiling, heavy-browed, had a wide pink face and almond eyes and a red nose and wore her dark hair piled upon her head. This painting always seemed to Barbara to encapsulate what wasn't quite right about Adele, the way she didn't fit in, which elicited in Barbara both tenderness and occasional irritation, as though she ought always to be looking out for Adele, when sometimes she just wanted to forget about her for a while.

With regard to Adele, Barbara always felt the awkwardness of her own position, after all: she'd been at Humberside Collegiate her fresh-man year of high school. And then suddenly, on account of some suc-cessful patents that Daddy and Uncle Edward had written, for the first time there'd been money—for the cottage, for new cars, for Mother's diamond ring (she'd never had an engagement ring when they were young), and for the silver mink and a lovely sheared beaver; and for Barbara, private school, the elevation to Bishop Strachan School for Girls, in tony Forest Hill, a whole new social set—Charley, Ellie, Trish, Disey—all of them from big houses in fancy neighborhoods, and not one of them used the same bathroom as their parents! Barbara had been a quick study—it didn't hurt that she was tall and pretty, but she learned the right music and books and movies to like, and she made the right jokes, and made sure she had the right clothes, even if they were sewn by the dressmaker and didn't have fancy labels inside—and by the eleventh grade, when Adele appeared, Barbara felt as though her friends had all but forgotten that she wasn't really one of them, and had accepted her fully into the fold (though only Charley and Trish ever took the subway out to Runnymede to come to her house, which was both far away and, for their world, unusually modest); and so Barbara, who *liked* Adele, felt at once an affinity with her and a responsibility—Adele did not have the right clothes or make the right jokes, needless to say—but none of Barbara's gang of friends could be bothered even to make the slightest effort with the new girl, and frankly, Barbara often enough wished she didn't have to. But Adele lived, like Barbara, in the

West End, and they took the subway home together many days; there'd been no escaping it.

And yet now, somehow, absurdly, blinded by love—or lust, was it?—she'd actually *married* someone whose relationship to the known world—to Toronto, certainly, but maybe to anywhere, Paris or London even—would always be, like Adele's at Bishop Strachan, askew, at an uneasy angle. And that meant, she was coming to grasp, living with him in uneasiness, which somehow she hadn't really considered. No wonder he dreamed about a life in the United States, which was anathema to her Canadian self (she'd said to him once, jokingly, Think how you feel as a Frenchman about the Brits, with whom you've been at war for a thousand years, and that's basically how we Canadians feel about the Americans), but he'd loved his time studying at Amherst, his first introduction to America, and he'd loved their time more recently living in Cambridge, Mass., while he was in grad school; in fact sometimes she felt that were it not for her complaints, he'd still be in that apartment, their cold little condemned walk-up on Emmons Place around the corner from Savenor the fine butcher, and he'd have kept on with the PhD—he'd done all the fieldwork and research, after all—and would have been willing, even, to become one of those dreary tweedy professors sipping sherry in a paneled room. Not that what he'd opted for instead seemed to her as yet any more interesting—nor to him, for that matter; quite the opposite—but at least he stood to earn a decent living, eventually. He'd packed all his notes and the eighty or so extant typed pages of his thesis about Turkey's political situation into a handsome leather suitcase that Mother and Daddy had given him for his thirtieth, in June '61, and he'd kept it by the bed in Paris and Gardanne and now in Geneva too, and he claimed in his letters both last fall and this that when he was alone he was working on it, that he'd finish it after all, and she made encouraging noises and pretended to believe him.

He'd started the job with the French aluminum giant Péchiney over a year ago, while she was in Toronto with her parents. That was one of the things he'd been so upset about, having to find the flat in Gardanne, outside Aix-en-Provence, by himself and move in—he claimed it was because he'd wanted them to choose it together, but really, mostly, he got depressed by himself and found everything an effort. And then Péchiney had offered to pay for him to do this business school year at CEI in Geneva, this strange, novel, utopian endeavor, but at least there were some Canadians involved—the Rileys, with their passel of little kids, and the Mowbrays, and the Schultzes, who were like Barb and François but reversed: he was Canadian and she was French—and maybe it would turn out to be the beginning of their portable but united home life in the way François dreamed when he wrote his letters.

Maybe. But she couldn't tell whether in her deepest heart she was really ready for that leap of faith. Would she go to the ends of the earth with him, without complaint? Oh, she sometimes felt she simply hadn't thought things through clearly enough. But it was too late now. And of course she loved him, and desired him—even his finger alighting on the inside of her wrist was enough to raise her pulse—but was all that enough? Or had Mother and Daddy been right when they counseled against, saying you don't just marry a person, you marry their family, and by extension their whole world, and what were the parameters of his whole world, after all? That there were no constraints sometimes frightened her, as if the very ground beneath her shifted. In any event, she certainly couldn't leave Mother and Daddy right now, not till Daddy was better, up and walking again, back home in his own bed—and if Dr. Ogryzlo wouldn't even give him a release for Christmas, then where did things stand? But Daddy, even in his awful state, was still his bighearted self, and he knew that she was torn between her two worlds, and before they'd left the hospital that evening he had had her sit on the edge of his bed and had told her that he and Mother had discussed it and they'd like to pay for François's airfare to come over and spend Christmas, so they could all be together.

"Oh, Daddy," she'd said, a little breathless, aware of the expense and the tension between Mother and François, wondering whether in fact this was a gift that she, Barbara, even wanted; and aware, too, that without it, François would be alone in Geneva for probably a fortnight, as the institute would be closed and most people traveling. Maybe the top brass at the business school, Haenni or Hawrylyshyn, would take pity on him and invite him for Christmas or more probably Boxing Day, but it would be a long, solitary stretch and he would dread it. "Oh, Daddy," she said again, and then, "Thank you, thank you." She bravely took his hardened hand between hers and brought it to her lips—could he feel her kiss or did the deadened skin mean he felt nothing? She could never ask of course. Why was so much unsaid or unsayable? What might happen if everyone actually spoke their mind?

Now, lying in the twin bed of her childhood—the very bed in which her ex-boyfriend Luke Whitworth had replaced her when she and François set off for France on the *Queen Mary* after their wedding—she considered the challenge before her: to persuade François, down the static-filled trunk call, that to come to Toronto for Christmas was truly a gift to him, to them as a young couple, and not a capitulation on their part. That's to say, that for him to accept did not mean that her parents had somehow won and he had lost. She knew that would be his immediate reaction—she knew him well by now—and for a fleeting moment she considered playing the trump card in her hand. All she would have to say was "But don't you understand, Daddy's dying!" and he would come without complaint. But she could not admit this to herself, much less to him, and she so feared the possibility of it being—of it becoming—a magic spell, the performative utterance of J. L. Austin's philosophy, that she knew she could not say it, neither aloud nor internally, and she banished the thought.

BUENOS AIRES, ARGENTINA

With the new year, a new job: she would become a travel agent. Denise, six months shy of thirty, in midsummer in Buenos Aires, played a round of golf at the Jockey Club with Fanchette and Estelle, along with Estelle's little sister, Antoinette, visiting, with her new Uruguayan husband, from Paris. Only Fanchette belonged: her father, the admiral, was friends with the fanciest Argentinians, hence her family's wangled Jockey membership—it was the club of all the country's presidents, and Denise had heard that the waiting list, always long, had ballooned since they'd hosted the golf World Cup the previous year.

Fanchette was the tallest and most imperious, as well as a couple of years older, so it made sense that she decided things. She had the right aspect, her beaky, owlish face and brushy hair already streaked with gray. Her vigorous stride compensated in its way for her strong but inaccurate drive shot. She also possessed an elegant set of red-handled clubs in a buttery toffee-colored leather golf bag that Denise couldn't help but covet. Fanchette, although she was bossy and annoying, and Estelle had become Denise's closest friends in Buenos Aires; golf was one of their preferred activities.

Before arriving in Argentina, Denise had never played nor even thought of it. But the French girls—women!—her age all seemed to, and the weather was conducive—never too hot, never too cold. And then Fanchette had taken her up. That's what it had felt like.

Denise had moved to Buenos Aires full-time to join her parents in late 1959: they'd already then been living there for over a year, ever since Papa, eager to leave his job in Morocco, had unexpectedly accepted a position in Argentina. Denise had been living in Paris, in the apartment her parents owned there, and had left it a few months after François and Barbara had abandoned her by moving to the United States, where he'd got a fellowship to pursue a degree in Middle Eastern studies at Harvard. Arriving in Buenos Aires, she'd been surprised to discover how big the French community was, with so many people her own age.

Needless to say, at first she'd not been in the best frame of mind—better than when she'd come to stay awhile with Papa and Maman in '58 after her hospitalization, but still not good. It had taken a while to get the lithium dose right, but now she almost never thought about it. In the beginning, she played the piano for hours each day, walked the glorious boulevards with Maman holding her hand, and went frequently to church. Beyond that, she'd rarely left the family compound in the suburb of Vicente López, a large gabled house with leaded windows, surrounded by high stone walls, with a large, empty, green garden containing several big old trees, including a spreading jacaranda that she loved, and a separate garage with an apartment above it in which the housekeeper, Señora Inés López, lived with her husband, Alberto, who occasionally washed the car and put on a suit to drive Papa and Maman to parties.

This was by far the grandest setup her parents had ever known. Papa had been made the director of a large porcelain factory that belonged, along with various other assets, to a Franco-Italian family long established in Latin America, with one branch in Argentina and another in neighboring Uruguay. Papa at last liked his work—he particularly enjoyed the Latin rhythm of the days, long lunches and a siesta before returning to the office until well into the evening. He liked his colleagues, too—many of the cadres were French or Italian, and he spoke Italian of course without difficulty. His Spanish, on the other hand, wasn't sophisticated, and poor Maman had learned only what little she needed to know to communicate with Señora López about menus and housecleaning. When Denise had first stayed with them, she'd barely had the sense that she was in a Spanish-speaking country at all (after all, growing up in Algeria, she'd never spoken more than a few rudimentary words of Arabic, although the cleaners were all Berber women and their French often patchy). Even for church, they attended the specially scheduled early French Mass in the Basílica San Pilar in Recoleta, where Denise could shut her eyes and hear the sung *évangile* in its familiar monotone, inhale the incense, feel her mother's warm thigh pressed against her own, and believe she was in Rabat or Algiers—not Paris, no, but Paris, in any event, was not and had never been home.

Fanchette and Estelle were very involved in the French congregation. Fanchette shared responsibility for the flower arrangements with a grandmother twice her age—but Denise didn't first talk to her there. No, they'd met at a ladies' tea with their mothers, because Papa and Maman were of course friendly with Fanchette's parents—though there remained, inevitably, a whiff of the former naval hierarchy, and a war-related reserve, on Papa's part. Fanchette carried in her body the haughtiness of her exiled parents, their social superiority and snobbery, even the competitive religiosity—two of her older sisters were nuns, one in the silent order of the Poor Clares in Syria, and even with a rosary-draped crucifix blessed by the pope hanging over her virginal bed, how could Denise hope to compete, her one sibling lapsed and married to a Canadian Protestant?

Next to the formidable Fanchette, Estelle was all joy, reminding Denise in spirit of dear Marie José, her close friend in Algiers, who, well before Algerian independence, had taken a post as a French teacher at a *gymnasium* in Stuttgart. ("But you *can't!* It's Germany!" Denise had protested. "Someone's got to teach them how to laugh," Marie José had replied with a wink. "I've never seen snow, and I can't stand wurst or beer, and with the exception of you, I've never much liked blondes, so it's probably a terrible idea. But the money's good, and we've all got to turn the page sometime, don't we?")

Estelle and Antoinette had grown up entirely in Argentina, though their parents were French, and they spoke Spanish effortlessly, sometimes unthinkingly, between themselves. Dark-haired Estelle was the elder, taller and more forceful than her languid, retiring sister, though nowhere near as bossy as Fanchette. She had a fat gap between her two front teeth and a naughty smile, as if she were always about to wind you up, but in truth she was very kind. A *garçon manqué*, she called herself, a tomboy, though they were grown women. And unlike Fanchette, who made being single seem the pious choice, Estelle behaved as though she remained unmarried at thirty simply for fun.

"I've got three brothers already, and now a brother-in-law in the bargain," she joked that afternoon at the Jockey, referring to Jean-Marc, Antoinette's mild and genial husband. "I've had to learn from the cradle how to defend my own interests, and Rule Number One is to keep the boys at bay."

"Come on." Fanchette raised a caterpillar brow. "You can't say you'd turn down a prospect as charming as Jean-Marc?"

Antoinette blushed winningly, as though she herself were being complimented.

"He's the perfect husband for my perfect sister." Estelle flung an arm around Antoinette's neck and planted a kiss on her sister's cheek, her olive skin and red lips vivid against Antoinette's pale freckles. "And if I ever meet the perfect husband for me—we'll see. I make no promises."

Denise was now too old to fall off her chair laughing the way she had at university, but here, at last, she could laugh. After moving away from Algiers in '56 to attend hotel school in Switzerland, she'd been through such a long, dark stretch—from the time of the hotel school internship onward, really, when the Liberian delegate at a political conference had energetically seized her breast with one hand and with the other grabbed her crotch in the bathroom of the suite she'd been cleaning at the Grand Hotel in Bern. She'd not told a soul the truth about the encounter besides the unknown priest in the confessional in Lausanne a week later. And then François's marriage in '57—she tried, she was still trying, so hard, to love Barbara like a sister; she prayed over it constantly, but chiefly she felt lonely and abandoned by her brother. And then of course the Paris fiasco . . . how thoroughly she'd fallen in love with Émile Rodier, her married boss, how poorly she'd hidden her emotions, and how carelessly he'd toyed with her, putting his hand on her knee, letting her bat her eyes and flirt with him over lunch, making her blush scarlet in front of colleagues, all just making fun of her, in the end . . . then on top of that heartache and shame, the situation in Algeria ever worsening and the sense that she'd had, for weeks, months, that she walked the streets of Paris in a gauzy cloud of disgrace, an object of derision at the office because of Rodier, and then in society on account of the mere accident of her birth, that in being *pied-noir* she felt she was seen by the metropolitans around her as a threat to their easy lives. She felt she was an unpleasant reminder, a stain.

"Mais comment ça, mademoiselle, vous parlez si bien le français!" she'd heard more than once, as though the piggish Parisians thought, perhaps, that everyone in Algiers spoke only Arabic? And she had certainly heard them say, at dinner parties, "To hell with the *pieds-noirs*, we've got nothing to do with them"—when they all carried the same passport! And she'd heard them complain about the *harkis*, the courageous Algerians who'd risked and lost everything for France, calling them *bougnoules* . . . but it turned out that France was not only indifferent but thoroughly ungrateful, unwelcoming—how to reconcile being French and not French at the same time?

After the generals' coup in Algiers in March '58, it was painfully clear to Denise, at least, that there would never be a way back, no future in Algeria for herself or her family . . . she realized only then how she had longed, unwittingly, eventually to return to their dear apartment, to the ever-changing sea light from the little balcony, to the sounds of her mother pottering in the kitchen and the neighbors calling or grousing or beating carpets in the street below, to the unthinking ease and safety that was *home*, and now would never come again. But already, of course, François was long gone, he'd never have returned to live there, not with Barbara; while Maman and Papa had committed to Buenos Aires and were arranging their transatlantic move. Even they seemed calmly to accept that the world and the life they'd known was finished forever— they said no more about it than a few rueful asides here and there, with much invocation of God and His invisible plans, which Denise tried her hardest to accept.

That was when she'd lost hope, for a while. She'd lost faith in the future. She'd looked back at the two years from '54 to '56 that she and François had spent together in the flat on the Rue Guillaumet after he returned from America, finishing their law degrees side by side, as the halcyon days of their youth. Once François was with her, even Gardel and Servier smiled at her, like switching on a light: she'd become visible. Servier even kissed her once on the lips at a party at the apartment, when he'd had one too many, just before he burned a hole in the arm of Maman's beloved sofa with his cigarette, which they'd found uproarious in the moment and cause for panic the following morning. They hadn't imagined, struggling to patch it, that their parents wouldn't see the sofa again for so long that the provenance of the damage could never be questioned. It was only now, at last, probably arriving in Paris, seven years later, along with everything else from the Algiers flat (their chipped coffee bowls; Maman's trousseau of embroidered linens; the deco bisque bust from the living room mantel of a beauty with flowers in her hair, her eyes closed in ecstasy; the armoire from her bedroom, the right-hand door of which hung crooked; the long narrow Berber rug from the hallway with its flashes of pink . . .) and nobody but Cousine Geneviève to greet the delivery . . .

All that darkness, year upon year of it. Had she really tried to kill herself, in August '58? That's what they said afterward—whiskey, pills, after many days totally alone. She'd been desperate: she'd left her job after the Rodier fiasco, too ashamed to show her face there, and then with François and Barbara had gone off to America, and always the shame, the shame of being *pied-noir* and feeling reviled . . . it got so she couldn't eat or sleep or bring herself to go outside. And after the pills, there'd been two months in that horrid *maison de repos* outside Paris—she was still mortified that she'd brought both her parents galloping halfway across the world, when Maman in particular hated to fly almost as much as she did herself, and when, in any case, they couldn't afford the expense.

Through all that time after the suicide attempt—her first stretch of recovery in Buenos Aires, and her short-lived attempt to live again in Paris, again so alone, the time when the doctors put her on lithium— each day had felt like a flat, featureless lava plain across which she was doomed to slog, without sunshine, without companionship, neither tree nor flower nor singing bird— Oh, not true, in Buenos Aires there'd been Fiamma the German shepherd licking her with her hot breath; there'd been Chopin and Mozart and the piano; there'd been Maman's soft arm across her shoulder or her warm plump hand to hold, and those piercing but always compassionate eyes, the blue of the sunlit Mediterranean, watching over her. But for so long, Denise hadn't believed there could be again pleasure, easy laughter, or hope, really—everything had seemed shrouded in ashes, leached of color, all life in abeyance. And then, at last, when they decided she'd live with Papa and Maman in Buenos Aires for good, the relief of knowing she wouldn't have to leave, that she could simply choose to be a kid again: she didn't *need* to live in Paris, or to succeed at work and build a career, or, most alarmingly, to meet a man and marry him and bear half a dozen squealing children. Her illness had exempted her from these requirements of adulthood. Christ smiled upon the weakest, didn't He? Unlike her brother, she was someone to whom little had been given, and so in return from whom little might be expected. It seemed that all that was expected was that she be happy, somehow. She could read murder mysteries in the afternoons, lying in the living room window seat; she could learn, from Señora López, how to cook, and teach herself Spanish at the same time; she could go, if she felt like it, to British library events to improve her English; she could make new friends and play golf with them—and she did.

SPENDING THE DAY at the Jockey Club in San Isidro, as she was doing this afternoon in January 1963—it was, for Denise, an ideal. Until recently, for two and a half years she'd worked at the Anglo-German bookshop downtown, where she'd been able to keep two days, besides Sundays, for herself, and she'd gone golfing at least once a week. She had, for a while, described herself as "mad for golf," and had purchased a pair of men's tweed plus fours and a matching tam, dressing up as if it were the 1930s; though she'd only bought the cheapest set of golf clubs, in a canvas bag— her bookstore salary was hers to spend, as she had few living expenses, but it did not allow for a set like Fanchette's. Over time, she gave up the costume, realizing she wasn't actually mad for golf as a sport but, rather, adored the glimpse it afforded of an ideal world: the club's rolling, emerald greens, interspersed with clusters of wavering trees and amoebic sand traps; the broad blue sky dotted with birds, whose songs and cries drifted among them—the rufous-bellied thrushes, the swooping swallows and martins, the plump-breasted doves. Out on the course, you couldn't hear the traffic, only occasionally the voices of the other golfers, and, from certain holes, the sounds of the clubhouse, where people dined in groups on the flagstone patio in the lee of the castellated brick building. After their round, the young women often sat at one of the glass-topped iron tables and drank Campari and sodas or whiskey sours beneath a flapping parasol, smoking and gossiping as the late afternoon sun cast ever longer shadows across the pristine course.

Yes, the expat life: Denise considered it at once as her real life and not quite real, as if it unfolded in parallel with an alternate French life— darker, damper, lonelier, more grueling—that she might instead have been condemned to lead. Not that nothing mattered, in Buenos Aires, but that things mattered slightly less, or differently: she wasn't quite *responsible* any longer; she was merely living, like riding on a fairground ride, allowing for God's invisible, implacable plans to unfurl.

For two and a half years, she'd thought her job at Pigmalion as much a part of the divine plan as the Jockey Club or the francophone Mass at San Pilar. Pigmalion: the bookshop's very name seemed to her the perfect expression of herself in Argentina, a statue brought newly to life. She hadn't seen herself as a woman ready to be made into the image desired by her mentor, though of course now she wondered whether that had been Fräulein Lebach's—Lili's—aim all along.

Back in the early days when Denise first came to live in the city, when she'd abdicated and was ready to embrace an easier existence, she'd decided that she might still expand her horizons by reading her murder mysteries *in English*—so that the pleasure would become also instructive, though not unpleasantly so. Someone—perhaps the American wife of her father's colleague Legrand?—had recommended the little Anglo-German bookshop down near the Luna Park auditorium on Avenida Corrientes, a few blocks from the Plaza de Mayo in one direction and from the university in the other. It wasn't the only English-language bookshop in town, Madame Legrand had said, but it was the best one, not least because of its formidable owner, a German Jewish émigré who'd arrived in Argentina just before the war.

The bookshop, from the first, had smelled delicious to Denise, of paper, ink, sawdust, cedar, cigarette smoke, and perhaps even a touch of mildew, though Fräulein Lebach ensured that it was kept impeccably clean. Denise loved the shop's cool gloom, its high, dark shelves filled with books, their spines glimmering like treasure, each the promise of an undiscovered world; and the three long tables down the middle of the shop, on which were laid out the new arrivals: an English table, a German table, and a third that blended the two. Fräulein Lebach, though Denise did not at first know her name, sat all but hidden behind a desk at the back of the store, surrounded by piles of books and papers, ledgers and notepads, usually reading, a lit cigarette either in hand or smoldering in the overflowing ashtray in front of her. She must have been in her late forties or early fifties, slim and elegantly dressed, always in a dark skirt and a light-colored blouse, often with a silk scarf tied at her throat, her wavy salt-and-pepper hair tidily pulled into a chignon. Gold rings on her capable freckled hands, a gold chain glittering at her collar, sometimes discreet gold earrings. Never silver. She had a gravelly voice and slightly the aspect of a bloodhound, a little jowly, with mournful gray eyes and bad teeth. But when she laughed, phlegm rolled cheerfully in her throat, and she was quick to laugh. She loved books and knew everything about English literature and knew personally all the literary stars of Buenos Aires, who came to chat with her in her shop.

When Denise first walked in, wandering the three tables somewhat indiscriminately, her fingers trailing over the sleek book covers laid out in rows, Fräulein Lebach looked up from her reading, over her half-moon glasses, and asked loudly, in German, "*Sind Sie auf der Such nach etwas bestimmten?*" And when Denise, startled, shook her head slightly, Fräulein smiled and repeated in precise, heavily accented English, "Are you seeking something specific?"

Denise, not wanting to shout the length of the store—there were other patrons browsing at the time—made her way to Fräulein's desk—as if she were a schoolmistress, she'd joked to her parents that evening—and explained her desire to read murder mysteries in English to expand her command of the language.

"So," said the Fräulein, briskly rising from her chair and striding to the English table, "This is not a real *roman policier*." As she said this, Denise was aware that Fräulein's French was perhaps even better than her English. "It is more a psychological thriller. But it is the newest from the best. Do you know the books of Patricia Highsmith?" She picked up and held out to Denise a hardcover with a gray background on which was drawn a face with, over it, what looked like shards of a shattered mirror. *This Sweet Sickness*, the novel was titled. Reading the back cover, Denise felt a physical jolt of recognition: it told the story of a man obsessively in love with a woman who had rejected him; the copy called it a "painful novel about obsessive imaginary love." As if Highsmith had taken Denise's story, her attachment to Rodier, had switched the characters' genders, and had turned it into a novel. She looked up at the Fräulein almost in fear: How in mere seconds could this woman have seen so clearly into her soul?

But the bookseller's gaze remained frank and easy, her gray eyes crinkling with pleasure. "I love them all, you know. You must have read *The Talented Mr. Ripley*? It was surely translated into French . . ." So she knew already that Denise was French? "And the first one, *Strangers on a Train*, made by Hitchcock into a film—perhaps you have seen it?"

Denise shook her head. "I've heard of it."

"Well, this will do to begin," said the Fräulein, taking the book back from Denise and moving with it to the wall of bookshelves on her right, which housed English-language fiction. "But if you're like me, this is only the matter of a single day. You shall need perhaps two more, yes?" She paused and turned. "*Vous préféreriez qu'on parle français?*"

Denise shook her head again. "I'm trying to improve my English." She said, of course, "Engleesh."

"So, we will both improve our English, so unexpectedly in this Spanish-speaking country. Come, let me offer you a coffee." And she led Denise back to her desk, where, from beneath a stack of books— German titles—she revealed an occasional chair, on which Denise might sit, and opened what looked like a cupboard behind her desk to reveal a hot plate plugged into the wall, and several cups and plates. She retrieved a jug of water from the WC down a little corridor, filled the octagonal moka pot with water and ground coffee from a tin, and placed it on the already glowing element. She shook several wafer biscuits onto a saucer, and as she held it out to Denise one almost slid off onto the cluttered desk. Denise blocked it with her hand but did not take it.

"I'd rather have a cigarette, if you don't mind?"

At which the Fräulein expressed delight, and offered her own box—Winstons—while in return Denise shared from her precious box of Marignys, smuggled in by the carton by every French friend who came to town, including Denise's own parents and herself.

That first afternoon, the two women smoked and talked for the better part of an hour, interrupted only by other clients making purchases. As she observed these transactions, Denise realized that Fräulein Lebach knew many of them personally, what they liked to read and had most recently read, how often they came shopping, and even what the other members of their households might select if they were present. She spoke English, German, French, Spanish without seeming even to have to think about it. And when Denise left with her package of three books— Margery Allingham's first Detective Campion mystery, *The Crime at Black Dudley*, and Ngaio Marsh's *Spinsters in Jeopardy*, along with the Highsmith—Fräulein charged her for only two, saying "There will be one you do not care for as well; that one, you may bring back to me."

"Like a library," Denise said, surprised.

"Just like a library. We always come back to the library. 'Bookshop' in your language, yes? *Librairie!*"

So began a weekly pilgrimage that swiftly became a friendship— Denise had never before had a friend almost old enough to be her mother, had her mother been a young mother rather than an older one, and it felt like having a chic and cosmopolitan aunt—and before long the friendship resulted in Denise's job at the bookshop. Fräulein's assistant, a long-nosed young man with floppy hair and an unusually thin neck, decamped for graduate studies in Chicago, known to Denise only as the place to which François's Fulbright friend from Amherst, Mouret, had also moved for further study—and Fräulein suggested, over Winstons (they couldn't smoke only Denise's Marignys, they agreed: they were too rare), that Denise come join her in the shop.

Within a few months, Denise came to know a little about Lili Lebach's life. The older woman, a child of prosperity, had fled Elberfeld, Wuppertal, for Buenos Aires in the late 1930s, when she was in her late twenties, and had soon been joined by her brother, Walter, already by then in Boston, USA. Having barely escaped in time, she'd come to Buenos Aires because Walter's business associates, who preceded them, had been able to arrange it. She spoke of her German youth with happy nostalgia, as if recounting a dream—the beautiful gardens of the Villa Freytag in Elberfeld; singing with the youth choir beneath the magnificent vaulted ceilings of the Stadthalle; bike riding with friends along the green banks of the Wupper, the spectacular suspension bridge looming above them—but she expressed no desire to return to the country of her birth even for a visit, even now that it would have easily been possible. In this way, she seemed to Denise a model of how to proceed in exile: she had retained within her and miraculously now, all these years later, without bitterness, the splendors of her youth; but she had moved on, and away, from that past. She was an émigré and a cosmopolite, a citizen of the world, and she carried her griefs—legion and enormous—locked inside her. But she was determined to live, fully. She had opened her bookshop in the darkest days, in '42, when it wasn't clear whether the Allies could triumph, and she had from the first insisted that she would carry both English and German titles because she refused to allow evil to claim the language and the literature that were native to her, that she so profoundly loved.

Pigmalion was down the road from the large Luna Park concert hall, where Argentina's fascists had held Nazi rallies before the outbreak of the war, although by Denise's time it had become chiefly a venue for raucous boxing matches, some even televised. Fräulein Lebach's wealthy businessman brother, Walter, with whom she was close, stopped by the shop occasionally to take his sister to lunch. Fräulein Lebach also maintained a strong bond with her niece Louise, a chemistry student at the university, and initially hoped that Denise and she might become friends; but their conversations never transcended the formal. Denise found in

Louise the more austere aspects of her aunt without the pleasures; she was a pale, luminous, reed-thin girl with beautiful almond eyes but no mirth. Her twiglike limbs and brittle hair recalled for Denise the period of her own greatest self-denial, an adamantine anorexic withholding not only around food but around life itself, precisely what Denise, in choosing Buenos Aires, had decided to put behind her.

Fräulein Lebach, on the other hand, fascinated her only ever more: she introduced Denise to the great writer Borges, professor of English and director of the National Library, who, though thoroughly blind, stopped by to sit on the same occasional chair Fräulein had cleared, the first day, for Denise, and to drink coffee, eat wafer biscuits, and discuss with his German friend the new releases and trends of European literature. One afternoon, the great and glamorous Victoria Ocampo, already seventy, swept in, her vast car and liveried driver waiting on the pavement outside, and later Fräulein told Denise about dinners and parties at the Ocampo mansion, and spoke of the glittering company of intellectuals. Ernesto Sabato and his wife, Matilde, came also to the shop, and the dignified Matilde in particular always smiled warmly at Denise, as if to communicate that she knew what it was like to be overlooked and yet to believe oneself worthy nonetheless.

It seemed to Denise that she had fallen into an idyll, a world she had been raised to revere, in which she herself had no, or very little, importance, rather as if she were Céleste, Proust's famous housekeeper. She looked at the writers who orbited Fräulein Lebach—or whom the Fräulein orbited—and felt their sheen reflected, just a little, in her own image. Papa and Maman, devoted lifelong readers and secret writers, hung eagerly on her stories of the bookshop, and found her new world and the society of which she was peripherally a part more compelling, it seemed, than their own.

"I'd much rather have supper with Jorge Luis Borges than with the admiral or Hersant," Papa admitted with a wry laugh.

"I'm not having supper with him, Papa," Denise replied, proud nonetheless. One afternoon when he'd stopped by unannounced and Fräulein had been out, she, Denise, had chatted with Señor Borges in English about forthcoming fiction titles from Great Britain, including a novel by an Indian chap from Trinidad called *A House for Mr. Biswas,* the shipment of which had been delayed by striking stevedores in Southampton. And he had remembered her name! Mademoiselle Cassar, he had said, and then, off his own bat, the family joke, as if he'd invented it: *"Faites gaffe! L'incassable Cassar, n'est-ce pas?"* It wasn't supper, but nor was it nothing. She felt as if by saying aloud the family name he had acknowledged also Papa, whose unpublished novel lay in a manila folder in the drawer of his desk, and whose genius, in which she and her mother so fervently believed, was similarly obscured by the mundane money-earning business in which he was forced to engage.

But life was ever thus: Fräulein Lebach was able to continue to lead an ideal literary existence only thanks to the money made from premium cowhides exported around the globe by her older brother Walter's company. It didn't seem quite fair that Papa's labors should enable, instead of his own literary endeavors, his wife's elegant dresses (though they were a first, really, in her life, and she was now seventy years old) or his daughter's freedom to read English murder mysteries and go golfing at the Jockey on a Thursday afternoon. Denise reminded herself, however, that her joy brought her parents joy, that especially after her illness they wanted no more than her happiness. For them, this entailed, fundamentally, marriage and children (for devout Catholics, how could it not?), but they were lenient, not having themselves married until Maman was thirty-six, and still hopeful that Denise would find the One.

For well over two years, between Pigmalion and the golfing girls, Denise's life seemed delicious, easily as much as the two receding years with François in Algiers. She swallowed without fail her daily lithium, and no moods surged too high, but none too low either; she didn't look ahead, or, insofar as she could manage, following Fräulein's example, behind her. She invited Fräulein—"Please, call me Lili!"—to supper in the garden at the house in Vicente López, where Lili charmed Papa and Maman and regaled them with stories of Buenos Aires in wartime, and riveted them, too, with details they'd never known about the kidnapping of Eichmann by the Mossad in the spring of '60. Denise brought Estelle—though not Fanchette—to lunch with Lili in a restaurant near the bookshop, and Fräulein Lebach asked Estelle with focused interest about her travels to the pampas, and to Ushuaia, in Tierra del Fuego, where she had herself never yet been. She advised Denise not only on what to read but on how to arrange her hair—because of Lili, Denise grew her short blond *coiffe* a little longer and waved it with tongs—and on what clothes to wear. She helped Denise, as she said, to find her style: "There is fashion," she said, "ephemeral nonsense to which you must pay no attention. And then there is your own style, which you must find and to which you must cleave."

She understood that Denise was devoutly Catholic, so she didn't press too hard, but she shared her passion for the teachings of Gurdjieff, the late, imposingly mustachioed Russian-Armenian guru who had encouraged his followers not to sleep through their lives. He exhorted them to seek what he called the Fourth Way, which would blend together the emotions, the body, and the mind in healthy balance. Lili practiced every morning what Gurdjieff called "the Movements," and, at Denise's request, loaned her an LP of Gurdjieff's music written with Thomas de Hartmann. Denise found the melodies lovely and soothing, but Lili described them as "sacred," a term that struck Denise as possibly blasphemous. Lili invited Denise to join her at a lecture on the legacy of Gurdjieff and Ouspensky, but Denise, unsettled by the cultish aura, declined.

Gurdjieff's aim, according to Lili, was presence and the development of consciousness. Not to be passive or absent-minded, but to be actively engaged, each moment, in living. Denise—who, having experienced the world as hostile, had worked so hard to rebuild herself—could not quite fathom how this would not bring great suffering. Sometimes, often, she felt that living inside her mind served as a great and necessary protection; and besides, of what, really, besides one's own mind, could one be certain?

Ah, countered Lili, but wait awhile and your mind alters, your perceptions change; to be certain of one's mind is to be deluded, she claimed.

They had various lighthearted versions of this exchange over the months following the military overthrow of Frondizi, when the atmosphere around them felt particularly precarious and Denise desired more than ever to limit how much she let her attention stray to the ungovernable wider world. Indeed, she reveled in being an expatriate and being able to tell herself that the political fate of Argentina, unlike that of Algeria or France, need not concern her: she could exist, or try to exist, outside it, alongside it, in a relieved state of semidetachment. It seemed, at times, that Lili was attempting to pull her out of herself, to challenge her worldview.

"Are you so devout because you really believe," Lili once asked, lighting Denise's cigarette with her silver lighter, as they sat in their familiar configuration on either side of the desk at the back of the store, "or have you simply insisted on belief because your parents are believers, because your religion was handed to you like the keys to your ancestors' house?"

"And why wouldn't I eagerly accept the keys to my ancestors' house?" Denise replied.

Lili made a fleeting gesture with her hand, like a swallow flying away. "Because religion has been responsible for a great deal of evil in this world."

Denise accepted this solemnly, as unarguable. "But also for a great deal of good."

Lili laughed her phlegmy laugh. "Maybe," she said. "I accept that you believe so. Literature——" She stabbed at the air with her cigarette, making smoke stream from her nostrils like a dragon. "Now, that's a religion I can believe in. That is perhaps my God."

IN LATE NOVEMBER '62, Lili literally opened her door to Denise. In an unforeseen step, she invited her cherished employee to supper at her flat in Recoleta. She lived in a beautiful art nouveau building on Avenida del Libertador y Posadas that felt to Denise like being in Paris: the gracious mirrored lobby, the marble staircase with its ornate banister curving like a snake around the clattery old caged elevator, and the regal crimson runner lapping the steps like a monster's tongue. Lili Lebach lived on the third floor behind an imposing set of glossy double doors: when she opened one of them, she appeared dwarfed by her surroundings.

Denise could see that her hostess had dressed for the occasion; while in principle she wore the same ensemble, her pencil skirt was of black raw silk, and her blouse, in a dizzying Hermès pattern of conjoined stirrups in caramel, chocolate, and vanilla, was of a heavy, satiny silk that draped particularly elegantly. Her familiar brown leather square-heeled pumps had been replaced for the evening by black patent ones that squeaked on the marble tile. Holding a tumbler of whiskey on the rocks, she turned with a conspiratorial smile to lead Denise down the little hallway to her living room.

Everything was, to Denise's eyes, in exquisite taste. The flat, in spite of the grandeur of the building, was relatively modest, though well proportioned. American jazz drifted from a hidden record player up to the high ceilings, with their molded cornices, and calla lilies stood in a vase upon the bowed marble fireplace. The room had space for a long sofa—upholstered in midnight-blue velvet, with a gold fringe—and two low-slung barrel armchairs in a 1930s style. The large windows, open to a small balcony and the blue dusk, with its soft breeze and intermittent seeping sounds of the city in the springtime, were hung with lined drapes of a bohemian green-and-brown pattern that recalled, for Denise, the artists of the Bloomsbury group, in whom Lili was much interested, Vanessa Bell and Duncan Grant; Lili had told her they'd painted everything at their house in the country, on England's south coast: the cabinets, the bathtub, the furniture. . . . The walls were covered by framed paintings and drawings, a checkerboard of artworks, some colorful, others pen-and-ink, inviting closer scrutiny. The room was dimly and suggestively lit by table lamps with heavy shades, several fringed like the sofa. On either side of the mantel, bookshelves, painted white rather than the dark green of the bookshop, held Lili's personal collection of books, inviting and initially mysterious. The shelves were accented, too, by intriguing knickknacks: a Chinese plate on a stand, painted with a water scene; a tiny alabaster amphora; a trio of netsuke carvings, one a bucking water buffalo, another a robed monk bearing a tablet, the third a woman squatting with a cooking pot. On the glass-topped rattan coffee table sat a tray with a glass, an ice bucket, a soda siphon, and a carafe of decanted whiskey, to which Lili turned her attention. A cigarette, half cinder, dangled unattended in its ashtray.

Denise felt something like wonder, and perhaps a little alarm, to be in the personal space of her adored employer. It wasn't a dinner party—of course not: Lili could hardly have invited her to dine with Ernesto Sabato and his wife, though Denise knew they'd been to Lili's for supper in the past. She might have invited her with, say, Augusto, the former assistant now in Chicago, had he returned to the city; or perhaps—but no. The nature of their friendship was particular, and exclusive. Denise wasn't up to the level of Lili's literary network, though she worked in the bookshop; and she was too young to be of interest to Lili's other friends, whoever they might be—presumably the artists whose works covered the walls, and musicians and designers and architects, and perhaps, through her brother, even a smattering of philanthropic businessmen and their wives. Lili had been in Buenos Aires almost as long as Denise had been alive; she might know anyone, everyone.

In intellectual circles, Lili was famous; Pigmalion was known to the French and Spanish as well as to the Germans and English. Why such kindness to her, Denise, whose only claims were her private proficiency at Chopin nocturnes and her mediocre par on the Jockey course? Sipping her peaty scotch, scanning the bookshelves while Lili disappeared to the kitchen to see to their supper (Franz Kafka, Heinrich Mann, Thomas Mann, Zweig, Zweig, Zweig—on the other side of the fireplace, Elizabeth Bowen next to Willa Cather, Jean Rhys next to Muriel Spark—), Denise scolded herself for her insecurity: Why shouldn't Lili have her to supper? Why shouldn't she entertain the older woman as easily in this delicious apartment as she did in the back corner of Pigmalion? Why, in these new surroundings, was she made so anxious? Uncertain, she drained her glass, then poured herself a substantial refill before Lili returned.

Served in a small dining room adjacent to the sitting room, lit only by brass sconces curved like a woman's body, at a round table covered with a purple damask cloth, the meal, though simple, was surprisingly tasty: lamb Argenteuil over rice, with a side salad and, as Lili put it, a single, powerful cheese. Instead of a sweet, she cut a tart apple into slices and fanned them elegantly on a delicate plate; and she brewed them stronger, better coffee than at the shop. When Lili was with her in the room, Denise inhabited herself fully, she felt *bien dans sa peau*. Only when Lili left— she insisted that Denise not help clear the table; perhaps the kitchen was a disaster?—did Denise feel fretful, almost overwhelmed. She excused herself at one point to the bathroom, where she dabbed her wrists and temples with cold water, but still her heart beat heavily in her chest.

After supper, as they drank another whiskey in the drawing room, Lili sat next to Denise on the sofa and spoke of Gurdjieff. "Each of us needs to be awake to the present," Lili reiterated, looking beyond Denise to the open window and the now-black night. "In all our senses, with our bodies and minds as one. Only then," she murmured, "are we in a state of sacredness." She offered Denise a cigarette, took one, lit them both, inhaled as if gasping. "Take, for example, smoking," she went on. "For you, as for me, each cigarette is a pleasure but also causes pain. It burns in the throat, it makes us feel the shape and limit of our lungs. We know, because we cough or grow short of breath, that it cannot be good for us." She nodded thoughtfully. "And yet the cigarette also slows down time, it opens a space in the fabric of our days, for contemplation or conversation. It defers what lies ahead—it defers death, even, you could say."

Denise, who had herself had the same thoughts about the habit, listened in silence.

"So you see, a small part of our day, of our bodily movements, can, if we pay attention, hold profound significance. We learn to pay attention to ourselves, so." Lili, leaning forward, put her hand on Denise's knee. "What does our body have to tell us?" she asked.

"What do you mean?" Denise could feel her heart beating in her fingertips, her belly, her earlobes.

Lili smiled, sat back, smoked. "Sometimes, we don't observe things about ourselves and yet they are apparent, even obvious, to the people around us. Because we are animals, you see, like a cat, or a dog, or a child. We learn to hide things from ourselves if we are convinced they are unacceptable—but like a cat, or a dog, or a child, we have innate needs and desires."

"I don't know what you mean."

"To live healthfully, we must learn who we are, and accept ourselves."

Denise could barely hear Lili for the pounding in her ears. She took another gulp of whiskey, but what she wanted was water. She was suddenly unbearably thirsty. "May I have a drink of water? I can get it—"

"No, sit." Lili went at once and returned with a tall glass. The water was tepid, and Denise drank it all in two gulps. As she placed her glass on the tray, she felt Lili's hand, electric, stroke the back of her head.

"Dear girl," Lili said, "there is nothing to be afraid of. We like women. We desire women . . ."

Denise flinched from Lili's hand and leaned away, complicatedly aware that her face expressed horror. "I think I'd better go," she said, fumbling on the floor for her purse.

Lili, unfazed, merely laughed. "Calm down, dear girl. Sit still and listen to what I have to say. You think I am trying to seduce you? That I want to ravish you here on the sofa? Nonsense. I feel tenderly toward you—I am enormously fond of you. But I have no desire to take off my clothes—nor yours, for that matter. Frankly, you are not my type. It is simply a privilege of my age to care enough and, at the same time, little enough, to tell the truth. And you, Denise, I've known you now more than two years. We've been together many, many hours, and have had many conversations. Wonderful conversations. We're good friends, aren't we?"

"Yes, but—"

"We know each other well. And I observe you, I know when you are happy, or hopeful, or frightened. And I know, the way a cat or dog knows, what you want." Lili stood, lit another cigarette, walked to the window, where she seemed to see something outside in the dark. "Your lovely friend—our lunch companion—Estelle, yes? With her funny teeth, that olive skin, those beautiful dark eyes. Do you ask yourself what she is to you? Do you ask yourself what your body wants?"

Denise, at this, stood also, and clutched her purse to her stomach like a shield. "I will not—I cannot—"

"Consider me your friend, as I am. I'm here to tell you that 'lesbian' is not an insult, nor a sin, nor a crime. You're surrounded by lesbians. In fact, you love lesbians—Virginia Woolf, Patricia Highsmith, I've heard even Marlene Dietrich—and, of course, me." She looked Denise in the eye, her expression both grave and amused. "You cannot love me less for knowing this? It makes no difference. In your heart you've known all along, *n'est-ce pas?*"

THAT NIGHT AS she lay in her single bed beneath her rosary-draped crucifix, alongside her open window, the glorious blooming jacaranda glowing in the garden outside, its branches like reaching arms wrapped in luminous tulle, she heard, still, her heart thumping in her ears. She held her hands between her thighs, at once to quiet and to excite herself, as in her mind she went over and over the extraordinary evening. Might Lili have kissed her, had she not flinched? What would she have done then?

Had she known all along, as Lili insisted she had? What would it mean to know now—what, if anything, did she know? And how, after this, could she return to Pigmalion?

SHE DISCOVERED THAT she could not return. She couldn't bear to face Fräulein Lebach—in her mind she had recalled at once the more formal appellation. She had her mother telephone and tell Fräulein Lebach that she wasn't well, and then the next week she sent a note by post to say she thought it best that she sever her employment. Fräulein Lebach sent in return a formal but pleasant note, wishing her improved health, along with a final paycheck. Denise did not know how to explain to her parents what had happened, and invented a lie about an aggressive male customer who had harassed her: she said that Fräulein Lebach had unexpectedly taken his part, that she and the Fräulein had quarreled over this, and that it was best to call a halt. She was aware that she was deploying a version of the sexual assault in the bathroom during her internship at the hotel in Bern, which remained a secret, to cover for another experience altogether; but this new one felt more unsayable even than the other.

Meanwhile, the bookshop itself, its artifacts and odors so beloved to her, its space the site of so much pleasure, became a place to avoid, and the loss of which to grieve. She felt fortunate that she had little reason to venture downtown, and in the weeks before Christmas, she insisted that she and Maman shop in the little district in Vicente López or in Recoleta, at times when she felt sure she would not encounter the Fräulein. Once, on Avenida Alvear, in the late afternoon, she thought she recognized from behind Fräulein Lebach's cream summer blazer with navy piping, but the wearer, when she turned, had a different aspect entirely. Initially, though, Denise's greatest anxiety was that Fräulein's heartless insinuation might spill over into the rest of her life, that she, Denise, would feel somehow tainted in her friendship with Estelle, as though she'd done—or, by thinking, had done; or, by revealing without even thinking, had done—something contemptible. What if Fräulein Lebach

were right, and somehow, unbeknownst to herself, like having halitosis, she exuded some unpleasant, desirous aura? It was, she told herself,
ridiculous. Besides which, although she could never have said so aloud,
love between women was no crime—Fräulein was right that many of the
great women writers Denise admired had private lives of which the pope
would sternly have disapproved. As for the Fräulein, if her morals and
religious beliefs did not forbid it, why shouldn't she take female lovers?
Or have taken them, presumably, in the past, as she was old now, meno-
pausal doubtless, and even to think of her in terms of desire, of desire of
any kind, seemed as alarming to Denise as considering her own parents
in that way.

But the reason she couldn't go back to Pigmalion wasn't because she
thought differently about Fräulein Lebach herself, but because she understood now how Fräulein Lebach (oh, but she wanted, still, to think of her
friend as "Lili"!) thought of her, Denise: as being in love with Estelle.
Which surely she was not, and would never be.

Eventually, after a couple of weeks of stalling, she mustered the courage to regain the golf course, at Fanchette's repeated invitation. Fanchette was rather like a pecking bird, persistent, for which Denise was, in
this instance, grateful; but at the same time, they knew her history, knew
her to be depressive, imagined she had suffered a setback, so when finally
she appeared they didn't ask questions.

She felt nervous when Fanchette and Estelle picked her up in Fanchette's little blue Renault: Would she behave oddly? Did she, as Fräulein
had suggested, reveal something untoward? But as soon as Denise slid
into the back seat—ridged black vinyl that burned through the thin
cotton of her golfing skirt—Estelle turned and grabbed her wrist and
squeezed it affectionately, and made a silly happy face, sticking out her
tongue. "Thank God you're back," she said. "Fanchette has been driving
me *crazy!*"

And Fanchette, grumbling in her deep voice, her eyes firmly on
the road: "So she says, because her golf game is lamentable—but

la-men-ta-ble!" She swooped into a U-turn, spun the wheel with a chauffeur's aplomb. "I've made her buy me a drink for every round she loses, and it's been free cocktails for the past fortnight. I'm no fool." Fanchette honked at a Mercedes that cut her off, and cursed.

"Stop, stop! No need to get enraged," Estelle giggled, winking at Denise. "Her temper gets no better with age." And again she reached and held Denise's wrist. Her fingers, in the heat, were a little damp. "We missed you, dear friend. It's summertime now. All shall be well and all shall be well." She turned back to face the road ahead, stretching an arm out the window, into the wind. "Look at the trees!"

And indeed, though it was the end of the season, they drove along a boulevard lined on either side by jacarandas, the roadside carpeted with fallen blossoms, a sea of royal purple: their musky scent filled the car.

"All shall be well," repeated Denise, rolling down her own window and putting her face to the breeze.

SHE TOLD HER FRIENDS the same lie that she had told her parents, and they moved on. She told her friends, and her parents told their friends, that she would need a new position; and when the three Cassars went for drinks on New Year's Eve to Estelle's parents' home—a large and elegant villa not far from the Jockey Club—Estelle was overflowing with excitement.

"Guess what?" she burbled, arm around Denise's shoulder as they headed for the living room, which in turn opened fully onto the beautiful garden. "I've found you the perfect job!"

"Don't tell me—chambermaid at the French embassy!" Estelle and Fanchette often teased Denise about her inability to pick up after herself, to wash a cup or make a bed.

"Absurd. No. This is for real."

"Okay?"

"Jacques needs someone at the agency. You'll be perfect. Look, here he is. You two can discuss it."

Jacques, whom Denise was meeting for the first time, was Estelle's younger older brother. They were six children in the family: Elizabeth, the firstborn; then Julien, then Jacques, then Estelle, then Antoinette, and finally Yves, the baby. Jacques, in his mid-thirties with a pretty blond wife and two little girls in smocked party dresses outside on the lawn, had several years previously opened his own travel agency, which was proving very successful. Apparently, one of his junior associates had decided to return to Paris, and he therefore had a serendipitous opening in his office.

Denise would never forget that first meeting—the way the midges danced in the long shafts of sun to the sound of children's merriment and peaceable adult chatter. The air was scented with jasmine from the rampant bush along the wall beside them, and with citronella from the little fuming coils along the path. She was aware, at the periphery of her vision, of the swimming pool's flash of turquoise. His face, when he turned to her, so like his sister's—that abundant black hair; those wide-set dark eyes, thickly fringed by lashes and filled, she felt, with humor and benevolence; his lopsided smile; the five o'clock shadow that darkened his already olive skin. His utterly conventional striped tie invitingly askew at the collar; his clean, brown, square hand, which reached out at first to shake hers—and then, at Estelle's urging *"Mais enfin, on se fait la bise, içi!"* the obligatory kisses instead, and with them, the whiff of cigarettes, vodka, hair oil.

She was certain, from the moment of their encounter and for many years to come, that God did have an implacable plan that she could not fully see. She was in that moment not yet thirty, still years younger than Maman had been when she married Papa. Her parents said, always, that they had been struck, simultaneously, by their *coup de foudre*, by the knowledge that, as in Plato's *Symposium*, they were in fact two halves of the same soul. Each had miraculously intuited that the other felt the same (for some reason Denise always thought, in this regard, of Mendelssohn's "Songs Without Words," as though their shared emotion were a melody that passed through and between them, a music only they could hear). And although it had seemed to the world that their union was impossible—Maman was thirteen years older than Papa!—they had— with, as they said, God's help—made it come to pass; and now, almost thirty-five years later, their marriage seemed clearly to have been fated, to be the masterpiece of both their lives. Whether Denise thought all of this in the exact moment when Jacques pressed his warm cheeks against her own she could not later truthfully have said; but it felt as though she had, as though she knew, from the first, that they were Destined.

Yes, of course he had a lovely wife, Maria Luisa—her thick blond hair in a spun-sugar bun on top of her head, her knee-length pale pink empire dress very Jackie Kennedy—and of course the two delicious little girls: one fair, like her mother, the other dark like her father, both in smocked Liberty prints with puffed sleeves and white lace collars, with long white socks and Mary Janes, picture-postcard children leading picture-postcard lives. She did not for a second entertain the illusion that they could be magicked away. What did she think, when he smiled and laughed and said he'd heard so much about her from his sister that he felt they were already family? She thought: "Destined"; she thought: "God's plan"; she thought, too: "Patience."

And when he offered her the job before even they'd finished their first drinks—and Estelle whooped so loudly that the rest of the party paused to hear the good news and applauded her, which made Denise blush ferociously but also grin—that was the only word for it, her mouth pulled so wide with glee that her very jaw ached—she felt finally, for the first time, as though the pieces of her life might fall into place, somehow, if she only kept her faith.

And again, a few days later on the golf course at the Jockey Club with Fanchette and Estelle and Antoinette, when Estelle praised Antoinette's husband, Jean-Marc, and made her joke about the perfect man and whether she'd ever find him, Denise felt her stomach flip, as if Estelle and she held between them a secret that the other two didn't know about:

that Jacques was, for Denise, the perfect man, her other, completing half, and that whatever it meant she would wait for him, until their time came.

To think that a few weeks earlier she'd felt the world around her to be precarious and inhospitable—as though Lili Lebach had cast her like a baby bird from her nest. She felt grateful, now, to Lili: a whole new essential chapter was about to begin, and without that strange, intense evening and its painful aftermath she would not be here, on the cusp of the rest of her real life. Awake, as Lili's Gurdjieff would have it, in every cell of her body. Remember this moment, she told herself, remember this day, as Fanchette teed up, wiggling her wide bottom like a settling hen, while Antoinette whispered something to her sister and Estelle giggled, her mouth slightly open and her tongue pressing at the fabulous gap between her teeth, all of them so casually and happily being together, belonging together, still young, their lives still ahead, as a white-tipped plane flashed overhead in the glaucous, honeyed summer afternoon light, and, a mere second later, its roar split the air.

JANUARY 1963

☙

GENEVA, SWITZERLAND

François had been back in Geneva for only a few days when Barbara's telegram brought the news of her father's death. The postman from the telegraph office came round by bicycle just after seven in the morning, when François was shaving, and so he answered the door in the paisley dressing gown he almost never wore, with a towel over his shoulder and only half his face done. The postman, skinny and a little greasy in his uniform, handed him the folded blue paper without looking directly at him, as if deferentially. Perhaps he knew it was bad news. François tipped him, but only fifty centimes. Everything in Switzerland was so expensive.

A week after receiving the information, he still wondered whether he should have stayed. In his heart, though they had all refused to speak of it, though they had insisted on discussing plans for travel—that conference in Ottawa they kept talking about—he'd known from the moment he entered the hospital room that Terrence Harold Fisk must soon die. The old man—gaunt, discolored, with a flatness to his gaze—had seemed barely and miraculously alive, held to the planet only by the constant ministrations of his loving wife and daughter.

But even when they were alone—not just alone in Barbara's girlhood bedroom with Mrs. Fisk downstairs, but alone in the whole house, or out walking the dog around Grenadier Pond, watching the mufflered skaters glide past like figures in a Victorian painting—Barbara did not concede even the possibility, let alone the likelihood; and François didn't feel it was his place, having arrived late to the vigil and certain to depart early, to force either her or her mother to accept the inevitable before they had to.

This posed a dilemma when he was preparing to return to Switzerland, just before New Year's. Even though Mr. Fisk had never been permitted to leave his bright white room at the General, and they'd even set up a little artificial tree in his room, complete with colored lights and silver tinsel, the conceit persisted that he'd be ready, within the fortnight, for Ottawa. François didn't know whether to offer to stay longer, invoking the unpalatable truth—that Barbara would surely wish he were there when the time came—or else invoking the preposterous, mythic version, in which Mr. Fisk would rise like Lazarus, and François might be welcome to carry his cane, as it were. Or whether, in fact, it was best to say nothing, to go along with the household pretense that little was at stake, and to head back, as planned, to the mountain of work that awaited him in Geneva.

Of the possibilities, this last was the one he had chosen, in part because Mrs. Fisk bristled every time he entered a room, and he could not bear it. Though when Barbara drove him to the airport and they clung to each other like children in a storm, he was almost ready to stay—almost. They did not speak of Death, who was with them in the car, just as nobody had spoken of Death in Mr. Fisk's white room at the General when François went to say good-bye, except that when the women were fussing over the dismantling of the tree, the old man had whispered, so that only François would hear, "You take good care of her, I know you do. Because you love her like I do. Her mother's a bit hard on her"—he had trouble saying so much at once and had to pause and gather the spit in his dry mouth—"and harder still on you. But she loves her too, you know."

Beyond that, they pretended about Ottawa, and they pretended that the Fisks would travel to Paris in May, and that maybe they would all go to Buenos Aires to see the Cassars—after all, why not? And once he had boarded the plane, he wished he could hurry back, just to say what hadn't been said; and then he ordered a scotch from the stewardess and let it go.

HE'D RETURNED TO Geneva all alone, with his compassion and his self-pity both, to the bald little flat on the Route de Malagnou (still no neighbors in the apartment across the way), to the dead mums he'd left in the vase on the table, the stink of their water and moldering leaves filling the air. They'd been a gift from Babs Riley when they'd thought, briefly and mistakenly, that Barbara might be returning for Christmas. And he settled in to work and to wait for his wife to come back to him, so that life, their life together, might begin again.

FRANÇOIS WAS HALFWAY through his business degree at CEI (Centre d'Études Industrielles), a year-long program run by the brilliant, quixotic Paul-Marie Haenni, a Swiss chemical engineer who envisaged his school as the training ground for a benevolent and holistic global capitalism. He believed in a future in which capitalism's prosperity was shared, in which the developing world had a stake, and in which the preparation of business leaders involved a broad cultural education—not just in economics but in science, letters, psychology, and sociology. This approach, Haenni insisted, was preferable to that of the technocratic American MBAs, and to this end, he invited an array of unexpected speakers, most recently the great French sociologist Raymond Aron, who would give a lecture the following week, on Tuesday, January 17. François, thrillingly, had been invited to be one of three student respondents after the talk.

He was in equal measure excited and terrified—he'd certainly never expected such an opportunity. Indeed, François had never wanted to pursue an MBA, but had been offered the chance by his employer, Péchiney, the aluminum corporation for which he'd been working since he left Harvard. Although Péchiney had presented the course as optional, François didn't feel he had a choice, because after almost a year in Gardanne, a crappy industrial town outside Aix-en-Provence, he and Barbara, especially, were keen to get out; and above all because he was impatient to be promoted. CEI was, of course, the preparation for promotion.

He'd been ambivalent about it, before he got there. Maybe, in truth, he was ambivalent about it still. Not long ago he'd been embarked on a PhD in Middle Eastern studies at Harvard, after all, and Sir Hamilton Gibb was to have been his thesis adviser—one of the great minds in his field. Even though he and Barbara had decided together that he must instead go into business, it felt like a comedown to be taking notes on a factory in Eindhoven or surveying the supply-chain logistics at the port of Rotterdam. At first, he'd condescended almost unwittingly to his CEI classmates, a motley gathering from around the globe—Tokyo, Port of Spain, Ottawa, Calcutta—but all of them devoted to the mercantile, all of them aspiring industrialists, eager to embrace their cogdom in the ever-expanding global capitalist machine.

Back in his lonely flat, in which, after months, traces of Barbara were few—her hairbrush on the bathroom shelf still sprouting a fiesta of strands of her glossy hair; her brown pumps tucked under the dresser; her floaty summer dresses in the closet—he had before him, poor distraction, the case studies to write up from the Netherlands trip in late November and, both excitingly and dauntingly, the reading in preparation for Raymond Aron's visit to the institute.

Haenni, CEI's director, had explained that Aron had last visited the institute a decade earlier, when it was new. He'd discussed his support for the Schuman Plan to create a European coalition for coal and steel— and he'd been powerfully in favor of this first, crucial step toward a European Common Market. Now Aron was returning at the moment when the Inner Six, the original countries to sign up for the Common Market, would be deciding the fate of Britain's application to join them.

Officially, though, he'd be there to discuss his latest tome, *Peace and War Between Nations.*

The amazing intellectual Aron, whose columns François had read as a teenager in *Le Figaro* at his parents' table, whose brilliance had been impressed upon him by his father all his adult life, who was revered in the Cassar household. François couldn't quite believe it. "If only," Gaston Cassar had been known to say, "if only Raymond Aron had given that radio address in June 1940, I wouldn't have hesitated to rush to London . . ."

For François, in this possibility of a conversation with the great man, so much was at stake: Aron, unlike so many of his peers, wasn't stuck in provincial hierarchies. Like François, he also loved America, had befriended American intellectuals, and had been inducted, while François was at Harvard, into the American Academy of Arts and Sciences there: they could even have passed each other in the Coop or on Mass Ave (though François knew they hadn't, as he'd have recognized that face anywhere). Aron, of all brilliant Frenchmen, might appreciate François, with his unusual trajectory, recognize him for a serious scholar, a genuine mind, stuck now in this strange business course—or, terrifyingly, he might not. He might just ignore him and move on. Because the event on the seventeenth loomed enormous in François's imagination, he seemed only able to procrastinate.

ON THIS FRIDAY, in the late afternoon—Friday the thirteenth, maybe just a bad-luck day?—he'd tidied the apartment instead of working. He'd folded and refolded his shirts in the drawers, arranged the glasses and mugs in rows in the kitchen cupboard. The two tiny rooms on the Route de Malagnou dismayed him—they were barely furnished, and the bedroom gave onto the busy road, so that even with the double glazing it was noisy from early until suppertime. In the beginning, when Barbara had been with him, the sparseness had seemed romantic, when he thought they'd build their nest together, adorning it with little gifts they'd give each other. Now its bachelor aura—too tidy, too spartan—depressed him.

Dusk in Geneva meant late morning in Toronto. He stood from the books and papers that had blurred before his eyes to turn on the lights. He turned the radio on, then off again. Leaning over the telephone, he hesitated—they couldn't afford it; they'd agreed they must save every penny; they weren't supposed to speak until Sunday night . . . just once a week—but her voice, just her voice. He needed to hear her voice.

Only when the phone rang at the other end did it occur to him that his mother-in-law might answer. It was her house, after all. The prospect roused a kaleidoscope of butterflies in his gut—they'd not spoken since her husband died, though he'd sent a condolence telegram. The funeral was the next day, Saturday the fourteenth, and he'd sent flowers, but she wouldn't have received them yet. He pressed the button to cut the call.

A little breathless, he lit a cigarette. This was ridiculous. How could he be afraid of his mother-in-law? A tiny, stout woman with hair like a gray poodle's. A tiny, stout woman who knew nothing of the world beyond Toronto, Canada! Who cared what she thought of him? God, though, he hated speaking to people on the phone. And in English, especially. He felt so awkward, uncertain of his words, anxious that his accent was stronger when they couldn't see him . . . and Mrs. Fisk, well, she was already tough in person. . . . But he didn't hate speaking to Barbara—he needed to hear her voice. He needed her voice like breathing. He'd brave Mrs. Fisk if he had to—if that's what it took to reach the balm of Barbara's voice.

But when he dialed again it was Barbara who answered.

"Darling," she cooed, when she realized it was him. "But is everything all right?"

"Everything's fine. I just wanted to hear your voice. To say I love you."

She hesitated a beat. By which he knew that she was at the wall phone in the kitchen—the other one was in her mother's bedroom—and that her mother was nearby. He could picture the scene so vividly—the bright winter sun reflecting off the snow outside, the checkerboard lino, the casual way Barb would flip the handle of the yellow can opener mounted next to the telephone while she spoke. "That's so dear of you," she said. "You know I do too."

"But you can't say it?"

"We're just going over the menu for the reception after the service tomorrow. So many errands."

"I'm sorry."

"Don't be sorry. Mother says they do it on purpose, give the bereaved lots to do. So you don't have time to think about it."

"I wish I were there. Well, really, I wish you were here."

Barbara sighed. "Did you get my letter?"

"I got it. Of course I understand." That morning , he'd received her letter saying she didn't know how long her mother would need her, that even after the funeral it might be a couple of weeks, maybe even a few. Stalling yet again. On the one hand, he understood; on the other, he wanted to tell her there would never be a good time to leave Toronto. She'd just have to do it. Unless she gave up on him, instead. "But I miss you."

"I miss you too, silly." She gave a little laugh.

He could hear his mother-in-law's voice obscurely in the background. He wanted to tell Barbara how nervous he was about the Raymond Aron event. He wanted to tell her that he missed her touch. He wanted to tell her that sometimes his heart ached in his chest, a physical ache.

"We shouldn't talk long now," she said. "I've got to call the caterers, and we're heading out to pick up the wine. Isn't it weird that you give a party when someone dies? But Daddy would've liked it. You know he loved a party."

"He did."

"The Collyers are coming from London, I think. And the Whitworths from Kitchener, and Eleanor from Ottawa. Thank goodness for Charley and Marnie, they've been troopers." The high school friends—he always felt in competition with them, often felt they were winning.

"Okay, I just wanted you to know how much I love you."

"You too, darling. We'll speak at the regular time on Sunday, okay?"

"Courage for the funeral, Barb. I love you."

"Bye-bye!" He imagined her nodding, even as she turned back to her mother, a way of conveying that she loved him back, but she didn't say so aloud. Maybe he was too hopeful.

AFTER HE HUNG UP, he felt, if possible, worse. He sat back down at the dining table, the Aron books and his notebook spread in front of him, now theatrically illuminated by the overhead light. He hated the winter darkness. He hated being alone; why was he always alone? Though when he'd returned from Toronto at the turn of the year, he'd been happy to rejoin his cohort, and the classes in the mansion on the Route de Florissant in Conches, by the bend in the lazy Arve River, now frozen over but where, when they'd arrived late last summer, a posse of little boys had waded in the water with their pants rolled up, busy panning for gold—or, rather, dredging for it with muslin cloths, in what François and Barbara had been told was a local tradition of generations' standing. They'd joked, that late-summer afternoon, that CEI, in its way, was teaching adults from all over the world to pan for gold, hopefully with more success than the boys; but certainly the sight had been utopian: the limpid, rushing river, with its sandy banks and jumbled, overhanging trees; the cheerful unhurried industry of the little boys; and, a stone's throw away, the sedate turreted mansion (its long, dark windows like mournful eyes, its rolling lawns and gravel drive of a Swiss perfection) that housed the institute, tucked behind its stucco wall and ornate iron gate . . .

Whatever François had imagined when they'd arrived in Geneva had proven to be nonsense, seeing as it had involved them being together as a married couple. Now the course was halfway over; they'd move on at the end of May, when the gold diggers returned to the riverbed, though what lay ahead, beyond that month, was still uncertain. After Aron's visit, François would travel to Paris to speak to his employers at Péchiney. When the course at CEI was done, they would send him wherever they chose; hopefully, he and Barbara were agreed, to the New World.

He thought of himself—it was essential to his self-respect—as different from the others. He hoped that Raymond Aron, in the blink of an eye, might recognize this: Aron, after all, was an intellectual, but not above visiting CEI. . . . François's parents had raised him to believe above all in the life of the mind, to disdain money, of which they'd for so long had so little, as a necessary evil. We must trust in the Lord, they said, like the birds on the breeze. Back at Amherst, his roommate, Rosie, had joked that he had the mindset of Rosie's Orthodox cousins, for whom Torah study was the great purpose of life, and the shopkeeping downstairs an odious sideline that had to be endured. He wasn't religious like his Catholic parents, or like Rosie's Orthodox Jewish cousins, but he did believe—absurdly, he was coming to realize—that money was beside the point. Or, rather, that money wasn't of itself interesting to him. He could see that it was interesting, even passionately so, to some, to many even, that men around him wanted to gamble and win, to accrue great wealth, to control others with the power those riches would confer upon them. But for him, fundamentally solitary and not much interested in *things*, money's only interest lay in what it might enable him, or Barbara, or their future family to do.

He'd left the PhD to go to Péchiney not because he aspired to run the corporation—he might not even stick with it for very long, maybe only a few years, as a stepping stone to something else, possibly even back to academia in time—but because it was time to stop borrowing from their parents. Besides, they wanted to have some freedom of movement, to travel, to raise children without, as his parents had had to do, scrimping and fretting and taking in lodgers and sewing and relying on the generosity of cousins in the country.

No, he'd said to Barbara that though he was sorry not to finish his doctorate straightaway—he just found his thesis on Turkish politics so *interesting*—he'd go into business simply to make sure that none of his descendants had to be schoolteachers. Because as soon as they were literate—his maternal grandfather had been illiterate—they'd become schoolteachers: his mother had been a schoolteacher, and her sisters too; and his father's mother had been a schoolteacher, and his father's brother, Charles, as well. And even on Barbara's side, her great-great-grandmother, who'd immigrated to Canada as a child from Cromer, in East Anglia, along with her five siblings and her parents, both of whom died on the journey leaving her, the eldest, the head of the household— even *she* had become a schoolteacher and, eventually, like his mother's eldest sister, a headmistress, the family's one claim to fame. A most worthy profession, needless to say, but one little appreciated and still less rewarded. He, François, wanted to free the family from the modesty and genteel poverty of their past, and in this time of change and new alliances, of the upheaval of old class structures and lives of limited expectations, when value was to be determined not by the circumstances of one's birth or the power of one's connections but by the ferocity of one's intelligence and one's will, by one's commitment to hard work and ingenuity, why shouldn't he be capable of *anything*?

Well, yes and no. That's how he'd felt for years, when he first went to America, to Amherst, when he'd traveled all the way to its southern tip at Key West and beyond, beyond to Cuba—why not *anything*? When he'd got that Fulbright fellowship, it was because he was determined not to be defined by his breakdown and flight from *khâgne*, that infernal two-year course for the advanced exams for the *grandes écoles*— he'd made it through the first awful, awful year, and had returned for the second only, like his only fellow Algerian classmate Derrida, to have to retreat again homeward in ignominious pieces halfway through. He'd renounced, desperate, miserable, and had worked like a dog just to get his head together, and they'd all agreed never, ever to speak of it, though he'd heard through the grapevine that Derrida, brave fellow, had gone back the following year, a third year, and, like a guy with a blowtorch, destroyed the competition. But not Cassar. And if Cassar had been denied triumph in the unforgiving French system—though he'd shone most brightly for so long in Algiers—then part of pulling himself back together had been to embrace the belief in a world beyond France's petty institutional waltzes, and to strike out for the New World, for Amherst first and then on to Harvard, the very signifier of triumph, its reputation unparalleled around the globe—he'd done that all on his own, he was embarked intrepidly on his own boat!

And then, yes, they'd taken the decision, he and Barbara (she'd been so adamant, and the Fisks glowered behind her shoulder, and he wanted, above all, to make her happy, as he'd never before wanted to make any-one but his mother happy), that he must turn instead to business. The logic was implacable, but still, in his heart, it caused him deep sadness. And it had also necessitated turning back to his father, satisfying at last Gaston's lifelong desire to be *right*.

From the beginning, when François was fourteen or fifteen, his father had said, "Study science and mathematics, do what I did, try for Poly-technique," but he'd held his ground, held steady: philosophy or nothing. He'd pushed, mightily, for *khâgne*. And even after he'd fled Louis-le-Grand and Paris, he'd maintained unflinchingly that he'd done the right thing. His father was always offering introductions and connections, old navy contacts now running university departments or programs, or unlikely enterprises or divisions of large companies—"It's how it's done," he'd say. "People want to hire people they understand!"—and for years, François had scoffed, behind his father's back, at these proposals—affectionately, to be sure, and not without respect for his father, but with the sense that Gaston did not understand the fire that François felt to suc-ceed on his *own* terms, to transcend the known, what had been offered.

He had no interest in math and science, nor in Polytechnique, nor in the navy, no interest in working like a brute all his life just to acquire a handsome apartment in the Seventh or the Sixteenth—no, he wanted

to *conquer the world*. Not like Napoleon but like Humboldt or de Tocqueville: he wanted to experience everything, from the rocky iguana-
covered outcrops of the Galápagos to the sumptuous palaces of Jaipur,
from a gelatinous platter of steamed sea cucumber in a restaurant in
Kuala Lumpur or a tear-inducing curry in Macao to the Inca ruins of
the Yucatán Peninsula, from the ancient churches carved in rock at Lal-
ibela to the dusk falling over Mount Olympus to the sun rising behind
the rusty monolith of Ayers Rock as it loomed out of the vast Australian
desert—he wanted to see and smell and taste and hear and touch all of
it. He wanted to read everything, learn about everything—gnosticism,
Byzantium, the Uighurs, the Chechens, Hatshepsut, Shackleton, Geron-
imo, Süleyman the Magnificent, the poetry of Li Bai, the writings of Ibn
Khaldun, of Ahmed Baba in Timbuktu, the lot of it, an infinite feast, he
longed to gorge himself on life itself, endlessly curious, ravenous even—

And yet here he was, at thirty-one, fallen into the company of men who
were amiable and intelligent and by any conventional measure ambitious,
but who in no way saw the feast laid out, did not notice or remark upon
all that lay beyond the here and now to investigate and absorb. With the
possible exception of his fellow French student Dufour, they probably
didn't even know who Raymond Aron *was*. And he was here in this situation because he'd allowed, for the first time, that money mattered and
that he didn't have any, or the prospect of any, that all the world's treasures might as well be on the moon if he couldn't even pay for an airplane
ticket to rejoin his wife for Christmas and had to rely instead upon the
largesse of his father-in-law, himself just such an amiable nonentity as
the business world seemed intended to create.

He'd only got the interview at Péchiney in the first place by capit-
ulating at last to his own father, and making use of his contact at the
company. He'd traveled from Cambridge, Massachusetts, during term
time to Paris to meet the men from the company—his father had paid
for that airfare, of course, to François's shame; as with so much else, he
had vowed to repay it—and the men from Péchiney, impressed by him

(and surely also by Harvard; in 1961, with JFK newly in office, wasn't the whole world impressed by Harvard?), had offered him a post and he had thought about it and he and Barbara had discussed it at length, and still he had thought more about it, debated, and finally in some confusion he had accepted.

The posting in Gardanne, well: it had been what it must be, an introduction to the business, to the factory that had, since 1894, alchemically taken iron-rich red bauxite—originally mined locally but later brought by ship from Guinea to the port of Marseille, then transferred by train to Gardanne—and had distilled from it, with the help of sodium hydroxide, the alumina that would in turn be deployed in the specialty steels that made the modern world. François had told himself that this was not, in spite of appearances, inherently less interesting than would be a visit to the Grand Mosque of Conakry. No, this was, in its deep strangeness, a different realm of fascination: the alumina extracted from the bauxite would then become aluminum, extraordinarily flexible and lightweight, and be used, in other factories in other towns and countries, either under the auspices of Péchiney or of other companies, to produce airplane parts and beer kegs, soda cans and window frames, toasters and refrigerators and electrical cables. This ancient red ferrous material, which was dug from the dry ground at Fria, in Guinea, and passed through the Gardanne factory, transformed and literally *created modernity*, a festive and forward-looking American lifestyle of Coke cans and keg parties and stadium seats.

In principle, François was fascinated; in practice, alas, less so. It was as if he stood so close to a giant painting of which he could see only a few square centimeters that he could not begin to make out what the larger work might depict, or how. The year at Gardanne humbled him, made him wish he'd studied science more attentively and for longer; but it also frustrated and enraged him, as the matters to which he was asked to apply himself seemed so far from his natural talents and skills. Though always pleasant, he remained reserved around his colleagues, primarily engineers and chemists, with a smattering of business cadres. It was a training, he told himself, and Barbara told him too, a means to an end, rather than his fate.

The CEI course came as both release and possible cause for alarm. Initially, the reality reinforced François's prejudices: his eager classmates, although international and diverse, spoke about outputs and balance sheets rather than philosophy, and carted with them their messy households—squalling children and their tired mothers, the odd cat or dog—which meant a lot of conversation turned to nannies, pediatricians, and depression. The seminars and lectures were a mixed bag, sometimes as dreary as arithmetic, earnest explorations of the most productive corporate structures. But to his growing interest and pleasure, like finding early flowers peeking through dead leaves, François discovered that CEI's director and his closest associates were practical visionaries, determined with the greatest optimism—indeed, one might even use the word "faith"—to create a generation of benevolent global capitalists who would refashion the world into a better one, reducing inequity, promoting growth even in the most far-flung outposts, and, alongside business, promulgating ideals of liberty, sovereignty, tolerance, and collaboration, as well as a broader Hegelian teleology, a belief in humanity's greater advancement toward the good. Haenni had set up CEI as a *laboratory for the future*, and invited his students to be part of a great experiment.

Professors and students alike believed supremely in "never again"— the Second World War was little more than fifteen years distant, and the Cold War raging around them. (Indeed, the Cuban Missile Crisis had determined the shape of their first semester: as he listened, incredulous, to the radio reports, about the Phantom jets lined up in Key West against the Soviet missiles in Cuba, François recalled those intense, sun- and drink-filled days, the pink hotel, its electric-blue pool, Broussard languorous, the bustling, flag-draped boulevard in Havana, the steamy blood reek of the cock fights, all of it forever melded in his memory: How could these delicious contiguous worlds clashingly erupt? Were they not, simply, the world as it was?) But more than that, here in CEI's mansion in Conches, they sought to create a *better* world: they believed, as fervently, in that possibility; the positive was as central a tenet to their worldview as the negative.

Hence the impending visit of Raymond Aron, of the great pendulous ears, naked pate, and kind eyes, at once mirthful and sad, a thinker unquestionably brilliant and, in these global matters, an important voice. Anti-Communist, Aron was in favor of the European Common Market, but skeptical; a supporter of de Gaulle, but not uncritical; and newly director of the European Sociology Center, funded by the Ford Foundation, aided by the young Pierre Bourdieu. François, whose father had raised him not only to revere Aron but also with the strict instruction not to venture opinions in ignorance, had set himself the man's full bibliography in preparation. The January 17 event would involve an early-evening lecture, followed by a small dinner, to which he and Barbara were invited, but which he now understood he would attend alone.

François wanted so badly to make an impact on the great man. He knew himself to be too reticent, too deferential to authority—a failing dunned into him by his volatile military father—and understood that lesser men often made a stronger impression. But what could he do now, about who he was and had become? Always an outsider, always on the wrong foot, he saw and understood more, he was sure of it, from his place on the edge; but he so often couldn't command the necessary attention. He could not abide small talk; he couldn't bullshit; he had no silken tongue and could not tell a lie. Above all, far now from Gardel and Servier, from Mouret and Broussard, with no longer any country, his family decamped to the other end of the earth, nor with even apparently much of a wife, he had no tribe: he was alone. Each man had his nature and his lot, and must live with it.

Would Barbara come back now at last? In her letter she'd spoken about her mother's prolonged emotional strain, and how alone she'd be when Barbara left. She'd reminded him how much work it would take to wind down her father's business, and how her mother needed her help. But somehow, at heart, it still felt to him like an excuse; he still felt abandoned.

He'd already rejected the pious voice of the radio announcer; the only other option was the record player, of course. Music did not possess him, though, the way it did some, and he selected instead from the record rack Tom Lehrer's funny songs. They'd been to hear him live at Harvard, where his satires were all the rage, and his biting, sprightly lyrics. At the sound of Lehrer's voice, François felt a wave of nostalgia and regret. He poured himself a small scotch (Was it too early? It was almost dark, after all) and lit a cigarette and sat on the stiff little sofa in the gloaming, feeling sad.

When, a few minutes later, the phone rang, he startled, and his hand shook a little as he lifted the receiver. For a wildly hopeful moment he thought it might be Barbara, calling back.

But it was Riley on the line, bonhomous Larry Riley, his favorite among his fellow students, a Canadian joker a few years his senior who worked for Alcan, with a beautiful wife also named Barbara (they'd joked about it, their blooming Canadian Barbaras, though Mrs. Riley went by Babs) and already a handful of kids—five!—with another due in the summer. (Needless to say, they were Catholic; their family size made perfect sense to him, but when they'd first met, Barb had made some snarky comment. She got that from her mother, who was prejudiced against Catholics as well as against all Europeans except the British and maybe the Swiss, which made him doubly reviled.) Riley was inviting him to supper that evening.

"We were just talking about you," he said, "Babs and me. The kids are driving us bananas—I took the afternoon off to take the boys for an outing, and they practically beat each other up in the car. I said to Babs, If I don't get some adult conversation I'll explode, and she said, Call up Frank. She says we've got plenty of fish pie to go around, and there's even some vanilla ice cream and a decent bottle of wine in the house, exceptionally. Whaddaya say? I can pick you up in half an hour."

THE RILEYS' LITTLE HOUSE, a modern bungalow behind a formidable hedge in Chêne-Bougeries, around the corner from the elementary school the kids attended and a few blocks' walk from the Institute, was the opposite of François and Barbara's apartment. Where theirs was sparse and impersonal, the Rileys' place was bursting with the junk and detritus of family life: a stroller under a canvas tarp on the porch ("Can't risk a snowdrift in baby Sally's barque!" said Riley) and a pile of snow boots, little and large, in the front hall. The closet could barely close over the array of ski jackets and snow pants, so Riley simply hung François's overcoat over one of the doors. The air was warm and fishy; the boys' treble racket at the dining table competed cacophonously with some big band jazz—Ellington, maybe?—from the living room. Maryanne, the elder daughter, a slender dark-haired girl of ten or eleven with her mother's bright blue eyes, wearing a large red apron, admonished her little brothers from the kitchen door: "Pipe down, kiddos. Our guest is here." Having carefully wiped it on her front, she came forward with her hand outstretched. "Nice to see you, Mr. Cassar," she said. "I'm just finishing giving baby Sally her supper, and the boys are pretty well done." She cocked her head toward the kitchen. "Mum'll be out in just a minute."

Her big brother, David, gangly in a ski sweater, his voice about to break, emerged and also shook hands before retreating to his bedroom.

"We'll give the girls a few minutes to prepare the second seating." Riley smiled as he shepherded François, after a quick wave at the boys, into the low-ceilinged living room, from which, mysteriously, all traces of children had been banished. The jazz seemed suddenly civilized and calm. "What can I get you to drink?"

Babs joined them a few minutes later, smoothing her hair with a sweet, nervous gesture, and she kissed François on both cheeks—"Why not?

I'll happily pretend I'm French if I get to kiss *you*, François!" But she sat with them for barely five minutes before darting out again. "I'll just make sure the little boys are getting ready for bed. They're quite capable of horsing around for an hour, and that always ends with little Gregory in tears. Maryanne's a terrific help, but it's a bit like herding cats, you know."

"Or you don't know," Riley said when she'd gone. "Because, frankly, before it happens, you can't imagine it. You can't begin to. Never again a serious thought, never again a quiet moment. Absolute bloody mayhem." But he said this with a wide smile, incisors showing, and François understood that Riley loved being a family man, reveled in the chaos. "You just gotta believe that more life is . . . more life!" Riley said, raising his glass. "Bottoms up!"

After his first swig, he asked François what he'd been up to, and François shrugged, his self-deprecating shrug perfected long ago at Amherst. "Oh, just the prep for that Aron visit on the seventeenth. There's a lot to read. The new book's as big as a doorstop."

"Oh, brother." Larry rolled his eyes. "Tell me about it—how to ruin a weekend, eh? How'd you get roped into that one? Haenni couldn't have *paid* me, but poor you, you got suckered. I'm sorry to hear it, my friend. Probably a good thing Barb's still away, eh?"

As he said it, he remembered about Barbara's father, and grew solemn for a few minutes; but he couldn't repress his ebullience, and by the time Babs returned, the two men were laughing, hard and silently, shaking in their seats with their eyes closed and watering, over an exchange earlier that week between Manley Schultz and Bob Hawrylyshyn about the quality of the food at the Royal York in Toronto, where François and Barb had had their wedding reception back in '57. It served traditional stolid fare of no culinary account, fruit cup and iced cantaloupe to start, or prawn cocktail if you really splurged, doused in a cocktail sauce that mixed mayonnaise with ketchup. Then chicken or steak, equally overcooked and dry, or rubbery scallops in a floury wine sauce. And Black

Forest cake, with its nasty layer of cherry jam, the provincials' emblem of luxury.

"You'd think it was the Tour d'Argent," Riley giggled, wiping his eyes, "the way Manley spoke—"

"My dears, dinner is served, such as it is. Our Friday fish, I'm afraid, François." Babs's apology was sheer politesse. "You'll have to come again on a steak night."

"Babs's beats the Royal York hands down, I promise."

She kissed him on the lips for that.

The two of them laughed a lot. They had so much fun. Their lives were clearly overwhelmed—François could hear the little boys' voices rising down the hall long after their bedtime, poor Maryanne telling them to be quiet or they'd wake the baby, and Babs all the time with half an ear in case she'd have to dash—but they didn't mind it, either. They wanted all these kids, adored them. They had their own traveling circus, as Riley put it—"We don't need any other friends," he joked. "We made our own. Literally!" And both of them erupted in laughter, as though he'd said the funniest thing ever.

Did François have fun like that with Barb? He thought they did; they used to. But maybe it was too long ago now—the past couple of years hadn't been easy. He sometimes felt she simply didn't *like* him enough, found him needy, greedy, smelly, too male, his hands like paws, his desires overbearing, as though she'd wanted a lapdog and been sent a Saint Bernard. And yet he knew that in the gamut of men he was fastidious, continent and discreet, always clean, didn't belch or pick his nose or even swear, particularly. Was he unappealing? Was he unfunny?

BACK IN HIS lonely bedroom with the shutters drawn and still the occasional sounds of night traffic on the Route de Malagnou outside, lying in his pajamas smoking a final cigarette in the dark after he'd brushed his teeth, he turned his thoughts instead to the positive: the Rileys were proof that parenthood wasn't the end. Barb had always said they'd never do anything interesting again once they had kids; but the Rileys had moved halfway around the world with five of them and were still able to invite a friend to supper at short notice. Proving it was all about your approach. Maybe Barbara wasn't as readily maternal as Babs; maybe he'd be less easy a father than Riley; but they wouldn't have six kids anyway. They'd left things too late already for that. Besides, how could they afford it? But two or three—just two, even. If she'd agree to it. If she came back. Couldn't they have as happy a family as the Rileys?

His other thought, before falling asleep, was of Riley himself, of his easy generosity and kindness. They'd known about Barb's father's death, they'd known he was alone in Geneva; they'd surely been exhausted at the end of their long week, so many kids, so much mess and noise all the time, the baby barely over a year and Babs pregnant again. And yet they'd made it seem like he was doing them a favor by coming over. Not just by saying so, but by seeming genuinely happy in his company. Friendship, he thought, was like a mirror: the other person reflected back to you an image, a version of yourself, hopefully a version in which your better features were accentuated. With the Rileys, he'd felt funny and interesting, a fine listener, an appreciator, forgetful of his shyness, wholly without bad temper or insecurity. He'd been someone he liked, a version of himself that Barbara liked— he'd been, indeed, like his hosts.

Larry Riley, he thought as he fell asleep, might not see all of him, his strangeness and isolation, the many ways he could never belong. He wouldn't see how much Aron mattered, in the world or to François. And Riley wouldn't ever understand how much it pained François, the following week, that Aron, after answering François's questions on the dais with such gusto, seemed utterly uninterested in conversing with him at the dinner afterward. Like he was a little guy, a nothing, which inevitably raised, for François, the possibility that he was those things. François, seated across the broad table from Aron, tried to engage him when the waiters were setting down the foie gras, hoping to continue the discussion about de Gaulle's just-announced opposition to Britain entering the

EEC; but Aron merely nodded politely and turned to speak quietly to Haenni, beside him. François tried a second time over the pigeon, but Aron, preoccupied with discreetly removing bits of shot from his mouth and placing them on the edge of his plate, perhaps didn't hear him properly, and didn't even look up. The third time was barely an attempt, really: François, ashamed, stumbled and retreated, articulating only in his head his observation on the potential consequences of the growing importance of English as a global language.

HE RETURNED THAT NIGHT to the Route de Malagnou despondent— How could he have blown his chance to make an impression? How could he be such a nonentity?—and rapidly downed three whiskeys before falling, his finest dress socks still on his feet, into his lonely bed. He would have talked to Barb about it, he would have allowed himself that—she should have been there with him!—but knew that now he never would. Riley, who would never see him crushed that way, wouldn't have understood if he did ("What's got you down, Frank? Chin up, life's beautiful!" he'd say), and François was glad of it, really.

But what Riley did see he accepted and appreciated. Just like that. He didn't demand more; he was never disappointed. A true friend. For almost fifty years, across continents and through joys and tragedies (oh, when Larry's boy David died in a sailing accident, and Larry called, and François got on the plane and went—), Larry Riley would remain his closest and truest friend. What could a conversation with Raymond Aron matter in comparison to a conversation with Riley, of which François was granted so many?

And as if the divine would bind them only ever closer to the end, Riley would share with Barb the awful fate of Lewy body dementia, both these beloved humans turned practically to stone, their minds still moving incommunicably behind the frozen statues of their bedridden bodies. François would not—could not—stay to witness this in its entirety—he could not bring himself to visit Larry in Ottawa after he could no longer speak, when Babs, a nurse by profession, sat and held his hand and read to him for hours each afternoon ("I know he's still in there," she whispered down the phone, as if sharing a secret)—but he knew, as he knew from Barb's neurologist in Greenwich, what lay in store, for his friend as for his own wife, the unbearable loss of it all. Riley would die just three months and ten days after François, and Barb, though still animate, could not understand what had happened to either of them, nor what it meant, both men, long lapsed in faith, suspended between belief and unbelief, hoping still to share some laughter in the afterlife.

PART IV

SYDNEY, AUSTRALIA

When we came home from the weekend trip with Daddy and Grandma, Michelle's little brother was dead. But that wasn't why I slept on the terrace. I started sleeping on the terrace a lot earlier, when it was still warm, because of the burglar. Not right away after the burglar, but soon, because obviously it was the safest thing to do. I didn't tell Mummy or Daddy or even Loulou because they would make fun of me and tell me not to, and I had to wake up earliest to climb back in the window before anybody else got up; but seeing as it was my morning job to waken Mummy anyway, that wasn't hard.

When Grandma came, I felt safer, even though her room was the farthest away, and I felt okay for a while to sleep in my actual bed. But after our trip and Michelle's brother, I went back outside. It was winter, almost the winter holidays, and the red tile of the terrace got very cold and the air in the night sky even colder, dark air with occasional moths and faraway stars and a sometime moon, with the scary quiet rustling in the fronded banana tree by Grandma's window downstairs. But if anybody climbed the metal grille outside her window, onto the terrace, I would hear them first, so it was important that I be there. I was the secret night watchman. I waited till everybody went to bed and the house grew quiet—sometimes I had to wait a long time—and I carried all my covers with me, along with Michka my bear, when I climbed through the window and wrapped myself round and round like a radish, with only my head and hair sticking out. I did not ever get caught.

I am in Miss Clark's third class, our first year up at the big school in Rose Bay, next to the convent. Two girls' schools side by side: our uniforms are gray and gold, theirs a beautiful turquoise. Miss Clark has a mean reputation, but she has never been mean to me. And since Michelle's brother she makes an effort with everyone. She has a square face with greasy skin and spots, and her hair is often greasy too—she isn't pretty, clean, and soft like Miss Dixon or Miss Fields—and I think this explains her reputation. But really she is quite kind. For example, when she is the playground lunch supervisor she tries not to see you throw food away, so you won't get in trouble.

I try hard not to get in trouble ever—I think of it as one of my jobs, really, because my job at home is to make people laugh and to get along, which they won't do if they are cross with me. I'm afraid of so many things but try hard not to show it, because then I would be a bother, I would be trouble, exactly, in a different way from being naughty, but with the same result. I am trying always to be invisible but better than invisible, if that makes sense. You see, my mummy is very busy because she goes to Law School, and my daddy is often away on important business, sometimes for weeks at a time. Last month when we took Grandma to the Blue Mountains he was stopped for speeding and the policeman told him he needed to have a proper Australian driver's license instead of an American one, and he told the policeman he'd only been here for three weeks. When the policeman had gone, he laughed a little sheepishly and said, "But it's true, you see, I wasn't lying—we may have lived here since 1971 but I've never been in the country for more than three weeks at a time." We all laughed too, but Grandma, who sat between Loulou and me in the back seat, sucked her teeth in a disapproving way and fished the roll of butter rum Life Savers out of her handbag so we could each have one. This is often what she does instead of speaking her mind. "I have learned," she says with a wink, "to hold my tongue and to keep sweet."

When Daddy gets home he's tired and can be cranky, as Mummy calls it, though the correct word is angry, really. Sometimes he is most amusing, as Grandma puts it; but Loulou and I are afraid of his bad temper and hate it when he and Mummy argue. I am afraid of other things, too, like when he squeezes my hand hard for a joke and it hurts. But he also taught us to stand on our heads in the dining room at dinner, and he can wiggle his ears when he's silly, and he makes lots of bad puns that make us groan and laugh at the same time. He says he is a mushroom, "that's a fun-gus," like fun guy, get it? And he always says, when we say his jokes are awful, that we'll miss him when he's gone. When you think of it like that I am trying to be someone you don't really notice when I'm there, but who you miss when I am gone.

I am seven and three-quarters years old and in third class and my sister, Loulou, is nine and a half and in fourth class. Sometimes I tell her, "You are not the boss of me," but we both know that in all practical ways that isn't true. When she wants to be, she is the boss of me. For example, she decides our afternoons, since Mummy is at Law School three days a week and now we are big enough not to have a babysitter. Last year, whenever the babysitter didn't come, we had to drive with Mummy in her little car to the uni, kilometers away, a sprawling modern campus, all concrete parking lots, where she'd leave us by ourselves for an hour and a half in the ugly yellow-and-orange cafeteria. I was always afraid that strangers might talk to us, and sometimes they did (though nobody like the man in the park when Mummy and Daddy were playing tennis, who asked us to stroke the pet that lived in his trousers. It was mottled and bald with a few dark hairs. Loulou, always braver, did it; but I turned away). Mummy would give us coins for the vending machines, to buy chips or a Violet Crumble, but it's way better to be at home in our pink brick house on the hill in Woollahra which turns its back like a semicircular fortress to the world, and opens its windows only to the garden and the pool in the back. But of course the burglar got in through the garden, didn't he, over the wall from the neighbors', and he robbed them too. I am mostly afraid someone will ring the doorbell of our apple-green front door, and what will we do then? Loulou calls me a scaredy-cat, so I don't tell her I'm afraid. It is understood that she is strong like a boy and I am weak like a girl. I got my hair cut short, hoping it would help me have more courage, but it did not, and now I miss my braids, which made me look prettier.

This year, until Grandma came, Loulou and I would take the bus home together to Edgecliff Road and then walk the rest of the way. If Loulou was tired—she is often tired—she would have me carry her book bag as well as mine, one in each hand, the hard vinyl banging against my legs as I trudged along, while she marched purposefully ahead of me up the hill. But when Grandma saw this she told Loulou she mustn't do it again. Before Grandma came, Loulou always fixed Russian toffee for afternoon tea, which you make by stirring equal parts brown sugar and butter together in a pan on the stove, producing a gold-brown grainy lava that you pour into a square dish and put in the freezer until it becomes solid. Only often we couldn't wait that long and ate it still liquid, with a teaspoon each, trying not to burn our tongues. We weren't supposed to use the stove when Mummy wasn't there, but Loulou always washed the frying pan and put it away in the cupboard before she came in, and Mummy was too tired and distracted to inquire what we'd had for tea. In the same way, we weren't supposed to swim in the pool without a grown-up present, but when it was warm, from January to May, we did anyways of course. We share the pool with the kids next door, pretty Gretel, who is my age and more my friend than Loulou's, and her skinny little brother, Jamie, and we'd all four play Marco Polo or have diving competitions. Even if she was at home, their mother wasn't looking either.

Grandma is my guardian angel. She arrived in early June and she is leaving back to Canada at the end of July, a week after Grand-père and Grand'-mère and Tante Denise arrive to stay. I haven't figured out how they will all speak to each other because Grandma can't speak a word of French and only Tante Denise can speak any English. Daddy says

Grand-père really can speak it and understands everything he reads, it's just that he has a strong accent and people don't understand him. What use is that, I wonder? We don't write down what we want to say when we're actually with someone.

Anyway: Grandma arrived at the airport and we went to pick her up. We ran across the slippery terminal floor when we saw her come through the sliding doors, and I buried my face in her bright blue coat—her "mid-season coat," she calls it, because our winter is nothing like a Canadian winter—which smelled of her perfume as well as of the biscuity smell of airplanes and a little of the bitter bug spray they spray through the cabin before they let you disembark (we always cover our noses and mouths because Mummy says the spray is as likely to kill us as it is the bugs, but the smell sticks to you anyway), and from that very moment I believe my life got better.

As in: Grandma saw on the first afternoon, as she waited at our garden gate while we came up Rosemont Avenue, that I had to carry Loulou's book bag, and she said, "What's that about?" and then told her to "cut it out." "She's half your size," she said to Loulou, which isn't true, though I am smaller in every way, small even for my age, just as she is tall, dark as she is fair, "a study in opposites," Grandma said once.

But also, when we come home to Grandma, she prepares different snacks each time, while Loulou only makes Russian toffee and Mummy wants us to eat only apple slices and dried apricots, Grandma sometimes gives us Sara Lee chocolate brownies and sometimes meets us at the bus stop and takes us for ice cream cones, and other times she makes her special cinnamon toast and milky hot chocolate. It's too cold for swimming but she'll bring out a striped folding chair from the garage and sit by the birdbath in the shade of the banana tree while we build our lean-to and serve cookies on banana-leaf plates, or play at being doctors with our dolls, whom we bandage carefully and medicate with perfume samples from Mummy's bathroom drawer. And if it's rainy she hangs up our slickers in the bathroom and dries our hair with a towel, and we climb into her bed, one on either side of her, just as if we were visiting in Toronto, and she reads to us from the old *Girl's Own Annual*s that Mrs. Young gave us.

She's the only person guaranteed to stick up for me and that is why I told her about my jumper, which she calls my sweater. I hadn't needed it for ages but in wintertime my school blazer isn't enough to keep warm. The problem started a long time ago, maybe in March, some freakishly cool day when I took my jumper to school in my book bag. But obviously not a day when Miss Clark was the lunch monitor, because I didn't manage to throw out the banana. Mummy should know not to give me bananas, as I dislike them intensely. I don't think I'm such a picky eater but the only sandwiches I will eat are tuna-fish salad or salami and cheese, both on white bread with soft crusts, and still she gives us liverwurst or ham with butter, a sickening slick and milky mush, or sometimes even prawn salad, and all of these things I must secretly throw away.

Many mothers make horrible lunches and many girls throw them away. I do not know whether a teacher noticed this herself or whether Mr. Robbins, the man who empties the rubbish bins, told on us, but either way they stationed a teacher by the bins every day at lunchtime. Which is a disaster.

On the day of the banana, that banana, I don't remember who the monitor was, but they must have been paying close attention. They must have caught someone just as I approached, and it must have been impossible to get rid of the banana. So I put the banana in my book bag thinking, "I will deal with it later." But I forgot.

And I did not need my jumper nor did I think of the banana, and the two things sat together at the bottom of my book bag, and over days and even weeks, many times heavy items, like schoolbooks and sandshoes, pressed down upon them both. Too late, I could tell that the banana, now blackened, and the jumper, once gray, had got mixed up, now a single item with a strong, sweet banana odor. And then the odor faded and the jumper, in a newly glued shape that I did not dare take out of the bag, became stiff, like cardboard, in some parts.

Mummy would yell, I knew, because our uniforms are expensive, and I had been naughty and then careless—I had committed two sins—and I would be both trouble and in trouble, which, like I said, it's important for me not to be. (Loulou, who is braver, is okay to get in trouble; but not me.) So I didn't do anything. I kept the banana jumper, my one school uniform jumper, buried in my book bag.

Then it started to get truly cold. I had goose bumps all up my arms on the bus after school and I said I was cold, and Loulou said, "Where's your jumper, then?" It was in my bag right there but I lied and said I did not know. "Did you lose it," she said, but in a sleuthing sort of way—I knew she was thinking she could tell on me, and get me in trouble, so I lied again and said, "Of course not. It's at home." But then I was stuck because of my multiple sins, and did not know what I could possibly do to get out of my predicament. Lying out on the terrace in the night, or before, awake in my bed waiting for everyone to go to sleep, I worried about my jumper. I have so many things to worry about.

I do believe in God, if only secretly. I can't tell if Mummy or Daddy do, and maybe I believe for all of us. He sees in our hearts and He knows all the wrong things we think and do and have ever done. But if we are good and try very hard, we can hope He will protect us. Every night I say the Lord's Prayer and a special prayer for everyone in my family to be safe. Nothing feels safe unless I keep watch. I remember a time when I had no fear; and then suddenly came the time when I was afraid of everything, when I could see Death and Disaster hiding in every corner. I pine for the time when I felt free; I think of it as being like Adam and Eve in the Bible, only I don't know when I ate the apple. I cannot remember what changed or when, for me, I only know it's different now. When I was smaller I thought maybe *I* was God, or a part of God, but now I know this isn't right. Is God in us? Above us? With us? If He is all-powerful, why do such bad things happen?

Mummy and Daddy aren't God, obviously, but if Loulou is the boss of me, Mummy is our boss and Daddy the boss of us all. They can both get very cross and it feels like God's punishment, like when Mummy made my birthday cake but it burned and she threw it very hard on the floor—the crumbs flew everywhere like confetti, and the glass dish shattered—and she said, "I will never, ever make a cake again in my life," and of course it was my fault because the cake was for me; and I also sinned by being secretly selfishly saddest about not having a cake after all. Or when I was six and Daddy yelled because he'd come back from a long trip and Loulou and I ran down the stairs to meet him, all excited, and the first thing I said was "What did you bring us? What did you bring?" That was the sin of being spoiled. Of course I didn't really care more about my present than about Daddy, but I was, as Daddy said later when he wasn't so angry, taking him for granted. But you mustn't take anything for granted because everything can disappear. Like Michelle's little brother. He was here—so cute, I remember him, with honey-colored curls and big amber eyes—and now he is gone. Maybe she took him for granted and that is why God took him away.

But my jumper—a disaster. Then when Grandma came, and saw straightaway how it was for me, I knew I could tell her and she would not punish me. I went to her one Saturday in her room, where she was putting on her jewelry, and "Grandma," I said, "I have a problem." And without asking what it was, she said, "I will help you."

Several things I did not expect: I did not expect that the jumper would ever again be clean. It wasn't really, because one side came out darker than the other; but after she soaked it for a time in the plastic tub of warm, soapy water and spread it on a towel on top of the washer, it dried soft and fluffy again and, in most places, clean.

I certainly did not expect that it would be too small for me anyhow, and that I would need a new uniform jumper not because of my sins but because I had been growing all the while, invisibly.

And mostly I did not expect that while she did not for one minute waver in her ever-so-kind gentleness with me—she loves to stroke my hair and my cheek—Grandma got cross instead with Mummy. I realized as I listened from behind the door to the laundry that even as a grown-up, Mummy was still Grandma's daughter the way I am Mummy's daughter. "What kind of parent are you," Grandma scolded, "that your own daughter, that sweet little girl, is afraid to come to you? What is it she's afraid of? You should ask yourself *that*, Barbara."

The way she said Mummy's name, I felt such guilt. I wanted to rush in to explain that I never meant to get Mummy in trouble. I wasn't telling on Mummy when I asked for Grandma's help. But everything you do has consequences, like the teachers always tell us. Trying not to get in trouble or to be trouble, I had caused trouble. I was glad that Loulou didn't hear them talking also, as she would have told me outright that this was all my fault. She didn't need to; in my heart I knew. It would all have been better if I had just been brave and taken my punishment. It is also a sin to be cowardly, and I am cowardly in every day.

I was cowardly on the trip, too. We were only meant to go for the day, not overnight, and when we set out I felt no fear. Mummy stayed behind to do her homework for Law School. She stood at the top of the driveway and waved us off, while Daddy and Grandma and Loulou and I went on an adventure. Only later did it occur to me that we took the trip just so that Mummy could do her homework. It had never occurred to me before that we got in her way, that she ever didn't want us there.

Daddy loves to go for a drive—his car, a brown Ford, has four doors, unlike Mummy's car, and the back seat is like a little sofa. Grandma sat in Mummy's seat and Loulou and I in the back, where at first, as we always do, we squabbled about where the middle is. We drove west through the flat, wide roads of the suburbs, past rows of little houses, then fences and low square blocks and shops, petrol stations, and warehouses, out to the country. Mostly Loulou and I weren't looking—"You travel like suitcases," Daddy always says—because we brought our books. I brought *Tintin in Tibet*, my favorite Tintin book, because of course Tintin finds again Chang his dear friend who is lost, even though everyone believes it is impossible, and *Prisoners of the Sun*, which I also love, because they are saved at the end by reading, by a scrap of newspaper that tells them when the eclipse will come, and this makes the Incas think they are gods.

Tintin's adventures were more exciting than ours. We drove a long way before stopping for lunch at a pub in a small town called Berrima. Because we are children, Loulou and I went inside only to use the evil-smelling bathroom: the big square room, with a painted tin ceiling and windows on all sides but little sunlight on account of the wraparound veranda, was gloomy and cold. It had rows of tables along two sides, and a green-topped billiard table. In the pub I could see only men, dusty, big men with their sleeves rolled and muddy green tattoos on their hairy arms. A couple of them at the bar wore Akubra hats on the backs of their heads, even though you're supposed to take your hat off indoors. One was Aboriginal—he turned and smiled at Loulou and me, his white teeth bright against his dark skin—and everyone else was white, or, rather, red, as the men all looked like they'd worked outdoors in the hot sun forever. I expect that their necks were dirty. The only woman we could see stood behind the bar, hardly taller than Loulou and wiry, with blue veins popping on her forearms and a nose sharp as a knife, her eyes too close together like a weasel's. (Back in the car, after, Grandma shook her head and said, "That woman's had a hard life," but did not explain what she meant.) The weasel woman smiled at us too and poured us each a fizzy lemonade in a bulbed beer glass, and Loulou and I took our drinks outside and sat on the edge of the veranda with our feet in the dust. I had on my brown suede zip-up jacket, which got stained on the arm by fairy floss at the Royal Easter Show—it was Loulou's fault—and my red sandshoes that turned brown in the dust, and the lemonade bubbled up and sprinkled my upper lip, like the foam from a wave. Grandma and Daddy brought out a bag of cheese-and-onion crisps for sharing, and cheese sandwiches wrapped in waxed paper, brown bread with butter. I don't like brown bread and I don't like butter on my sandwich—at school

I would definitely have pitched it in the bin—but I was afraid they would be cross so I ate all my sandwich except for the crusts. Daddy ate his sandwich pacing around the parking lot, not talking to anyone, stopping to examine the different cars and utes.

While we were eating, the two men in Akubra hats came out, hitching up their pants and laughing, and got into a Dodge truck the color of mint toothpaste, the Black man at the wheel. He waved out the window and honked the horn as they pulled out onto the road, sending us a cloud of red dust.

Back in the car, in addition to her comment about the lady behind the bar, Grandma said, "They don't fly very high around here" and "All descended from convicts, are they?," which made Daddy laugh.

"That's not right," I said. "The Aborigines have been here much, much longer, thousands of years before Captain Cook."

"Of course, dear," Grandma said. "But that was just one fellow."

"And the way things work around here, that probably wasn't even his truck," Daddy said. "He'd be a hired man on a local station."

I wanted to tell Grandma about the Dreamtime, about the Aboriginal myths Miss Clark was teaching us at school, about the Rainbow Serpent and how the kookaburra got his laugh, and the Mimis, like fairies, who live in rock crevices in the outback. Loulou shook her head at me: the grown-ups didn't want to hear, and it was hard, anyway, to try to talk from the back seat to the front. But I insisted.

"Grandma," I said, leaning forward between the front seats and tapping the shoulder of her blue cloth coat, "do you know the story of the Rainbow Serpent?"

She patted my hand. "No, dear. Sit back all the way in your seat, okay? And tell it to me in your loudest voice."

The Rainbow Serpent, who is both a girl and a boy, came up from underground and made the world the way it is. Before, the world was flat and empty, and by slithering all over the land, the serpent made the mountains and the valleys. Then the Rainbow Serpent summoned the frogs and tickled their bellies to make them laugh—there's a different story about a particular frog named Tiddalick, but that's later—and when the frogs laughed, water came pouring out of their mouths and created all the rivers and streams and lakes. And the Rainbow Serpent said, See how nice it is? And if you obey me, you can be a person, and if you don't, you will be a stone.

"I would much rather be a person than a stone," said Grandma with a little laugh.

"But you need to know," Loulou said, "that the story doesn't end there. Because in Aboriginal Dreaming, the Rainbow Serpent is the boss of us all, like the Greek God Zeus, and even now the Serpent moves from water hole to water hole around the bush, and if we anger him, or her, or whatever, then great storms will come, and floods, or droughts."

"Aren't their myths fascinating," said Grandma. "Who'd like a Life Saver?"

"It's an extraordinary culture," Daddy said, his eyes on the road. "While you're here, we've got to make sure you hear their music—the didgeridoo. Look—" He pointed to the open land ahead on the right, where among the wavering dry grasses a posse of kangaroos grazed lazily. "Wildlife in the wild."

Grandma peered out and turned her head as we went by. "Funny creatures," she said, "with those huge back legs and thumping tails, and then those little shrunken front paws, like hands . . ."

"I wonder what the local myths are"—Daddy had forgotten the kangaroos and was thinking again about the Rainbow Serpent—"because the valley near here was a lakebed once, hundreds of thousands of years ago, and around Wee Jasper they go fossil hunting. According to the guidebook, there's an abundance of extraordinary marine fossils."

"Who cares about fossils?" Loulou said. "They're dead, right?"

"Very dead," he replied. "Though they tell us what used to live here."

"Like the Rainbow Serpent turned them to stone," I said.

"Just like that," Grandma said. "Fossils are basically stones."

I returned to my reading, satisfied. Not long after, we stopped in Goulburn to visit an old house. I like museums that are houses the way people used to live in them—Grandma took us to one in Toronto where the tour ends up in the kitchen and a lady in a long skirt with a bonnet on her head puts out trays of soda bread with butter and blackberry jam, all of it made the old-fashioned way right there with a butter churn and boiling the blackberries on the wood-fired stove, with sugar. We wondered whether she wore the dress to churn the butter or was actually lying and bought it at Loblaws. I loved that museum and hoped this would be the same, but it wasn't. It was just an old house full of furniture and dusty knickknacks and a fat lady with a loud voice who seemed to live there, who droned on boringly about the history—it was built in 1857 and then it was a pub, but it became a boarding school after, for boys only, called Garroorig-ang. She told us some pupils had got famous, including one who became a cricketer and another a painter who went to Paris and was friends with Van Gogh and Monet whose pretty-colored pictures Daddy reminded us we saw at the art gallery in Paris with Cousine Léone, and a third who fought valiantly at Gallipoli in World War I, which is why we have Anzac Day. And all those people were at one time in this funny musty house in the middle of the bush, wearing formal clothes and drinking tea, living as if they were in London or Bristol. Then it was a private house where some daughter of the explorer Hamilton Hume had lived. The fat lady, who wasn't even wearing a costume, asked us if we'd learned about Hamilton Hume at school and when we shook our heads she seemed shocked. And there weren't any snacks at all, not even for sale.

Loulou and I got back in the car grumpy and hungry for a snack, but without Mummy we didn't like to say so. I had finished *Tintin in Tibet* and started *Prisoners of the Sun* by the time we got to Yass, where Daddy stopped for us to walk around and get some afternoon tea. We bought lamingtons in a plastic package from a general shop next to the petrol station, where the young man wearing dungarees ("Is he a mechanic?" Grandma asked disapprovingly. "Probably," Daddy replied, amused) pointed us the way to the town park, by the river, so as, Daddy said to him, "the kids can run around a bit." We'd been "cooped up in the car," he said, which was an expression Mummy and Grandma used, and I had the feeling he was trying to show Grandma that he knew what to do with us, even though we never did anything just with Daddy, not ever.

The park by the river was named after Banjo Paterson, maybe because he was from there, but Loulou, who sings well ("Such a pretty voice," Grandma says each time, and never for me, because I sing off-key, so I don't sing at all now) burst into "Waltzing Matilda," and sang all the verses. She danced around on the brown grass, twirling while she sang, so I did too, but even with my jacket zipped to my chin I was shivering—the weather had gone cold and gray, and fat drops started to fall from the sky.

Back in the car, I lay down halfway on my side—I did not put even a finger or hair over the imaginary line down the middle—and I closed my eyes, tired by the long drive, lulled by the roar of the motor and the calm voices of Daddy and Grandma, whose words I couldn't quite make out. It was already late when we left Yass, though nobody spoke of the time, and I reckoned we were headed home, back to the highway. But later I understood that Daddy wanted to try to see the fossil field, near Careys Cave, he said. I guess he'd wanted all along to go there, though he hadn't mentioned it before. Or maybe he'd mentioned it to Grandma—Loulou and I just do as we're told. But I guess he didn't count on how quickly the winter darkness falls, and he didn't count on how fast and thick the rain would come down, and when I opened my eyes the world outside was fully black, and the green neon *D* from the transmission hovered in the sky, reflected on the windscreen, blurry from the raindrops. The wipers made their soothing swishing sound, but there was a grave hush in the car: headed downhill, we were barely moving. Sitting up, I saw that Loulou sat up very straight on her side of the car, behind Grandma, her eyes looking ahead, wide open. Even in the dark, I could see how blue they were.

"What's going on?" I asked.

"Nothing dear," Grandma said from the front. "Would you like a Life Saver?"

Loulou nodded at the road. We didn't answer Grandma. I could see the row of taillights, four cars at least, maybe five, and other cars joining the queue from another, smaller road on the right. Gum trees loomed on the verges. The rain fell hard, but it's good to drive slowly when it rains; that wasn't the problem. The problem was a gushing river over the road at the bottom of the hill. Grandma had a map open on her lap but it was useless, too dark to see.

"Thank goodness it's not the real river," she said. "We crossed the big bridge a kilometer or two back."

"It's real enough," Daddy said, and I could tell from the sound of his voice that his mouth was a thin line.

"It's what they call flash flooding," Grandma explained, without turning back. "It's when the rain comes down too fast for the ground to absorb it. Especially when it's dry."

I thought of the field of wispy brown grass, earlier, on which the kangaroos had so thoughtlessly nibbled. "Are we going to be okay?" I could hear that my own voice was small.

"Don't be silly, fraidy-cat. Of course we're okay." But Loulou didn't stop staring through the windscreen, and Daddy and Grandma seemed not to have heard me.

One at a time, very slowly, each car inched forward to the bottom of the gully and pushed its way, surging smoothly through the water that fanned out around it in waves perpendicular to the rushing current. Each time a car pulled through the river and up the far side of the hill, I wanted to cheer. It didn't look so hard; but both Daddy and Grandma were taut with nerves. Another, and another, a ute, the water barely sucking the top of its fat tires. The rain drummed furiously on the roof and around us. So much water.

"I just don't want to flood the engine," Daddy said, as if to himself.

"They're getting through okay." Grandma sounded a little uncertain.

"The last three have been trucks," Daddy said.

I knew it was time to pray. I was the night watchman, but I hadn't properly kept watch. I was the storyteller, and made the stories end happily. I had allowed myself to fall asleep, as if we would be safe, and we were not. But should I pray to Jesus or to the Rainbow Serpent, who was surely—we all understood this—the God in charge here? This valley had been a lake and perhaps now again would be a lake, if the Rainbow Serpent deemed it so. Was I allowed to pray to the Rainbow Serpent, who was not my God? When I'd crossed myself with Holy Water in Grand'-mère and Grand-père's Catholic church in Toulon, Loulou had hissed in my ear, "You can't do that! You're the wrong religion!" Because we are C of E. So maybe I should pray to Jesus, who loves the little children? Might Jesus and the Rainbow Serpent know each other? Would they get along? I thought of Mummy, back home in Sydney, sitting in the armchair in the living room or making tea in the kitchen: she didn't know we were in danger. She would never have let us go if she'd thought Daddy and Grandma couldn't keep us safe. Or maybe she herself wasn't safe, because we weren't with her? If I wasn't keeping watch, might not anything befall her? Maybe I was the one who kept people safe? In which case, I was present now and praying now and God and the Serpent would heed my prayers; but who was looking after Mummy? My breath shivered in my throat.

When it was our turn to go down into the dark water, Daddy changed the gear so that a green *i* floated ahead in the sky, on the windscreen, and he proceeded slowly forward into the gully. The rain drummed overhead and the river thundered around us, our tires made monstrous sucking noises and the waves we created made wide swishing noises, all of it an intense water symphony like being in a car wash in Hell. I thought of the book *The Water Babies*, and wondered what it would be like to dive under the surface and meet all the water creatures; but then I remembered that the little boy in that story turned out, at the end, to be dead and to have been dead all along.

By the time I thought this we were already climbing up the other side. Daddy put his foot on the accelerator and the Ford surged forward up the hill, spitting gravel behind us. The drumming rain now sounded like applause.

"Well done, François," Grandma whispered.

"That was pretty scary." Daddy was smiling now; I couldn't quite tell whether he was joking.

"How come? What could've happened?"

For a moment, neither grown-up answered.

"You just don't want the engine to get flooded," Daddy said. "Because then the car stalls."

"What happens then?"

"The engine has to be running for the car to go." I felt like he was answering me without properly answering: What did that mean?

"Yes, dummy, then the car stops in the deep water, and then the river carries the car away and we all drown," Loulou said. Then, scornfully, as if only I had been afraid: "But it didn't happen, did it?"

Thanks to my prayers and the Rainbow Serpent. "Where are we, anyhow?" Looking out the rain-spattered window I could see only blackness and wetness, the occasional looming pale trunk of a gnarly gum caught momentarily in the car lights.

"We're on the road to Wee Jasper," Daddy said.

"What happens when we get there?"

"God knows." Grandma sounded as though she was rolling her eyes.

"We'll look for a place to stay," Daddy said, as if it were obvious. "I don't think we can drive the whole way back in this. It's over three hundred kilometers."

"But what about Mummy?"

"Your mummy will be just fine. We'll call and tell her where we are."

A terrible mistake, an awful miscalculation. We were supposed to have been home for supper. What would she do without us? I kept my eyes open and my face to the glass on the journey to Wee Jasper, praying for her and for us too. Whenever you let someone slip out of your thoughts, when you weren't vigilant, that's when bad things could happen. It was as if a thread stretched from me to God and from God to Mummy, and if I let go of my end of the thread—well. Attention was everything; keeping everyone in sight, in your mind, was so important. The effort was exhausting.

At the lone pub in Wee Jasper—rightly called the Stables, Daddy said, because we were knackered, like horses—the white-bearded owner said he'd open up one of the summer cabins for us for the night. Behind the main building, four dark little shacks stood scattered between the trees. Before he showed us to ours—a single large room for the four of us, with a scuffed yellow lino floor and a fluorescent overhead strip light clotted with moth corpses, a large bed with a metal bedstead where Loulou and I would sleep on either side of Grandma, and a small bed under the window, a cot really, for Daddy, all stale and even the electric heater smelling of dust when the old man, rain puddling off his beard and his sheepman's oilskin, plugged it in for us—before he showed us the room, anyone could see that neither Daddy nor Grandma was happy, though what were they to do? It was, the old man said, the only accommodation available in town, and at least the cabin had a little green bathroom with a sink and a toilet, and anyways, we would sleep in all our clothes except our shoes under the blankets "of questionable cleanliness," as Grandma said with a sniff, adding, "This certainly *is* an adventure," in her darkest voice, and she gave Loulou and me each a butter rum Life Saver at the moment when we would have brushed our teeth—but before all that, when the old man's wife offered to make us scrambled eggs, fried bread, and bacon, a swagman's high tea, as she called it, Daddy asked if we might use the telephone and said we'd pay for the call, and the old man took us into their private kitchen and pointed to a large black phone hanging on the wall, with its receiver like ears, its see-through dial like a mouth agape, and its dangly twisted cord.

We clustered around as Daddy dialed, and he interrupted dialing to bat us away with his strong, square hand. It was the first bad temper he had shown all day, but Loulou and I knew, as we know how hard it is for ourselves to be good, that it took a lot of effort for him not to lose his temper, and that every so often the anger just had to come out, it couldn't be helped, like farting. So we stepped back and couldn't hear her exactly when she answered the phone. I was so frightened that she wouldn't answer, so afraid that something bad had happened to her, that I almost cried when it was my turn to speak. Her voice sounded tinny and small, but also sleepy, the opposite of worried.

"Are you okay? Mummy, is everything okay?"

"Of course, dear. I'm just at home doing my homework for Law School. What an adventure you've all had. Maybe you can write it down as a story, when you get home? You must be hungry now!"

I wanted to say, "We could easily have died," and I wanted to say, "You, too, could have died!" But just as I'm old enough to understand that everything is precarious—the word was in the newspaper; Mummy told me what it means—I am also old enough to understand that we are not allowed to say so, that we must all pretend that we aren't stepping, each day, along a tightrope over a fire-filled gorge that would at any instant swallow us. So I kept my terror and the weariness of my vigil to myself and I said, "Yes, very hungry, and the nice lady here is making us eggs with *fried bread*." (I didn't mention the bacon because I don't care for bacon. Loulou loves bacon but she detests scrambled eggs—it's the white squiggly slimy bits.)

"Don't eat too much of that, darling," Mummy said. "Fried bread is very greasy and you might get a tummy ache."

And then I handed the receiver to Grandma, who told her we'd been good as gold, and nobody ever knew that my emotion was as thunderous as the storm, and as vast.

WE DIDN'T HEAR about Michelle's little brother until Monday at school. The Rainbow Serpent came for him. By which I mean, he drowned. Not in the huge storm in the night on the road to Wee Jasper, in the Goodradigbee Valley, where the Murrumbidgee River runs from Lake Burrinjuck all the way to Canberra, but in Michelle's grandparents' bright blue kidney-shaped swimming pool in Parramatta, where Michelle's family had gone to spend the day on Saturday for a big reunion with her uncle and aunt in from Perth, along with her cousins Eric, Edwina, and Joey, the youngest, who is thirteen and who Michelle adores more than anyone. It's wintertime and when it started to rain the kids dropped their game of Stuck in the Mud—Michelle has a sister and three brothers, though that's just two brothers now, and she's the youngest but for Andy, the afterthought—and came inside to play ping-pong and listen to records in the basement. The grown-ups thought the kids had Andy, and the kids thought he was with the grown-ups upstairs in the lounge. But Andy, just three, went off by himself. Maybe he never even came inside. Maybe he was leaning over to pick up a leaf from the pool's surface, or following the ripples made by the raindrops, or maybe he was running around the rim and tripped, or— They didn't even notice he was missing until teatime, and it was Michelle's dad who saw him first, his red-and-blue jacket puffed up in the water.

I would like to make up a different story, one with a happy ending, the way our story had a happy ending. I imagine things all the time, but I did not imagine the story of Michelle's brother, until after it happened. She has not come back to school yet and as there's only a week till we break up I doubt she will. Mummy and Daddy both say I have an overactive imagination, but I believe that if I imagine the worst things I can keep them from happening, just like I believe that if I notice everything and think of everything ahead of time—if I tell the story beforehand—I can keep us all safe. Everything is precarious and the fire or the water can rise up and swallow us, or the plane can drop out of the sky, or a country can stop existing or a war can break out, or a person can go away and never come back. They can turn to stone if I'm not watching, or the burglar can slip in the back window and stand in your very house, in your parents' bedroom, looking out at you as you arrive home laughing from school and the library, and he can still be in the house when you walk in the door, just at the other end of the long hall, and he can swipe all your Mummy's jewelry, including her gold snake ring with the green and blue enamel scales and the ruby eyes, and get away down the trellis and over the back fence before you ever knew he was there. The vigilant one wins.

Everything is connected, if only you could float up high enough into space to see it, if you were God or the Rainbow Serpent. While we were in the car in the storm I knew something was wrong, I knew to be afraid, but I thought it was for Mummy when really it was for Michelle's brother. The little boy painter from the school in Goulburn didn't know yet in that house that he would grow up and go to France to teach painting and be friends with the artists my French relatives take me to see in a museum in Paris, any more than our relatives could know that just by chance Loulou and I would stand in the schoolroom in the middle of nowhere where that boy who would become an artist maybe first drew a picture. When *he* was a boy, maybe Banjo Paterson stood right on the riverbank where Loulou danced, singing "Waltzing Matilda," not knowing yet that he would write poems and that one of them would become a song that every Australian would sing and that Loulou would stand on that spot and sing it. In the same classes with Mummy, she says, is the first Aboriginal woman who will ever graduate in law from the University of New South Wales, and in a photo that was in the newspaper, taken at the airport, our daddy was walking in the background behind the American music star Liberace, who, the paper says, is the most highly paid musician in the world. My friend Lizzie's dad came to Australia from Budapest in Hungary during World War II, when he was a little boy, and my French grandparents have been to Budapest for a holiday and now they are coming here, and will visit my school, maybe even at the same time as Lizzie's parents, without them ever meeting. All the connections we see and do not see. Sometimes we feel alone but we are always more closely connected than we think. If you understand it all, maybe you can be like God, and protect everyone.

✤

SYDNEY, AUSTRALIA

B arbara with her Suzi Quatro shag and her navy windowpane wool bell-bottoms and her amber and seedpod necklace with its large beaten-silver medallion, with her snazzy Mini Cooper and her wide-mouthed laugh, accepting a puff of a joint from a fellow women's libber on the steps of the lecture hall, did not feel like the old Barbara, uptight and anxious to please, that she'd been for so long. For the past two years, she'd driven the fifteen minutes from the house on Rosemont Avenue to the UNSW campus as though the Mini Cooper were her chrysalis— transformation underway as she drove past Centennial Park, where they spent so many Saturday afternoons with the kids, past the Randwick racecourse, where she'd still never set foot (even though Loulou's best friend's father had a stud farm up in Mudgee and bred racehorses)— and she emerged a butterfly, untrammeled by the cares and stifling roles imposed upon her—by the kids, by François, by her *life*—so that by the time she unfolded her long legs from the tiny car, in one of the many sprawling parking lots surrounding the school—an institution that in its very architecture, its hideous, brutalist concrete, seemed also to have shed the fustier trappings of a more formal and constraining education— she felt revivified, exhilarated, free.

The drive home after classes might have felt like a reimprisonment, except that usually she was in such a rush, and so tired, fretfully aware of the girls rattling around alone at home—Loulou was very responsible, but nine wasn't really very big—of the food shopping still to do, of the acrobatics of trying to fit in her homework, those soporific case studies in their vast tomes, weighing down her tote bag, in between being a mum and a wife and a hostess and a housekeeper. Having her mother visit had made some aspects easier, others more challenging—nobody could evoke more effectively than her mother the trammeled and unconfident Barbara, even though she was forty years old, for God's sake, and not long to forty-one! But the kids adored their grandma, and she them, indulging them with endless sweets and late bedtimes after watching old movies on TV, and for Barbara the relief had been intense. She hadn't even recognized, until it lifted, the strain that had gripped her— worrying whether they were safely home from school, worrying about getting dinner sorted, whether François was home or, as often as not, not—and suddenly, all anxieties evaporated; plus she had help with getting the girls to bed, and much appreciated company, frankly, of an evening when François was away.

Mother and François had at some point over the years buried the hatchet sufficiently to be able to make each other laugh, theirs a sweet-and-sour relationship in which they needled each other but compensated for the nastiness with little acts of kindness: François brought his mother-in-law Chanel No. 5 or kid gloves from the duty-free at Charles de Gaulle, and she'd arrived in Sydney with, in her suitcase, a large tub of Bassett's Liquorice Allsorts, his favorite.

But Mother was one thing, and the French crew, PaManDe, all three of them at once, entirely another. At least they'd arranged their arrival so that she'd finished her exams—but barely forty-eight hours later they'd appeared on the doorstep, and she was pressed back into that ill-fitting costume of "*la femme française*," for which, as she always said to François, "my feet are just too damn big." (It was true: try finding shoes for size 10½ feet in that blasted country, where all the itty-bitty elegant women had itty-bitty little feet, and looked down their noses at her for being so galumphing and for having an accent when she spoke French, and for being from Canada, which they routinely disdained, and about which the only thing they ever had to say, cussedly, was *"Il fait froid là-bas, n'est-ce pas?"*) But here she was, halfway round the world, and when Monsieur and Madame Cassar showed up—mercifully now, with the kids, she could just call them "Grand-père" and "Grand'-mère" too—Barbara was cast immediately back to those early married years. Three-course meals, the linen napkins, the bloody siesta, the rituals as ineluctable as Catholic Mass. The agony of it. She longed to feed them fish and chips in greasy newsprint at four in the afternoon or, more blasphemous still, simply to skip a meal altogether.

And Denise, that relentless bonhomie, the constant smoking, the bottomless cough, her prominent yellow teeth like a nag's, and the whistling! Interminable, tuneless meanderings, while she was reading the newspaper or peeling potatoes or, as so often, just smoking and staring into space . . . and only this time had Barbara really noticed her infuriating habit of reading aloud every street sign or shop name or billboard they passed in the car—"Double Bay . . . Rose Bay . . . New South Head Road . . . La Traviata Italian Cuisine . . . Milk Bar . . . Morrison's Travel Agency: You can go anywhere with us! . . . Yield . . . Sun and Surf, it's all so great, here in Queensland Super State . . . Belton's Hardware . . . Stop . . . Kemeny Pharmacy, Schwarzkopf gives the world to you, in lemon lime and baby blue . . . Stop . . . Macleay St . . . Stop . . ." Stop! Jesus H. Christ, enough already.

Maybe she only did this in anglophone countries to practice her irritating English, the way she read only English-language books when she was with them, this time a recent bestseller, *Jaws*, that she'd carted all the way from France (having ordered it from W. H. Smith in Paris after reading a review somewhere), then all the way across the continent from Perth, where they'd landed—her copy of *Jaws* had been to Ayers Rock, for God's sake—and now it sat abandoned after her departure on the coffee table in the living room, hardly the right book, or perhaps too much the right book, for kids to see daily in a city where great whites regularly sidled up to shore bloodily to dismember the swimmers at Bondi and Manly.

Barbara hated even that Denise, every morning, greeted her by saying, brightly, *"Bonjour, ma beauté!"* because it reminded her each time how plain Denise herself was, a woman for whom, in early middle age, few genuine compliments could be found about her appearance; whereas Barbara knew—Hoped? No, knew—that her own looks, such as they were (like Ingrid Bergman's, she'd been told when she was young), had not yet abandoned her. Only a few weeks ago, Ben, the bearded young lothario in a tie-dyed tunic in her torts class, no older than twenty-eight, had asked her out and whistled through his teeth when she'd laughed— with the open-mouthed, head-thrown-back laugh she had only at the uni—and told him she was very much married, with two little girls, too.

"Aw, come on," he'd said, "that doesn't have to mean anything, nowadays. It's the age of free love! Love is not a pie!"

And she'd laughed some more, in a way she intended to be both non-chalant and definitively off-putting; though she'd thought about the exchange a hundred times since, wondering— But Denise, yes, plain and pious and full of exhausting sunshine (every meal Barbara prepared was *"vraiment délicieux,"* every kids' playground *"tellement agréable,"* every bloody supermarket aisle *"une merveille"*), yet now that both she and Mother had departed, Barbara wished them back again. Having Denise around, for all that she was a pain in the neck, was easier than being stuck just with her parents. Not only had François been able to take only a few days off work, he'd been saddled with an unexpected and unavoidable trip with one of the bosses (French, but from New York) to see the Comalco project at Weipa, on the Gulf of Carpentaria, with a quick flit down to Aurukun, where they had a new mining lease.

Bloody Péchiney and their endless appetite for bauxite—last year it had been the industrial action, a.k.a. strikes, at the plant that had claimed so much of François's time, and she'd wondered, from the vantage of her law student self, whether she ought not morally to have been supporting the workers rather than her husband, Péchiney's Australian CEO—but no matter, she simply resolved to keep her lives separate, the only traces carried across the divide her fashionable hairstyle and her clothing.

So now she darted around the kitchen with Julia Child open to the fat-spattered recipe for *boeuf bourguignon* that she ought by now to know off by heart, chopping and assembling and stirring and seasoning, an eye periodically on the clock to be sure to get the rice on in time, wondering whether yet to summon the girls to set the table and make the salad (Loulou was very proud of her vinaigrette). She'd got cooked prawns from the fishmonger for prawns in half an avocado to start, but had yet to prepare the avos, one of which was manifestly bruised. She'd got artichokes too, for another dinner—tomorrow, maybe?—so perhaps they could start with those, instead? Though they, too, needed preparation—why, oh why, the three bloody courses?

The kids were down the hall in their bedrooms but Grand-père and Grand'-mère—never, never could she bring herself to call them, as they'd desired, Papa and Maman—sat just through the wall in the living room: every so often she could hear their murmuring voices, and then again silence for a time. She was doubtless knitting—what had the old woman been thinking, to arrive with a knitted shawl for Loulou and nothing for Chloe, so that now, to make up for the dismay (Chloe's piteous expression, when she realized she'd been forgotten!), Grand'-mère was like the maiden in Rumpelstiltskin, working frantically against the clock to finish a shawl for Chloe before they left to return to France. Grand-père would be reading, of course, his glasses, always smeared with fingerprints, halfway down his nose, through which he breathed noisily, his little belly rising and falling beneath his buttoned crimson vest. . . . How could she feel so annoyed that they sat there enjoying the calm and private industry that was forcibly denied her? (By the time she ever got to sit down with a book, including a law book, her eyelids were so heavy she could barely hold them up, which was one reason she smoked in bed at night, to keep herself awake long enough to *read* something.) But how could she be so resentful of their quiet and at the same time so full of dread lest either of them should come around the corner into the kitchen and speak to her, let alone offer to help?

Surely not everyone felt, at her age, that their in-laws were totally alien beings with no idea, no way even of *conceiving* of who Barbara was? They loved to tell the story of how Grand'-mère, in Nice, before the war, had decided to try to learn to drive, and he, Grand-père, had agreed to teach her. But during the first lesson they quarreled, and during the second they quarreled again; and Grand'-mère, whom they all loved to describe as a "lay saint" (with a piety that in itself repulsed Barbara) had sagely announced that she would not, after all, learn to drive, because never in all their marriage had she and her husband quarreled, and she did not wish now to create an occasion for disharmony. Lay saint or damn fool? Honestly, the way they all talked about her, as if she had a halo, the Virgin bloody Mary, when all these years she just seemed to Barbara like an inscrutable cardboard cutout—her mother-in-law was, Barbara thought, a damn fool, the upshot was that the woman had never learned to drive a car and had remained all her life totally dependent. As Barbara said to her friend Carol, "She was born in the nineteenth century and she never got out of it."

As she'd tried to explain to Carol, "They're good people, fine, but they're so self-righteous, with their Catholic certainties and patriarchal pieties—literally, they believe women are put on this earth to marry and bear children! This is our whole purpose in life! And you'd think that François's sister—she's a lawyer, for God's sake, and single, and childless—you'd think she might say boo to a ghost, that *she* wouldn't be a male chauvinist pig like her father—but no! She toes the family line, her precious Maman is perfection itself, always respect the hierarchies and the husbands rule the roost." What chance did she, Barbara, stand in such a setup? Furthermore, as the mother only of daughters, she sometimes felt that the old woman, with her glittering clear eyes and luminous smile, pitied her, Barbara, almost as much as she pitied her own daughter, Denise, because while having children at all was a blessing, daughters were alas second best.

She called Loulou and Chloe as loudly as she could from the front hall, heard in return their muffled "Co-ming!," popped her head into the living room, where Grand'-mère and Grand-père toiled silently and apparently satisfactorily in the penumbra.

"Mais vous avez besoin de lumière," she said, dashing around turning on the lamps. *"Le diner sera servi dans dix minutes."*

They both looked up, smiled in assent, peaceably—but, she thought, with a tincture of condescension, and she felt her jaw set, a little, as she smiled in return, and withdrew to put on the broccoli and cut up the avocados—rather than manage the bruised avocado, she'd resolved to make a quick timbale, so there'd be enough to go around. Would Chloe eat it? She'd gone off avocado for a while.

Here they were, the girls in their matching blue jeans and jumpers, one navy, one red, as though even on holiday they wore a uniform, just a slightly different one, Chloe as always with the top button of her shirt done up because she was convinced that this way people would know she was a girl. Here, the bowl for the dressing, Loulou, then sending Chloe out the kitchen door to shake the washed lettuce in a tea towel to dry it, while Loulou got on with setting the table. They cleared, too, and often helped to dry the dishes, as it should be, helping that is, and yet some sense of indignation rose in her that this was all women's work, to which they were being trained from the get-go—had François ever dried a dish? He certainly didn't now.

How could she have tied herself to this strange French family in the first place? But if she'd married boring Luke Whitworth, as her mother had wanted—well, she'd be a member of the Granite Club with a house in Rosedale, but Mother also said he'd got fat and ruddy with drink, a pompous bore, and she'd never have seen a thing beyond Highway 401. François she still found sexy, even their fights seemed to her sexy sometimes, though with the girls looking on, judging them, judging him, in particular, sparring had come to seem less like foreplay and more like a showcase match, rigged for the audience. It changed the tenor of things. What was pushing them apart, at this point? The law school; his constant work travel; the girls themselves . . . maybe the question was, What *wasn't* pushing them apart?

Just as she called, *"À table!"* and heard the old couple muttering to each other through the wall—she pictured them hauling themselves up from their armchairs, in Grand'-mère's case a feat, as she was a substantial woman and becoming rather unsteady on her pins, adjusting their buttoned cardigans as they advanced deliberately to the dining room— just at that moment the phone rang, and of course it was François.

"Hello, Daddy!"

Carrying in two plates of avocado-prawn timbale to set in front of her in-laws, who, already seated, were busily fussing with their array of pills and ampoules, a veritable pharmacy alongside their water glasses, Barbara heard Loulou's delight at the sound of her father's voice: he was to them like a rare god, a firebird, largely mythical, and in equal measure amazing and terrifying.

"Not much," Loulou was saying, speaking quickly, "we tried out the skateboard in the park. . . . No, no, they didn't come. Grand'-mère was too tired. We went while they were lying down. . . . I don't know. Do you want to . . ."

Chloe danced at Loulou's elbow, trying to snatch at the receiver, and Loulou batted her away with just the gesture François used when he was similarly annoyed.

"It's dinnertime—they're already at the table," she was telling her father. They all knew it was out of the question for Grand'-mère or Grand-père to get up to come to the phone. ". . . Yes, here she is."

Loulou held out the phone not to her sister but to her mother, who took pity on Chloe. "She just needs to say hello, and then they'll go sit down. One second only," she said simultaneously to François and to Chloe, who was now crestfallen.

"Hi, Daddy," the little girl said, attempting brightness. "Loulou said I'm not allowed but— . . . Yeah, pretty fun. . . . I don't know yet. When do you come home? . . . I love you!"

Barbara shooed the girls to the table. "Tell them not to wait for me," she said. She had an eye on the rice, almost done; the broccoli still to drain—the cord would stretch if she held the receiver between her neck and chin—she'd just skip the first course, at this point.

"What did you say?" He'd said something surely important; she'd been pouring the broccoli into a colander in the sink, her face enveloped in a cloud of steam from the boiling water, and the receiver had slipped a little. She dropped the pot with a clatter and grabbed the phone so as to hear him better.

"There's been an accident," he said again.

"What do you mean? What sort of accident?"

"A head-on collision, two vehicles at an intersection on the site."

"Are you okay?"

"I was in the air, on the flight from Brisbane with Morisot, when it happened."

"What happened?"

"Basically a tractor—like, a bulldozer"—she knew he did not have the words in English; why would he have these words?—"hit a fuel truck. A full fuel truck. One guy in each vehicle."

"But you're okay?"

"There was an explosion. They both died, Barb. The two guys both died."

Barbara looked at her reflection in the window behind the sink—it was dark out and all she could see were the kitchen cupboards behind her and her own face, flushed from the steaming broccoli water. "Oh, François," she said. "I'm sorry."

"It's pretty awful. There hasn't ever been anything like this at Weipa—nor anywhere around here, for years—"

"Where are you?"

"I'm in the motel room. I've got to pick up Morisot in twenty minutes for dinner—the plant manager, Borromeo, was supposed to have us to his house, but I think we're just going to the one restaurant in town. We can't ask him—he's lost two of his men."

"And probably his job, too," she added reflexively.

François sighed. "I just—it's been a tough day. And with Morisot, too." The French boss, in from New York.

She'd put him in a taxi to the airport a little after six, she in her blue velour dressing gown, still in a fog of sleep; he distracted already by the tasks ahead, having gulped his coffee at this very sink and having left uneaten the egg she'd prepared. Had she even kissed him good-bye? She'd been annoyed, mildly, to have to get up an hour early, and annoyed to be left to entertain his parents. "I'm just so sorry. What happens now?"

But the rice! She turned it off, removed the pot from the element. She transferred the broccoli from the colander to the square serving dish, squeezed lemon juice over it, and salt, all with the receiver tucked again in the crook of her neck.

"The regional doctor flew in, about the time we arrived, but he was just pronouncing them dead. They were badly burned, both of them. The whole place is . . . everyone is a mess."

"I'm so sorry," she said again, but now Loulou was at her elbow, carrying two empty appetizer plates and asking, in a loud whisper, "When are you coming? When?"

I'm on my way, she mouthed back. Chloe lingered behind her sister, bearing the other two plates. She'd brought the forks, too, by mistake—they'd need new forks. Had Barbara ever put the wine on the table? Surely she had. She pointed to the broccoli and the rice. "François dear—I'm afraid—it's just that we're at table—your parents, I haven't yet—they're abandoned . . ."

François sighed again. He sounded deflated and small, none of the joker or the pugilist in him. She felt a surge of protective love, ever rarer for her. "I'd better let you go," he said.

She could tell he did not want to, but for his parents, he understood. She tried not to think that he'd be less understanding if she had Carol and Rob over for supper instead, or Laura and Pete. That didn't matter now—he was suffering.

"It's not your fault," she said. "You know that, right? This isn't your fault."

"Depends what you mean by fault." His voice was quiet. "I run the company here; the buck stops with me."

"You weren't even there when it happened—you don't even know these employees—"

"It's a bigger question than that. There are safety protocols—this should never even have been possible—"

"It'll turn out to be one guy," she countered, now desperate to get to the dining table. "One guy who was tired or high or had a heart attack or something. It's a freak thing. Try not to let it consume you too much. I love you. I've got to go."

"Of course," he said. "I hope I'll still be home tomorrow night. I don't even know whether we'll go to Aurukun in the morning. I'm not sure how things will go."

"I do love you."

"Me too."

She took up the *boeuf bourguignon* in the lidded tureen from their wedding china. She only ever used it when her in-laws were visiting; somehow their regular dinner parties involved silver platters rather than dowdy tureens. He'd sounded terrible, putting her in mind of the French word *aplati*—flattened. No need for the kids to know. She pictured a fireball—there would have been a fireball. She'd only seen photos of that strange terrain at the northern tip of Queensland, the blue water and the flat red earth, a vast spit of land all of dust, from which the bauxite was extracted, and they'd built the enormous plant in the middle of the plain like something from a sci-fi movie, all the metal silos and pulleys and extraction buildings themselves turned red by the dust; only the surrounding waste ponds were not red, filled with what, in the business, they ominously referred to as "liquor"—a slick rainbow of autumn colors, glimmering toxic striations of white and gold and russet and black. Before that, what had been there? Not nothing. It was an Aboriginal tribal homeland: before it had been transformed into a dystopian hellscape, it had been untouched for thousands of years, the people there living as lightly and resourcefully upon the land as the animals and birds.

Péchiney didn't own the plant, hadn't built it; they owned a subsidiary that collaborated with several other international companies on this project. Borromeo wasn't even François's employee, strictly speaking. Let alone the two men who'd died. It was a terrible, terrible accident, and awful that it had happened on this of all days, when François was visiting, and with Morisot too. She'd call Judith, his secretary, in the morning, to find out his revised itinerary.

The girls ate their beef in jig time, though Chloe kept chewing bits vigorously and then, rather than swallowing, putting them on the side of her plate, gray blobs of mush.

"It's too stringy, Mummy," she whined, and Barbara didn't have the vim to insist. They didn't want dessert. "We want to go listen to my new record, Mummy, please?" Loulou wheedled.

"You know whom you must ask," Barbara replied.

"*Grand'-mère, est-ce que je peux quitter la table, s'il te plaît?*" Loulou asked in a singsong, her pronunciation excellent. At this point, in spite of many after-school lessons in the living room of Madame Hiscock's diminutive flat, this was perhaps the only long sentence she could say in French.

Grand'-mère turned to her with that luminous smile, her eyes alight— but somehow vague, too?—"*Bien sûr, ma chérie.*"

Chloe repeated the invocation, less perfectly but with determination;

both girls cleared the dishes, brought the dessert bowls and fruit salad, kissed their grandparents' leathery cheeks, and vanished in a flurry, leaving Barbara and the elders, who would surely soon tire.

"And how was François?" Grand'-mère inquired with her almost quizzical formality. The conversation had reverted, without the girls, fully to French.

Barbara explained that there'd been an accident—a tragedy, she even said—in Queensland, that François was fine but shaken.

Grand-père, while plowing doggedly through his chilled melon balls (cantaloupe and honeydew, with a sprinkling of ginger and a sprig of mint), offered a memory of his own work life, a chapter she hadn't known, twenty years prior—also a fatal accident, this time in the Sahara, where he'd been responsible for an exploratory oil dig.

"I wasn't there either," he said. "I didn't witness the accident. I had nothing to do with it, but it's stayed with me all my life. The guilt, as if somehow I could have done something. They weren't even my employees—it was one of my employees who hit them, though, in a sandstorm. One of them was just a boy—he was severely maimed. The other had a small child, and he's the one who died." He shook his head and slurped another spoonful of melon. His wife, a Mona Lisa half-smile playing on her lips, seemed to be remembering happier things. "I had to fight for it, but in the end we gave the families some compensation," he went on. "But to me that almost made it worse. As if a life could be compensated for, as if money alone made things better."

"I'm sure the money did make a difference, though," said Barbara. "They were workmen—they had so little." How alien and depressing it all seemed. "François is worried that he's responsible for the tragedy. But he's not, of course, as I told him."

"No." Grand-père put down his spoon quite deliberately, though there were still melon balls in his bowl. "He is quite right that he's responsible. As the chief executive officer in the country, he must carry this burden."

"But it's not even a Péchiney project—it's a joint venture."

"Better that each CEO take responsibility insofar as he can. And he's got Morisot with him, so it's on Morisot as well. Even more so; he's the more senior executive. The problem of our century—or maybe just the problem of mankind—is a refusal to take responsibility, to lead properly. Look at Péchiney—that merger with Ugine Kuhlmann is one of political expedience. It's not a sound business decision, and never was—that's a failure of leadership right there. Péchiney was the flagship of French industry, our largest multinational corporation, and its electrolysis technology is the envy of the world—of the aluminum world, at least. And Ugine Kuhlmann? What are they? A failing chemical company with an interest in uranium, the nuclear sector."

Barbara tried not to look at her watch. Her mother-in-law dabbed at the corners of her mouth with her napkin, before rolling it up and reinserting it in its silver napkin ring. She smiled gently, encouragingly, at her husband, but offered no comment.

"And now, between the bottom falling out of the aluminum market and this massive oil crisis—" Grand-père threw up his hands. "Mark my words, if they don't come up with some alternatives, Péchiney will be in trouble."

Barbara was torn between not wanting to encourage him overly and, oddly flattered that he was telling her more than François usually did, curiosity about what he was getting at. "What do you mean, alternatives?"

Grand-père glanced at his wife, her encouraging smile. "I don't want to bore you. The nuclear aspect that Ugine Kuhlmann brings, yes, that's an alternative, or it could be. But fundamentally, it will mean investing in downstream products."

"Sorry?"

"Péchiney makes aluminum and sells it. If the prices of your product aren't competitive, what do you do? If you're small, you can get out of the business, put your investments elsewhere—but a company the size of Péchiney, thousands of employees, tens of billions of francs in turnover each year, it's like turning around an ocean liner. They aren't nimble.

They need a strategy that will be put into action over years, maybe a decade. They need leadership, a vision. The CEO I knew, Marchandise, had a vision, and arguably Morisot did, but Ugine Kuhlmann wasn't part of it. Somehow they got strong-armed.

"So the other thing you can do, if you can't get out of the business, is change your relationship to your product. It's hard to sell? So don't sell it, or sell it, if you will, to yourself: use it instead of selling it. Don't stop at the raw product; produce the finished goods. That's what the branch in Greenwich does, Howmet—engine turbines, hugely successful. Buy companies that make things—maybe construction materials, or kitchen goods, or, I don't know. More downstream."

As he spoke, Barbara was thinking as a law student about the implications of ever-expanding international corporations with carefully drafted legal relationships to their local subsidiaries on different continents, like a creeping vine making its way insidiously through the cracks in a country's walls. After all, the boards and directors of corporations were legally bound to act in the interests of the corporation, even if those interests were in conflict with the common good—like the tobacco companies still flogging cigarettes (in fact, she was herself even now smoking one) long after the surgeon general's 1964 report—that's to say, even if the corporation's success might be fatal for ordinary people, the leaders were constrained to act for business success. She thought of her pro bono student internship the previous spring, defending in court that poor girl who'd stolen a bottle of shampoo from the Woolworth's at the Warringah Mall—she'd stolen it literally to be able to *wash her hair* at the public showers at the beach; she slept rough, nineteen and a heroin addict, a runaway. A near innocent, hapless and alone. Miles from the corporations, and yet the system favored the corporations. But François would—did—call her sentimental, and even Grand-père, if he could see inside her mind, wouldn't, for all his devout Catholicism, take the side of Christian charity but would instead pat her on the head and tell her that it was the role of women to care, maternally, for each lost soul but that the brutal world of work was not for them.

Meanwhile, Grand'-mère's lids were fluttering—still, the luminous smile, as if pasted there, but she was falling asleep at the table. Her husband took her wrinkled hand between his two and brought it to his lips.

"*Ma chérie*," he whispered, reviving her, "*C'est l'heure.*" And to Barbara: "You'll forgive me for having gone on at such length. But I worry, rather, for François. I encouraged him to go with Péchiney, all those years ago. And certainly they've done well by him, by your family. But for the future, I don't know. We shall see." He smiled and shook his wife's hand as if greeting her. "*Ma chérie!* It's past our bedtime." He rose and helped his wife to her feet. She leaned, with considerable weight, it seemed to Barbara, upon his arm. "Thank you, as always, for such a delicious supper." He bowed slightly. "You will forgive us if we retire?"

"But of course." She, too, rose, then kissed their cheeks, that too part of the endless ritual of their lives—she'd probably kissed her mother-in-law more times than she'd kissed her own mother!—and waited until they'd withdrawn to set about clearing the table. She wouldn't call the girls back to help with the dishes—let them enjoy their records: she could hear the music vaguely, its regular beat, drifting down the long corridor from Loulou's room.

THERE SHE STOOD, herself suspended at the midpoint of her life, between the older generation and the new, in service to them both, unable to hold her husband (his familiar body, the smell of him!) in his hour of need—he would still be at supper with his boss, wherever they'd gone, and eventually back in his motel room on the Gulf of Carpentaria, over three thousand kilometers away, a room he'd told her before had orange shag carpet and muddy brown wallpaper, like being trapped alone inside a vat of bauxite liquor—and unable freely to be herself.

She thought of how her girls had clung to her when they'd returned, a few weeks ago, from the ill-fated adventure to Wee Jasper, their little arms in a monkey grip around her waist, their little silken heads (Snow White, Rose Red) pressed hotly against her ribs: their flesh, her flesh. She thought of her mother, now returned without company to Toronto, of the hemorrhage she'd sustained in her eye on the long flight, "macular degeneration" the doctor called it, "the wet kind," and of how she now would never again see clearly through her right eye. And she thought of this old couple that she resented so profoundly—but why did she? They were goodness itself, as her mother said of them. Even with their shortcomings, they were just people who loved her husband and whom he loved—he adored his mother fiercely, she knew—and they were aging—their little pile of medicaments at every meal, their unsteady steps, their game efforts, having traveled all this way, she over eighty, simply to sit at the table with their granddaughters and to kiss their fresh cheeks . . .

No, though the laughing youthful law student with whom tie-dyed Ben had flirted so breezily was only a few weeks in her past, he seemed, she seemed, a dream, a figment: in reality, like Gulliver, she was immobilized by so many little threads, the lines of love and obligation that had always made up an adult life. For her, at least, the Age of Aquarius was a lie: the rebellious voices suggesting another path were speaking nonsense. Love *was* a pie, and all her pieces spoken for.

As she stacked the dishes in the dishwasher, scrubbed the pots and put away the leftovers in containers in the fridge, leaving for last the washing of the wedding tureen, with its pommel-handled lid, a vessel of French culture unchanged in its design for centuries, she acknowledged, for just a moment, in her marrow, that just as she had been unable to resist the ties themselves—just as she had capitulated to marriage and, eventually, to motherhood—even as she struggled against her bonds, she couldn't fully regret any of it, any of them. She would never leave, would not, could not, break free of all that tied her. She would have to work within the limits of the possible; she hadn't the ruthlessness to do otherwise.

With the greatest care, she dried the porcelain tureen and its cumbersome lid with a linen tea towel and placed them gently upon their high shelf before setting off down the hall to chivy her darling dancing girls to bed.

✣

SYDNEY, AUSTRALIA

He had not been able to sleep—how could he sleep? As Lucienne snored softly in the darkened room, lying on her side beneath the mohair blanket, her mouth slightly open, making occasional fretful moans as he watched over her, he had dressed without turning on the light, all but his socks and shoes, and had walked outside in the gray dawn to step barefoot across the prickly lawn. It *felt*: his feet now so rarely touched the ground unsheathed, moving like large pale fish among the moist blades and tufts, his soft skin registering each pebble and earthy clod, each piercing burr that the little girls called "bindi-eyes." In spite of the pain, even relishing it, he made his way as far as the stone steps to the swimming pool. Its turquoise water, shiny in the gloom, made little sucking noises, lapping at the filters, as though alive. Alive!

He turned back to look at the house, a pink brick semicircle, all windows, with its wide veranda upstairs that made a shady overhang below. A bird rustled in the foliage by the wall, but otherwise all was still— almost. Suddenly, upon the veranda, he became aware, startlingly, of movement, what looked like a small tent rising from the ground— blankets, maybe? And then a head, short dark hair askew around a small pointy face—the little one. What was she doing there? Wrapped up like a mummy, she had seen him, too, and came to the railing, extracting a spindly white arm from her dark covers to execute a small wave. Then, with a smile, she put her finger to her lips—Shh!—so he did also, both of them committed to silence; then she turned, with her bundle of bedding, climbed through her bedroom window, and disappeared.

Weren't children funny. Did she make a habit of sleeping outside in winter? It seemed uninvitingly cold—his white feet had reddened from the chill dew—but perhaps to a child somehow magical. This little walled garden, visited by birds and butterflies, soothed by water, cloistered from the world, felt so safe, a haven. Illusory, of course, but why not? If only the girls could be permitted, for some time yet, to enjoy it.

He himself had not been so fortunate—he remembered the shabby row house off the Boulevard Trumelet in Blida, to which his family had decamped after his father abandoned them, when he was about Chloe's age. He had slept there in one bed with his much older brother, Charles, while Yvonne slept with their mother in the other—Marie Louise had already run off by then—and the one window at the front gave onto a busy street where horse-drawn carts and motorcars threw up dust, which coated the sheets and furniture and their clothes. By the time he was Loulou's age, the war had begun, and all the other fathers vanished just as his own had, leaving the children in a world of women and death.

Again, when François and Denise were small, no idyll to be found— the constant movement and disruption, the bombardments—thank God these little girls could sleep in peace and frolic in the grass or in the lovely swimming pool: What else had it all been for, was it all for, this endless struggle, if not for that?

He ran his broad, pale hand over his face; was it to keep from crying? Who would see his tears, besides the Lord, Who could see them whether he shed them or not? We trust in You, he said to the presence to whom he had given his life, like the birds in the air. We cannot know Your plans for us; we trust in Your wisdom. But grant me the fortitude. To see his little granddaughter peeping over the railing at dawn, with her impish smile and not a care—that was the proof of His goodness.

But for himself, the challenges, could he rise to them? His cheeks, in spite, remained dry, and he stepped back across the garden to the door to their room, where he would soon waken Lucienne, and they would prepare for their departure.

Strange to think that he would never again visit this house, this city, this country even: the family would not be here long enough. So many places he had been, and lived, and had cared about—he recalled with such joy the retreat L'Escale, at Broummana in the mountains above Beirut, those hot summer afternoons, or walking through the cedars to the little chapel in the fresh of the morning to hear the Mass in Aramaic. . . . He'd had a letter not long ago from lovely Charles Hélou, that wise and gentle friend from those days, who in the storm of 1940, as the British approached, had offered to smuggle him to the mountains for a while so he might retreat from the conflict—but what would he have done about Lucienne and the children? It hadn't seemed possible, as though he'd have simply been saving himself—though as with de Gaulle, in retrospect, he'd perhaps been mistaken. How different would things have been? Or the afternoons in Zannas's garden in Salonica, a glass of retsina or of ouzo, the urgency of their conversation and the dread, not knowing what was to come . . . where was Maliszewski now? Gaston had corresponded not long ago with dear Zannas, who'd lost his brother to lung disease in an Italian camp but had himself come home after the war and resumed running the Greek Red Cross. Or the nights at his half brother Guy's in Dakar, the big round dining table in that high-ceilinged room, the fan turning lazily overhead, Guy's fair British wife particularly lovely to look at by candlelight; or the pleasure of his drive to work each morning in Buenos Aires, peering out through the hazy, golden air at the beautiful boulevards, like Paris but southerly and warm—all of those places now locked, soundly, in his memory only; and of course at his heart, his beloved Algeria, forever lost but seared in him, not just the sprawling white city that he so cherished, arrayed on the hillside around the azure bay, but the hinterland, the mild arable fields, the rolling slopes, the rocky gorges, Constantine like a fairy-tale city perched on its spiny ridge, buffeted by winds, the glory of the wide desert, the Roman ruins by the sea at Tipasa or the great interior city of Timgad, all but intact, grids and columns and endless mosaics, and, of course, his treasure, springtime in Tlemcen, the almond blossoms drifting like snowflakes along the avenue, her hand at once cool and warm in his, palpitating like a little bird—he could feel it even now.

He must go waken her, would again take in his hand her precious fingers, as he had all these years whenever he could, his greatest solace, the meaning of his life. He'd known from the first that their marriage was special—as he'd said to her, in the darkest of the war, when all else seemed lost and they had nothing, "Perhaps our love is the masterpiece of our lives?" But only with a lifetime of observing those around him had he come to see how rare, in fact, it was to want nothing more than this, to feel this one person completed you, as if you were Platonic spirits, only together fully one.

And so, what now? He stroked her hair, ran his finger along the shell of her ear. She opened a brilliant eye, smiled, raised her hand to pat his arm.

"We travel today," he said. "A long journey."

She sat up, suddenly. "I'd forgotten—must we—"

"The cases are ready. I finished them last night. I've laid out your clothes for today on the armchair—" He nodded; she followed his gaze.

"Thank you, my dear one. I must—" With some effort, she slid her legs around and put her feet deliberately to the floor.

"Lean on me." He stood before her holding her forearms. Looking down, he could see her mottled feet, the ankles swollen, and his own feet, pale, the bottoms of his trousers darkened by the dew. How similar their feet looked; and how different. Did she remember that they were leaving early? Of course she must—he couldn't help but sigh at her back as she shuffled to the bathroom. It was now fully day, but gloomy, and the room felt weighted by his sadness. He sat at the end of the bed to put on his socks and shoes, and heard the water running and splashing behind the bathroom door, the dear sounds of her morning toilette.

Of course he had always *known* that the age difference between them would one day matter; he'd assumed this burden from the day of their first tentative confessions beneath the canopy of white blossom. But now, forty-seven years later, the reality was upon them. Her malaises and migraines had begun years before, before even they left Algiers, maybe even when the children were small, in Beirut or Salonica, so long ago anyway that these sufferings were simply part of her. And how long since she'd first complained of constant weariness—her legs were tired, she hadn't the energy. . . . At home in Toulon, to counter this, Odet, their devoted housekeeper—like a second daughter, they all agreed, to Denise's annoyance—brought her each morning at eleven a tray upon which sat an orange madeleine (her favorite) and a small glass of Coca-Cola, the sweetness of which she loved, into which they secretly squeezed the blood of a raw steak, to give her protein, and strength. (Almost a decade later, she would leave this world while eating her morning madeleine, in her armchair overlooking their infinite, glimmering Mediterranean; and he and Denise and Odet would save in a glass candy jar with a domed lid the remainder of the biscuit, her teeth marks visible. They would place the jar safely in the kitchen cupboard above the washing machine, next to the cereal boxes, the cocktail crackers, and the little tins of peanuts, and it would remain there for many years, until he, too, died.) But how long had it been since she stopped writing the letters? When the little girls were barely able to read, and certainly not in French, she had written them loving notes and long letters too, like the one in which she explained the history of Saint Bernard dogs, the saviors of the mountain passes. She'd always understood children and how to delight them—she hadn't for nothing been a schoolteacher in her youth—whereas to him the grandchildren seemed another species, like puppies, lovable but utterly alien. He looked forward to when the girls would be old enough and, inshallah, fluent enough to converse with him as people. But when did she stop writing? That was already a year ago, or even two. She now just signed her name, adding "with love," at the bottom of his letters—"*J'ai la flemme*," she'd say with a little apologetic smile. "I'll write more next time."

At least the knitting—this was proof, surely, that she was still okay, that she could count the rows and keep the stitches and follow the patterns? They would have to send Chloe's shawl by post, now, when they got back to France. If they'd only had the final week, as planned—it didn't matter now. Denise was all that mattered.

Lucienne emerged from the bathroom, fresh-faced, her hair combed, wearing the navy tweed skirt suit and cream blouse he'd laid out, all her jewelry on. Just the lipstick missing. "Wait," he said, "your lipstick," and found her purse and rummaged, then opened the tube and handed it to her. She smiled her beatific smile as she swiped on the lipstick without a mirror. Was it possible she had not remembered?

"Shall we go up for breakfast now?" he, asked, offering her his arm. She struggled each day with the stairs. She'd refused a cane, just as she'd refused a hearing aid, because she didn't want to seem like an old lady. He knew this was about her pride but also that these were gestures—sacrifices—that she made for him, as though after all these years, his continued love depended on her youthfulness and elegance. She still always sprayed her wrists with eau de cologne before bed.

Halfway up the stairs—he walked behind her, to make sure he could steady her if necessary—she paused to catch her breath, and turned and said to him, "We must trust in Him."

"Of course," he agreed, uncertain of the context.

"She will be fine. The doctors will take care of her until we get there, and with God's help and our love, in time she will be fine." She said this very calmly, as if he were a child who needed reassuring. Her faith had always been greater than his. So, she had not forgotten: she simply was not afraid. He felt, too, that she was telling him not to be afraid about their future either, hers and his: if you trusted in the Lord, He would protect you. You would not be subjected to more than you could bear. So this was perhaps the lesson of the day: to lose your wife—at least to lose her as you had known her, though still (for how long?) to be able to hold her precious hand—this was grief, but it was not tragedy. To lose your one daughter, barely over forty, a woman alone in life without a husband or children, as if her life had not yet quite begun—that would be a tragedy. That she had survived, that the doctors believed she would survive—already God had smiled upon them.

"It's a long journey," he said, referring to the travel that lay before them.

But her swift reply showed she was thinking not of themselves but of Denise. "The Lord will help her every step of the way," she said, putting her foot with triumphal certainty on the top step, on the checkerboard parquet of the front hall.

THEY'D BEEN SCHEDULED to sail home, a week later, on the SS *France*, in luxury, but were instead setting out at noon across the continent for Perth, there to pick up the long-haul flight they'd arrived on a month before, the so-called Kangaroo Route: Qantas to London, with refueling stops in Singapore and Bombay. Then from London to Marignane, almost home, but for the hour's drive to Toulon. Denise was in hospital in Toulon, thank goodness, and not Marseille, so they'd be able to drop their suitcases and wash before going to see her. But that was still far away, in space and time both.

Barbara had set the dining table, as she had every morning, and put out yogurt, fruit, croissants, toast, and jam, as well as butter, because she herself liked it, and she stood ready at their elbows in her plush dressing gown, with the coffeepot and hot milk, like a waitress, to pour into the coffee bowls reserved just for them. He knew that this was far from their usual routine—he'd seen them standing by the kitchen sink wolfing toast before running out the door—and he appreciated the effort.

François, to please his mother, wore a tie under his sweater even though he was not going to work—it was Wednesday, but he'd taken the day off. He tried to speak brightly, to make a silly joke about the Kangaroo Route, but his face, too, was haggard with worry.

What a week they'd had—the company's misfortune in Queensland, and now this. But even without these dramas, all wasn't well with this household, Gaston knew, could sense. Barbara was too taken with her law course, with some fantasy that she could will away her family responsibilities and return to the twenty-five-year-old self she'd long ago ceased to be. Not that he begrudged her intellectual stimulation—far from it—but he felt her priorities were awry. What did François break his back for, if not to be certain that his children could come home after school to their mother? And instead they were latchkey children, just as he'd been a latchkey child almost sixty years before, his mother always out at school till well after he got home, a deprivation François and Denise had never had to endure, even when Lucienne was on her own.

Though as Lucienne would remind him, they were not there to judge what they could not understand. He'd always believed that one should marry someone of a similar background and culture, to be as mutually comprehensible as possible: communication was hard enough, language so slippery (What did "family" mean to Barbara? Or "faith"? Or even "breakfast"? How could one know?), that the only hope was to set out from a shared starting place. But François hadn't felt that way, not ever. He had Gaston's restlessness without his father's groundedness. He still carried the wounds not only of his wartime deracination but above all of the dark sojourn at Louis-le-Grand—"depression" was the only true word for it, though in his presence that word had never been uttered. What, exactly, had happened there? Nobody knew, or spoke of it; nobody found the words to ask. Still, what François had taken away was that France, the French system, had rejected him—and that Paris was a cauldron of misery—with the perhaps unsurprising result that he had cleaved to North America—or, that is, not to Canada, which he found provincial. No, he loved the United States, felt that with the Fulbright to Amherst and the master's from Harvard, he'd been accepted, endorsed even, by the New World in ways the Old had denied him.

Even in '69, at Péchiney in New York, before this transfer to Sydney, he'd lamented to his father that everyone around him who got promoted was either an aristocrat with connections or from one of the *grandes écoles*, usually l'X. Or both. What could Gaston do but sigh? He'd told his son at fourteen to push for l'X, but no, he loathed math and physics, he wanted to study philosophy and languages. How to impress upon a boy at that ungrateful age that when you came from nothing, as they did—Lucienne's father was an illiterate *garçon de café*, his own mother an elementary school teacher too poor to retire even when she was unwell—and when, in the bargain, you had a foreign-sounding surname, no matter how often you insisted on your Christian ancestors, you were simply going to have to jump higher, push farther, do better, be better; he, Gaston, had no real interest in math or science either: he'd wanted to be a *writer*, a novelist—yet that hadn't kept him from seeing clearly how the world worked, from getting the top marks in physics in his year in all of Algeria, the second marks in all of France, not because he was a gifted scientist but because he was a clever boy who worked harder than everybody else, thereby securing his ticket to Polytechnique and his dramatic ascent of the social ladder.

There still hadn't been any money in those days, not till well after the war, and in the beginning he and Lucienne would skip meals and delay the rent to pay for his navy uniforms, so he'd look as smart and elegant as all the sons of admirals and doctors and bankers. People like us, he'd tried to impress upon his son, make our way by hard work and strategy, not by fantasies alone. Though he'd made a few connections in his time, Marchandise among them, and he'd helped François get his foot in the door at Péchiney; he still wouldn't accept that it had been a mistake. This house, with its beautiful swimming pool; these little girls, with their nice manners and carefree, playful ways—and François wasn't even halfway through his working life—anything should be possible, no? Well, that was the hope.

Gaston looked at his boy, balding, but elegantly, getting jowly, a bit heavy in the middle, too much wine at supper, always a scotch or two beforehand, and not enough walking, with all the plane travel for his work. François drank his coffee black, with an ice cube. Gaston loved him intensely, and yet always felt also an irritation that Denise had never provoked, something in his heart like the bindi-eye in the sole of his bare foot earlier that morning. François so adored his mother; with him, Gaston, he was beyond dutiful, always eager to please, but rebellious, or resistant, too. Fathers and sons—he had nothing, himself, to go on, having only once seen his father after the age of eight, at his grandmother's funeral.

But he'd had Charles, his older brother, Charles, might he rest in peace, his funeral barely two weeks before they'd departed for Australia. To see him, these last months, eaten by the cancer; they'd told him at first he had a rheumatism, a stiffening, but when they did the X-rays it was everywhere, he was riddled with it, further wasted and shrunken with each passing week in his sterile hospital room—Gaston realized, suddenly, that this was the very hospital in which Denise now lay, in a room no different, the same pink linoleum floor, the skimpy synthetic curtains on rails between the metal beds, the nurses prim and harried, their lips often pursed as they rushed from room to room, and those kidney-shaped metal dishes for pills or sputum, the stink of the lanolin they rubbed on Charles's parched skin, the smears on the window, the superhuman statue of Mary inside the entrance that did little to reassure, and in that place served rather to announce suffering, so much suffering. When Charles died, finally, for him a release—but poor Tata Paulette, his widow, with her crown of gray plaits and her enormous bottle-bottom glasses, dissolved at the graveside at the Cimetière Lagoubran in the brutal June sun, not a scintilla of shade. He'd worried that Lucienne might faint. . . . They were chalk and cheese, Charles and he, his older brother as resolutely irreligious, a committed Communist indeed, as he himself was devout, a schoolteacher who scorned professional ambition—in many ways, Gaston could argue, they'd felt the friction, and the love, of father and son, ten years between them after all. And he would miss his brother.

And his son, alive before him; he'd miss him too; he'd hoped for the extra week, had fantasized (surely) that they might take a walk, the two of them, that François, so secretive all his life, might confide in him, about his marriage, about his work . . . and even (absurd!), he'd fantasized that perhaps he, Gaston, would speak to his son about Lucienne, about the growing lapses—surely François had noticed, though he hadn't said anything, her tendency to ask the same question ten minutes apart or to repeat an anecdote—though perhaps François had been so little with them after Denise left (and in Denise's lively company, somehow, the lacunae showed less) that he hadn't noticed—could that be? No matter, they wouldn't speak of it now; and perhaps it didn't matter, as what was to unfold would unfold just the same whether they spoke about it or not.

"Is there any more news?" Barbara was asking. She'd vanished for a while to dress and had returned, having replaced her velour robe with those extraordinary checkered trousers. It still amazed him when women wore trousers.

François looked irritated. "Of course there's no news. Think of the time difference, Barb. It's eight a.m. here, which means it's midnight there."

Barbara started to clear the table. Gaston could sense annoyance in her gestures, but her voice remained smooth and pleasant. "Well, I guess that's a good sign, isn't it? Because if her condition had worsened at all, they'd have rung in the night. Or whenever."

François nodded thoughtfully, tapping a cigarette on the tablecloth before lighting it. Gaston couldn't understand why both his children smoked so heavily. Both of them coughed as if scraping bottomless wells.

Lucienne, setting her coffee bowl carefully on its saucer, spoke up: "We know she'll be fine. We just need to get back to her."

AT TEN O'CLOCK at night, on Monday, the telephone had rung. It wasn't a usual hour for a call, except sometimes when François was away and ringing, as Gaston understood, to say good night to his wife. But all the adults were sitting together in the living room, chatting vaguely about Australian politics, the reelection a couple of months previously of Gough Whitlam (what sort of name was "Gough"?), not fully a surprise, but by no means guaranteed—the oil crisis, after all—but then the telephone, and François rose to take it, although he wanted Barbara to do it.

"It's probably for you," he said in English.

"Never, so late."

He shrugged. "I *hate* to be bothered at home——" he said to his parents as he left the room.

Then they heard his mumbled voice in the kitchen, the tone, which changed. And a long silence, then more mumbling, but the tone—they could all, except perhaps Lucienne, who was quite deaf, detect the warning, the wariness of his timbre. And because of this, a tacit anxiety that filled them, they did not pretend to converse but sat still and silent, awaiting his return.

"Papa, can you come through a minute," François said quietly from the doorway, a tremor in his voice. They stood in the sallow fluorescence of the narrow white kitchen, Gaston aware of his son's five o'clock shadow, of the smell of tobacco and Eau Sauvage, of the little cleft in François's chin that he'd inherited from Lucienne. The men spoke barely above a whisper.

"Tell me," Gaston said, his eyes on his son's sorrow-filled eyes.

"There's been an accident." The very words, according to Barbara, that he had used the previous week. "That was Brieux"—the *gardien* of their *co-propriété*. "Denise is in the hospital."

"Of course." From the moment his body had registered his son's change in tone through the wall, he'd known it would be Denise. Charles and Yvonne were already dead. Only Denise wasn't with them. "What happened? Is she——"

"In critical care, right now. A car accident, this morning, on her way to Marseille."

The journey was a little over an hour, on the *autoroute*. She traveled it several times a week, in her little Renault, which she blithely called *"ma boîte à sardines."*

"What happened?"

"Brieux wasn't too clear. I guess the hospital was trying to reach you, and called him when they couldn't get through. We need to call the hospital ourselves. He's given me the number."

Gaston only now realized that François, all this while, had been fingering a small piece of paper. He reached out to take it from his son: the burden was his.

"Let's call from my study." François led him down the long, curved hallway. Their feet made no sound on the carpet. "What about Maman?"

"I'll tell her that Denise has had an accident. There's no need to mention critical care. We just need to get home now."

When he called the hospital switchboard, he was put through to the head nurse in critical care; she was only somewhat helpful. Denise was indeed a patient on her ward, sedated at this time. She'd been brought in by ambulance at eight-fifteen a.m., with multiple fractures and internal bleeding; she'd had surgery straightaway. She'd come through well, but her injuries were serious. She had been conscious, yes. She was sleeping now. She would be in critical care overnight, to be monitored; assuming there were no complications, she'd be moved to telemetry in the morning. The nature of the accident? No, no, a single-car accident. What did that mean? Her car had gone off the road. She was alone in the car. One wouldn't wish to speculate, but perhaps she had fallen asleep at the wheel . . . ? Off the *autoroute*, yes, westbound, between La Ciotat and Cassis, before the stretch along the cliff, just after seven-thirty in the morning.

At bedtime that night, he'd told Lucienne there'd been a car accident, that Denise was in the hospital; that he hoped to speak to her by phone the next day—this wasn't untrue—but that reasonably, given the time difference and that Denise wouldn't even be awake until their Australian day was over, they ought to go ahead and change their plans and head home early by plane. Lucienne took the news fairly calmly, her hand over her trembling lips, her eyes wide, but without tears. Though he was aware that she went to sleep clutching her rosary beads, in prayer to her last conscious breath. That first night he had lain awake beside her, too warm beneath the blankets and too cold outside them, thinking of their daughter, poor Denise, of all she had surmounted, of the courage it took for her to forge ahead through each new day, of how he recognized the torments of her spirit—his mother, his sister, had suffered such torments. Of how he wished for his sweet daughter only peace and love. Of how he was convinced but would never say aloud to a soul that she had not fallen asleep at the wheel—in the evening, perhaps, it would have seemed plausible; in the morning, never.

The next day, with the help of Judith, François's lovely secretary, he'd dealt with plane tickets and travel logistics, and had alerted the travel-insurance company of the unforeseen change in their plans. There was no immediate promise of a refund of the cost of the stateroom on the SS *France*, but he was assured that they would consider the claim promptly. Would they, he wondered, require photographs of Denise's mangled Renault or of her broken body in traction? He and Lucienne had assembled their scattered belongings and made their suitcases essentially ready, all while he kept up a cheerful patter to assure Lucienne that the situation was not as dire as their preparations might suggest; but she surprised him by seeming neither to forget nor to escalate the narrative he presented to her, and by believing, with almost unnerving calm, that as soon as they could hold Denise's hands, one each, she would be restored.

At four in the afternoon, which was eight in the morning in Toulon—a midsummer morning, back at home, the cicadas sawing, the gardeners watering the flower beds by the compound gates, Brieux already at least an hour in his little booth, waving the residents off to work as they drove out, and the cleaners and workmen in as they arrived. Eight—usually the time at which he himself set off to the *centre commerciale* for his daily shopping, the panniers empty on the back seat—was a terrible hour at which to disrupt the *gardien*, but he was too impatient to wait any longer.

Brieux, whom he could picture at his broad desk, in his royal-blue boiler suit, his sparse gray hair dancing wispily above his temples, his thick mustache carefully brushed, was respectful and sorrowful. Gaston knew his wife—fishwife!—for a gossip—the entire apartment compound would already have been apprised of the accident—but Brieux himself always kept decorum. He repeated what he knew, which wasn't much.

Denise had set off sometime before seven that Monday morning, too early for him to see her go; but he knew she was taking her houseguest—her friend Estelle Gabin. They'd chatted at the gate on Friday afternoon, and again by the *petit rond* on Saturday morning when he was delivering a package to Madame Aletti in Bâtiment D, as she had broken her ankle, and the women had explained that they were old friends from Denise's Argentina days. "But you speak such good French," he'd observed, and Madame Gabin had said, "But I *am* French! There are plenty of us in Argentina!"

Yes, so that friend—with the gap between her two front teeth? asked Gaston, to be one hundred percent certain, though he was already certain, of course; yes, with the gap—so that friend was catching the Mistral up to Paris, to stay with her sister for a while, and Mademoiselle Cassar was to go on to Marseille—she'd complained about having to stay there for much of the week for her job; she'd said she'd missed the sea view and the breezes, especially in the *canicule* of July, when she was in Marseille, where her little flat caught not a whisper of wind.

So: she would have been happy, surely, spending time with Estelle—they adored each other, laughed together like teenagers. Why an accident on the day of her dear friend's departure? Perhaps she had fallen asleep after all, up late chatting, smoking and drinking, pretending they were younger than they were.

He'd called the hospital for an update, that Tuesday morning, and had been told she was improving, all signs positive, she'd had a good night in critical care and they planned to move her, by noon, to telemetry—yes, that was a definite improvement. She wasn't out of danger yet, but—no, he could not speak to her—yes, they would tell her that her parents were on their way.

Now, the following morning, breakfast behind them, suitcases in the trunk of the Ford, time to set out. Five hours on the plane to Perth. Three hours to wait before the flight to Bombay, with a refueling stop in Singapore, for a sixteen-and-a-half-hour leg; then another two hours before the ten-hour flight to London. In London they would wait almost four hours for the flight to Marseille—a final two hours. And then the drive home. François's secretary had kindly arranged for a car and driver from Péchiney, because everyone was agreed that it was too much for Gaston to rent a car after such a long journey. François had said, gently, *"T'inquiète pas, papa. Je m'en occupe."*

In something like forty-three or forty-four hours from the takeoff in Sydney, heading backward in time, they would arrive at their flat in Toulon, inshallah. (If only they could travel more quickly backward in time, quickly enough to stop the accident from happening!) So perhaps in forty-five or forty-six hours they would at last, as Lucienne so happily anticipated, stand on either side of their one beloved Poupette, each holding her hand, stroking her hair, and she would smile at them and tell them not to worry, not to worry.

She'd been so often ill, as a child, so nervous, all pallor and bone, with her trembling fingers and her long blond braids like switches, her light blue eyes behind their glasses so easily startled and moist. She needed protection now just as she had done then. How they'd hoped she would fall in love, find her own protector, so that they might depart this earth in peace. Without a miracle, she was doubtless too old now for children of her own—though Lucienne, always strong, had been forty-one when Denise was born—but she surely wasn't too old to marry. No, men, widowed or even divorced, often sought a new life companion . . . his own brother, Charles, having so sadly lost his own Lucienne young (yes, so easy to forget, she too had been named Lucienne, dead three months before Gaston's own wedding!), with kids to raise, had found in her stead stalwart, frog-faced Paulette. And theirs had been a happy union—excepting the tragedy of their one son together, the awful Jacky, who hadn't even attended his father's funeral.

No! No thought of funerals. The little girls came to wrap themselves fleetingly around their grandparents' torsos, then flit away. It made no sense for everyone to venture to the airport: Barbara would have had to take the girls in her Mini as they couldn't all fit in the Ford; and what if the terminal was crowded and they couldn't find one another at check-in? No, it made sense to say good-bye here, on the street, so Barbara and the girls stood at the front gate, the pink house behind them showing its fortified self to the road, its verdant garden and terraces hidden away, as if in purdah. Loulou certainly had a tear in her eye—dear girl, she seemed to him one of them, familiar; whereas the little one, cute, yes, but always performing, less *true*—it was hard, yet, to know.

And Barbara, after whom the little one more obviously took, smiling and waving, with her strange new unbecoming haircut—it made her nose look longer—and those outlandish trousers. . . . But how he loved them all, and his son, his own flesh, how he and Lucienne loved them, their future, the little girls unbelievably the generation that would carry the family—if not, alas, being girls, the family name—into the new century, that unimaginable, inevitable place that he, and most certainly Lucienne—he squeezed that dearest hand; how long had they already held one another's hearts?—would never see on this earth; into which even François and Barbara and, inshallah, Denise—please God, Denise—would step only trepidatiously, much of their lives already behind them. For François would be, in the spring of the year 2000, sixty-nine years old, exactly the age Gaston was himself on this August day of 1974, a man on the cusp of frank old age, the hill well crested behind him; but still—please God, please God—with a meaningful portion of life yet to live.

INTERLUDE

✣

TOULON, FRANCE

At dawn on August 22, a late-summer Tuesday, a milky mist hung over the indigo sea, caressing the horizon and the farther dark promontories along the coast, like giants' hands fingering the open water. By breakfast time, the sun had burned the sky clear, its impeccable blue lighter, brighter than the reflecting waves beneath, fringed by occasional whitecaps, dotted by vessels and buoys, a surfacing submarine in the distance, its little men lined upon the deck, all the visible universe a kaleidoscope of blues from Prussian to celeste. From the dining room, the infinite blue vista was punctuated in the middle distance by the long dark cones of cedars and the rippling, brainlike crowns of the marine pines atop their tall, hardy trunks. As the morning unfolded, the odd wasp floated in the window, along currents of hot-smelling summer air that bore the sounds of splashing, diving, children's joyous cries from the swimming pool below; while from the hallway, the clicking sounds of the elevator outside, the shuffle of feet, the bell's repeated ring (again, again), the opening and closing of the door, the bustle of parcels and voices, then from deeper within the apartment, the kitchen, came the clang of pots and cutlery.

The cocktail party: this night before the big dinner, when only immediate family would gather on the large terrace upstairs, the eight of them including Mrs. Fisk, and very dearest friends, and those cousins who had already arrived. The big dinner was for the twenty-third, their actual fif-tieth anniversary, in the large private dining room at the three-star hotel in the shadow of Mont Faron: guests were traveling from near and far, fifty guests for fifty years.

On Tuesday after lunch, as soon as it reopened for the afternoon at two-thirty, Lucienne and Denise visited the hair salon in Cap Brun, wedged between the pharmacy and the *bar-tabac*, to have their *mise-en-plis*, and sat for over an hour side by side, holding hands, in sticky vinyl armchairs beneath the humming domed dryers with rollers in their hair. During this time, François and Barbara (who were sleeping in a borrowed basement studio in the building adjacent to his parents') stayed with Mrs. Fisk, who could no longer read on account of her macular degeneration (or knit, or sew), and who therefore needed company. Gaston, although Denise was sleeping for the week on the saggy velvet-covered sofa bed in his study upstairs (the room generally thought of as hers having been allocated to Mrs. Fisk), managed to claim a couple of hours at his desk, where he was working, as he had been almost daily for five years, on the family memoir for his granddaughters. It stretched to almost fifteen hun-dred pages in his even hand, blue ink on unlined paper in five red binders on the shelf above the sofa bed. Now very near the end, he had long ago told himself he would finish in time for this anniversary. He hadn't made this artificial deadline—no matter; the girls wouldn't read it for years, probably decades—but he still felt it urgent to strive for completion.

"Trust my father," François had said to Barbara sotto voce, after Gas-ton had risen almost stealthily from his siesta and mounted the staircase. "He doesn't waste a minute."

In the sitting room—a half flight of stairs down from the dining room, which overlooked it—Mrs. Fisk, almost stupefied by the heat, fanning herself with a purple Thai Airways fan saved from the Sydney days, sitting deep in the fat satin armchair near the windows. The metal blinds, lowered to the ground against the brutal sun, created a soporific gloom; but the floor-to-ceiling windows stood open and the sounds of kids playing filtered in alongside the cicada song. One of these insects, apparently resident in the window boxes just outside, sawed particularly loudly. Barbara, close to her mother on the neighboring sofa, leaned forward to read aloud, in her clear, high voice, the gothic stories of Isak Dinesen, a.k.a. Karen Blixen. Lenore, who hadn't asked to listen, wondered whether a midafternoon in August was quite the moment for them, but did her best to concentrate, to take in and imagine the distant worlds created for her out of words.

François, as was his wont, marauded. He roamed in the temporarily quiet kitchen, nominally seeking an ashtray but also checking out the trays of hors d'oeuvres delivered by the *traiteur* for the evening's cocktails: tiny quiches and puff pastries stuffed with asparagus and goat cheese; little pizza squares, each with its withered black olive; smoked salmon on brown bread circles with sprigs of dill; little bamboo skewers of crudités and others of fruit; a large and odorous platter of deliquescing cheeses, surrounded by grapes and nuts. . . . He filched a few of these, then drifted through the girls' room, where their clothes lay strewn across the lower bunk as if they'd turned their suitcases upside down, except for their two party dresses, hanging at the ready inside the open cupboard. On the dresser top their jewelry and hair clips, gewgaws of girlhood, glittered in a jumble. He stopped at the door to his parents' room, the blinds down there too, the rust-colored wallpaper rendering the room womblike: the crucifix he'd always known, draped with a rosary and olive branch, rested on the wall above their low bed; the brown-and-turquoise cushions that his mother had knitted were the only concession to vanity. On the walls, the oil paintings of his childhood—a pink rose, amateurish (perhaps his mother had painted it in her youth?); a peasant girl with a kerchief, in profile, who looked as though she might be of the family, but had in fact been picked up at a flea market in the early years of his parents' marriage. And the family photos, of himself at his Péchiney desk, a professional work photo he'd sent them not long ago; Denise laughing, in profile, outside at a restaurant;

Barbara and the girls down at the little beach at the bottom of the cliff, from one of the winter visits in the Sydney days; the girls in their Kambala school photos, fading now, probably taken the last Australian year, Loulou carefully groomed and looking wiser than her years, Chloe with short hair, a mess, and her tie askew, a new side tooth glimmering like a fang. His father's light suit for the evening hung on the cupboard door; his mother's dress was laid out on the bed, doubtless arranged there by Odet before she left, the black pumps she'd wear on the floor at the bed's edge, their shape distorted by her bunioned feet. A joyful day, and a sad one. He returned to the dining room, ashtray in hand, and lit himself a cigarette. Barb was still reading aloud, although Mrs. Fisk had closed her eyes and was possibly asleep. For a while he stood at the dining room windows, where, having noisily raised the metal blinds far enough to see the swimming pool (while, at his feet, the aging dachshund Big, who'd outlived his Toronto cousin Small, lay heaving on the cool marble, his breathing raspy and his umber flank rising and falling in heavy protest against the heat), he watched his daughters and their new friends happily cavorting.

Chloe had been with them for over three weeks already, having been picked up in Lyon by Denise after her month of summer camp in Saint-Palais-sur-Mer, and had managed to take up at the swimming pool with a girl her own age named Nathalie, visiting from Paris, the granddaughter of Commandant Dessault, under whom François's father had, at the end of the war, served at Rue Royale in Paris. Through Nathalie, or with Nathalie, the girls had become part of the roving band that claimed the grounds of the compound day and night for their games. The Nicolet family on the ground floor of the Cassars' building, whose two younger kids, Arnaud and Florence, were at the gang's core, seemed to have an open-door policy, allowing all the young to tumble in and out, listening to music in their basement or devouring the contents of their kitchen: Jeanne Denis, the eldest of the group; Louis and Alexandre, best mates; Mireille Colombo, Jeanne's younger cousin, from next door; the beautiful

Moreno kids, José, Jorge, and lovely Marisol; then the junior contingent, weird Invernizzi's skinny boy Yves, and the Largents' grandsons, David and Benjamin; and from that same building—was it I? or H?—General Bourret's grandkids, the other Nathalie, and Adrien . . . of all of them, only the Nicolets, Louis, and Yves lived there year-round. The rest piled in from elsewhere, Paris mostly, but some from Geneva, and now Toronto too.

Down at the pool, the kids dived and chased each other in the water, pushing one another's heads under with great triumphant whoops, grabbing each other's legs, flirting and giggling, then flopping over the side to lie on the slatted wooden deck in the sun, the ocean wide behind them, below them, their lean brown bodies drying quickly in the sea breeze; then a call from one, and back to the water; or up the steps to lean over the bridge above the pool and dare one another to jump. The girls thrilled to this belonging: in these precious days to be welcomed in the loose group of French kids past whom they'd walked in previous summers unnoticed, eyes down in embarrassment—there could be no greater honor. To bend to help little Benjamin tie his shoes, to referee the earnest tennis match between Yves and Louis, to pick pine nuts along the drive while gossiping with the other girls, or to lounge on the Nicolets' purple sofa listening to Bob Marley; to rush out in the dusk after supper to join the others, and then to play hide-and-seek for hours in the dark, running, feet slapping, along and through the footpaths, parking lots, garages, ground floors of all the compound as far as the gate, sometimes even on the tortuous unlit paths down the cliffside to the beach—each night the girls got butterflies at the dinner table in anticipation, peering surreptitiously out the window as they cleared everyone's plates to see whether the other kids had yet started to gather above the illuminated pool—then waiting, waiting, while the adults droned on, and picked their teeth, and drank and smoked endlessly and barely touched their congealing food. Might they escape before coffee? Before dessert even? Eyeing their mother for signs of assent, then, still, as they always had since they were small, asking

Grand'-mère's permission. She never denied them, though sometimes she seemed to pause thoughtfully and consider it.

This night and the next night they would have to forgo their night-time games; they both bristled at the sacrifice, because how could any grown-up party matter as much as these precious hours, and only five more nights until they'd leave for Canada—in less than two weeks they'd be back at school in Toronto, Chloe in her second year at UTS and Loulou back at the French school in her gray-and-navy uniform. For the afternoon, though, they could pretend they had nowhere else to be; they did not look up to see their father standing at the window above them; they looked up only much later, when the sun had fallen low in the sky, its wan light fully off the pool, and Tante Denise, her hair an immovable wedding cake, called them from on high with a small wave: "*Mes chéries, c'est l'heure!*" Then they scrambled guiltily, gathering up their towels, T-shirts, flip-flops, because if she was summoning them, they were late: the photographer was to come at six, the guests at six-thirty. Thank goodness Loulou's watch said just after five, though Odet had already returned, in her party dress and heels, her round, frank, brown face exceptionally brightened by a dash of lipstick and her ears by small golden hoops.

When the girls slipped into the bathroom to wash and change—both of them at once to save time; the bathroom was big enough, though still they bumped and squabbled—Odet went in to help Grand'-mère put on her dress. Mrs. Fisk also was dressing in her room, and Denise upstairs, hastily, clean slip, silk blouse and skirt, aware that anyone might appear, at any moment. Gaston, always with military forethought, had shaved a second time and put on his sports jacket—saving the suit for the big party—well beforehand. He now sat in the thronelike hard armchair by the dining room window, Lucienne's chair, and watched the afternoon shadows grow longer as the pool below emptied for the day.

Soon, soon, the photographer arrived, a small, tanned man in his for-ties in a short-sleeved shirt of dazzling whiteness, wielding a large black bag of equipment. In the not inconsiderable time it took to hoist Grand'-mère up the narrow steps to the terrace—Odet above her and Gaston below, holding and supporting her in unexpected places as she emitted modest moans of terror, like a small dog, with each step, the air around them all vibrating with *angoisse*—the photographer set up chairs on the terrace and envisioned the shape of his portrait: the girls in their party dresses at either end, flanking their parents, with Denise and Mrs. Fisk at the center behind the happy couple, ancient but regal in their chairs. "Fifty years!" he marveled as he tinkered with his lenses. "Now, that's something to celebrate!"

And even as they smiled—"Look natural!" cried the photographer, surely aware this was an impossible request—downstairs Odet, her apron over her fancy clothes, heated the oven for the platters of savory treats and arranged the crystal glasses on a doilied tray, the fanned pile of embroidered napkins, the bowls of nuts and chips, and climbed the steep marble staircase again and again to deliver these necessary elements of the imminent party and arrange them on the white-clothed table, along-side the vase of scented lilies, their waxy white petals splayed to reveal quivering moist red stamens.

After the photographs, the photographer swiftly dispatched, Grand'-mère was installed on the pink cushioned porch swing with, beside her on a little ledge, a tumbler filled with Perrier and a dash of bitters to give the illusion of a cocktail. Gaston chatted briefly with Mrs. Fisk in his exe-crable English, just as the guests began to arrive: Paul and Catherine the very first, their oldest friends, with Aurore but not the little boys, deemed too young and rambunctious for this party; then Gaston and Léone, then Christiane and Dominique, then Louis Boileau and his wife, then the Musset cousins, Guy's daughter and her husband, Jehovah's Witnesses, surprisingly, whose many children who would join the dinner the next day. And Xavier and Joëlle, Charles's boy, with pretty Mireille, their youngest, who'd spent a month in Canada with François and Barbara and got on famously with the girls; though not Michel or any of his brood, as

New Caledonia was too far to travel from; and none of Geneviève's sons, who were at the traveling age and elsewhere. Not to mention Gaston's brother, Charles, gone; his sister Yvonne, gone; his sister Marie Louise, gone; his half brother Guy, gone; Lucienne's sisters, Tata Baudry, Gaston's mother, Lucienne's old father Sposito—all of them, long gone . . .

The clear blue evening settled around them all, their animated faces lit only by the electric light from indoors, glowing golden through the windows; and beneath the hubbub of their conversation the soughing breath of the sea far below, lapping inexorably on the pebbled shore, the rocky coast, singing of eternity. There at the tip of the promontory just below, the Anse Méjean, in front of the little chapel, the white statue of the compassionate Virgin, her hands open, gazed out to sea, transplanted from Oran's Cap Falcon and standing there, so near, in memory of all the families—his, hers, a mere droplet—buried across the rippling ocean in Africa, their earthly graves sealed, like so much else, in memory.

The missing not forgotten, then, but present in the sea's rhythms, in the night air, along with the unspoken miracles of those whose cheeks could still be stroked, hands held, those who might have slipped into the realm of the shades but had been stayed, for a time, by love, or God, or Fate. In recent years alone, young Aurore had lost her husband suddenly and tragically, yet she burned only more brightly in his wake. Dominique, younger still, had almost died of an intestinal disorder; Denise, of course, held in her the scars of the accident on the road near Cassis, that August morning now several years before; while François had only the previous winter almost succumbed to Ludwig's angina, a dental abscess that had spread overnight into his neck and chest so rapidly and with such intense swelling that he'd been unrecognizable, his wife only really aware of the gravity of his condition when he began to hallucinate. She'd rushed him to the ER at midnight on a Saturday, leaving the girls alone overnight, although they were too young yet. Later, when she'd asked the surgeon what might have transpired had they waited till morning, he'd joked grimly, "You wouldn't have come at all"; and François, allergic to penicillin, had spent three weeks at the Toronto General, three floors and a corridor from where Barbara's father had died, wandering the hallways in his hospital gown, dragging his IV pole at his side, waiting for the massive infection little by little to subside. . . . No, many were gone, but many miraculously present, *present*, and for Gaston, perhaps even for Lucienne—though she could not always any longer carry on a conversation beyond the moment itself—How was your journey? Isn't it a beautiful night? What—gesturing to the platters, the bottles, the glasses—is missing from your happiness?—always her gracious spirit, her luminous smile, such kindness; though the girls, on the cusp of the ungrateful age, made mock of her behind her back (forgive them Lord, they know not what they do!)—surely, in her body, in her blood, she remembered, as he remembered so vividly, this day exactly, fifty years earlier, their marriage at the *mairie* of El Biar, and then the next day their religious wedding in the simple church of Sainte Croix in the casbah, the church that had been (and now again it was anew) the Djama Berrani, the mosque for those from outside Algiers, known to have existed at least since the seventeenth century (mention is made of it in 1653) and at various times a café, a Christian school, a French barracks, and then a church, the tabernacle of which was built from the fig tree that had grown in the square outside its doors, from which, at one time, the heads of slaughtered Christian slaves had been suspended. This day, August 22, in 1928, after the civil marriage at the *mairie*, Lucienne's father, Sposito, the illiterate cook and waiter, recently retired manager of the Restaurant des Sept Merveilles at Telemly (following his financial ruin and the loss, at the turn of the century, of the hotel and small vineyard at Castiglione that he and his wife had worked their lives for), a widower by then, cooked their wedding supper with his own hands, and poured for his guests, for Lucienne and Gaston, the last two bottles of wine from the *terroir* at Castiglione, bottled before Gaston's birth, drunk in honor of the marriage of his youngest daughter. (That Lucienne's parents had been ruined by an ill-advised loan made to Gaston's runaway father, the ironically named Constant Cassar, was not mentioned even then, in 1928; nor would it be mentioned in 1978, by anyone.)

And after the long delays for dispensations from the navy, from the city, from the Vatican, the latter two safely in hand well ahead of time but the former dispatched in error in a mailbag to Indochina, long awaited, traced only belatedly, and hastily reissued in Paris at the last minute, as without it the naval officer could not marry—and after, on the twenty-second, the aged priest belatedly explained he was too hard of hearing to take the couple's prenuptial confessions, and so sent them scrambling in the late afternoon to the priest at St. Augustine's (how apt, they always thought, that the emissary of their great compatriot Saint Augustine should have heard their admissions), who wrote for them each a ticket of confession delivered betimes to Sainte Croix. And so, on the morning of August 23, 1928, at ten a.m., the old deaf priest blessed their union, Lucienne Sposito in her simple white dress and Gaston Cassar in his white navy uniform, standing together in that humble, unadorned sacred space before a tiny assembly, just seven including the bride and groom, lucky seven—Father Sposito in the colonial helmet he always wore in summertime, and Gaston's mother, Marie-Thérèse, and his sister Yvonne with her husband, Léon (though he wouldn't remain her husband much longer after that), and their little boy Gaston, then just five and a half, his limbs like twigs, his long brown neck craning above his white collar, his jug ears, his kind, mournful eyes.

And at noon on that same day, the newlyweds boarded the *General Chanzy*, bound for Marseille—they'd booked a good cabin, and the maître d,' husband of an old colleague of Gaston's mother's, took special care of them and slipped them a complimentary cognac. The night of the twenty-fourth they spent at the Hotel Victoria on the Boulevard de Strasbourg in Toulon, a few kilometers from where this party had assembled, then the city's second-grandest hotel, for them a great luxury; and by eight a.m. on the morning of the twenty-fifth, Gaston had reported for service to his demanding mistress, the French navy, to work in transmission services on the appropriately named *Provence* under a commander—Ollive—known among his men as *"le gai Gaulois."* It was what Gaston for so long loved second only to his wife, the navy, that and his beloved country; though in time he had to learn to love other things instead, except his wife, his darling wife, and even in his speech at the big dinner on the twenty-third—it did go on a little, he was always a tad loquacious, pompous even, but charming, he was so very charming—he read from Lucienne's letter during their courtship, it was so sweet, Lucienne had written, "I implore you, always be assured of my love—no matter the circumstances, never doubt, never doubt my love, this love which is my splendor and my torment, because a Great Love is always a serious thing." And he said he never doubted and she never doubted—not one day, not when they were separated in the war for months; never. And Lucienne, dear thing, not much left now, she smiled through his speech and gazed at him with such adoration that everyone knew that even in her dotage, even without her wits about her, she didn't doubt or question, she loved and was loved, fully and entirely, devoutly even, with a love almost hallowed, a beautiful thing.

And of the seven on that wedding day in 1928, his nephew Gaston was the only one who stood to toast his uncle and aunt fifty years later on the terrace by the sea in Toulon, all that life, all those years (his grandmother Marie-Thérèse and his mother, Yvonne, both institutionalized outside Toulon in their last years, with persecution mania, and eventually interred, years apart, like the rest of the family not dead on Algerian soil, in the Cimetière Lagoubran on the other side of the city) lived through together and apart, this one boy, now man, bearing witness to the long arc of their great love.

BUT WAIT: WHAT was that in the older Gaston's happy speech—joyous even—that next evening, at the hotel, in front of all the guests, the fifty friends and relatives in the hotel dining room, everyone sated by rack of lamb and little sheaves of carrots and green beans, a wee round tower of yellow rice on every plate, the wine, a fine rosé from neighboring Bandol, sweating in bulbed bottles on the tables and in their glasses, their gilded chairs pulled back from the white tables soiled by crumbs and sauces, belts and collars loosened, high heels abandoned akimbo beneath the dangling tablecloths, women wiggling their numb toes, the floral centerpieces wilting, the littler children tearing up and down the carpeted hallway outside, under the watch of a pair of deputed fathers with bloodshot eyes, the aura fully that of the end of the wedding, a combination of exhaustion and inertia in the guests, who wished now to be at home but hadn't quite the energy to rise from their chairs and make for home or their hotel rooms, everyone feeling at once wistful and relieved that this long-planned event, so looked forward to, was suddenly over, in the past, a memory already, but didn't it go off well, the catering a success, the hotel well chosen, the cake—a splendid and delectable croquembouche, its golden spun-sugar tower decorated with real flowers, something that back in El Biar they might only have dreamed of—was delicious, its profiteroles fresh and moist, its *crème pâtissière* divine, but we really shouldn't have had that last bite, that last glass . . .

How to leave when who knew when they'd next be reunited, the cousins from Pau, from Lyon, from Brest, some who'd not seen each other in over twenty-five years—was it last at the apartment of the Cousines Breloux near the Place du Gouvernement? It must have been '59, no? They ended up in Alsace of all places, those three old spinsters—is the last one, Laure, still alive? Gaston would know. Wasn't it their mother who condemned the marriage? That was always what we were told. Or was it even earlier, the funeral of Tata Baudry, the midwife in L'Arba who lived to be over ninety, dear thing, God rest her soul, you know Gaston credits her with his whole life—it was she who paid his fees for the lycée, and the boarding, too, after his mother committed to them without a penny of her own, madwoman, a single mother and at the time just a substitute teacher, can you imagine, in the elementary school in Blida— but that little old lady, Tata Baudry, wizened like a nut—she'd saved and saved, for those two kids of hers whose lives were so disastrous—the son, Émile, who got in trouble with the law and fled to Brazil, where he changed his name—to Edouard Garcin!—and died young, in 1930— her letter returned to sender from the Hospital Villa Curupaity in Rio de Janeiro . . . and the daughter, Auguste, unfortunate girl, never married, could never hold a job, she lived off her mother, she too died young, of a lung complaint we think—and for what did Tata Baudry work so hard delivering babies—village babies, country babies, Muslim, Christian, Berber, Arab, French, Spanish, Italian, Maltese, all babies loved by her brown hands, and when she was paid money she saved her coins, so she could give them to her relatives . . . she paid for Gaston's schooling, then she helped to pay for their wedding, and still later helped them buy their first furniture for the apartment in Toulon, Boulevard Léon Bourgeois, where François was born, yes, that rather heavyset bald fellow over there, smoking—without Tata Baudry none of this would have been possible, *sage femme* indeed, and she was honored on this night, Gaston spoke of her and thanked her; and they toasted, even if not by name, all the others who had gone before, Lucienne's eldest sister Fée, who became the head-mistress of the teachers' college in Constantine, though her own father couldn't read, and Joséphine Sébile, their mother, who married Sposito and with him bought the business in Castiglione from old Malacamp, *en viager*, the inn and restaurant known as the Hotel de L'Orient, with its vineyards, all that they would later lose on account of deceitful Constant Cassar—he, too, was there, behind the toasts, invisible, all of it a world now dusty and faded, the worn memories of the parents of most guests, or grandparents even, of another time long before their time. These two the last of a lost generation and she, she, poor thing, still so pretty, even approaching ninety—but she must be, she was born in the nineteenth century, something like 1892, yes, it's true, a massive difference between them, thirteen years, is it? Must have been quite the scandal at the time. But what did he say? What did he say?

Because we weren't listening so carefully ourselves—the exhausted children, the tipsy husbands, the mothers discreetly rubbing their sore feet or sneaking one last gulp of rosé, or worrying they'd suddenly got their period and might stand to reveal a bloodstained skirt, or listening to the whispers of the old woman or old man next to them, a second, almost complementary flow of verbiage, just quieter—what did he say that prompted Barbara, much later in the night, back in their basement studio with the metal blinds lowered and the little bedside lamps casting shadows on the floor through which a millipede most decidedly darted (Barbara saw it from the corner of her eye), to say to her husband as she flossed her teeth standing while he arranged and rearranged the small soft pillow of his little single bed, "Why didn't you tell me? I can't believe you never told me. If you had told me," she said, "I never would have married you."

And he raised his eyes, his sad green-and-amber eyes, which carried by now within them a lifetime of hurt and grief and above all the terrible burden of being alone, of not anywhere belonging or being understood or seen lovingly—had their marriage, unlike his parents,' been a mistake, then? He still refused to countenance it—he raised his eyes, wounded all but mortally by her coldness, by the provincial judgmental spirit that looked at him and deemed him irredeemably *unacceptable*, and he said quietly, "How could I have told you what I did not know myself?"

And when Barbara had finished flossing and had brushed her teeth at the minute sink in the tiny bathroom, had washed her face with the rough face glove that hung on its metal hook above the sink (hers with a red stripe, his with a blue one) and had rubbed into her cheeks the verbena-scented cream from the little green pot beneath the mirror by their shared tooth glass, and a little of the excess cream into the backs of her still elegant hands, she went without pausing to her own single bed, where she did not smoke her nightly bedtime cigarette while reading, but instead turned onto her side—she calmly turned her back to him—and turned out her bedside lamp and murmured, so quietly that he did not hear her, "Good night then, François."

PART V

CONNECTICUT, UNITED STATES

A s he sat in his cracked black leather armchair in his basement study
reading—or "reading"—François could not stop thinking about
it. All the reasons for it: poor dear Larry's poor son David, dead on Lake
Michigan last summer, and Larry and Babs desperate with the loss. Or
the collapse of his office around him. Or the probably still-seeping radi-
ation from Chernobyl, even a few years later. Or his own entrapment—
wasn't he allowed to lament it, his own entrapment in this house, in this
marriage, in this life? Who else would?

Barbara was at the library's Book Design Committee meeting—in
the company of that pallid, bony WASP she was so taken with, a minor
heiress of some sort, who reminded him of the Tin Man in *The Wizard of
Oz*, and the obese Bryn Mawr alumna whose tentlike dresses somehow
contrived barely to touch her vast body—and she would then go shop for
supper at the Food Emporium ("Not fish, please!" he'd requested) before
coming home, leaving him alone for hours on this squalid Saturday
afternoon. Alone except for Waffles, the one-eared, stump-tailed, ball-
obsessed Jack Russell for whom, after they'd had lunch (for François, the
ham and cheese sandwich, with mayo, that she'd left on a plate on the
counter covered in foil and for Waffles, seven small cubes of Gruyère, for
which he'd had to sit, and stay, and lie down, and twirl, and then back
through the routine to sit, all the while roundly insulted by his master),

François had thrown the tennis ball several times down the corridor, though not, to Waffles's dismay, with Barb's zeal.

After less than ten minutes, François had retreated to his basement lair, his reading lamp alight at two in the afternoon, the silence punctuated momentarily by Waffles's tapping paws on the wooden floor overhead and then, after the dog curled up to sleep in a crescent on the living room sofa, only by the sound of the water trickling in the downspout by the window and the wavering percussion of raindrops on the flagstones outside.

Early March: the rain, melting the snow, had shrunk the drifts into isolated dingy hummocks fringed with soot. It had revealed the sodden dead scruff of grass beneath, tussocks floating in black ice water. All the branches still bare. At one point Laddie, the neighbors' bulky Labrador, trotted gracefully across the yard past the window, a bright, wet blob in the murk, mercifully unseen, upstairs, by Waffles, who detested him.

François pretended to read *The Muqaddimah*—to reread it, that is, after thirty years, because some time back Chloe had brought her copy home from college and left it here, and Barb, recently clearing out clutter from various corners, had been preparing to take it to the book exchange at the Greenwich dump, prompting in François a wave of protective nostalgia for Ibn Khaldun, fourteenth-century North African luminary and companion of his scholarly youth. He had sequestered the fat glossy yellow paperback in his study. What for, if not to read it? So he "read" it. Had it always been so turgid? What relevance could he possibly find in these thin, dense pages? And his mind—his body too, eventually—strayed to the kitchen upstairs, where he'd placed his tumbler upon the counter (Corian, mind you, the latest thing; Barb had very much wanted it when they renovated the kitchen, and had chosen pale blue, her favorite color). His tumbler: the kids mocked what they called his OCD, but surely in this house for which he had earned every penny (for which, when he thought about it, he had *sacrificed* his life, because how long had it been since he'd enjoyed a single day?) and yet in which he was consigned, like a monster or freak, like the Minotaur, to one room in the basement, might he not at the very least claim his one drinking glass as his very own, and insist that no one else touch it? He had drunk water in it at breakfast time, and water in it at lunchtime, and now at two, at three, three-thirty, the clock progressing with such impossible lassitude, the water outside dripping, the day ever darkening, all he could think of and all that he wanted was a drink. Just one. Not scotch, which he preferred after dinner; not gin, his favorite but also his shame; just a little, untraceable snifter of vodka. He'd rinse the glass, retreat downstairs, a cigarette or two in the course of an hour, a little mint—a sharp green Pastille Valda, the embossed tin brought in his luggage from Paris— and who would be any the wiser? Waffles wasn't telling. What would it matter? Just one.

But he'd promised himself none before the cocktail hour—correction: he'd made himself that promise after he'd failed to keep his earlier promise, not to drink except modestly when in restaurants or at work functions; which was after his failed promise of January not to drink at all. Which had lasted all of seven days. Though the lapse had hardly been his fault— the magnitude of the disaster was immediately clear; no, it had proven more disastrous still than he'd imagined then, the consequences only now beginning to unfold—how could he not be forgiven for requiring some small help to get through it all? He climbed the stairs, he heard the dog stir, and patter, tags jangling, to the kitchen, where François insulted him, and paused to take the Absolut from the freezer—it grew viscous in the cold—and to unscrew its metal top, and to pour an inch—no, if just one drink, then maybe two?—into his special glass, which stood alone on the meticulously clean countertop the way he felt he stood alone in his life, and then he carefully screwed the top back on and opened the freezer and laid the bottle gently on its side, next to the frozen peas and the Tater Tots. (When they were younger, even when the girls were at home, Barb would never have sunk to Tater Tots: she prepared everything herself all those years, from scratch; but this bag in the freezer was a concession to midlife, a minor freedom, and in truth they both quite liked them.)

Waffles, throughout, waited patiently, eyes on his master, body quivering with intensity. When François looked at him, he sat without being asked, so hopeful.

"Stop trembling, you little creep." François's insults were affectionate. He shook a few peanuts from the jar in the drinks cabinet and threw them one at a time in high arcs for Waffles to leap for and catch in midair. (When Waffles failed to intercept the peanut before it hit the ground, François called him pathetic and stupid, but affectionately.) In between throwing the peanuts, he took significant medicinal sips of his vodka, as though it were cod liver oil, and each time closed his eyes and winced as the cold, bitter fluid slipped down his gullet. He gauged perfectly the consumption of peanuts and vodka so that both he and Waffles finished their treats at the same time. He washed his glass at the sink in hot water with dish soap. Rather than leave it in the drainboard, he dried it with a dish towel and returned it to its place on the counter. Waffles continued to shiver expectantly.

"Finished," François said sternly, wiping his hands together in a gesture meaningful to the dog. "Finished."

Waffles, sorrowful, turned and slunk back to the couch.

Getting on for four-thirty. She'd be back within the hour. He both longed for and dreaded her return. Over Christmas, when he'd been railing about something, one of them—was it Chloe—had asked, "What's wrong? What is it you *want?*" And the words had burst from him without hesitation—he remembered grabbing both sides of his head as though his skull might explode: "I want to be left *alone!*"

But this was only half true. He wanted to be seen, accepted if not understood; he wanted the companionship his parents felt—he always had, and had never felt it. So he wanted not to feel alone, but how was this possible, when his family seemed always to reject him? He wanted, so desperately it lived as an itch beneath his skin, the very itch that drove him to unscrew time and again the metal tops of his various toxic bottles, he wanted to be relieved of the pointless, grueling busywork that consumed his days, had consumed them for decades, that had stolen his best years—so many airplane flights, so many hotel rooms, so many meetings, so many tours of plants and factories, so many phone calls, so many fat printed reports with vinyl covers, their contents exponentially more turgid than *The Muqaddimah*, so many backstabbers, manipulators, liars, dirty cheats, so much grubbing for attention, position, promotion, connection, like ants swarming their hill, climbing over one another, heedless, insatiably but meaninglessly driven—Camus, his soulmate, had had it right—crushing his own ability to think and to learn, to follow his interests and exercise his mind. It had once been a good mind, a fine mind even; had Sir Hamilton Gibb not written on his paper, in that pristine hand he recalled so well, that François's was the finest analysis of contemporary Turkey that he had yet encountered? But so what? He had lost that interior space, that intellectual gift, like a sports car rusted irreparably over years in a garage or a prisoner kept in the dark in a tiny cell, and how could he even know, now, what it would be he might want, without having had, for longer than he could remember, an iota of mental space in which to pose the question?

And what had this sacrifice given him in return but money enough (though never quite enough) and the recurring resentment of his wife and daughters, who seemed to find him unseemly and repellent, who never stopped to ask themselves how they came to enjoy their fine educations or their pleasant home, who seemed rather always to find fault. . . . When they'd first moved in, Barb had had stationery printed that called this place "Tikki Takki House"—she'd spelled it that way instead of "Ticky Tacky" because she'd thought this faux-Polynesian flavor more amusing, in any case a reference to that Pete Seeger song of their young, "And they're all made out of ticky-tacky / And they all look just the same"— because she was ashamed to be in a town house in a cul-de-sac in a condo development in Greenwich, Connecticut, when all her friends in Toronto lived in sprawling Victorian houses in Forest Hill or Rosedale, and by such measures only, in her world, were a person's triumphs known. That she had seen the sun rise over the Mayan temples in the Yucatán, that she'd had her photo taken in sun hat and bathing suit by a giant cactus on a rocky outcrop in the Galápagos surrounded by a thousand lazy-eyed yellow iguanas, that she could read any book she chose and procure any food, that she owned a closet full of clothes she barely wore—none of it, it seemed, was enough. That she did not even begin to understand what it had cost him, what it cost him now. That she did not seem even to care.

He consulted his watch. Not time for another glass, not if he wanted to be sure she didn't find out. He very much didn't want her to know. He didn't think Chloe had told her about Christmas, though who could be sure? Barb hadn't referred to it, and she wasn't good at hiding her feelings. Then again, maybe she was trying to be more sympathetic, kinder to him, because of the scandal at work.

Christmas, then, his own scandal; January, a scandal from which only he, among his senior colleagues, seemed likely to emerge unscathed. Both of them, in his head, unfaceably enormous. Maybe there was, after all, time for the smallest sip more of vodka—Barb always ran late. But he had to pour it into the glass—he'd promised Chloe, rather than himself, that he would; and he didn't intend to fail her. So: a small serving more, the opening and closing of the freezer door, the opening of the bottle, the patter of Waffles's feet, no peanuts this time, just the gesture— "Finished!"—and Waffles's mournful resignation.

François downed this second serving in a single swallow: the way that fat Book Design lady's clothes barely touched her body, the liquor barely touched his mouth, his tongue, catapulted instead directly to burn his esophagus (so that many years later, twenty-one and a few months, to be exact, Death would come for him in the form of esophageal cancer). It was still raining.

At Christmas, they had all been gathered in Grandma's apartment in Toronto—because Grandma, now almost fully blind and not far off ninety, was on medication for heart failure that had her needing the bath-room always nearby and hence could not travel; because Loulou, at law school in Nova Scotia, seemed, in this time, with familiar (indeed famil-ial) Canadian fervor to eschew all things American, including the house in Greenwich; and because it was as easy for Chloe, studying in England, to fly to Toronto as to New York—and thank goodness, as she might oth-erwise have been on that very Pan Am flight—103, the flight she'd taken several times—that blew up over Lockerbie, crammed with American students just like her heading home to their eager families. And because of course nothing pleased Barb more than being in Toronto, at any time.

He'd had meetings in New York until late on the twenty-third, had stayed at the Middletowne, that loathed hotel near his office in which he'd essentially lived for several years in the late '70s, Monday to Friday on his own each week, while Barb refused to move back to the States because, she said, they couldn't uproot the girls yet again after moving them from Australia to Canada; and because she had to finish law school, seeing as her idiotic compatriots had refused to allow a single credit from her just-completed Australian law degree, even though they were both common-law countries; and because she couldn't abandon her poor blind mother—all these reasons that were surely valid but that also spoke chiefly of her lack of interest in *him, François,* her lack of love, indeed, her unwillingness to put him first the way time and again he had put her first, a disparity as old as their marriage: he'd applied to go to Can-ada from Sydney just to please her, though it was a demotion, "profes-sional suicide" as Larry Riley had said, incredulous, when he'd told him. But he'd done it, had swallowed it all, had barely complained when the goddamn Canadian government hassled him about a visa—though he'd been married twenty years to a Canadian! And Péchiney just dealt with it, quite sensibly, by promoting him back to New York, the much bigger market, the radically better position, where he should have been all along but where she perversely, for years, refused to join him. . . . But Christ-mas: he'd worked in the morning, the only one in the tomblike office, but he wanted to finish the paperwork before he left; and then he'd flown up on the Saturday afternoon, Christmas Eve itself—not sooner? Barb had asked on Friday, but again, like now, the double-edgedness of it all, he'd wanted to be with them, but at the same time he couldn't bear it, they all disappointed him, hurt him, their love always conditional, barbed, as if they poked him with a thousand tiny darts, by now he knew it and anticipated it, the way he hated Christmas because he so loved it, because each time he hoped it would be different, each time the long-suppressed wonder and anticipation of his boyhood welled up in him—how, in the war, when they'd had *nothing*, somehow his beautiful mother (dead now six years, dead only three weeks before Christmas indeed) had saved money enough to buy him colored pencils and a notebook, sheet music for Poupette, how she'd have saved a letter from his father to slip inside his shoe in the night, and an orange, round and firm, its juice the tangier because it was both longed for and a miracle; and from Tata Baudry somehow an egg or two, and from the wealthier Cousines Breloux some flour, and for Christmas an olive oil cake filled with dates, so moist and sweet—the Christmas Mass at night by candlelight, and again on Christmas morning—and the little crèche set up on the table in the front hall at the Rue Guillaumet, the stable a cardboard box on its side decorated, by him and his sister, with gilded paper, each year a little fresh straw from the cheesemonger on which to lay the plaster baby Jesus, his bright paint chipping with time, and arrayed around him his praying parents, but also the cow, the sheep, the donkey; while across the table, moved a few centimeters closer with each passing day, the three wise men approached, bearing their gifts . . . and the year he was leaving for Amherst on his scholarship, a young man by then, his mother had pressed into his hands a tin box filled with cotton wool in which was nestled a miniature version of the crèche, "So it will be properly Christmas," she'd said, "even when we aren't together."

All those memories, that rush of gratitude and amazement, yes, he'd always felt amazed, wondering that in the midst of weeks, months, of relentless darkness and struggle, a day of lightness could be found, the scent of an orange, the consoling mumble of a congregation in prayer, a haunting canticle, the sweet taste of the dates. But from the first, Barbara had a different idea of Christmas, certainly once the girls were born—the garlanded tree with its garish tinsel and flashing lights, the inundation of meaningless gifts, signifying chiefly unnecessary expenditure, the heavy English Christmas dinner, with its dry bird and mushy salted vegetables, all the northern European weightiness married to North American tat, the wonder turned instead to gluttony and consumerism.

So yes, he dreaded it each year, could each year foresee—they could all foresee—that the festivities would derail, the only questions being when and how. But this year was like a setup, cramming them all into the small flat, the two girls on the sofa bed in the TV room, he and Barb in the guest bedroom, where, between the bed and the chest of drawers and Barb's childhood desk, they could both barely stand at once, and Grandma in her slightly larger master bedroom at the end of the little corridor, with its en suite bathroom and sliding doors to the balcony. The bodies alone—four women's bodies and his own—filled the space, the air; stifled him. Outside the weather was bitter, but he'd opened the window in their little bedroom to smoke, holding his cigarette close to the sill so the curling trail would weave out into the night rather than filling the apartment, because now that she was too old and blind to smoke herself, Grandma complained of the smell. Not to mention the girls, of course, whose criticisms never ended. Over time, he'd become defiant about it, in spite of the killing cough, the hawking he had to undertake morning and night over the bathroom sink, like shoveling snow from the pathway to his lungs. Because why not? Why shouldn't he kill himself smoking, if he chose? Why couldn't anything at all be granted him without judgment and condemnation?

At dinner, the five of them crammed around the table that had once sat elegantly in the dining room on Grenadier Heights, now stuffed into an alcove of the sitting room so that the girls practically had to inhale to slide into their seats against the wall—at dinner he'd been overcome by a great weariness of the soul, and with it, their chattering voices faded into general noise, a conversation he could no more follow than he could have climbed Everest, but they weren't soothing, they irritated him, he knew it was wrong but they did, the banalities, holiday shopping in Yorkville, the illness of Mrs. Sims and her daughter's carelessness, the woman named Lyuba on the twelfth floor who celebrated Orthodox Christmas in January, would they go out to the church for the late service—St. Martin-in-the-Fields, most likely, on Glenlake, just past Keele, not *their* church, but who was going to drive all the way across town to their old neighborhood, to Grace Church on-the-Hill—and none of it matters, he was thinking, because it isn't even church, actually, just their wishy-washy Anglican pretense that she'd forsworn when they married, just as he'd forsworn Catholicism (the Latin Mass!), but it hadn't turned out that way—and all the while, if he were honest, as they bugged him more and more, the bottle of Tanqueray in his suitcase under the bed in the guest room had called to him the way the Absolut called to him from the freezer this very afternoon, and as they blathered and cleared the main course around him, and blathered some more, Barb's cheeks flushed from the champagne, the tip of her nose a little red, even Loulou, often so quiet at home, quite talkative, what was she talking about? Her friend Lisa, off in Japan to teach English—could he have picked that girl out of a crowd? He could not, had no idea who she was, and how could he be expected to care?

"Excuse me," he'd said, "I'll be right back," as if going to the bath-room, unusual only in that he excused himself, but it didn't cause so much as a ripple in their chatter, and all the while Barb, who flinched if he so much as kissed her cheek, scratched Waffles between the ears as he posed blissfully by her chair, the dog so loved by his mistress that he was smug-gled secretly into Grandma's No Pets apartment building and carried up and down the fire stairs, eight flights, every time he needed to pee. Oh, to be the dog!

He'd shut the bedroom door but not all the way. First he'd tried to quell this infernal itch with a cigarette, smoked again out the window—hadn't he done this all those years ago at Amherst, leaning down to exhale through the wee opening between sash and sill to please his roommate, Rosie, back then, and now to please this gaggle of women that was his family—but inevitably the itch could not be stopped, and so he knelt down and unzipped his leather case and withdrew the fat green ridged bottle with its white label and swooping black script, his familiar, the friend of his solitude, and being without a glass or cup and with half a thought to the duration of his absence, he unscrewed the top and took a hearty swig. And then he had another cigarette; and then—just as today, he could not resist—another swig, quite a big one. And alas to his shame—Or was it, even, in the moment? Perhaps not shame until later; but certainly to his surprise and irritation—there was a knock, but the door pushed open at the same time as the knock, and his younger daughter stood there, gaping, even as he upended the Tanqueray into his mouth.

For a second she didn't say anything and nor did he. He could not look her in the eye and so did not.

"Oh, Daddy," she said, all of twenty-two but sounding like a disappointed parent, "how could you?"

"What is it?" he said—because he did not know how else in this moment to behave; and it seemed paramount to assert that he had done nothing wrong, nothing that it was not fully within his rights to do.

"Not even a glass? Like a bum in the street. Not even a glass." She sounded very sad, rather than angry. It was worse. She was again silent for a moment; he did not look at her; she sighed. "Promise me that, at least. Promise me you'll have the dignity to use a glass, next time."

At which, indeed like a scolded child, he nodded and said, "I promise."

She then retreated, pulling the door to but not shutting it, just as it had been before, and he got down once again on his creaky knees (as if in prayer!) to stuff the bottle back into his suitcase, wrapped in the towel he kept for that purpose so the glass would make no noise when the case was moved, and he zipped the case closed and sat for a few moments on the edge of the bed, running his thick fingers over the stitching of the bridal quilt, a red-and-white patchwork made by his mother-in-law's grandmother at some distant moment in the nineteenth century, as if over a crucial message in braille that he could not decipher, letting the wave of his despair—and shame, yes, terrible shame, though it quickly subsided—wash over him, before setting his features in a mode of bland indifference and returning to the noisy table.

After that, how could he not have committed to sobriety? He felt such pity for his memory of himself on that night, worn out, exhausted even, alienated from them all, and they did not even notice. Holding his tongue, always, never sharing his misery, never bothering them with it. He felt grateful, too, that it had been Chloe rather than Barb or Loulou who'd come looking for him. He still did not know—would never know—what had been in her eyes.

And back in Greenwich, after the turn of the year, he had determined he would start anew. He could not tell Barb how hard it was—how fucking impossible—because whenever, over these years, she had suggested that he drank too much, he had insisted that she was talking nonsense, that he could give up at any time, just like he could lose twenty pounds if he wanted to or could take up his Berlitz Spanish tapes and really learn the language. That's to say, the itch and the role of the itch—which she kept trying to call "alcoholism"—could not be acknowledged.

But then, there'd been the public scandal, the scandal that even now shadowed their days—thank heaven he had no part in it, but practically speaking that was small consolation as he lost his colleagues one by one. The rain seemed to have stopped for a bit; François decided to take Waffles for a walk, just as far as the covered bridge. That way, when Barb got back, harried and late, she would thank him at least for that. He put on his windbreaker and a tweed flat cap just in case. Having a wet head was only more unpleasant without hair. Waffles, who didn't like the rain either, was reluctant—but surely he could hear that the drumming had stopped? François took the old green leash, not the new stretchy one that unspooled automatically from its plastic casing, the better to drag the dog along with him.

Could he himself have been dragged with the rest of them? How many times since January had he asked himself that question. On the good days, he assured himself that his probity had been indelibly manifest to all his colleagues—Yves, Dominique, Jean, Claude, and even Eric—and they'd kept him in the dark out of a healthy combination of fear and respect, because they'd known he would dissuade and perhaps even report their infractions: insider trading was against the law both in the United States and in France, and had latterly been much in the news. But then, on the darker days when his spirit mirrored this afternoon's weather, he told himself that they'd excluded him simply because that was what they'd always done, that he'd never fit in, that they'd concocted and disseminated their account-fattening crooked plans without him because they thought him unworthy, an irrelevance. Not that they chose not to tell him, but that they never considered it.

This scandal went to the very top, not just of Péchiney, but of all France. Thank goodness for the boss, Aubert, who liked him, and whom he liked—though not as much as he'd liked Besse: Besse had been his favorite boss in all the years, a kind, solid, brilliant man, like François not from the elite, though he'd been to all the right schools. And what had he got for his labors but a terrorist bullet on his front doorstep, his young daughter looking from the window, awaiting his return . . . that after he'd left Péchiney, of course, and was the CEO of Renault, in '86; but he'd been no older, poor guy, than François was now, and had vanished in an instant— Thank goodness, anyway, that Aubert had been untarnished—how many times this past year had François flown with him to Quebec, or to Chicago, or down to Wichita Falls, Texas, to the thriving Howmet plant, in the corporate jet—this, of course, he now believed, the reason he'd been deputed to go each time, because you couldn't leak information that you didn't know, he and Aubert—whom Barb called the Grand Panjandrum—like two stooges, kept clean for a reason . . .

Yes, the scandal was much bigger than Péchiney; it was all of France: that Pelat guy, arrested, Mitterrand's closest confidant, they said, first arrested and then suddenly dropped dead, his great friend from the German POW camp, that stocky little pugilist on the news a renowned commander of the Resistance—François had laughed aloud incredulous, not with mirth but shock: What was it Pelat said to the journalist? That the last time he'd been arrested it was by the Gestapo! But suddenly the shoe was on the other foot—a metaphor that came to mind because, on this soggy tour of the condo development's circular drive, François had stepped carelessly in a puddle and the water had seeped through some crack in his deck shoes (Weren't they supposed to be waterproof? Wasn't that the whole point of them?), soaking his left sock . . . the shoe was on the other foot and Pelat was a crook, an American-style, Ivan Boesky sort of crook, and the fact that he'd been in the Resistance forty-five years ago couldn't save him. And along with him Beregovoy's senior aide—the fucking *finance minister's* senior aide, that creep, Boublil, or the Booby, as Barb had taken to calling him—and Max Théret, the moneybags of the Socialist Party—they were by no means the only ones, but the most public. By American standards small potatoes, perhaps, but nonetheless, the biggest insider-trading scandal in French history.

The story had broken in that first week of January. At the office, they'd had only twenty-four hours' notice. It all came back to the New York team, to the group of men he saw each day, with whom he sat in meetings, and ate lunch, and even occasionally—though not with anything like the regularity with which they saw one another—for dinner. At the center of the scandal was the purchase of Triangle Industries, the parent company of American National Can, the crowning triumph of Péchiney's decision both to expand in the American market and to continue its investment in downstream products. With Aubert flying in from

Paris, they'd started the negotiations in June of the previous year and had come to a final agreement in November, just before Thanksgiving: the No. 3 aluminum producer in the world buying up America's largest can manufacturer ("A can in every hand, that's America!" joked Barb, with her snarky Canadian superiority); Michel Rocard, the French prime minister, had called it "a great economic development for the nation!"

Yes, well. Except that within three weeks of the deal, the American SEC had launched an investigation; a month later it was all over the press in both countries; and by February they were indicting senior French figures in the case. The facts were irrefutable: in the week before the announcement, Triangle shares, trading at ten times their normal volume, more than quadrupled in price. In just the last three days, a few buyers snapped up two hundred thousand shares. A Lebanese banker named Traboulsi was linked to both Boublil and Pelat; he, too, was indicted. The Socialists, Mitterrand included, were publicly painted with shame, their caring image irredeemably slimed by their greed; but this came as no surprise to François, who had long ago decided that all, or almost all, politicians were corrupt. No, his shock was at his colleagues, five men with whom he'd thought, after a decade—more than a decade they'd worked alongside one another, since his return to the States after Sydney and the brief Toronto detour—to have shared principles, his misjudgment born of all the other concrete things they did share: elevators, rooms, chairs, files, and even, now, computers. But when he said, "Christmas," he'd learned, he meant something different than Barb did; when he said, "devotion" also. And with these men, while they might all have spoken of loyalty, and honor, and honesty—his own dictionary definitions were taken from a different text, an abandoned volume, remnants of a lost century, another, more naïve world. He wasn't fit for this one.

The rain started up again when he and Waffles were only halfway back from the bridge. It fell now at an angle, hitting him in the face— the word *crachat* came to mind; though to whom might he say it? To whom might he say any of it? Waffles, though sprightlier on the return journey because keen to get home, grew irritated and paused repeatedly to shake himself dry, apparently not understanding that the wettening water fell continuously upon them. François felt like Waffles: the fool who persisted in believing he had agency when in fact forces on high determined his fate.

Barb had told him about a new board game, like Monopoly, but called Corruption—"The game for America in the eighties," she'd said with a bitter laugh. And of course she hated France, she'd always hated France; to her, this fiasco seemed fated. But, he wondered as he shut the door against the now-persistent downpour, dried Waffles head to toe with the worn towel left folded on the front hall table for this purpose, and then hung his own wet garments in the front hall washroom, maybe it wasn't that she disliked France per se, or even America per se, but that she disliked them because they mattered *to him*, because perhaps like his colleagues—he'd always thought they liked him!—she disdained him in her heart. All he'd ever wanted was to love and to be loved, to have the mirrored perfection of his parents' marriage. Even after all the years, so many arguments and harsh words, so many recriminations, so much disappointment, he kept trying: Barb was the love of his life, he'd never doubted it; he couldn't believe, not really, that she thought their life together had been a terrible mistake.

Last month, he'd taken her to Florida, to Miami and Key West, his first return since his long-ago student visit with Broussard and Mouret back at Christmas of '52. A lifetime. He'd thought it would be fun— the girls grown now, both off at their graduate programs; the Connecticut winter brutal and demoralizing, all the more so with the scandal at work. Last minute, mid-February, a sort of Valentine's trip. He'd even suggested, only half in jest, that they might find Florida a pleasant alternative for their retirement, remembering as he did the azure water and the clear, hot days, the long narrow causeway to the Keys with those strange little tufted islets visible among the waves. . . . And in his memory, Miami had about it a Latin charm, the white and ice-cream-colored art deco hotels near the beach, and the rather sleepy downtown. . . . But when they returned, the sleepy city had been usurped by massive steel-and-glass skyscrapers: the Southeast Financial Center, the I. M. Pei–designed CenTrust Tower, the Government Center building, the Miami Center, the Courthouse Center, the Lincoln Center, everything a center but the Palace in Brickell, the streets below baking and forlorn as traffic zipped along the avenues. Then the long drive to Key West bumper to bumper, the horizon from the causeway shimmering drunkenly in the haze of exhaust smog: they had to choose between the frigid AC roaring in their rented Buick LeSabre and the stifling stink of hot fumes if they opened the windows. They argued about lunch—he got hungry and pulled over at a dirty fish shack, which she complained would give her food poisoning; he demurred, and over an hour later they ate Big Macs in the car, which, he contended, were just as likely to make them sick.

By the time they'd reached Key West they were both surly. The hotel the travel agent in Stamford had booked was supposedly a fine one, the tallest building on Duval Street, the brochure had said, dating from the 1920s. But as Barb complained, it didn't seem as though much effort had been expended since on the upkeep. Their room at the back of the hotel was small and dark, and its lone window gave onto a view of parked cars and roofs, and the sticky carpet's dark paisley pattern, Barb said, had likely been chosen chiefly to hide a multitude of sins. "I shudder to think," she added and, for effect, literally shuddered. The air-conditioning, as in the car, too loud and too powerful, did not allow a less aggressive setting. The bathroom mirror and the sink were both cracked, and the plug for the tub was missing. ("Not that I'd climb naked into *that* without a gun to my head," Barb said.) Most upsettingly of all, they'd asked for a smoking room ("There's your mistake," she said. "Who smokes anymore, besides you? We're lucky they didn't put us in the basement!") and the reek of old tobacco clung to the bedding and upholstery, along with the tang of bleach and a distinctly recurring Floridian mold smell. Barb could not stop: the hotel was ghastly, but no less so Duval Street itself, along which, after dark, hordes milled from bar to bar. ("Men naked from the waist down," she read aloud from a poster outside one; and when they turned onto a side street to escape the crowds, "Oh look, 'For Sale by Onner'—who do you suppose Onner is? Have you met anyone named Onner?") They ate perched outside on barstools at high tables under strings of multicolored Christmas lights—Barb's cheeks glowed alternately pink and blue, depending which way she turned her head— while a small country-music band played ("Stand by your man . . .") loudly and poorly on a raised stage near the entrance to the kitchen, sparing them the effort of conversation.

He liked it all as little as she did (upon their return he lodged a complaint with the travel agent: no guest, he said firmly, should under any circumstances be sent at that price to that hotel!), but he disliked her attitude more. He took it personally on some level, as though he had decorated the hotel room, as though he'd invited the crowds and cooked the rubbery calamari himself. So he tried his best to pretend the adventure was acceptable, or at least anthropologically interesting, which only set them more firmly against each other. And so it continued, five days door to door, the lone rose he bought her for Saint Valentine's (always a lone rose, emblematic, to him at least, of the red rose he'd bought from the gypsy outside Harry's Bar, near the Opéra, on the night he proposed in late March '56, after she'd magically said yes and they'd floated out into the spring night, aware of the superiority of their youth—young, in love, in Paris! Though that, too, in retrospect, had doubtless signified quite different things to each of them), in America a strangely odorless rose, and more strangely still a thornless one, left behind in the tooth glass on the scuffed dresser in their dingy hotel room.

HERE SHE WAS NOW, his valentine, his bride, struggling with the grocery bags in the doorway from the garage to the kitchen, the big garage door rattling shut behind her, her wide mouth drawn in a nearly lipless line.

"Here," he said, reaching out for the bags. "Let me help you."

"I'm fine." She brushed past him to unburden herself at the counter. "You won't like it," she said, "but I got fish after all. Well, scallops." She started unpacking, still in her coat. "I thought, You actually *like* scallops, if I do them with white wine and lemon, over rice. You'd rather have that than a pork chop, I know you would."

He wondered whether to try to assist her, as she piled items at speed into the fridge and the cabinets; thinking better of it, he retreated to the far side of the island and stood, alongside Waffles, in wait. "Scallops are just fine," he offered amiably.

"You've no idea the cost of things, François. The steak was absurd! Three dollars a pound! Only in Greenwich, Connecticut. Highway robbery. The scallops were on sale—half price."

He wondered if that meant they were going off; her tightfistedness around household purchases annoyed him. It reminded him of his mother-in-law. In his parents' house, they always ate the best food they could afford. Was she then suggesting that they couldn't *afford* a decent piece of steak? Was it yet another veiled criticism of him, of his ability to provide? Let it go. "Aren't you going to take your coat off?"

She stopped unpacking and looked at him intently for a second, then resumed her bustling. "I've still got to take that damned dog out. In the rain, too."

"I've taken him."

"At lunchtime? That's too long already—"

"No, we just got back"—he consulted his watch—"less than half an hour ago."

"Well," she said brightly, "thank you. That *is* a surprise."

And again, more intensely, he found himself irritated by this response. As if it were unimaginable that he would do a helpful thing. The nerves all through his body jangled—this the sorry result of that little bit of vodka wearing off, his brain's subtle call for him to numb them again with a renewed dose; but he resolved not to let any of it show.

"Well, okay then," he said, rubbing his hands together and affecting a mild and placid expression, "I'll stay out of your way. I'll just be downstairs—I've got a chapter to finish."

"That's fine," she said, turning on the radio as if he'd already left the room: WQXR, the radio station of the *New York Times*. "It'll only be half an hour or forty minutes."

But surely they both recognized the almost imperceptible edge in his voice, and he knew, they both knew, that once activated, the irritation almost never subsided unexpressed, just as the itch for a drink almost never subsided without a drink; that's to say, they both knew—suspected, feared—that the evening, no matter how tasty the scallops and how prompt their preparation, would devolve into the familiar scene of François roaming the room as if it were a cage, delivering an ever more incensed monologue, railing against the world—whether about Barb or not was immaterial, as it was delivered *at* Barb, like a prolonged tempest that circled her until finally the winds subsided—while Barb, throughout, pulled her chair back from the table, lay her hands in her lap, and hung her mute head, retreating inside herself who knew where, enduring.

Calling a kid could change the inexorable trajectory, especially if it went well. The odds of a spontaneous chat with Loulou weren't good. Chloe, maybe? Was she still in Cambridge, or had she left for France? On the way to Easter with Grand-père and Tante Denise in Toulon, she had plans to visit friends in Paris for a few days. She would make a pilgrimage to the haunts of their own youth, the places that they'd told her about, all still there more than thirty years later, unaware of all the precious memories they held: the Rhumerie, the cheap and cheerful Restaurant des Beaux Arts, the Café de Flore . . . but not Harry's Bar, not their most special place, they hadn't told her about that. It was on the Right Bank, for one thing, where she would barely go, too fancy for her student budget. Possibly it no longer even existed; they hadn't checked in years.

"Shall we try Chloe?" he asked, with a glimmer of hope.

"I don't know that we'd get her," Barb said, though he could see that she was tempted. "Was she leaving today or tomorrow? If she's in Paris,

I don't know which hotel . . ." Barb was finally removing her coat; she walked down the hall to hang it in the front hall closet, and her voice drifted back: "I don't know. It's after eleven over there anyway, even if she's in Cambridge . . ."

"She never goes to bed before midnight. We could just try."

"Okay," Barb agreed, but doubtfully. She turned off the radio, in case.

Though he willed it, and knew that Barb, too, willed it, both as forcefully as they were able, they could not magic their daughter into her room on Jesus Lane on Saturday night. Maybe she'd left already, or maybe she was out on the town with her boyfriend or a group of friends. They could imagine anything they chose, joyful or anxious; but could hear only the flat, British double ring echoing down the tinny line. As he eventually replaced the receiver, he saw the disappointment in Barb's face—he felt it too—and he paused to caress her shoulder.

"Well," he said, "I guess we won't catch her tonight. I'll go finish my chapter. Just call me when it's time." There'd be half an hour till drinks time, and he thought that perhaps, in the compassion of their shared small sorrow, the trajectory of their evening had been altered after all.

TOULON, FRANCE

She was glad that Chloe and Oliver had come—how could she not be? She considered her nieces to be her own daughters, and their future husbands (Surely he was a future husband? Chloe would not be bringing him otherwise) were to be embraced and welcomed into the family. Of course she made jokes about the *pièces rapportées*—who didn't?—but from all accounts Oliver was everything you could wish for, including the son of very devout parents, though inevitably, being British, they were Protestants. The father, a university professor of some sort, had also recently been ordained, apparently, though what this meant in practical terms she did not know. She had liked the idea of Oliver better for knowing these facts about his family; and now that he was here, she liked him a good deal, though his French wasn't very good (on the first day he'd referred to the binoculars as "*les binoches*," immediately adopted as a family joke), and Papa, between his deafness and his own execrable English, had difficulty following the conversation at table. She kept having to repeat and explain things for him. But she was glad, of course she was. It was just a rather stressful time.

Her sleep had been disrupted for, well, a few months. Maybe it was menopause, but she didn't think so. She slept now in the airless little room off the kitchen and often felt as though she'd only just fallen asleep when her alarm went off. She took her coffee at the table in the kitchen at six-thirty, usually just that (she couldn't eat much these days, just like she couldn't sleep), her large bowl of coffee, black with sugar, and a cigarette or two, as the day dawned, before she hastened to wash her torso with a cloth in the chilly bathroom, to dress and slip out the door for work.

She didn't like to encounter Odet in the mornings—Odet arrived by seven-thirty. They irked each other more and more since Denise had moved back into her father's apartment, now over a year ago. That Odet disapproved of this did not need to be said overtly; Denise could feel it. And did not think it was any of Odet's business. She had moved back in before, after all, when Maman died, in '83, and had stayed over a year, then, too. What was wrong with taking care of family, while they also took care of you? What was family, if not for that? Papa, whose legs were bad, had had a fall (mercifully a minor one), soon after they'd returned from Chloe's college graduation in America, and in her worry she felt it vital to be near him. He protested, but she knew he was grateful. And besides, alone in her flat she was afraid and could not sleep . . . okay, so it was closer to two years she'd been there, perched in the little bedroom cubby that had once held the girls' bunk beds. Since they'd grown and had been given the larger room to stay in, she didn't care to sleep there, even though they so rarely came. She felt safest in the little room; and it was closest to Papa, so she could hear him if he called out in the night, or got up to go to the bathroom.

And so what if she couldn't bear to be in her own apartment just now? She supposed that Odet and Barbara and all the others who judged her harshly thought she should rent or sell it, that it was wrong to leave it empty for so long. But what had she bought it for—or yes, if she were fully honest, why had François bought it for her—if not for her to have the freedom to do with it what she pleased? She asked for very little in this life. She submitted without complaint to many small humiliations, to being always the extra wheel, the single woman, the undesired; she had devoted her life to her mother and father, joyfully, and when her beloved mother had died and she had doubted all her decisions—when, yet again, she had been assailed by the futility of her existence—she had prayed to God to tell her what her life was *for.* And He had told her that she was the night-light, the small companion in the darkness, to assist others when they needed it, but not to call attention to herself. And she had said, Yes, Lord, I can do that, I can be that, and had recommitted to her path of sacrifice—but if the Lord (and her brother) had granted her a space on earth of her very own—she couldn't articulate how much she loved that space, how much it meant to her, even if, at present, just as she couldn't really sleep and she couldn't really eat, she also could not live in it—then wasn't it her prerogative to use that space as she chose?

Sometimes, just sometimes, she would tell her father she had a lunch engagement and wouldn't be home at midday, or that she had a meeting or an errand to run that didn't really exist, and she would park in her own allotted space outside Building H and would slip up the darkened stairwell to the second floor, stepping into her beautiful, still apartment, empty of people and demands, hearing her heels click on the marble floor and the hum of the refrigerator, and the sound of the fountain in the koi pond outside the window. Her heart would fill, and she would sit on the sofa for which she had so carefully chosen the upholstery fabric, a less expensive replica of a blue-and-red chinoiserie pattern she'd seen in British *House & Garden*, and simply breathe. She would sit unmoving, which she never otherwise did, rushing here and there always, for work, for her father, for the church, hosting guests, and for a few minutes, she would take in all the pleasures of the flat, the colorful fabrics she'd chosen, the Oriental scatter rugs and the pictures on the walls, each one meaningful in a different way, her stone, porcelain, and papier-mâché egg collection on the dresser next to her smaller but no less loved tortoise collection, all of the tchotchkes souvenirs of disparate people and of places, manifestations of secret memories and loves. She'd then water the plants, both inside (where they congregated on a painted table by the window) and on the balcony. A line of Baudelaire always came to her in these quiet moments: *"luxe, calme et volupté."* How fortunate she felt to have this beautiful private place. But she could not be in it for very long, and when, in the evening, she returned from the office to her father, she felt grateful for that, too, to have a companion for whom she must find resolve and good cheer, and meaning, which she couldn't seem to generate on her own.

Looking at Chloe and Oliver, how happy they seemed with each other—they would surely get married, wouldn't they? So many young people didn't anymore—she wondered how her life might have been had she found someone. No, the hard truth: if the someone she had found had reciprocated her love. Many years, over ten indeed, like a spider building an intricate and beautiful shimmering web tethered to the world in only a few tenuous spots, Denise had created her beloved, and their love, from the slightest evidence—the occasional letter from Jacques in Buenos Aires, a few gatherings at his sister Antoinette's in Paris, once a dinner just with him at an elegant bistro in Marseille, when she still worked there, and she had felt herself almost trembling with joy in his presence, noting the curl of his stubbled lip and his shiny teeth when he smiled, the way he gestured broadly while still holding his fork, his intent gaze, his lovely darkly lashed eyes; and he'd been so funny, and kind, had remembered so many details of her time at the agency, the sailing day she'd spent with his family, when she'd consoled his youngest daughter, Isabelle, after she tripped and bumped her head coming out of the little cabin on the boat, and Denise had held the wisp of a girl in her lap and rocked her, had kissed her forehead countless times and sung her little songs to distract her from the pain—he'd remembered that; and their first meeting at the party in the garden at his parents' house, so vivid to her still; and the particular black-and-white portrait of her parents in profile that she'd kept in a blue frame on her desk at the travel agency— all of that remembering seemed so clearly a sign of care, an acknowledgment of their impossible but abiding love. . . . She'd considered him her Tristan, she Isolde, devoted forever though honor and duty kept them apart. She'd spoken to nobody about her passionate devotion, though she'd kept a diary in which she wrote to him, or wrote about him, almost every day. He lived permanently on a distant continent, in another hemisphere; he was married to a lovely woman whom Denise admired; he had three, and then four, daughters; but she wrote and believed that none of this mattered, that their love was divinely ordained—Had Maman and Papa's love not been divinely ordained? Were not all Great Loves gifts from God?—and that therefore it did not matter whether they were physically together, ever, because their union, spiritual and potentially complete, transcended all worldly trappings. It was enough, she told herself, that he was alive on the planet, and she could love him the way she loved God, with a sacrificial devotion.

And then that terrible summer of '74, when Estelle came to visit. Denise didn't yet then own her flat, and she was still working in Marseille, where she rented a depressing studio in a sunless narrow street. So the friends had stayed instead in her parents' apartment—they were still in Australia, but she'd returned early, unable to take more than three weeks' vacation. And dear Estelle had come for a few days, in the middle of a longer visit with her sister in Paris. Olive-skinned, gap-toothed Estelle, whom she adored, and they'd done together at forty all sorts of things she'd not enjoyed for years—they'd spent a day lazing at the beach, wading occasionally into the cool salt water, and had eaten pizza in their bathing suits under a fronded umbrella on a terrace by the sea; they'd gone, for dinner, to a lively restaurant on the port and had drunk a liter and a half of wine between them—Estelle cheerily struck up conversation with two men at a neighboring table, a sort of light, flirtatious banter, and only as they meandered back to the car did she screech with laughter, bent double, and hoot, "Trust me, trust us, to flirt with the only gay guys in the place! Honestly, we're ridiculous!" And Denise, too, had laughed—how she adored her friend! But later that night, as they sipped scotch and chain-smoked and swung their feet in the glider swing on the roof terrace of the apartment beneath the great canopy of stars, with the beating surf far below them as regular as breathing, Estelle had confided in her—"I've not even told Antoinette," she whispered, as though a listening ghost hovered nearby on the night air—that she'd discovered the facts of her brother Jacques's affair, that he'd been having a relationship with the chief secretary at the agency, Blanca, and that it had been going on for years, maybe even as far back as Denise's time in Buenos Aires, yes, over a decade, certainly not long after, because Blanca had a little boy, born in '66, was it, just turned eight, and Estelle had always admired Blanca for being such a fine single mum, but now that she understood the situation, she felt Blanca was much more difficult to admire: the child was Jacques's, at this point he powerfully resembled him—who could mistake those eyes, those lashes? And she'd confronted her brother about it, and he'd shrugged, all charm—he was fatally charming, her brother, wasn't he? Everyone adored him, and he knew it—and he'd said, "Can I help it if I have a surfeit of love?" and, further, "Don't worry, I take good care of all of them," he'd said, and winked, which made Estelle wonder whether there weren't other mistresses about, or even, heaven forbid, other children. "And to think," she said, "my poor sister-in-law going through four pregnancies—five, if you count the awful miscarriage—to try to give my brother a son and heir! And with Blanca, he has the son on the first try, but the son can never be his heir. It's like Shakespeare!"

Like Shakespeare indeed. And all too familiar, the story of her paternal grandfather, whom she'd never met, the inconstant Constant Cassar, who'd left his family of four children when Papa was just a boy of eight, for the other family in another town that he'd kept for years on the side. Papa saw him again only once after that, at his grandmother's funeral, and of all the sins in the family mythology, his was the greatest, the absolute betrayal of his wife and children, of his duty before God. For Denise, the revelation had come like a hurricane, destroying in minutes the delicately spun and so long preserved shimmering web of her love affair—yes, she'd considered it all these years a love affair, though they had never held hands, let alone kissed; but she'd spent time each day thinking of him, praying for him, imagining his life in Buenos Aires . . . she'd been a fool, enamored of a figment, had created the soul of a man who never existed—

Denise could not linger any longer in that memory; it still burned. If it had all ended then, her life, as she'd intended—but God had other plans for her. And here she stood on the little balcony off the dining room, watching her niece and her niece's boyfriend, down below at the pool, leaning over the balustrade and gazing out to sea, their backs to her. How many cigarettes had Denise smoked, standing here? Her father, she could hear, was pushing back his chair at the desk overhead, and soon she'd hear his heavy but uncertain steps on the narrow marble staircase. In his mid-eighties, he was unsteady now on his feet, and she worried constantly about him falling. She'd read that simple falls were the most likely catalyst for an older person's final decline; and if she had a purpose on the planet, it was to protect him. She found it hard to believe that just four years ago he had traveled on his own to Buenos Aires, to revisit for the first and last time the city and people who had made them so happy. He'd made his plans just a scant year after Maman's death, had traveled in the early spring of '85, with a dogged, even cheerful, commitment to continued life that had impressed, even amazed her. He hadn't understood why she'd refused to accompany him—she knew it had seemed both like a failure of character and a failure of care—but she simply could not do it. She could not.

Chloe, by the side of the pool, looked up and waved, tapped Oliver on the arm, so that he also looked up and waved, squinting in the sunlight. She wore shorts; dear girl, she was getting rather heavy, since puberty had those heavy legs, though she'd been such a skinny child—Denise understood all too well what that was like—perhaps if she took up smoking? It had worked for Denise. But who was going to suggest that to the young today? Did she need to gesture to summon them for lunch? No, they'd turned, they knew simply by her presence that it was time; she could see that they moved toward the stairs.

Behind her, with a clatter of silverware, Odet was finishing setting the table. Should she have helped her? No, for God's sake, she'd worked all morning on the conveyancing contracts for the company's newest tract of land: they would build a compound inland for the first time, though they were known for their luxury sea-view condominiums—but with the lean recent years, the company had made slightly different calculations. . . . Denise had her job, and Odet hers: again, like the use of her flat, Denise felt that this, which to her was a natural and logical boundary (Odet was, after all, *paid* to set the table, as well as to prepare lunch, and to clean, and to do the laundry), was by her very North American sister-in-law and nieces tacitly called into question. They, unaccustomed to having paid help, always felt obliged to launch in and lend a hand, oblivious to hierarchies, little understanding how this self-aggrandizing precedent ("Look what a thoughtful and generous person I am!") disrupted the long-standing order of the household, making *her* question whether she was entitled to enjoy a cigarette at the window, in her brief lunch break, rather than take on the housekeeper's tasks. It was most provoking. She could hear through the wall the clicks of the elevator in its shaft as it climbed to their floor; anticipating the young people's return, she unlocked and opened the door, as her father, who had gone into his room, then the bathroom, emerged also into the front hall.

Over lunch—prosciutto and melon, a beautiful orange flesh so juicy and redolent it was almost high, followed by quenelles in a *sauce armoricaine* and a well-dressed green salad (Maman had taught Odet how to make a proper vinaigrette), of which Papa made his usual joke ("I don't touch the stuff—it's full of microbes!"), followed by yogurt and fruit—they spoke of the kids' plans to walk to the Mourillon in the afternoon, perhaps the following morning a trip to the market downtown; they could take the bus from outside the compound: they discussed, to Oliver's delight, that in the outbound direction, homebound if they were downtown, the bus's destination was Terre Promise, the Promised Land—and lunch on the port—yes, Papa would come: she could leave work early to pick him up, though could they plan, then, for the kids to meet them at the edge of the Port Marchand, to walk with him from there to the restaurant—she'd make a booking—because from the lot it was too far for him to walk, and she did not trust him on his own if she dropped him off, his legs weren't what they used to be. (She could see on his smiling face both his mild irritation at her insistence—he disliked any suggestion that he was an old man, not yet, having all his life been *young*, so much younger than his wife—and his delight at being fussed over, taken care of.) Yes, if they wanted, after lunch they could stay, but they'd be on their own, as she'd have to run him home for his *sieste*— even as she suggested they'd be free to wander, she thought, as always, of all the steps from the apartment parking spot up to the lift and then to the front door—seventy-two: they'd counted them long ago, even before they became too much for Maman, who'd spent the last two years of her life housebound on that account—and she knew that the kids couldn't stay downtown—what would the point be, anyway, when all the shops were shuttered until two-thirty or even three?—because she couldn't spare the extra twenty minutes it would take to accompany him laboriously up all the stairs and get him settled for his nap . . . here, he balked: "You are being ridiculous! Every morning I go on my own to do the shopping, often to three different *centres commerciales*, at this point." But that was first thing, she pointed out, before his legs were tired, and did he not remember last autumn, with Madame Jolivet, when Denise had left them to walk to the café while she parked, only two hundred meters, not even, and he had crumpled to the sidewalk like a tower in an earthquake? The bruises, the weeks of pain—did he not recall? By now, though still smiling, he was truly annoyed: the day had been exception-ally hot, he recalled . . .

What she didn't say, fingering a red pimple like a welt under her chin, only faintly aware of her knee tapping furiously under the table, was that both her boss and her doctor had encouraged her to take this fortnight off from work—"nervous exhaustion," the doctor called it; her boss had

observed only that she seemed *"bien fatiguée,"* by which he was referring to the fact that she'd lost her temper too many times in the previous week with her two incompetent juniors and the blasted receptionist,
that vain little bottle-blond airhead who kept forgetting to give Denise
her phone messages and had thereby created a minor but very real crisis. . . . It almost seemed as though Morel and Muli were in cahoots to
try to push her out of the office, when the conveyancing contracts were
at their most demanding stage and, in addition, there was the upcoming hearing for the lawsuit against the concrete-cladding company over
the complex in Cassis—no, she couldn't possibly take time off now. The
doctor, Muli, had been quite insistent: she'd lost too much weight, she
smoked too much, she wasn't sleeping (it was true; she wasn't sleeping).
Why, he wanted to know, had she fallen out of bed and cracked a rib,
already now two months ago, but still? The answer of course was that
being unable to sleep she had taken a sleeping pill, possibly two—why
not, at last, on a Friday night, with neither work nor Mass the next day?
Did any of them understand (certainly not these blithe, spoiled adult children!) all that she, Denise, had to manage, and what faith and tenacity it
took for her to smile and joke and add to her burdens, uncomplainingly
and with a show of delight, the extra effort of taking them all for lunch at
the port downtown? She could feel her heart pounding in her chest as if
she had been running, rather than merely eating lunch.

Meanwhile, somehow, the conversation had turned to Algeria—how
could this have come up now, when already her shoulders were up to her
ears, her body's tension like a singing wire? But she had to remind herself
that if these kids knew no history, understood nothing of the past, didn't
know where they came from, it was because this was what François had
wanted for them, marrying Barbara and raising their children in a different language, a different—or no!—religion, and an unrecognizable
culture, so that for all their endless lessons they still had foreign accents
and searched for their words—if they didn't have the vocabulary, how
could they be expected to know who, by accursed birthright, they were?

While Denise's mind was elsewhere, Chloe had obviously volunteered the accepted truism that the French presence in Algeria had been fundamentally wrong—as if well over a hundred years of people's lives—and deaths, for that matter—could simply be dismissed with a vague ideological wave of the hand, rather like telling a child she was a mistake and should have been aborted! Insisting that a person had no right to exist, to be who they were! Denise could feel her hands clenching, that strange detachment of rage, like a wind through her. "Do you have any idea? Of course you can't," she burst out. "When we came here, almost a million, nobody wanted us. All our lives we'd been told, 'You are fully French, part of France, it's a *département* like any other.' France is France from Dunkirk to Tamanrasset, de Gaulle said it as late as 1959—but then he threw away our lives and our history because it was *expedient*, because of public opinion, the opinion polls of arrogant people in the metropole who couldn't find Algeria on a map, who didn't even know we spoke *French*, for God's sake."

She took a breath. Even in the flight of her speech she could see the expressions of alarm on Chloe's face, on sweet Oliver's, yes, even on her father's—they considered her intemperate, did they? "And don't get me started on the *harkis*, the poor noble Algerians who *supported* us, who *supported* France in the conflict—at great risk to themselves and their families, might I add, and they had to flee, they had no choice, leaving their land and their communities, throwing in their lot with the supposedly beneficent French nation . . . and how were they treated?" She paused for effect; she could see the alarm still, but persisted: "Like *shit*, that's how. They should have been welcomed, and thanked, and instead they were locked up in what were virtually concentration camps—"

"Yes, it's true," her father said, breaking in. "This country should be ashamed of how we treated the *harkis*." He had about him a supreme patriarchal calm, like the Buddha; she could feel him willing her to let go of her rage, to return to them at the table in the warm, placid spring afternoon, to relinquish the memories of those terrible months in Paris, before she joined her parents in Buenos Aires, a history that gripped her like a fever—he continued to speak in the low, even tone of a teacher: " . . . was the French presence in Algeria wrong? Certainly it was born of highly questionable impulses, justified by highly dubious reasoning—basically, France owed a good deal of money to Hussein Dey, the Algerian leader, and rather than pay it, especially after he insulted us by hitting our consul with a fly whisk, we invaded the country. Which hardly constitutes a fine basis for future relations. But what about the Spanish in Latin America? Or, more relevant to the discussion, what about your own home country, the United States? Or your childhood home, Australia?"

"How do you mean?" Chloe appeared baffled, the set of her jaw resistant. But Denise, her temperature now lowering (she could feel the color in her cheeks; she was now aware of her wildly tapping foot, and put a hand on her knee to still its dance), felt a surge of gratitude for that bafflement, as for her father's calm disquisition: of herself, of this uncontrollable emanation of her heart, she felt ashamed, now, a flush of shame as sudden and inevitable as her anger. Why must she be herself? Why was it so unacceptable to be herself?

Her father, with his infuriating wry smile, continued to speak: "Americans love to consider themselves blameless. I don't accuse you of this, my child, but it's our responsibility to know the history. There are various forms of colonialism, you see, of greater or lesser intrusiveness. In West Africa or in Indochina, France never sought to do more than govern and administer the people—"

"And exploit their resources," Chloe broke in.

"Yes, though I think 'develop their economies' is how it was articulated at the time. Anyway, just as the British in India or Kenya had no intention of moving in wholesale, in Indochina, aside from a small contingent of enterprising adventurers, we aimed largely to run things.

"Whereas when France embarked upon the Algerian undertaking, it was in the spirit, exactly, of the British in America or Australia. That's to say, it was with a belief in new possibilities for the French population, a desire to start an outpost of France itself—or Britain—overseas. It was to be a settler colonialism, rather than a purely administrative one—"

"And you're suggesting that's somehow better?" Chloe's ire was audible. Denise, still trying to calm herself, shut her eyes briefly.

"I'm making no suggestions," Papa continued. "I am simply laying out the facts. A set of facts by which, logically, both Australia and the United States should be returned to their rightful inhabitants."

"But it's not the same—"

"Is it not? Might we not acknowledge that Australia and the United States are simply more *successful* examples of settler colonialism—no less unjust, no less brutal, simply with a fuller obliteration of the native cultures? And this, of course, without turning our attention to slavery, that ineradicable shame of the country of your birth."

"But nothing of what you say justifies colonialism—or its racist brutality. We're talking about Algeria, so what about Frantz Fanon? Have you read Frantz Fanon?"

He sighed. "I confess that I have not. But I'm not seeking to justify—that's beside the point. And, we must all agree, impossible. We must consider the facts; they can't be willed away. We started from the premise that in the case of Algeria, at least, the decisions of 1830 cannot be justified by anything other than France's perceived self-interest. But self-interest is generally humanity's motivation, no? All I'm trying to impress upon you is that your happy and free United States of America is, at root, no different from French Algeria—merely, for the colonizers, a more successful iteration. After the Spaniards, the British, and the French came successive waves of settlers, vast numbers of them, eager to start again in the Land of the Free. But the Land of the Free was in fact no more a blank slate than was Algeria. To create that mythical land required also the subjugation of peoples."

"So you *do* agree that it was right for Algeria to gain its independence?"

Denise watched her father's face closely; his calm did not waver. "It was—or, rather, sadly it became—inevitable. I say 'sadly' for myself, for our family, rooted there for over a century. We might have wished for a happier ending, one that would have made it possible for everyone to live in harmony, to build a nation together. But wishing does not make it so." He paused. "I'm a man of faith above all. I trust in God, and believe that His will is done. We are mere mortals, endlessly fallible and misguided. I loved Algeria—I grew up and lived more than half my life considering it my home. I loved the very land itself. Unquestioningly. Your grandmother and I were formed by it, our love was born there, and we expected to grow old and to die there. We are Mediterraneans, above all, and Catholic, and we consider ourselves blessed to live out our days within sight of Mare Nostrum.

"I don't say all this to argue for empire—though I was born into that tradition and lived much of my life in its service—I am, and therefore you also are, a colonial product. No, in the name of empires, countless atrocities were committed, and they must not be forgotten. No, I've said all this to try to show you the danger of hypocrisy. We are always already guilty. If we don't know history, we're doomed. Let him who is without sin cast the first stone. If only we actually lived by our principles."

Denise attempted to gauge her niece's response—surely she was forced to accede to her grandfather's irrefutable logic. Denise felt still the embarrassment of her own outburst, and the irritation that she should feel embarrassed. But that, now, must be suppressed.

"Speaking of India," said Oliver, always peaceable, looking at Grand-père, "I saw on the shelf above my bed"—he was sleeping upstairs on the sofa bed in Papa's study, that least comfortable berth—"a copy of *Thy Hand, Great Anarch!*, in English—is it yours?"

"Oh no," said Papa. "That's Denise's. My English isn't up to it, I'm afraid."

"Yes." Denise took up the gambit, grateful to this wonderful young man for changing the subject—please God the girl might marry him. "Barbara sent it to me. You know they'd like to visit India, so she's been reading. And I, too, have always dreamed of going—"

Odet appeared suddenly from down the hall, having removed her work smock and slippers, back in her street clothes and clacky sandals. Of course here she was, claiming the floor as soon as Denise started to speak.

"Okay everybody, I'm off," she cried brightly, fumbling in her bag for her bus pass. "I'll see you tomorrow morning."

Chloe pushed back her chair with a screech along the marble, and darted over to embrace Odet on both cheeks and to thank her, effusively—this wearisome theater of gratitude! Which prompted Denise to do the same, enveloping the still smaller woman (they were both small, after all) in her arms: "My beauty, thank you, thank you, thank you! Is it Madame Michel this afternoon? Make sure she drives you home, okay?"

"Good-bye, good-bye!"

How exhausting it was, Denise reflected as she regained her chair, simply to be alive, well past life's midpoint, alone in her heart, and every interaction a labor. She looked at her watch. "Maybe I have ten minutes to lie down before I go—" Though she wouldn't—couldn't—sleep. "Papa, do you need a hand?"

"I do not."

"I'll just take ten minutes, then, in the armchair."

As the house fell into its siesta silence, she tried to quell the worries and disappointments spinning through her. Listen to the sea against the shore, she told herself. Listen to the cicada song. Listen to the desperate shih tzu on the ground floor barking in his yard, to the gardeners' motors and thready voices drifting up from the hedges by the pool, to the trapped fly, desperate too, buzzing up and down the giant windowpane. Try to forget. Try to forget. It is time, again, always, to go.

⚓

CHANNEL CROSSING,
CALAIS TO DOVER

They'd begun digging the previous year, but the tunnel under the Channel wouldn't be finished for eons. Still, the choice was between the bus and the ferry or the train and the ferry, the former recommended only by its cheapness. Place de Stalingrad, the terminus from which the lumbering coaches departed nightly, felt sinister at all hours, and the toilet facilities on board were indescribable. So we paid half again as much for the dusty overnight train from the Gare du Nord, from which we'd have to disembark at Calais from the depths of slumber—wakened, first, by officials banging peremptorily through the midnight carriages, carrying with them the echoes of wartime. Nothing surely had changed in the intervening forty-five years—certainly not the carriages themselves, made up of six-person compartments, their two banks of filthy velveteen seats facing each other, the armrests worn bare, the smeared windows half-covered by dusty accordion curtains, and outside, sheer blackness, broken every so often by a whizzing abandoned station or the flickering sulfurous streetlights of a sleeping town.

Our bags, which barely fit on the overhead racks, loomed precariously above us, while we were forced by lack of floor space to play footsie in the dark with our fellow passengers. Odors old and new mingled in our nostrils, residual sweat and gusts of tobacco from the corridor, followed by the pungent stink of garlicky fat when the rangy, vulpine youth by the window took from the sack at his feet a waxed-paper packet of cervelat that he stuffed between hunks of bread and into his mouth, chewing noisily. We dozed in the penumbra, heads lolling to the train's rhythmic rattle, never quite asleep, waiting always for the high whine of the brakes. We'd left Toulon in the morning on the TGV to the Gare de Lyon, escorted to the station by Tante Denise, her workday interrupted for us. We'd planned the return route so as not to have an expensive overnight in Paris: the whole journey, door to door, would take almost twenty-four hours, though of course Tante Denise and Grand-père believed I was traveling farther still, all the way back to Cambridge, to my digs in the yellow brick student house on Jesus Lane, rather than stopping with Oliver in his tiny room in the cluttered shared row house in Herne Hill, South London, where we clung to each other in a single bed pressed beneath the chilly window, and where the five disparate residents wrote their initials on the eggs in the fridge.

We were powerfully aware that we traveled from sunshine back into gloom, from comfort to discomfort. During our stay from Easter into April, the blooming bright oleander and electric bougainvillea burst in a froth over the golden stone walls and along the highways, a parliament of birds filled the trees with their songs, and the fat honeybees began their dogged pollinating rounds. We'd sat in the sun on the terrace till our cheeks and shoulders burned, while in Paris and London a damp chill still prevailed, in spite of the cherry blossoms and municipal clusters of brilliant tulips.

Easter: to please my grandfather and above all my aunt, we'd accompanied them to Mass in the gloomy church down the hill on Easter morning; even Oliver, raised in endless religious ceremony, was uncertain of the droned rituals of Catholic Mass in French. I'd felt self-conscious remaining in the pew at Communion but knew that for us to step to the altar along with the rest of the congregation would have horrified our aunt, for whom our watery Protestantism was no faith at all, and our confirmations null. Just as the British were snooty about American education, the Catholics dismissed any religious traditions but their own, and I was considered, as it were, incommunicable. This annoyed and amused me in equal measure.

But I wanted Oliver to know and understand me, which was impossible without time in Toulon. My grandparents' apartment remained the one geographical constant of my wanderer's life, their inviolable routines and Grand-père's unwavering calm and humor, like my Canadian grandmother's generosity and sharp tongue, the fundaments of my existence thus far. They might frustrate me—like the oblivious appropriative emphasis with which my grandfather had, a few days earlier, taken in hand my newly purchased copy of Derrida's *Éperons* ("Ah, he was a schoolmate of your father's!") and, opening it upon the dining table, irreparably flattened and broken its spine, making it, in a single decisive gesture, a book no longer new, and a book no longer mine—but I believed in their wisdom, and their gifts for happiness, or at least contentment, gifts that had eluded the next generation of my mother, my father, and my aunt.

My grandfather, after all, had for fifty-five years adored and treasured his wife. He had cared for her with unflagging devotion through the ravages of her dementia, making sure not only that she was always comfortable and lovingly surrounded but that, with Denise's and Odet's help, she was each day perfectly coiffed and *maquillée*, an elegant illusion that her impeccable, inalienable grace and manners served to the last to uphold. And yet, once she died, he had nonetheless seemed (to me, at least) placidly resigned to her absence. More than that, he'd confided (only to me, in Paris, where I studied in the spring of 1985, at a caviar restaurant at which he abandoned me for ten minutes to chat with our young waitress by the bar) that when he'd returned to Buenos Aires earlier that year, a sort of swan-song trip, he'd asked Denise's old friend Estelle, she of the infectious gap-toothed smile, whether as she, too, lived alone, she might not consider marrying him. He'd suggested that it might potentially be a happy companionship for them both. She, he told me, cheerfully declined, her lightheartedness salvaging the exchange from mawkishness; but they'd both agreed, and might I also please agree, to keep this particular conversation from Denise. After all, he'd said to me—I was then not even nineteen—if Estelle had said yes, he was convinced that after some inevitable initial discomfort Denise would have seen the advantages of the union between her dear friend and her father; but as things had turned out, she should be spared having to consider it.

I agreed to keep the story quiet. I couldn't see that Denise would ever have been reconciled. But I marveled at the freedom of the old man's imagination, at his certainty that all would've been fine. He'd told me, around the same time, when I'd announced that my friends mattered more to me than anything, that I spoke out of youthful ignorance and would discover, in time, that family was all that ultimately mattered. I'd bridled, ethically outraged, but wondered too what he might know that I did not; and considered that this marriage proposal, to me so inappropriate—something from a Victorian novel, the binding of two different generations!—had been an ancient strategy to cement Denise's dear friend into the family, to ensure that even after his death—he was at the time eighty years old, and a realist—the two women were forever formally allied. Somehow—maybe it was religious faith or simply temperament, a sort of supreme confidence (though we were told that his ferocious temper in earlier years had far outstripped our father's, with the implication that our father learned his rage from a master)—he seemed to float through life a pure optimist, sage, compassionate, an inveterate believer in pleasure and, above all, in love.

How differently from me my grandparents and aunt lived, formed and bolstered by their beliefs—in God, in patriotic hierarchies, in antique social constraints—and by a lost world order. Theirs was a small tributary of the past, somehow continuing into my present. Whereas my father, who'd never spoken a word to us about his childhood, who never uttered the name Algeria (anything we knew we'd heard from Tante Denise or Grand-père), who seemed to have sprung, fully formed, into his life as a faux-American adult, had chosen to leave the past behind. As the old saying went, he had turned the page. He'd renounced Catholicism (though I'd once caught him with tears coursing down his cheeks when the pope delivered the Christmas Mass on television; when I'd asked why, he'd explained that when he'd last heard the Mass in Latin, he'd thought he had a religion, and a country—his only mention ever to me of these two primal losses); he'd largely renounced France. Jaded about the world, he had no known politics, no friends from before the age of thirty, no discernible past before he'd met my mother.

I considered these things in the darkness, as the train to Calais chuntered toward the coast, my grandfather's surprising happiness and the equally unexpected unhappiness of his offspring. I thought of Tante Denise, whose chin, from the stress perhaps of hosting us, had broken into a rash of red spots and who—she'd confided this only to me and, like her father, had asked that I not reveal it to anyone else—had been told unequivocally both by her boss and by her doctor that she *must* take a *congé* for her nerves, several weeks perhaps, which would begin right after we left. But this alas not before she'd disastrously lost her temper, on the next-to-last day of our visit, with long-suffering Odet.

The two women hated each other, rivals for the old man's love. Oliver and I had been in town that day for lunch, just the two of us, a special dispensation for courting lovers, and so had missed the outburst. Both women, we learned, had wept. Odet had, in high emotion, called Denise *"une garce"*—a bitch—and Denise—though strictly here she overstepped her powers—had told Odet that she was fired, after seventeen years. Odet had replied that as much as she loved Monsieur and revered the memory of Madame (who had taught her everything she knew, may she rest in peace), she no longer wanted to work for the family if it meant working for Denise. She'd stuffed her work smock and her slippers into a crumpled plastic bag from the drying cupboard where they'd been hanging and had stormed from the apartment, hiccuping sobs. We'd returned from our stodgy couscous and desultory window-shopping—on the bus, no less, to the Promised Land—to find Denise also vanished, returned sans *sieste* to work, and Grand-père uncharacteristically grave and mournful.

It was, of course, unthinkable that Odet should leave them—his whole life depended on her generous assistance—and now he'd have to sort out the mess his daughter had made. No, Denise was not happy in her life; nor, for all she tried to cast her memories in a rosy glow, did it seem that she'd enjoyed much happiness—the daily lithium by her water glass, my mother's muttered recollections of the breakdowns over the years, her disdain for Denise's life lived alongside her parents: a child to the last, my mother observed, with some sour combination of derision and pity.

I thought again of my far-off father, whose fierce stoicism immured him—in the daytime he spoke very little, almost not at all—and whose only release came with a surfeit of drink; I thought of how his raging, damaged soul oppressed and pained us. Unlike his own placid, jesting father, mine, though also a joker, suffered torment (Would he guzzle Tanqueray from the bottle if he were happy?), as did my mother, and I felt the burden of their misery like a magnet at once drawing me home (Might I be able to alleviate the misery?) and repelling me, geographically (Was escape my only hope? How far could I reasonably go?). My two years in England, along with my degree, were drawing to a close—I would graduate in June—and I had, the previous week, from the little post office at La Serinette, down the road from my grandfather's apartment, mailed my acceptance to the MFA program at Syracuse University.

I was determined to be a writer. My father blanched at such naïve fantasy: Grand-père had also wanted to write, had, in the 1930s, finished a novel and a collection of stories politely rejected as "uncommercial" by several Paris publishers, and had quietly renounced his hopes. Only in retirement had the old man sat down, with his lifelong military discipline, to write for his granddaughters the stories of his young married life. François had allowed himself no such flights of fancy: from the time he'd ruefully renounced his doctorate at thirty, he'd understood his role to be that of a provider. I knew he wanted to spare me his own disappointments. "But CloClo," he'd said to me, sorrowfully, when at sixteen I'd announced yet again my ambition, "only geniuses can be writers."

My mother, her own literary ambitions channeled into reams of witty, detailed, and compulsive private correspondence, quietly encouraged me. She'd been the one to receive and open the letters from the writing programs, and had spoken to each of the program directors on the telephone—charmed by some, doubtful about others. Syracuse was the obvious choice, for its faculty, for its funding, for its location (my parents now spent a lot of time driving from Connecticut to Toronto to care for my grandma, almost totally blind and nearing ninety, and Syracuse was along the route), and for its legacy, too.

Raymond Carver, who'd taught at Syracuse, had died the previous August. Just six weeks before our trip to Toulon, in February, on Valentine's Day (our second together: our first had been spent at a Waterstone's reading by Toni Morrison from *Beloved*), Oliver and I had taken the train to London to attend a memorial reading in Carver's honor. Students, we huddled and gawked in the back of an auditorium dotted with actual people whose books we read—Amis, Hitchens, McEwan—was that Richard Ford?—many of them standing to read or speak in tribute. One of these was Salman Rushdie himself, author lately of *The Satanic Verses*, which was causing such a stir, and who, by the following morning, the subject of the Iranian ayatollah's *fatwa*, was whisked into hiding by Scotland Yard.

My mother spoke to me on the phone about the MFA programs, but in her long letters she wrote about Rushdie. As the train rattled on, and Oliver stirred, asked mumblingly where we were, then fell back into sleep, I tried to imagine Rushdie's days, presumably cowering in some safe house in the foggy English countryside (Could he walk in the garden? Ramble through a field of sheep?) or moving, by armored car, behind tinted windows, from bolt-hole to bolt-hole, his life destroyed, his family and friends now mere voices on the telephone, if that, the bodyguards his only companions, as if he'd been kidnapped from his own life—he *had* been kidnapped from his life—a punishment from afar for *blasphemy*, all for a novel, for a *fiction* . . . it seemed impossible, medieval. It had never occurred to me, as it had surely never occurred to him, that mere words, an invented story, could in this era have such an effect, prompt riots and bombings in cities across the globe. Auden had insisted that "poetry makes nothing happen," and didn't we all believe him? And yet this, this was proof of the opposite; proof, too, that in our one world, in the same earthly moment, people inhabited different centuries, the culture of the ayatollah's *fatwa* harkening back to a realm irretrievably distant in Europe or North America, a time when stories had the power of spells or magic, when the utterance was still performative and saying made it so—I'd studied Austin in college; I could remember snippets of his thought, as I carried snippets, too, of Saussure: the signifier, I had said to Oliver, regarding *The Satanic Verses*, had been conflated with the signified.

Rushdie now could not have walked through the Gare du Nord wearing a backpack or played footsie with a sleeping ancient in a worn compartment en route to Calais. Maybe he would never again wander in public. He might live in hiding for decades. Or maybe they would find him—even some members of the British Muslim Students Association bayed for his blood, volunteered for the slaughter—and he would end his days a martyr to art and to liberalism, to freedom of expression. . . . He had not perhaps thought to become a martyr. Few did.

My stomach grumbled loudly and I pressed upon my flesh in hopes of quieting it, as though it were a voice. We were embodied, animals still and always; our words emanated, became separate from us—wasn't this precisely the magic of writing, to send a construct of words into the world, to share the abstract as if it were, as if it had been made, real, had become a concrete experience, the way a composer and orchestra created music or an architect and builders a tower? Only in the case of stories, expressly to be translated back into the minds of others, de-concretized, made portable, so that we might all share (and yet individually create) an experience as real as if it had been lived . . . *this* was communication, my religion's communion, the sharing impossible when tribalism held sway (whether of the Catholics at Mass or of the ayatollah and his *fatwa*), a secular and necessarily open-minded sharing in which the self was subsumed in the invention, in which metaphor and irreality were understood *as if*—a reality that wasn't real, the tension of it delicious and vital. But it relied, too, on a sophisticated contract, a pact with abstraction. Rushdie had thought he wrote on such a plane, and yet this had proven, more than the book itself, so literally taken, to be an illusion. A writer and his readers, in different realms.

After we'd stammered to a halt and gathered our belongings (the backpacks fell like heavy fruit from the racks above), we trudged among the addled horde—the young and the poor, chiefly, as the journey could be made less painfully if more expensively by day—through the bleached corridors, the immigration queues, to the ferry itself. The boat was glaringly alight, canned spots blazing from the panel-tiled ceiling. The deck on which we settled offered plum leatherette booths and swivel chairs scattered around a neon-trimmed snack bar, at which a bleak selection of wilted sausage rolls sweated beneath a heat lamp, overlooked by a scrawny pallid youth in a paper cap and crooked bow tie. The dingy patterned pub carpet was tacky underfoot, and my sneakers gave little sticky squelches with each step. From the windows, the port's lights glittered day-bright on one side; on the other, all lay in darkness. Oliver and I claimed a table, loaded our bags onto two round leatherette chairs— they swiveled slightly with the weight, like fairground cars—and tried restlessly, ourselves, like a dog turning in circles before settling, to dispose of our inconvenient limbs in such a way that we might sleep.

The ferry, I could tell, was a "good" one, though its duty-free kiosks remained shuttered and the snack bar offered, in addition to the sausages, only a stack of Kit Kats and Tetleys or Nescafé. Taking the same route by bus, I'd been once on a much smaller "unstabilized" boat, alerted upon embarkation to the rough crossing ahead by the white paper sick bags abundantly on every flat surface and the pervasive sour odor of vomit. On that trip, taken the spring I studied in France, the spring my grandfather confessed to me in a Paris restaurant, I'd traveled to London in the company of two other American girls, one from my university course and the other, a friend from back home, working as a nanny in the Sixteenth. In so many respects an ill-matched pair, they'd both turned green within minutes of setting sail and had vanished for the duration to the reeking slick-floored lavs, leaving me to guard our pyramid of bundled belongings and to choke down the bile in my throat—which, with great concentration, I managed to do, even as the ship rolled and bucked across the fierce black channel, overturning drinks and raucously sliding all movables from their tables to crash upon the tiled floor. This time I knew from the carpet alone, from the clean tabletops (no paper bags in sight), from the youth with his sausage rolls and bland gaze, that we would fare better; but still, unable to close my eyes (Oliver was asleep before even the Tannoy announcements about life jackets and muster points), I kept an eye on the crew, and on our fellow passengers, alert to absorb any anxiety they might betray.

This, too was life: if the train carried in itself the sounds and textures of history, all of us anonymous in the dark, all of us trapped on the thundering rails, hearing even in the European stations the mournful cries of separated families or the military march of troops echoing through the air, floating beneath the cavernous ceilings with the greasy-winged pigeons—*We are all the same,* the echoes whispered, *History is always around us and in us*—the clamor of the officials pushing along the aisles from car to car, the whine of the brakes on a midnight siding, all of it known to us by osmosis, the trappings of grief and fear—if, on the train, we were subsumed into general invisibility and a sense of the inevitable, of History, then the boat, surely, approached an analogy to the future.

Here I was, on the cusp of my real life, committed now to leaving this beloved sleeping man beside me within a couple of months, indefinitely, for a studio in a high-rise by the interstate in icy Syracuse, New York, so that I might persist, might shackle myself, all but literally, to my writing dream, force myself into a place where I'd know nobody and nothing, a sort of monastery among strip malls, to live without distraction (not even a television!) on the mad wager that it might be worth it, that someday, miraculously, perhaps decades hence, I might write something that merited the gamble. How turbulent might the crossing prove? Each of us carried to the shore by all that had come before, then launched upon the wide, dark ocean.

Look carefully, I thought, as I eyed the lean couple in bright cagoules eating peanuts singly from a little plastic sack; and the tired mother whose sleeping toddler dangled weightily in her arms, his small soft body engulfing hers, her fine dark hair mussed, strands stuck upon her cheek; or the three American sportsmen, students like myself, recognizable even here by the scale of their muscled hairy calves (in shorts, despite the cold) and the whiteness of their teeth, even if they hadn't been wearing sweatshirts emblazoned with their colleges' names: Hamilton, Colgate, Union.

I looked at them and felt both kinship and alienation: they weren't from Syracuse, but being from upstate New York they might have been. My strongest link to Syracuse till now—besides the drive-bys on the highway en route to the border crossing at the Thousand Islands Bridge just past Alexandria Bay (home, I knew, to Fred Exley, author of *A Fan's Notes*, now in his dark alcoholic decline)—had been the tragedy of Lockerbie, Pan Am Flight 103, one that I might have taken, that I had on several other occasions in fact taken, and in this case a flight on which thirty-five Syracuse students, returning from their semester abroad, had perished. We were linked then in my mind, Syracuse and I, by this tenuous thread, by the juxtaposition of my own luck and the tragic misfortune of those many students who might easily have been me, who might have been these three boys: we were on the one hand interchangeable and on the other each our selves.

Look at all the others with whom you share the boat. Beyond the most immediate, you can't choose your companions for a crossing or a generation. You can't know the weather in store, the size of the waves. All in this strange eventful history is uncertain.

That season, all was in motion, listing from side to side at ever greater speed as if the very boat might founder. Our actual ferry may have crossed uneventfully—we dozed uneasily and disembarked bleary, gassy, distorted, our hair and clothes askew, for the final leg to London, glimpsed through dirty windows, the emerald fields and toy villages, then the sooty, sprawling southern reaches of the vast city, past the little attached Herne Hill house among thousands of similar houses, to the smallest room of which we would eventually return—but the thrilling tumult was already underway.

In the brief weeks of April we'd spent sequestered at my grandfather's flat, our attention largely on the sea and the light and the dance of domestic tension, the world burst, like the tumbling bougainvillea, into a froth. We followed nightly on the small television set in my grandfather's bedroom, the volume turned to its highest setting. On Easter Sunday, the Soviets under Gorbachev held the first round of their first free—or partly free—national elections, and in the second round, on April 9, Boris Yeltsin triumphed in Moscow. Other new deputies included the dissident physicist Andrei Sakharov, the trapeze artist Valentin Dikul, and the weight lifter Yury Vlasov—each, like a character in surrealist theater, with a role to play in leading the USSR from a time of *glasnost* and *perestroika* to the exhilaration of democracy. On April 9, the same day as the Russian elections' second round—a day on which Oliver and I had forgone morning Mass to sunbathe on the terrace and I, after pretending to read Derrida's *Éperons* in spite of its broken spine, had fallen asleep—the Soviet army crushed the popular democratic demonstrations in Tbilisi, Georgia, killing twenty-one and injuring hundreds, in a tragic debacle that led to the fall of communism there. On April 17—the following Monday, when Tante Denise took the afternoon off from work to drive us to Aix-en-Provence, where Grand-père read the papers on the terrace of the Deux Garçons while we walked up the hill to visit Cézanne's atelier—the Poles legalized Lech Wałesa's Solidarnosc, the trade union fighting for democracy; while just a couple of days before, on the fifteenth, the great democratic protests started in Tiananmen Square.

By the year's and the decade's end, back in my grandfather's bedroom in December, gathered with him and my aunt around the grainy, deafening television (Odet by then safely restored to the family bosom, thanks to my grandfather's loving diplomacy), we would watch over days the fall and then murder of Nicolae Ceaușescu, marveling that every Romanian the TF1 reporters approached in the streets of Bucharest spoke perfect French. By the time I left them to find Oliver in London, just before New Year's, the great playwright Václav Havel had been made president of Czechoslovakia. The Berlin Wall had come down the month before, on November 9, a Thursday, and I'd heard about it on the radio that night after my last class, in my Syracuse studio, where I then, as every week, saw no familiar face besides the clerk at Store 24 until my next class Monday night at seven, and instead chattered excitedly of world historical events on international phone calls I couldn't afford.

Within a few years, soon after my father's early retirement in 1992, the newly created Russian oligarchs would wrest domination of the aluminum market, undercutting the price so dramatically that they would force, in time, the demise of Péchiney, that hundred-and-fifty-year-old flagship of French industry, symbol of France's industrial might, swallowed by Alcan, its Canadian rival (my mother's national team, so long scorned by my father, then triumphant), only for Alcan to be swallowed in its turn, just a few years later, by the behemoth Rio Tinto, which would eventually decide to wind down the bauxite operations in Weipa,

Queensland, with the stated aim of restoring the site to the management of the indigenous peoples there.

The boat, on this late-twentieth-century crossing, was far from stabilized, and many things fell from their places. But, inshallah, there would be a next voyage, and a next, traveling forward into an invisible future. None of us could predict where those things, or ourselves, might land.

PART VI

⚜

LA NAPOULE AND

CANNES, FRANCE

W hat a relief to have forty-eight hours away from the vigil. When they arrived at La Napoule, just before lunchtime, and Chloe and Oliver emerged from their artists' residency to join them for lunch at the café under the plane trees in the village square, Chloe asked blithely whether they were having a nice time in Toulon.

"What sort of question is that?" Barbara couldn't help but snap. "We're on a deathwatch."

Chloe, flustered, stammered an apology. But honestly, she was over thirty years old; surely she had the wit to understand that life wasn't all Pollyanna good cheer.

Barbara and François had arrived three weeks before, only a couple of weeks after the kids started their residency—only an hour and a half's drive from the Toulon flat, but it felt like another world—and they were to stay until, until. . . . It hadn't been specified between them, but everyone tacitly understood that she and François (retirees—imagine!) would stay now to the bitter end. Yes, a deathwatch.

He couldn't get out of bed any longer. This stage had been reached just in the past week. When they'd first arrived, he still shuffled laboriously down the corridor to the dining room, attended at either elbow, to sit, propped upon cushions for his raw bones, in his dressing gown and slippers in the hard armchair they all still thought of as his wife's, fifteen years after her death; and he still looked out to sea for long stretches, keeping track of the autumn sailboats and ferries, the submarines and hulking aircraft carriers, all the busy marine traffic on which his life had long been founded and which he loved even in this late, blurry senescence. Who had ever believed that he, of all people, could be reduced to so tattered a rag, the gestures of his thick hands faint and shaking, his eyes filled with sorrow?

Now, though, he slept much of the day, and when he was awake, they hoisted him into a sitting position while he emitted yelps, whether of pain or mere terror nobody was quite sure. The current housekeeper, Fatima, and Denise took turns holding large spoonfuls of sustaining beef broth to his trembling mouth—half of it inevitably dribbled down his chin, glinting rivulets in the folds of his now-scrawny neck, spotting his pajama top. He wore a diaper, like a baby, and still Fatima labored endlessly boiling sheets and changing the bed in an effort to keep him clean and sweet-smelling. Though it was now November—almost Barbara's birthday: they'd come to La Napoule to celebrate Oliver's and hers together, All Saints' and Guy Fawkes, as Chloe had noted, two very different traditions—the days weren't yet cold (at the little beach by the castle at La Napoule they could see swimmers in the sea) and Fatima kept Grandpère's east-facing windows open the whole time she was there, from eight to four, so the room was brisk with sea air. Sometimes, though, the wind came up and snatched at the old curtain, whipping it about like a loose sail, and the noise made Grand-père cry out in fear, the same sharp cries as when they moved him in the bed.

Barbara went in morning and night to kiss his shining, well-moisturized brow, but otherwise kept a distance, at most hovering in the doorway behind François, while Denise covered their father with noisy smooches or made exhausting bright jokes to try to cheer him or herself. Barbara knew she ought not to be, but found herself repelled by his stubbled chin and rank breath, the flittering white chest hairs emerging from his bedclothes, by the dark bedroom, a cave of death, by the rosary-draped crucifix above his head, and by his two pairs of warped street shoes, poor man, lined up beneath the dresser, as though he might, at some point, step into them and head off once more to the *centre commerciale* with his panniers.

No, death was appalling, to sit in wait for it appalling, all the more so when you were halfway through your sixties with breast cancer already on your report card. Denise, who still smoked like an incinerator and had no voice left to speak of, had somehow never suffered any ill health at all—except her utter madness, of course, the wearisome depressive phases everyone got so worked up about. She clearly believed, like a child, that her fawning and theatrics made some difference, improved his dying man's lot; but Barbara had attended enough deaths now—including her mother's, so expeditiously handled by the doughty and indomitable Lenore Fisk, who had simply decided, when her macular degeneration had advanced to the point where she could no longer distinguish day from night, that "nothing's any fun anymore," to stop taking her heart failure meds, and had been dead within a week—to know that there was no advantage to maudlin sentimentalizing. The proper response was to cleave only the more strongly to life. Of course, Gaston needed love and attention, but at this stage he slept at least eighteen hours out of twenty-four, a body enduring. He had manifestly embarked on his journey away from them, and Denise's attempts to hold on to him, to keep him *present* and *in the room* seemed to Barbara, well, appalling. Self-indulgent. Stiff upper lip was her own family way, and be quick about it. Her own father had always wanted her and Mother, when they left the hospital, to go somewhere special for dinner and to eat something delicious for him. He didn't want them lingering in the sickroom—he wanted them to *live*. Well, Grand-père was past saying anything like that, and anyway, charming as he was, he'd always been a vain so-and-so—always thrilled to be the center of attention.

She hadn't said any of this to François, for whom, in spite of his impossibleness, indeed his awfulness, she felt now tenderness and compassion. She would have suggested that they go for long walks to escape the molasses-like stasis of the apartment, but his legs were so bad—he was in such constant pain; lumbar stenosis was the diagnosis, and the only possible remedy a major operation that terrified him—that to take the shady switchback path down the cliff to the beach had become unthinkable, let alone to walk to Cap Brun or to the fort or to Sainte Marguerite. So they spent most of their time at home, except for doing the shopping, and as Denise, at least up till now, was still going out to work, this meant spending time with taciturn Fatima and now, too, the awful Angéline.

Barbara wasn't sure how long Fatima had worked for the family. A year, certainly—she'd been the housekeeper when Grand-père returned from the rehab hospital after he'd fallen and broken his hip the previous winter. But she was the third or fourth replacement since Odet and her ne'er-do-well husband, Francisco, had finally packed it in and returned to Portugal.

Barbara missed Odet; she'd always felt that she and Odet stood in essentially the same relationship to the family—that's to say, warmly embraced but condescended to, and effectively exploited—and she'd loved for years the sense of their mutual affection and disaffection, how they could discreetly exchange glances about Denise's histrionics, or even complain to each other about cleaning up her overflowing ashtrays . . . but at some point Odet had just got too fed up and too tired, and doubtless Francisco had conspired to force their departure. He'd been on workers' comp for *years*, and had then, about a decade ago, implausibly enough, taken a mistress, which drove Odet wild, until she realized that she paid all the bills and her lazy husband was her dependent, at which point she told him he could go off with his tart and earn his own living, but that if he wanted her, Odet, to continue to support him, he'd have to give that woman up. And straightaway, docile as a lamb, he'd given up his girlfriend. But maybe the savor had gone, the sense of France as a place of possibility—because from then on, from the time of their reunion, they'd plotted their escape. She'd been gone over three years now, and they all spoke to her often on the telephone—her funny pidgin French!—but mostly they just missed her, and nothing was the same.

Fatima, middle-aged, skinny, and sallow, with Brillo-pad black hair and darkly lined eyes, neither spoke nor smiled much. She was impressively efficient but did not wish to be drawn into the family theater. Denise never threw her arms around Fatima, never touched her in fact, stood a slight distance away and spoke respectfully and formally, and when asking a favor did so with some trepidation. Unlike Odet, Fatima had no difficulty saying no when something did not suit her. Grand-père too, for as long as he'd been able, had been particularly punctilious about the pleases and thank-yous for Fatima, the compliments on a dish well prepared or a successful flower arrangement, but the doting affection showered for years on Odet was nowhere in evidence. Fatima accepted these politesses quietly, without display.

Not so Angéline: Barbara had tried to speak to François about that one, that strange, insinuating addition to the household who behaved, despite her own recent arrival, as though François and Barbara were interlopers. She'd been sent by an agency, apparently a sort of home health aide, when Denise had recognized, in late August, that her father wasn't well enough to be left alone from four, when Fatima left, until seven-thirty, when she herself got home. And that, indeed, he needed the help of two people for most things, having, in spite of all the weight he'd lost, a formidable carcass.

You'd have thought, Barbara had whispered to François in their room with the door shut—the girls' room, with its virginal twin beds—that any proper agency would have sent, under the circumstances, a strapping young person, a man maybe, who could hold Grand-père up alone if need be, who could bathe and dress him so that the laborious tasks needn't always fall to Denise and Fatima, neither of them much over a hundred and ten pounds. Instead, they'd sent an aged child, a creature withered on the vine who, no taller than Denise or Fatima, had considerably greater embonpoint, and who dressed as though she were performing in the circus, in frilled bright frocks covered with large flowers and twirly flounced skirts. Although a woman of sixty or so—her chins a dangling, freckled wattle—she wore her hair half piled on her head and half around her shoulders, in the style of a little girl at a birthday party, adorned with ribbons and bows. Her eyebrows were drawn on in an expression of permanent surprise, and her painted mouth was a little Cupid's bow. She had a mincing step and spoke in a breathy baby voice, like a cartoon character. In practical terms, the woman was useless—she could neither lift nor carry; she did not cook or clean—but somehow, somehow, she had charmed both father and daughter, indulging Denise's whirling anxieties and, in the early days of her tenure, listening with rapt attention to anything Grand-père had said, flattering his vanity, so that now, when he barely registered who was in the room, and Barbara bridled at the babblings of this circus clown, in the evenings Denise would remind them, earnestly, "She's been just wonderful. Papa is so fond of her. He's said so many times"—thereby claiming Angéline as part of the family.

When, at lunchtime a few days ago, Denise had broached the subject of the funeral—"It's important to be practical," she'd said when her brother had winced and shut his eyes, "and we all know it's right around the corner"—Angéline had, to Barbara's horror, made herself central to the conversation. She'd had opinions about the undertakers, about the sort of Mass that would be fitting—decidedly a Communion, she'd insisted, for so devout a patriarch—and Denise had leaned forward, all attention, as though the baby voice were oracular. Afterward, back in their bedroom, Barbara had again demurred: "François, watch out for that one. Maybe she thinks there's money to be had. Otherwise I don't know what it's about. But she's very strange. And she's preying on your sister in a time of vulnerability."

François shrugged, his heavy shoulders mournfully resigned. "What can I do about it?"

"Well, at some point you'll have to put your foot down. Otherwise she'll be giving the eulogy at the funeral and claiming she's entitled to the silverware."

"Don't be silly."

"I'm not being silly—you have to ask yourself, If she's not an adventuress, what *is* she doing? She's a very odd duck."

François sighed. "I expect she's a lonely single woman approaching old age, just like my sister. More eccentric, less functional, but there you go. And she's been made to feel she belongs here. My father is leaving us. My sister will be alone. This woman is stepping into the breach."

"Your sister won't be alone. You've always been the best brother on earth to her. I could say that you've taken better care of her than you have of me."

"Don't," he said, not angry but plaintive.

"Watch out," she said then, returning to the matter of Angéline. "That's all I have to say. Watch out."

That had been on Monday; now it was Wednesday; tomorrow would be Barbara's actual birthday. Muli, the doctor who came by most weekday evenings at the end of his rounds, with his old-fashioned spectacles and natty black case, had assured them that they could go away for two nights without concern. He'd said that there was at least a week to go. How did he know, Barbara wondered. Was it like betting on the horses, or was it more like being a butcher or a fishmonger and just *knowing*, after years in the job, the weight of a pound in your hand? Could he measure by the hue of the skin or a light in the eye? By the pulse or the respiration? Or was he just guessing?

She'd been reminded powerfully, in these weeks, of the long-ago death of her own father, whom she'd adored. Almost forty years ago—a lifetime. Who had she even been? She recalled the belated moment when she'd realized what he actually *looked like*, realized that he'd wasted to a death's-head without her having seen it, as for weeks or even months her love had projected onto him a long-lost capacity for health. She literally hadn't seen it coming.

In this case, of course, with her father-in-law, the situation was quite different. He'd always prided himself on his clarity of vision, on not harboring illusions (which enabled him, of course, to hold tightly to the illusions he held dearest): in consequence, he'd been saying for several years, "Now that I am getting very old" or "Now that my forces are diminishing," and since his fall the previous year and the broken hip, he'd been saying, "Now that I don't have so long," and even when they first arrived, "Given that it's soon my time." He didn't say these things fearfully; rather with the supreme calm of the faithful, as if he were observing someone else's decline.

Except that life—or death—had caught up with him after all, and his animal self was triumphing now. Soon after they'd arrived, he'd been shouting in the night, still embroiled in his nightmare: "Don't put me in the grave!" he'd cried. "Can't you see I'm not dead! It's not time! No, don't put me in— No!"

Barbara and François, roused by his distress, had from the hallway glimpsed Denise, by the low wattage of a night-light, leaning over him in her nightgown, speaking softly, soothingly, his Florence Nightingale. She'd told them the next day that he seemed not to remember, which was a relief. But since then, he'd begun moaning when his limbs were moved, his little yelps of terror. He was no longer observing himself declining, dying; he was, rather, declining, dying.

Barbara was reminded of childbirth, that other time at which the portals between life and death were flung wide. Reminded of how, all those years ago, she'd made wry jokes and self-deprecating asides about her pregnancy and, before Loulou's birth, about her fear of the delivery— what woman had no fear, beforehand?—and of how, then, so suddenly, her body had been seized by the forces of Nature. Her brain, her will, her dignity suddenly irrelevant, herself a puny buoy on the tempest-tossed ocean of animal imperative. She'd been subject to the great wave of life's longing for itself, had been tumbled, gutted, devastated, split apart— and then granted first one, and then almost two years later, another, perfect miniature being. She could still summon the sensation of their soft newborn skin, the fervid grip upon her finger of their tiny hands, those minute pearly nails she'd nibbled off for months, the scent of their necks, the warm weight of their limbs—yes, after that momentously effortful subjection, there'd been new life. And after this one, only death. But just as she had herself been in the hands of Nature, so too Grand-père was now laboring, as she had labored, to a different end. Dying was long, hard work.

Thank God for the children, even now. Thank God for the respite from the vigil. They were halfway through their artists' residency in this peculiar castle outside Cannes—they slept in a turret, overhanging the blue sea, and dined with the others (writers, painters, potters, even a composer) in the cavernous, beamed dining room surrounded by the grotesque sculptures of the rich American artist who had, almost a century before, installed himself there. But they were happy to abandon their desks for a day or two, to sit and chat, to wander along the seafront in Cannes. As her birthday gift, François had booked for two nights a room at the small hotel near the castle, though climbing even the single flight of stairs to their room pained him greatly. When she asked the kids about walking together the few miles along the water from La Napoule to Cannes, he'd looked so crestfallen—he literally could not have done it, her husband *could not walk*—that she'd shelved the idea and agreed they'd all go in the car. But at the same time, maybe she'd only suggested it because she knew he couldn't do it; she knew herself capable simultaneously of compassion and sadism. She knew that she loved and hated him in the same instant.

They sat, jacketed but not cold, under the plane trees, then, espressos in tiny cups before them on the table, the autumn sunshine stretching its warm fingers through the greenery to cast them all in dappled light.

François smoked a numbered cigarette—he allowed himself five a day now, though the bottomless cough, the sound of furniture scraping along a floor, was not alleviated by his continence; and one of many reasons why he kept putting off his back operation was that the doctors insisted he'd have to stop altogether for at least three months beforehand, which was like asking him not to be himself. She observed him as he placidly watched the odd car or the odd pedestrian drift by. It was off-season at the seaside and the gift shops were shut. The café had only a few other patrons, including a carefully made-up octogenarian who reminded Barbara of Catherine Deneuve, with a fluffy dog trembling at her feet. These French women, elegant even when parodically geriatric.

The garçon—if a man of forty could be called "the garçon"—brought the bill on a tray and placed it with a flourish before François, who picked up the tray with both hands, his cigarette dangling from the corner of his mouth. What nostalgia that small gesture prompted in her—how glamorous and sexy it had seemed to her for years, from almost the first time she'd met him, this handsome Frenchman with his Gallic habits, his insouciance, how it had seemed to her to promise a glamorous life, a fantasy—and indeed, wasn't she here, by the Mediterranean in November, living a life that as a girl in Toronto she would have thought the stuff of dreams? She recalled her first time in London, in '55, giddy on a Routemaster bus, lurching around a corner into Trafalgar Square, astounded that *she*, Barbara, was physically *in Europe!* And then soon after, Paris—ah, well. All of it, the dreams; and the reality not the dream. What was the line from the Bible, sold your birthright for a mess of pottage? Had her life then just been a mess of pottage?

It wasn't over yet, of course; though most of it was past. This impossible, restless, overbearing man—not a fantasy, all too real, the stinking socks in the laundry, the rages, unpredictable (likely a disorder, she often thought, and told him, in a person also sweet and funny), the unmentioned vodka bottle under the bathroom sink and the gin in the suitcase when he traveled; his large, grief-stricken, endlessly needy self.

He'd swallowed and swamped her, belittled and criticized her, had also wept and sworn his devotion—and she'd held her heart an icy shard for decades, had tortured him as he'd tortured her; in her way, she'd have said, by withholding, she gave as good as she got. But nevertheless, or because of this, they'd grown together like Baucis and Philemon; no matter the bitterness, they couldn't be separated now. She'd thought for years that she'd one day leave him, just as he'd surely thought that one day he'd stop drinking, but the time for such illusions was now past. During their college years and after, her girls had said to her, over and over, "Leave him, leave him! It's not too late to start over!" But that was over a decade ago now, and it had already felt too late then.

They didn't say it anymore. If anything, both of them, now married, seemed to look at her differently, to judge her almost—not that they'd withdrawn their love; she knew they loved her readily, easily; she was, she'd always been, easy to love; but that they thought her childlike or shallow. "It's like you think someone should come along and save you," one of them had said, in a harsh moment. Perhaps it was true. Her mother, fierce Lenore, used to roll her eyes and say, "God help you, Barbara, if you ever have to file your own tax return."

"That's right, I'm a ninny, stupid Barbara," she'd respond—but even *she* couldn't tell how much she believed what she said, how much she'd internalized this sense of her inadequacy, how much she just used it as a shield.

"It's a kind of abuse," one of the girls had said, now long ago, though he'd never raised a finger to her. To tell her she had the intellect of a moth, that her opinions weren't worth hearing—yes, it was surely a kind of abuse, though she always felt when he said such things that he was actually talking to himself, criticizing himself. What upset him most was that she kept parts of herself to herself. The only child in her, treasuring her privacy. She knew that he had no sense of boundaries, that he thought of her as, wanted her to be, inseparable from himself. That had always been the struggle: his parents, this formidable dying man and his tiresomely saintly wife, had done everything in concert. The Bobbsey Twins, she'd called them for years, as in "Why do we have to be the Bobbsey Twins, like your parents?" But that was François's fantasy, his ideal, just as it had been Denise's, a sort of courtly love from medieval romance—fated, mythic, enormous. And *that* fantasy, even more than a fantasy that you were marrying Jean-Paul Belmondo, was doomed to disappointment. She'd been a constant disappointment, then, simply for being herself. But he still loved her, or claimed to; whereas she—well. She'd say that she did still love him, whatever that meant—just about. She cared for him, and worried about him, and felt pity for his suffering, and wished she could take away his pain. But she believed, wholeheartedly, that this had all been a mistake, that if she could call back in time to the girl she had been, dazzled by the dashing Frenchman on the bus in the rain at summer school at Oxford, she would say: "Don't! Don't do it. Walk away. Go home. Break up with Luke Whitworth too, take the job at the *Globe and Mail*, and cling to it with all you've got. But whatever you do, *don't marry him*."

"If ifs and ands were pots and pans, there'd be no work for tinkers' hands," her mother, queen of the ready adage, had always said. No point imagining a life that wasn't. There was plenty of good in this one, even with the glass half empty. And the kids—she couldn't imagine her life without the kids.

IN THE CAR on the way to Cannes—a quick trip, and on this late-autumn afternoon there was little traffic, the whole corniche asleep, as little La Napoule was asleep, hibernating now for months before the season of movie stars and the new Russian oligarchs with their yachts—Oliver and Chloe told them about the other members of their residency, and in particular about the Russian filmmaker Ilya and his wife, Tanya.

The son of a celebrated Soviet director, Ilya had been in the industry since boyhood, and only a couple of years previously, at just over fifty, he'd had an international success—his last movie had been nominated for an Academy Award. But then he'd suffered, in the middle of it all, a heart attack, a fairly serious one, and now, convalescent, had come to the castle with his wife—as charismatic and talkative as he was retiring—to work with her on the next screenplay.

The castle was, it transpired, as full of fascinating characters as it was of the former owner's hideous artwork; but the anecdote that chiefly captured Oliver's imagination, and Barbara's too, when he told it, concerned Ilya and Tanya. To finance the residencies, the administration rented out the great hall to film companies for parties during the Cannes festival, and sometimes, too, in the off-season. Because of this, all the artists had been dispatched for a weekend to a charming hotel in Aix-en-Provence. There, Ilya and Tanya, on account of his nomination and his heart condition, had been assigned by far the nicest room, but it was on the top floor, and the hotel had no elevator. Ilya, who had been suffering chest pains, realized once he reached his room that he could not, would not be able to leave, until it was time to return to La Napoule.

Ilya's world-weary aspect, Oliver explained, recalled Astrov in *Uncle Vanya*; blousy Tanya, his second wife and a decade younger, devoted her passionate energies to reviving him. Plus, that October Saturday was Ilya's birthday, his fifty-third. So as he lay on the hotel bed with his eyes closed, the French windows open to the afternoon breeze, Tanya nipped down the winding stairs to the front desk to demand, in her best French, that they locate a doctor on call to visit Ilya in his hotel room. More importantly still, she ordered, from a nearby café, a large tray of oysters and a bottle of Veuve Clicquot, in celebration.

Oliver relayed with exuberant delight Tanya's vision, from the balcony of their bedroom: one waiter in his striped trousers and black waistcoat and jacket, his hair brilliantined (she could see the top of his head) holding aloft the vast metal tray of ice and oysters as he swooped gracefully—like a dancer, she'd said—through the Saturday evening promenaders toward the hotel entrance, while a few steps behind him, his colleague, barely less perfectly choreographed, snaked his own path, bearing a smaller tray with an ice bucket containing the champagne, and two flutes.

"I couldn't help thinking of Chekhov," Oliver said. "I mean, not just because Ilya *looks* a bit like Chekhov. But also because here he was, in this foreign hotel room, and he wasn't *actually* dying—he's in the château working right now—but she'd convinced herself he might—the doctor was on his way—and remember that the last thing Chekhov did when he was dying of TB in a hotel room in Badenweiler was order up champagne."

"And then he said, in German, '*Ich sterbe*,'" Chloe added. "Weren't those his last words?"

"But luckily not Ilya's!" Oliver laughed. "Apparently he perked up a lot with the oysters and champagne."

"He's cheery now because their daughter is coming to visit. She's getting married here," Chloe offered. "In Cannes, or maybe in Nice? Maybe to an oligarch?"

"I don't know," said Oliver, "certainly the fiancé is very wealthy. They're going to stay in a hotel on the Croisette—Tanya's quite excited; the fiancé has booked them a suite with a sea view."

"How nice for them all," Barbara said. François, scanning for a parking place, said nothing. Barbara was aware that he might, at any moment, erupt in irritation: the streets were narrow, and the other drivers, in their element, irascible and aggressive.

"There's a place down there," she offered, "on the right."

He made a clicking sound of exasperation, but turned sharply into what amounted to an alley. The trick was to park half up on the curb, but the single-lane roadway was so confined, lined with parked cars on both sides, that he had little room to maneuver.

"Why don't we hop out," Barb offered, "and wait at the corner. Then you can pull up as close to the wall as you need to."

He nodded grimly, without answering. How well they knew each other. If she could keep the kids away while he parked, he'd be fine, and the afternoon would be fine; but if he had to park with them in the car, the strain would show, and he might snap, and then Chloe might lose her temper too. Family life, like playing chess, involved always thinking several steps ahead. They piled out and left him, to stand at the corner of the slightly larger road, looking down toward the water. They couldn't see the ocean, but even so the end of the long block burst with light, a golden spill of it.

Seaside light: it felt to Barbara like hope, always. But then, a second thought: perhaps the opposite was true. Seaside towns, the end of the land, the chosen home for the aged, retirees—the end of the line. Maybe even Cannes, for all its glitz, was secretly bleak? She was turning sixty-five; Oliver had just turned thirty-three. She was almost twice his age. And the millennium not far away—how she dreaded *that*, which felt not like a beginning but like the end. A threshold, like the seashore, but to what?

She turned back to look for François, who'd managed to squeeze their car into the small space, up onto the curb. He pushed in the wing mirror, always meticulous, and she saw him check his watch, though they had no appointments and no deadlines. He was obsessed with the time and the weather, keeping track. And where everything was put, even the placement of a ballpoint pen on his desk. Nowadays they'd probably call it a disorder—OCD or something. Probably he'd light another cigarette, if he thought they weren't looking—no? No. But she watched him as he walked—or, rather, limped—the length of the alley. How stiff he was; how burdened; as if he carried the weight of the world. And wincing; she could see, each time he lifted his right leg forward; a frisson of pain crossed his face, regular as a windshield wiper. He looked up and saw her, and he smiled, but his smile was brave and sad, and made her want to cry.

"We want you to choose a birthday present, Mama," Chloe said, at her shoulder. Chloe was looking not at her father but, rather, in the shop window of the elegant store on the corner where they stood. The window was white, the display—an Italian brand—of fine camel knits and dark skirts, neutral and chic, enviably smart. But a quick glance at the card on which the prices were handwritten made immediately clear that this shop was not an option.

"Not here," she said with a laugh.

"Why not? Let's go in—"

"Don't be ridiculous. I don't even *like* these things."

"Come on, Mama, no Filene's Basement here! It's your sixty-fifth!"

François joined them; she knew he was grateful that their chatter distracted from his limp.

"Daddy agrees, don't you? Won't we find something nice for Mom in here?"

He too would worry about the prices. She saw him notice the card. The kids didn't have any money. They themselves didn't have money for this kind of thing. It was ticklish, though, because you didn't want to seem to spurn their generosity or condescend to them.

"I'll tell you what," François said. "These streets are full of boutiques. Why don't we have a look around, and your mother can see if there's a place she particularly likes. Salespeople can be pushy. That way she can be more sure before she goes in."

Barbara was grateful. She touched his arm to say thank you. But she also knew he could not walk even three or four blocks without agony. She would do for him what he had done for her, grant him an out. How strange and unimaginable that at this stage of life even the good parts felt hard.

"I don't know about you guys, but I'm desperate for another coffee," she said. Then François could sit and wait for them, the way for years, until only a year or two ago in fact, his father would sit and wait for them—all life and the generations suddenly collapsing like an accordion. Oh, how she longed still to be young. How, in that moment, she wished for it all to come back, to be carefree, the way her daughter's most pressing thought was a birthday present, the way they told the story of their Russian filmmaker and Chekhov as though death were just a story, something out of a beautiful book, even as Grand-père's arduous labor of dying—with its odors and effluvia, its stark insistence and inescapability—was well underway even in this moment, just down the highway. To be sixty-five was to know that you dreamed the lazy lunch beneath the plane trees and window shopping along the Croisette, but that death was what was real; to be thirty-two, as Chloe was, meant you could still pretend the inverse was true. And still, why not, for the afternoon, dream?

"Let's find a terrace where we can see the world go by," she said brightly, forging toward the light, aware that her daughter would be rolling her eyes at her husband.

"The coffee will cost twice as much," said François, mildly.

"It's our birthday outing, isn't it?" she said with a nod to Oliver—it was his also.

"Of course it is. We're treating," said Chloe.

"Nonsense." François, though still mild, was firm.

In the event, they left him with the latest issue of *Le Nouvel Observateur* purchased at a kiosk, and his second coffee. While they were walking, he would surely allow himself another cigarette. Though she harangued him to quit, she hoped he'd have one.

Eventually she capitulated and let them buy her a silk scarf. Even Oliver insisted. It wasn't *too* expensive—less than the cost of lunch— and pleased her enormously. It had a caramel-and-cream geometric pattern against a black ground, and was made of a smooth, weighty silk that furled elegantly around her neck. She didn't have it wrapped but, rather, wore it out of the shop—a narrow shop that sold only scarves, shelves and drawers full of them, with a single window to the street and, at the back, a counter behind which the saleswoman, of about Barbara's age, brassy-haired and smiling, seemed to be trapped. But a flap of the counter, hinged, swung up surprisingly to release her, and she had cheerfully unfolded a dozen scarves and had tied half of them around Barbara's neck in front of the oval mirror on the right wall. She had rather bad breath (this was always Chloe's joke: France, the land of beautiful sights and bad smells) but was so cheery that Barbara didn't mind.

When the trio, mother, daughter, and son-in-law, walked back out into the light, and back along the boulevard to the café, Barbara, her hand at her throat, gently stroked the silk. Glimpsing her husband from afar—his coat gathered tight now around him, half-moon glasses halfway down his nose, bent over his magazine, engrossed, oblivious, alive—she felt a surge of emotion. Was it purely joy or also relief? That they were rich, still, in minutes, inshallah still in years, that the now-chill air could still kiss them, that they could fight, dither, joke, read, laugh, complain, be. Her mother had lived almost to ninety-three, Grand'-mère to ninety-one; while Grand-père, at her current age, had been recently returned from Argentina and had just moved into the Toulon apartment, where it seemed he'd now lived forever. No, she wouldn't be maudlin—it was almost her birthday.

"François, do look," she called out as they neared his table. "See what a beautiful gift they've given me!"

He turned and looked up over his glasses. When he caught sight of them he smiled, fully, with his eyes as well, those hazel eyes she knew as well as her own. "Show me," he said.

TOULON, FRANCE

Waking in his sister's bed, next to the space where his wife had been: the strangeness of life. The room was still dark, the reflected light from down the hall playing on the white wall opposite him as Barbara opened and closed some door, as if in an inscrutable silent art film in a gallery. Denise's apartment—which he had essentially given her; in which she did not live, had not essentially lived for years—felt in that moment of waking peaceful, unencumbered.

He was not, exceptionally, in pain. He raised his arms over his head to stretch them and they encountered an object on the wall. A slithery hard thing fell on his bald head and slipped down his neck. Denise's rosary, of course. Draped over the carved crucifix above the bed. Never unencumbered, in fact.

They'd moved down from the big apartment when the others arrived. Loulou and Pavel were staying now in what had long been the girls' bedroom, with a folding cot for little Ines. Barbara had asked, upon entering Denise's room, whether they might remove the body of Christ from the wall above them for the period of their stay.

"It gives me the creeps," she'd said.

"It's her bedroom. We're her guests. Just try not to think about it."

"That's been your strategy for a lot of things," Barb had replied. He hadn't taken the bait.

He could hear her in the kitchen, making breakfast. This day, another to be got through. So many sensations—were they emotions? He tried, now, not to register emotions, not simply in this period of his father's final illness and now his death but in this stage of his life. Because so few of the emotions were welcome ones. He sometimes felt that getting older was like inhabiting a mansion you couldn't afford, so that you were forced to shut down one room after another, eventually entire wings, until you huddled in the kitchen, breaking up the furniture for firewood. How to catalog all that had been lost, even before his father's serious fall, just under a year before? How to begin to sift through the memories that caused him pain?

No, better to move forward, even in agony (walking had become *an agony*—the sciatica, unpredictable and crippling, as if an invisible nemesis shot mercury through the veins of his leg), than to dwell on the past. What had the expression been, back in the day—his own family was already long gone, but the *pieds-noirs* used to say "the suitcase or the coffin"—that was it. And he'd chosen, time and again, the suitcase. Pack up and move on. Keep it packed, indeed, so you're ready at any moment. And as the years went on, make sure there was a bottle of something in the suitcase at all times.

They thought he drank too much—they harped on about it, the girls especially. Barbara less now, but even Denise had made comments; just the other night she'd said, after dinner, "Are you sure you need another?"— but she was one to talk. No, what none of them understood was how much he *didn't* drink, the phenomenal feat of self-control that marked the rhythm of his days. He woke up in the morning and he *did not drink*. His body, in pain, called out for relief, but he didn't grant it. Each long day, he waited till sunset. He punished himself, his soul's longing for rest and for oblivion, just to *forget*—to forget that everything hurt, that his beloved mother, the only spirit that he'd always felt loved him unconditionally, was long dead, that his wife and often his children seemed to despise him, that all his lifelong efforts had not saved his sister from her misery, from herself . . . not to consider the professional side: retirement was often tough, he'd heard that beforehand. Feeling stripped of your identity, of respect, underutilized, bored—he'd read the articles. That hadn't stopped him: he'd leaped as early as he could financially, perhaps too early, even, but he couldn't wait any longer, miserable at the office those last years after the insider-trading crisis, and then watching the company crumbling around him, the whole world, it seemed, crumbling—not just the aluminum business, taken over by Russian bandits from the Wild West that was the post-Soviet East, but everything that had made sense to him. Mammon was indisputably king now—not knowledge, or brilliance, or innovation, and certainly not honor or wisdom. All of it a far cry from Haenni's utopian capitalist fantasy in Conches, back in '62. And most disconcertingly, no respect for actual *things*, for manufacturing or engineering, for mining or building—no, the fortunes of the future, of the present, were abstract, virtual, digital code flickering in the ether. Everything he'd known and done apparently dispensable. . . . Now the dot.com boom, crazy all around them—thank goodness for his Fidelity retirement funds—but what was it, and where would it end?

As he shaved, trying hard not to look at *himself*, focusing instead on his chin, its cleft, the fleshy line of his jaw, the meeting of his razor and his lathered skin; then combing his hair, what he had left, all white now and kept short, and rubbing his cheeks with an unguent—Givenchy Homme—so known he didn't smell it, it was *his smell*—but never allowing his eyes to meet his eyes in the mirror, never permitting himself fully to take stock, afraid, yes, of what he might see there, a bottomless space for which there was no word, though the closest word was "grief" . . .

No, how had it come to pass that all his determination and his courage, all the fortitude of the boy he had once been (his mother's gentle verbena-scented hand against his cheek as she kissed the top of his head, that long ago day in L'Arba, early in the war, when he had carried Denise so far upon his back, his legs jelly when they at last arrived home to Tata Baudry's, and their mother, instead of scolding him in her worry, had blessed and embraced him and called him *"mon brave garçon," "mon fils chéri,"* and told him he was remarkable for having so lovingly taken care of his sister) seemed now, in the eyes of the world—in his own eyes, let's be honest—to have amounted to so little. He'd worked so hard, as a boy— only once in all his elementary years did another kid displace him from the top of the class, a kid who subsequently died of influenza—and he'd succeeded in spite of bombs and bunkers and months of school cancellations. Off at seventeen to Louis-le-Grand—and there, must he recall it, his first encounter with true despair, the first failure. All these years later, he still felt the same about Paris, a visceral dread—the cold, the damp, the isolation and hunger, the brutality of the school and its competition, never enough even to eat and the cats howling in the alley outside at night—above all the *darkness.* Like a plant, he could not live without the light, his Mediterranean, African light, that was to him the same as *being alive.* "This is hell," he'd written to his mother, asking that she not show the letter to his father, who would think him irretrievably weak, "and I am dead here." And his mother, he would never know how, had persuaded his father that he should come home, that it was the only solution, that otherwise he might die, actually die, which had felt true; and so he had come home. And in the fifty years since, nobody had ever spoken of it. The page had been turned; the door to that room had been closed.

He had determined, fiercely, that it would not be his ruination, that it would not shape his path, that it wouldn't limit him, even though France was so rigid, its routes to success so narrow. This his father had impressed upon him from earliest childhood, his father, who had told him not only that he must always work his hardest but that he must be the *top,* the way his father had been the top, that not to be the top was to fail. The letter, in 1940, he'd never forgotten, in which his father told him that the victory of the Nazis over France had come about because the French hadn't worked hard enough, not individually and not together, that the stakes, even when they seemed small, as they might for a nine-year-old at school, were always the highest, because the accumulation of small failures could lead, as it did in 1940, to the end of the world as they knew it.

So he had turned, then, to the States, had applied off his own bat for the fellowship nobody in Algiers had heard of, the Fulbright. He had been, in his time, the intrepid adventurer, impressive, even rash, to his school friends, off to an unimaginable life in English when his peers, stuck in the past, refused to learn it, off to Amherst, to Oxford, then eventually to Harvard—and he'd managed, better than many, better than most, a career bestriding the Atlantic, one foot in France, the other in North America. He'd been, until the botched departure from Sydney, a rising star in the corporation, headed perhaps even for the top, or close.

He'd made that terrible move for her, for Barbara, because she'd asked him to; and he'd never reproached her. She never understood what it had cost him, how even as he was repeatedly promoted in the subsequent years, he'd forfeited his chances—there were those who mistrusted him, thought him erratic or flawed or weak, because of that incomprehensible self-destructive decision to go to Canada . . . instead she'd berated him for taking the promotion to New York so soon after they settled the kids in Toronto.

Those long, hard years of commuting, in New York from Monday to Friday, so many dinners and evenings alone, the empty bed, despairing—like Paris, he used to joke, just with more light—only to arrive home exhausted on Friday night and feel that none of them even wanted to see him, that their faces fell when he came through the gate at the airport, that they were happier without him. Not welcome in his own house, just the ox to plow the field, the beast of burden.

At least, he thought—as he buttoned his white shirt, knotted the dark tie he'd packed in his suitcase in Connecticut weeks before, knowing that when he took it out and unrolled it, his father would have died—at least things were not like that now. He and Barbara had weathered the storm—those terrible first years in Connecticut—the awful fights—all of it a dark blur. Probably, certainly, he'd drunk too much, alone in the bleak

Middletowne Hotel on Fiftieth in those long commuting years. And then had relied too much on his old friend Johnnie Walker to get him through the early stretch in Connecticut. They'd been so happy there when the girls were tiny, before Australia, and he could never quite believe how things felt upon their return, like *Who's Afraid of Virginia Woolf?* or Sartre's *No Exit*, as though they were locked alone in awful combat. She so unhappy, and nothing he could do or say or give her was enough, none of it made a difference. As though he would only be lovable, forgivable, acceptable if he performed a series of Herculean tasks, the exact nature of which was never disclosed to him and seemed always to be changing: I want to stay in Canada, I want to travel more, why don't we have more friends here, I can't stand all those hoity-toity French wives, when are we leaving, when can we go back to my mother, who is all alone, or to London, I'd like London, when are we leaving?

Better, in many ways, in the six years since he'd retired—and yet. Working all those years, he'd never felt the pain that had dogged him since. He'd never woken thinking of the bottle in his suitcase. Always blindingly busy, lurching from airport to office, from Grand Central to Greenwich, from kid's graduation to dutiful parental visit, paying the bills, polishing his shoes, repacking his suitcase, always exhausted, always responsible. He'd never thought, for years, about the rooms he would, then could, no longer enter, entry to which was no longer even imaginable—to think that he might have been a scholar—that he might even have been an artist (Why not? As a little boy, he'd loved to draw and paint—he remembered his mother, in a particularly impoverished wartime Christmas, finding somehow for him a set of colored pencils and a notebook, when even the paper had been precious! To think! . . . And later he'd loved taking photographs, had imagined for years that one day, in retirement—but no) . . . that he might have felt at home somewhere, anywhere—though home, of course, as his father would have said, was a matter not of geography but of family, and his sister would have added that he was always at home *with them*—but how to articulate, to them or to himself, the terror and misgiving that had, for almost all his life, accompanied his love for them, profound as it was? How to convey that even if he could belong with them, he needed not to; or, rather, he needed to find somewhere else or someone else to belong to; and that there, of course, lay the greatest sorrow, that Barbara did not, could not open her arms to him. She could not give him home.

When his mother died, sweet husk that she'd become, lost to dementia for years before her body gave out, he'd said to Barbara, "This is the saddest day of my life so far." And yet she'd almost seemed not to hear him, certainly not to understand. She had, all these years, performed respect for her mother-in-law but had always feared her. Perhaps she was envious of his simple love for his mother, unfamiliar herself with a love that gave much and never punished. Perhaps she felt it as a reproach. Barbara's own mother had all her life punished her daughter, and Barbara in her turn punished him. A Protestant thing. But she could see how easy his mother's love was, how boundless, and how alien; in any case, she rejected it. Of his father, more complicated, she'd always been more fond. She was genuinely sad, now, that he had died.

He could hear her in the bathroom, surely putting on her makeup. While his sister never left the house without carefully painting her face, Barbara rarely wore makeup at all, and looked to him a little strange when she did, the strong lines of her face smudged somehow. He stood in his sister's living room, hearing the fountain outside trickling, shot his cuffs and adjusted his black tie. He hadn't turned on a light. He was getting fat and his collar pinched. His fingers, always thick, looked to him clumsy, pale chipolata sausages in the gloom.

"Are you nearly ready?" he called. It was almost eight. Up at the big apartment, the undertakers would soon be arriving to take his father away. He wanted to be there, to say his last farewell, to kiss, one last time, that high bony brow. He dreaded the walk uphill, and then all the steps, a torture for his legs. He'd take another Doliprane just now. She hadn't answered him. "Barb, are you nearly ready?"

He could just about hear his own irritation, though it reached his ears muffled by the irritation itself: he was essentially *in it*, rather than *observing* it. But he'd come over the years to understand that his anxiety reached her as ill temper, and that she then responded with ill temper, and that he should try harder to widen the wedge between his impulses and how he behaved. He called again, more softly, "Barb? I don't want to be late."

"Do you want to go on ahead then?" she called from behind the door.

He did not. He wanted to climb the hard hill together. In his imagination, she might even hold his hand. He was climbing, after all, to see his father put in his coffin. He, who could barely walk. Surely he wouldn't have to go alone? A literal calvary. Why would she deny him? How could it be that he did not even merit this small solace?

"It's okay," he said. He went to the kitchen to get a Doliprane. His neck and shoulder hurt too, on the left side. Not just his leg and his back. He coughed. Always. He wanted a cigarette but wouldn't have it—five a day, on this day, would require serious discipline. A crock. Sixty-seven and a crock. He would not complain. That he had long mastered. He might be full of rage at the world, at shitty politicians and crooks, at the general idiocy, but he did not complain about his own lot. She did enough of that for them both.

They were, they always had been, so different. Maybe he'd thought that in marrying her, he could escape who he was, could transform into, say, her father, a bluff, unthinking, unintelligent, unself-conscious man who liked sports, cars, and playing cards and was interested in money. Or maybe he hadn't thought anything, had simply been felled by her good looks, her wide mouth and long limbs, her slightly awkward laugh, and the way she lowered her eyes when she spoke. . . . Maybe he'd wanted chiefly what he shouldn't, the new, his insatiable desire for the New World, to escape once and for all from the hideous fettered conformity his father desired for him, the constraining definitions of success that had seemed to him like death. After his time in Paris, he wanted *anything* but Paris, and his father kept insisting that the only path to success was Paris,

and the destination to which the path would lead was . . . Paris. So he'd
fallen in love with a woman who was the anti-Paris, as far from Paris as
she could be, who hated Paris more than he did, or at least who hated
"the French," whatever they were.

But his father, this formidable old man against whom he had long
struggled (history, nationality, politics, religion, all of it) and yet whom
he loved fiercely, whose opinion had always mattered to him more than
he knew it ought— for years he'd sent him the children's report cards,
for God's sake, he couldn't quite believe it, but he had—that father, born
into poverty, had made his life's work becoming, then being a Frenchman, a French gentleman no less—a colonial French gentleman, perhaps the most fervent sort, the way a convert is more zealous than a born
Catholic. He'd insisted that nothing would stand in his way, not the humble circumstances of his birth, nor the father who vanished when he was a
boy—a Maltese father, indeed, by no standards of the time a white man,
by no standards of the time a plausible gentleman—not his distance from
the metropole, not his unexpected and uneasy choice of a spouse, not
the fact that in the beginning they had to choose between paying for his
smart white naval uniform and having enough to eat—he hadn't let any
of it stand in his way. But he too had failed, in his time: his run for political office in Algiers hadn't succeeded, nor his oil exploits in the Sahara.
He'd been buffeted by History, every bit as much as his son. But in the
end he had chosen to remain a French gentleman, to believe, cheerfully,
unwaveringly in his country and himself. He had thrown in his lot with
the persona he had willed into being, and his wife had believed in him
always, maybe that was all it took, a cult of two, and he, they, had been
happy. In spite of everything, they'd been happy. He and his beloved
wife had held hands through it all, which had been, perhaps, most certainly, their happiness.

Here she was at last, his own wife. Barbara. They'd have to hurry,
though he could not move fast even when he wanted to. She wore her
black dress suit, a pale lipstick. Even now she took his breath away—she

never aged, as tall and slender as she'd been on the bus that rainy day in Oxford, forty-three years ago. She smiled at him, tenderly, adjusting her new birthday scarf at her throat, its black background fitting for the day.

"Is that okay?" she asked.

"Perfect. It looks just right."

Even if she did not reach for his hand or begin to understand him—as he could not begin to understand her, even after all these years—still, now, she walked alongside him, out into the cold morning. Which was not nothing, was something. They had surely accomplished something.

TOULON, FRANCE

So strange, to be totally alone in the big apartment. Possibly in all my thirty-two years I'd not been alone there, certainly not in wintertime, at night, the wind buffeting and rattling the vast windows on all sides. I considered lowering the metal blinds against the immensity of the storm-filled night, but I feared feeling trapped—entombed even— more than I disliked the flapping and banging. I resolved to give in to the storm: exhausted, I'd sleep regardless, though I decided to sleep under a blanket on the broad living room sofa, rather than tucked away in one of the bedrooms. There was nobody to tell me not to.

Just a few days before, the rooms had been crowded and lively in spite of the mourning spirit: Loulou and her husband and their little girl, Ines, just a year old and newly on her pins, squealing with the joy of it; and me and Oliver of course—we'd abandoned our turret with only a few days left in the residency, and had been allotted that old lumpy sofa bed in Grand-père's study; and Mama and Daddy, who'd, paradoxically, slept in Denise's abandoned flat while she herself stayed on in the alcove bedroom, perching, as she'd done for years, as if still ready to leap up in the night for her father.

Nobody had stayed in his bedroom, of course. Or, rather, when we all arrived, *he* stayed still in his bedroom. Fatima and Denise had bathed and scented his body and dressed him in his best suit, and he lay on his side of the bed, near the door, with his head on two pillows and his hands crossed over the white sheet. All around him they piled the bright wreaths and ribboned bouquets sent in his honor, so it seemed that he lay in a bed of flowers, and they kept the window wide open against the possibility of a smell. They might then have closed the door so that the rest of the apartment stayed warm (the heating was pathetic at the best of times) but Tante Denise felt strongly that this would be tantamount to shutting him away, as if he were irrelevant, when he was, in spirit but of course also in body, still utterly with us, indeed the reason for and focus of our gathering.

When first I had turned the corner to see him there—was it him? Or was this no longer the proper pronoun to describe the waxen figure, gaunt, almost mythic, all bony nose, and his white chick's hair fluttering gently at his ears in the cold air. . . . When I first saw him, I could not quite believe that this was he, that he was dead. "Doesn't it look as though he's moving?" I whispered to Oliver, who did not want to look.

It felt very not-American, very not-Protestant for us to walk and play and eat and chatter within a few feet of this effigy, this decaying immobilized reduction of what he'd been, the core and center of us all. I knew without discussion that my mother must be horrified, repelled, as she'd been all those years ago when, in the same season, in the same room, Grand'-mère had also died, and they'd done the same thing. In North America you called the undertakers and they vanished the body and returned a strange waxwork, jaw wired shut, reeking of embalming fluid, propped in a satin-lined box like a jewel, and visible only in that curious institution, the Funeral Home, which *pretended* to be your own home, but uglier, with sky-blue broadloom and rustly drapes, dotted about with lugubrious solemn attendants in dark suits who clasped their hands together in front of themselves and spoke in whispers. That, of course, a farce all its own.

So I also understood my aunt's logic: How was it different to be dying, to be dead? Each of us lived in and was loved by a family, and just as you loved and were loyal to your family in spite of bad temper or poor choices or halitosis or OCD, you loved them also in death as in life. You were sensible to the agony of that final parting—the moment, on the morning of the actual funeral, when the somber men came to place him nonetheless in his satin-lined coffin—and you wanted to delay it as long as you could. Just as a mother monkey whose baby has died will groom its lifeless corpse and hold it close sometimes for several days, or as elephant mothers carry in their trunks sometimes for weeks their departed children; or as the orca whales also carry aloft their dead, so too, I understood, humans, also animals, reasonably, in traditional societies, mourn with the bodies of their departed.

In high school, in my brief theater days, I acted in a play by the Irish writer J. M. Synge, *In the Shadow of the Glen*, in which I played Nora, a widow keeping vigil in her isolated country cottage over the dead body of her difficult husband. That was before even Grand'-mère died, and I had not seen or known death for myself. I'd considered this vigil then an ancient custom far from my own modern world. In the play, of course, the difficult husband only pretended to be dead, and revived in a tragi-comic fury. But Grand-père wasn't playing at being dead. He'd been ninety-three, after all. We'd known he must leave us. You could even say he'd prepared us, diminishing into frailty without losing his humor or his wisdom. Though preparation wasn't really possible.

My parents had asked if I could stay on a week with Tante Denise, who needed an investigative surgery, her first ever adult hospital stay— something about polyps—and was afraid to be alone for it. I'd said yes, of course—how could I not?—but when my father left the room I'd asked my mother, "Is this the same thing you had a few years ago?"

"Pretty well, I think. They need to take them out, make sure they're not cancerous."

"So it's a *procedure*, right? I mean, it's hardly surgery, right?"

"There's anesthetic involved. She's nervous about that."

"Sedation or general anesthetic?"

"I don't know. It's a different medical system, a different culture. I don't know which it is. Does it matter?"

"Well, one's got a lot more risk involved. I get it if she's afraid of general anesthetic."

"But you don't get it if it's not? I'm not sure the fear is rational, quite."

"No." I said this in a knowing and judgmental way, as if we could agree a priori on Tante Denise's craziness. It was something shared, with Loulou too, but not with my father, who did not ever gossip about anyone and above all not his sister.

This time my mother surprised me. "Give your aunt a break," she said. It was the day before the funeral. "She's about to bury her father, whom she's taken care of for the last fifteen years. Maybe she just doesn't want to be alone, right?"

"I *said* I'd stay."

"Yes, and thank you. But maybe try to do it gracefully, too?"

I sighed and bit my lip. With the older generation, I could never quite grasp the shifting allegiances. Or my mother's, at least.

Now, this night, alone with all the familiar furniture, the paintings and tchotchkes—to which my aunt would not return: she'd confided before she went to the clinic that she planned never to spend another night there, that she could not wait to return to her own small flat—I felt for Denise a particular sympathy and confusion, after reading that afternoon, a diary I'd never been meant to see.

THE DAY OF Grand-père's funeral was clear and cold. The sea glistened deep blue, the headlands etched dark against the light sky. The men came early to put him in his coffin and take him to the church—"to box him up," as I said to my sister, trying to be amusing, desperate to laugh a bit. (Thank goodness for her little daughter, whose jolly antics allowed repeatedly for laughter: Ines thought the gathering of grown-ups existed to admire her.) The coffin could not fit in the lift, and the men had to maneuver it down the stairs. Initially, in haste, they banged it against the wall at the first turn, chipping the stucco. Tante Denise, already on edge, yelped loudly from the landing, her cry a louder version of his own late yelps, as if she herself had been hit. The cry echoed down the stairwell and I was sure could be heard in the lobby, several floors below.

"Don't worry," my father said quietly at her side in his dark suit, "it will all be okay."

But she threw up her hands and muttered, irate. Then creepy Angéline, already arrived, wearing a crimson felt cape over her frilly black dress and a matching hat with a feather, threw her arms around Denise, whispering soothingly into her neck, "There, there, mademoiselle, don't cry! He's with the Lord! It's a great day—he's in heaven!"

Embarrassed, we drifted back into the apartment, still hearing the undertakers' clattering descent.

"Honestly," my mother, standing by the dining room window, said to Oliver and me, as my sister chased her squealing daughter down the steps to the living room. No more than that, but we knew she was referring to Angéline, to the ensemble, to the emphasis on religion that so reassured our aunt. Tante Denise, like her parents, slept always beneath the crucified Christ—literally. We almost never spoke of it, but our agnosticism was to her a great sorrow. "There are no atheists in the trenches," she liked to say.

The night before, my mother had told my father that Angéline must not be invited to the lunch after the funeral. This after it became clear that she would travel to the church and thence to the cemetery in the minibus my father had arranged for simplicity's sake. My father, usually so forceful in his opinions, was in this moment, with his sister, eyes wide, meek as a lamb: he wanted only for her wishes to be granted, for her to feel that the obsequies had been handled with due honor and respect, in her eyes and those of this community to which he, and we, didn't belong. As if he'd ceded his grief to her. And she seemed to want Angéline at her side.

"After all," Oliver pointed out, "we have each other, and Loulou and

Pavel have each other, and your parents have each other; but your aunt is on her own."

"I can't say I much want Angéline to be part of our family," I replied. "The sartorial misfortune!"

But we all understood: Tante Denise was likely to be unmoored, now.

In the end, though, Angéline came to the graveside, along with our small group and very few old family friends—and cut quite a figure in her cape and what looked like flamenco shoes, her hat's vermilion feather waving above her head. She herself announced that she would not come to lunch. "You'll forgive me," she explained in a confidential tone, in her baby voice, before we even left the flat, "but I have a prior engagement. I would not miss your father's funeral *for the world*," she said to Denise, once again ignoring *my* father, as though he were no relation at all, "but directly afterward I must leave. I have arranged for a taxi to meet me at the cemetery."

And when the time came, a black Mercedes with tinted windows, its light off, awaited her at the entrance to the Cimetière Lagoubran. We watched her slip into the back seat, shut the door, and effectively vanish. In the following days, as my sister and her family decamped for their home in Moscow, as Oliver and I returned briefly to the castle to retrieve our large suitcases and I saw him off at the airport in Nice, as my parents, in a more languorous but no less determined fashion, packed up their month's worth of clothes, books, and papers and set off back to their house and their dog, Waffles, and their regular life in Connecticut, over all these days, the better part of a week, Angéline made no sign of life at all. She *had* vanished. My mother, always suspicious, told my father to count the silver. My father suggested blandly that contrary to my mother's suspicions, Angéline was simply an effective aide, one who provided emotional rather than physical support. Though useless at cooking or cleaning or carrying, it was shockingly true: she'd been a remarkable presence for Grand-père and Denise over these last months. Her job here done, she'd doubtless moved on and taken a new assignment. She hadn't, he pointed out, been paid to attend the funeral; she'd done that on her own time. But she still needed to earn a living. For my aunt, Angéline had been heaven-sent, her name a clue to her provenance and purpose.

TWO DAYS BEFORE her entry into the clinic, my aunt was left alone with me. She still slept in the cubby bedroom. I, meanwhile, once my sister and her family departed, came down from the study upstairs, where it was very cold at night, to sleep in our old girls' room. In my grandfather's bedroom, my aunt had laid on the coverlet the old framed black-and-white photograph from Buenos Aires of her parents together in profile, all dressed up, not young but not old, in the late joyful middle of their lives, in the late middle of the century, when it had seemed that at last the worst of the tempest was past. She kept the small bedside lamp on his side of the room alight night and day, and its red shade cast a warm, muted light: the cave of death had become a cave of memory. The whole apartment had become, with everyone's departures, a cave of memory.

That first evening we were alone together—neither of us much good in the kitchen, we'd agreed I'd make a salad and she an omelet, and together we'd have a meal—the medical clinic sent a technician to check her vitals and make sure she was ready for the procedure. The plan was that she'd go to the clinic—we'd go together—the following afternoon, and she'd spend the night there, monitored, before being taken to the operating theater early the next morning. The operation would be done by lunchtime, and yet they'd keep her overnight to be sure she was recovering well. I could escort her home on the morning of the third day.

The young man who came to take her blood pressure and heart rate, a shaggy blond guy about my age who'd whistled in the hallway, was visibly unsettled by the flat's strong smell of cigarette smoke. As he unpacked his kit at the dining room table, he admired the view—though it was already dark, you could see lights winking here and there, and intuit the great ocean from their absence—and then he asked, "What's wrong with your voice?"

Nobody mentioned my aunt's voice—or, rather, lack of it—to her face. A couple of years before, when I'd sprained my ankle and gone to see her physical therapist, I'd heard him call me "Louis Armstrong's niece." Ashamed that I'd caught this line, he explained that this was her nickname in the office, because her vocal cords were so wrecked by tobacco. Her voice was a gravelly rumble, an unlikely emanation from this bird-sized older woman. While I'd repeated this to Oliver and to my parents, I hadn't ever told Denise about it. Her voice was something we were all aware of and knew politely to overlook.

"I beg your pardon?" She was deciding whether to get annoyed. But she was, in a basic way, too frightened to be angry.

"I asked what's wrong with your voice?"

She laughed uneasily, that too a rumble that provoked a cough, the bottomless cough she shared with my father. "Cigarettes," she said. "My chords are—well, rubbish."

He frowned. "It's not normal, you know."

She smiled apologetically.

"Have you had it checked out?"

"Well, they've been checking me out all over for this operation, so I imagine if they were concerned, they'd have ordered some sort of scan."

"You should have it checked out, though." He shook his head a little as he puffed the blood pressure cuff around her arm. He was quiet till it reached its peak, and he made a notation on his clipboard. "It's not really an operation, to speak of. More like an investigative procedure. Not as demanding, thankfully. But didn't they tell you to stop smoking beforehand?"

She opened her hands flat to the ceiling, importunate. "I've done my best," she said. "I've cut down by half in the past week . . . it's been difficult."

"My grandfather just died," I explained. "The funeral was two days ago."

"My condolences." He pressed his stethoscope to her outstretched, upturned wrist, which looked pale and naked and vulnerable. He was again quiet, again wrote in his notebook. "And do you consume alcohol regularly?" he asked, reaching for another little gadget, to clip over her forefinger.

"Hardly," she said. This was the sort of lie my father told; the sign of a drinker, to deny it. When we were younger, she hardly drank, but these days she had her scotches—two, sometimes three—with almost military regularity. Nobody begrudged her. "She has a hard life," we always said, which was true—if not necessarily compared to many other lives, then certainly in that it was manifestly hard to live in her skin. But for her to say to the young man that she hardly drank—especially given the lithium, which she'd taken for at least as long as I'd been alive—seemed a telling feint.

I looked to see if he was skeptical, but he was preoccupied with the oximeter reading. "Your oxygen levels aren't so good," he said.

She looked alarmed. "What does it mean?"

"They're just— You need to stop smoking," he said. "You really need to stop."

"But for the operation?"

"You'll be fine. They'll check everything very carefully beforehand, don't worry." He looked at his watch, hastened to pack his gear in his tidy backpack. He was still zipping it as he made for the door. "You'll be fine," he said again as he stepped into the dark hallway and pressed the *minuterie*. "But you need to get your voice checked out. And you really need to stop smoking."

As soon as he'd left, she lit a cigarette and poured herself a sizable whiskey in her favorite cut-glass tumbler. "As if I didn't have enough to worry about," she said. "Chin-chin!"

WHEN WE SIGNED her into the clinic the next afternoon, her bravado had evaporated. She clung to my arm like a child in a busy train station, terrified of being separated from its mother. She was so small (never tall, she was shrinking with age: "The osteoporosis!" she'd grumbled. "They tell me the smoking makes it worse . . .") and so slight. She listened carefully, wide-eyed, to all of the instructions. She asked where she might be able to smoke while she was there, and was told she'd have to step outside: we'd passed several patients in their hospital gowns, one dragging an IV pole, along with some tired-looking nurses, smoking outside the entrance. Up in her room—my father had paid for a private one—they asked her to change into the gown and get into bed, though it wasn't yet six p.m. When the nurse had left us, having taken Tante Denise's supper order, she laughed her rumbly laugh: "Do you think this rigmarole is supposed to distract you from being nervous? Jumping through all these silly hoops!"

"It makes it easiest for them, I guess," I offered doubtfully. It did all seem very involved. I'd had to have a minor surgery at home in the States a few years before, for which I'd shown up at the hospital at dawn and been released, barely sentient, by noon: I'd slept away the day in my parents' king-sized bed and woke at suppertime in agony, to be plied, by my mother, with the painkillers prescribed. There'd been no hospital bed, no nurse, no gown. I wasn't sure whether this palaver was standard—sending the young technician to the house!—or whether Denise's frailty was particular cause for the doctors' concern.

The nurse kindly brought a supper tray for me as well. While my aunt fiddled at length with her elaborate bed to find a comfortable sitting position, I sat in the fat vinyl armchair, of an institutional pale blue, and after we ate, in principle, we read. We'd selected a few new magazines—she loved the home décor ones, and we'd picked up *Paris Match* for fun. I, reading *War and Peace*, was uncomfortably at the point of the death of Prince Andrei Bolkonsky. Our "reading," however, was a farce, hers because she was so frightened that she shivered and her teeth seemed to chatter, and mine because I was powerfully distracted by her suffering and my impotence to alleviate it.

I realized that she felt certain, unreasonably certain, that in the morning she would die. Whether on the operating table or in the recovery room, she would simply give over to death, the way, in Tolstoy, Prince Andrei gives over to death. This wasn't a rational thought but a visceral experience, and an imaginative one. She didn't want to talk about it, but she quickly put aside her magazines and looked instead at the walls, the ceiling, out to the hallway, as if waiting for someone. It *was* like being a child, I thought: her logic was associative. Her father had died; now, in this moment directly afterward, when she couldn't yet imagine her future, it surely seemed obvious that she too could die, might die, would die.

The future, a faith in it, I thought, had to be the line to pull her through. Before my eyes, in black and white, Prince Andrei had lost that line. "You'll come to visit us in the summertime," I said then, as a fact rather than a question. "You'll come see our apartment in Washington, D.C., and we'll take you to all the monuments."

"I don't see how I can do that," she said, with her sad smile.

"Why not? You haven't been able to come for ages because of Grandpère; but now, you must."

"Earlier this year, Air France banned smoking on the New York flights. I don't see that I can ever go to the States again. Given how I feel about flying in the first place . . ."

"But look," I said, "it's almost nine, and we've been in this clinic since five; and soon you'll go to sleep and you won't smoke in your sleep, and that will easily be longer than the flight to the States—"

"That accursed ocean," she said. "I've never understood why we live on opposite sides of it."

Because, I thought, my father had wanted—needed—to get away. Or because he didn't realize he was leaving when he left—but that made no sense. Time and again he had chosen: the fellowship, graduate school, my mother, the work postings outside France. . . . Even now, in retirement, though his pension came from France, he insisted that he couldn't possibly live there: the taxes were too high, he claimed. But really he just didn't wish to, he had never wished to. He had all his life been torn between his filial duty and the desire to run away, to be free and himself. Of course I didn't say this. I said instead, "But you've crossed the ocean so many times—and we all crossed the ocean to get here. I'll cross the ocean myself in just a few days, and you'll see, I'll arrive safely on the other side. I believe I will. And you will too, come summertime."

She sighed, coughed her bottomless cough. "Well, maybe," she said. "First things first, though. I've got to make it through the next twenty-four hours."

"You will."

Again, the sad smile. "We hope."

"Just like I know I'll make it back to Washington, D.C., on the plane, I know you'll be fine with this. You'll be fine." I hoped, as I said this, that I wasn't wrong: certainty always alarmed me. But my aunt was mollified, at least a little. "Would you like me to stay here overnight?" I asked.

Relief bloomed across her face. "Would you?"

"If they'll let me," I said. "I think the armchair reclines."

"We'll ask when next she comes. But she wouldn't send you away—" She spoke of the nurse, so kind: "She sees how I am. . . . Will you come downstairs with me while I smoke? Just one."

I thought of the technician's insistence the previous evening, and of how little I wanted to stand outside with her in the winter cold, of how little, really, she herself must want to stand outside in the cold. But she was trying so hard. "Okay," I said. "Let me get your dressing gown."

THE NEXT MORNING, I left the clinic after she was wheeled away on her gurney—but not before they'd given her an intravenous sedative that made her drowsy and calm, so that she smiled as she held my hand before she went.

"Pray for me," she said.

I nodded, though I didn't pray. "No atheists in the trenches," I thought. I drove her tinny little car for the first time—the ashtray overflowed with butts and the black gearshift was gray with ash, a layer caught in its vinyl folds as though a tiny volcano had erupted nearby. When I got back to the flat, I opened the door using the house key on the heavy ring it shared with the other keys—to the *cave*, to the gate, to the beach—a ring that I'd known all my life but that had never before been entrusted to me.

It was early morning still, and gray. My footsteps echoed on the marble. I could hear the kitchen tap dripping from the front hall. I'd slept poorly, and little—my small aunt, given a *calmant*, had snored as loudly as a motorcycle engine—but when I lay down briefly, I remained wide awake. Infected by Tante Denise's anxiety, I needed to hear that she was safely out of the operating room. They'd given me a number to call in the late morning.

I made coffee in the ancient stuttering coffee machine, and heated some UHT milk on the flickery gas element—it sizzled against the sides of the pot when I poured it—and I wandered the cold apartment holding with both hands the large bowl of café au lait. The rooms seemed almost to tremble in anticipation of everyone's return: Where was little Ines, shrieking with joy? Where was Odet, in her work smock, wielding a bucket of soapy water and a mop? Where was my grandfather, shuffling along the corridor in his misbuttoned cardigan, his moth-eaten shawl draped over his shoulders? And where was my long-vanished beloved grandmother, shuffling too, her dyed hair flat at the back where she had lain against the pillow, her blue eyes at once clear and vague? Where were my sister and myself as little girls, one blond and one dark, in our matching sleeveless pantsuits and Mary Janes, squeezing onto the tiny balcony off the dining room where the railings were so close that the grown-ups could not fit? Where was Big the dachshund, lumbering down the hall, dog tags jingling, nails tapping, to flop on his side in the sun? Only silence, everything in wait for life to resume; life holding its breath.

I thought to look upstairs in my grandfather's study for the traces of our lives, for the evidence that until only a few moments ago we had all been here. Glassed in on two sides, the room took so much sun that everything in it had been leached of color: the once-crimson curtain faded to pale pink; the dark green velveteen bedspread faded too; the few photographs on his desk curled and faded almost to white, their subjects merely ghostly outlines. I knew so well the objects in this room that hadn't moved or changed in my lifetime: we'd played as children with the desiccated painted maracas, with the small beaded Indian doll whose face had long ago worn off. We'd wielded my grandfather's scabbarded Polytéchnicien's sword, and had doodled on foolscap with his stubby double-sided red-and-blue editing pencils. We'd flipped wearily through the old photograph book of all the French navy's ships at sea, learning and forgetting their names, but more often through the stacks of cloth-covered family photo albums, interested only in finding pictures of ourselves. We did, though, also love the oldest album, of cracked leather held together with frayed black ribbon, which held photographs of our father and aunt as infants, as children. In one, our father, eyes enormous, perhaps one year old, was propped plumply on a white fur rug, wearing only a glinting medallion on a chain around his neck. Even in black and white you sensed the powdery texture of his skin. In that album our grandfather had dark hair and wore huge flapping suits, while our grandmother, her hair rolled at the nape, smirked coyly at the camera.

Older, I'd discovered on a low shelf behind some stacked paintings my grandfather's early multivolume edition of Proust, foxed and tattered but intact; and, of course, on a shelf above the divan, the five large red binders containing the family history he'd spent years writing for us, for my sister and me, fifteen hundred pages of blue ink in his steady, even, clear hand, interspersed with photographs and letters and receipts and telegrams—a trove beyond my reach but that I knew one day I'd read entire—it was our inheritance, after all, addressed to us. (I did not then expect that it would take me almost twenty years.) There between the shoeboxes stuffed with ancient postcards of lost places—Constantine, Oran, L'Arba, Blida, Bougie, Tizi Ouzou, Sidi Bel Abbès, Tipasa, Tlemcen—lay the stacked thin brown folders of our grandfather's largely unpublished essays (along with his series on the Maghreb that *Le Monde* had printed in the '50s), years of work on Europe, North Africa, and the Middle East, handwritten, then typed out on onionskin, along with lists of the people to whom he'd sent copies. Then, in other file folders, particular correspondences—with old friends from Greece and Beirut with whom he'd taken up again in the '70s; with regional and national politicians, some of whom wrote back long personal letters and others of whom—Valéry Giscard d'Estaing!—sent brief formal notes signed by their staff. He had saved a fat file of his correspondence with a historian of communism named Annie Kriegel, of whom he'd spoken more than once; and a fatter file still of carbon copies of letters he'd sent to the newspapers—*Le Monde, Le Figaro, Var-Matin*—with, when occasionally they'd been published, the clipping pinned to the carbon with a now-rusted straight pin. Everything was dusty, the piles of magazines (art, politics, history), the shelves of Spanish and Italian paperbacks, among which a few English titles lurked (*Thy Hand, Great Anarch!*).

Slipped among these as though it were a foreign novel, I discovered a sliver of a notebook, spiral-bound, ancient, with a Spanish crest upon the cover and, inside, graph pages on which I recognized, in varying degrees of looseness suggesting varying degrees of haste, Tante Denise's familiar hand in the blue fountain-pen ink of all her letters to us over the years.

The first entry was marked "B.A.," which, given the date—March 1962—I took to mean Buenos Aires. I knew few details of any of their lives before our births, but we'd always been aware of the happy decade in Argentina, before even we could find it on a map. When we were teenagers, there'd been a hit song on the radio by Dalida that my aunt whistled or sang endlessly: *"Hey, j'ai dansé un soir de carnaval, / Dans l'enfer de la nuit tropicale . . ."* The next lines were *"À Rio, do Brasil, à Rio de Janeiro"* and then *"J'ai laissé mon coeur auprès de toi . . ."*—"I left my heart with you." She would often say, "But *I* danced in Buenos Aires," and we understood that she had been happy there.

But now I understood also that she had left her heart there: for well over a decade she'd kept an intermittent record of her feelings for this unnamed man. At first he was a work colleague, her boss in fact, and in the book she recorded the couple of times a month when they had lunch, often with others, or when she was invited to supper with his family, or particular jokes he'd made at the office. Often the entries were addressed directly to him, especially in those early years, a collection of unsent love letters.

I sat cross-legged on the sofa bed in the cold gray study and read the diary through. She wrote about how people—her parents, in particular—kept setting her up on dates with other men, but after each outing she could think only about how her date had fallen short, about how he was not *you*, about how much more delicious and exhilarating the same walk, the same meal, the same conversation would have been *with you*, her beloved, for whom she was destined, she believed, by God. But it was enough, she wrote, to know that you were in the world; she did not need to possess you. A nun does not possess the Lord: she gives herself to him, in spirit and mind. The body is transient, base, unimportant.

I calculated in my head: Denise had been my age in 1965–66, at the height of her unfulfilled passion. She had lived intensely an undeclared, one-sided love affair that buoyed and enlivened, filled and consumed her; but unlike my sister or me, she lived it only in her head: no hand to hold, no warm body. Imaginary, it seemed unimaginable—and yet I didn't have to imagine it, because there, in my lap, was the evidence, these unsent love letters—the stuff of medieval courtly romance. Our unmarried aunt, our devout Catholic spinster, *had* loved—she'd kept her secrets but had written them down, and she had kept the notebook all this time, more than thirty-five years . . . I couldn't help but think of Flaubert's devastating line about Félicité in *Un Coeur Simple*, a novella to which I had latterly been writing, in the castle turret, my homage: "*Elle avait eu, comme une autre, son histoire d'amour.*" She'd had, like any other, her love story. I couldn't stop tears from pooling in the corners of my eyes.

In the second half of the decade, after 1968, when she and my grandparents returned to live in Paris, the entries grew sparse: an evening with
him at the home of his married sister, her friend Antoinette, in Paris; the
account of a letter from him about a book she'd sent, containing photos
of his growing daughters; details from a dinner they had, just the two of
them, in Marseille, once she was living there: the way he spoke with his
hands, gesticulating while still holding his fork; the intensity of his gaze,
his heavily lashed eyes, his laugh.

And then suddenly, after a long silence, a rabid attack that had almost
torn the paper, in a demented hand hardly recognizable as hers: *ALL
LIES! ALL ASHES! I AM A FOOL! IT IS FINISHED!*

What could have happened? What revelation? The page shocked
me in its extremity and disorder. I closed the notebook and placed
it on the velvet coverlet. My coffee, at my feet, was cold. I checked
the time: close to eleven, when I was to ring the clinic. In my belly,
dread. She would never have wanted me to read these pages. It was as
if I'd been inside her head. And yet surely she'd hidden the notebook
there for someone to find, the stuff of novels: if she'd wanted it *never*
to be found, then she would have thrown it away. What was writing
for, if not to communicate? There was no such thing as writing that
did not signify. If it had been fated that I find it on this of all mornings, did that imply—in some great fictional narrative, like *Tristan
et Iseut* or *Le Roman de la Rose*—that she would not have survived
the anesthetic? Her lungs, we knew, were in a terrible state; that I'd
blithely assured her that she'd be fine seemed suddenly an ill omen,
a harbinger.

I managed to frighten myself. My hand was unsteady as I dialed the
clinic from the rotary phone in the front hall alcove. The switchboard
operator put me through to Tante Denise's ward, where the phone
rang unanswered until I was transferred back to the operator. She tried
another extension. My breathing sounded loud and shallow in my ears.
Eventually a man answered; he didn't know my aunt's name; he found a

colleague, a woman, who went to check. She returned after what seemed an age, to reassure me that my aunt, though she had not yet been brought back to her room, had come through the procedure fine, and was resting in recovery.

"I suggest you don't come in before three or four," she said. "She'll be sleeping. It takes a while properly to wake up. Visiting hours last until eight."

Life, I reassured myself upon replacing the handset, was not a fiction. When I read a novel or watched a film, I could so often predict what would happen next. Plot felt to me inevitable. But in life, turns were not programmed or decided, and we had agency over only some small aspects of our stories. Implacable chance ruled. As passengers, we could not determine whether the plane crashed; or as patients, whether the operation proved fatal. Imagining did not make it so— thank goodness. But how much of our lives did our minds control? And what of love? Of what had my aunt's long love consisted? Was it the less real for existing only in her head? Or were her years in love as wonderful, for her, as, well, being in love? What of my parents' love, if love there was? They had now had a long and very real life together, shared hours and weeks and years, but was their love therefore more real than my aunt's, or was it simply that their often unhappy life together was more real?

Tante Denise, that afternoon, though barely awake, was cheerful. The procedure was done, and the doctor came by to say that while they'd need to await the official results, he could assure her that he'd found nothing threatening. She was thrilled by this reprieve: she had survived! She would survive! I, again recalling the technician's insistence about her voice (he seemed, to me, our Greek chorus), wondered whether we should ask the doctor to scan her vocal cords; but I could not bring myself to mention it. My aunt, when he left, fell asleep holding my hand. I stayed later, to watch her eat, and having warned her that I would go back to the flat that night, when she again dozed off, I left her.

THUS THE NIGHT of wind and storm, me alone with all our ghosts. In the dark, I lay on my side in the fetal position on the living room sofa, beneath a mohair blanket, its itch reassuringly familiar from childhood, and looked out the window at the writhing black branches, the scudding clouds. The racket—not only the rattling but the beating surf and great moans of the gusting tempest—paradoxically seemed a protection.

What was this place now, I wondered. All my remembered life it had been our family's one unwavering home: we'd lived many places and belonged nowhere, except with our grandparents in Toronto and Toulon. But when we were still children, our Canadian grandmother sold her house and moved into a condo on the ninth floor of a new-build by the High Park subway station—and then, though we still belonged *with her*, we didn't belong in the same way to her *place*. Whereas this apartment—it held fragments of all my remembered life. Every item in it was known to me: the photographs of us as toddlers, as teenagers; the ancient shower-head in the bathroom of our girls' bedroom that had sprayed thinly and spat at wild angles for more than a decade; the square linen pillowcases trimmed with lace that our grandmother had embroidered for her trousseau; the tiny silver spoon in the silverware drawer that had been hers as a child in the nineteenth century—every moth hole, every worn rug, every lampshade falling off its ring, every squeaking hinge, I knew— and the smell of the kitchen in the mornings, the draft at our feet by our bedroom window, the clicking of the elevator in its shaft, climbing, climbing, all the way to our floor. . . . In the common gardens, I knew every skewed flagstone, every wild lavender bush, every cypress, every splintering slat on the deck of the pool, and along the path to the beach, each hidden stone bench, even when obscured by overgrown foliage, each subsidiary path interrupted by rockslides, and halfway down, on the right, the giant, weary, ever-expanding aloe into the waxy flesh of which we'd carved our initials twenty years before.

What would it all now become? What were these things, without us brought together around them? Having been repositories of history, of family, of a kind of private magic, would they now simply become again *things*, the dingy, broken detritus of an anonymous past? If nobody lived here, if nobody opened the books, switched on the lamps, ate off the chipped plates, sat in the hard armchair by the window to watch the sea night and day in its ceaseless rhythm—then what was this place? And, more urgently, without *him* in this place—he who had assured me, when I was young, that family was all that mattered, that family, for the itinerant certainly, for those with no country, was *home*—who were we?

PART VII

RYE BROOK, NEW YORK

For a long time she knew him by the splotches on his bald pate, the ones that were skin cancers and the ones that might have been, and the scars where the cancers had been removed. After the time when he almost died, when they lived together again, they made almost a whole person. He needed a cane and could not walk anywhere to speak of, but she could not drive anywhere (they told her it was on account of the macular degeneration, but really she often forgot how to get where she was supposed to go, or even sometimes forgot where she was supposed to go), and so they managed together: they walked from the apartment door to the elevator, from the elevator to the car in the underground lot, and then he knew where to go and sat in the car while she went inside to do the shopping. Sometimes he would get cross that she took too long in the shop, but it could be difficult to find what she wanted; it seemed that the shopkeepers moved the merchandise each time—Where was the butter? Did they still carry English muffins?—and of course sometimes halfway through she remembered the guests who were coming for supper—How could she have forgotten?—and had to go back to all the places in the store she had already been to get more of everything. Only for him to rail—that terrible temper; she'd have known him on that account even if she hadn't had the sun spots as a clue—and insist that nobody was coming, nobody.

But how did he explain then the voices in the other room, the people who hid in the cupboards or behind the door when she went looking? They were *his* people, that was for sure, she wasn't certain which relatives they were—French-speaking though, she could tell that much. If he didn't want to feed them dinner, then that was his affair. She would never have treated guests so rudely—when she could hear them talking, she set places for them at the table, a little tricky because how many were they exactly? But every time he'd lose his temper—sometimes it was François but others it was an old man she didn't know who sat at the table—rickety now, they should never have bought such a cheap little table—and castigated her until she took the extra place settings away. Well, it rattled her, of course it did, but afterward he always spoke soothingly, kindly, and stroked her arm. As though he was afraid of the guests in the other room, and maybe he was right to be; they wouldn't show themselves, and they were *his* people. So be it. They came and went as they pleased. She never knew when to expect them.

IN THOSE MONTHS, Chloe and Oliver drove down sometimes from Boston with the kids and stayed in the Hyatt up the road. Because the little ones loved the indoor swimming pool there, steamy and stinking of chlorine, but also because it was too much to have them in the cramped apartment for more than a few hours. When the younger generation came, they all went out to supper—there were a couple of spots off the Post Road where the children didn't seem too much of a ruckus and François always paid. It was nice to have the change of scenery—"Do you miss having a drink?" Chloe asked one time, and he was utterly sincere when he said he didn't miss it at all; but it depended on the moment, really— and when they sat in the booth, Barb would reach beneath the table to find his hand and lace her fingers with his own. When she did this, she gave a little secret smile, for him alone, as though they were young lovers getting away with something. Each time it made his heart jump. All his life he had wanted this, a love like his parents', and now, as he was losing her—who could blame him for wanting, occasionally, a little nip, when he was losing her, and losing, perhaps, his own battle—it was at last granted him. As if God, if there was a God, were saying, You've worked hard all these years, in spite of everything, and you may have this longed-for treat before you sleep. God—a North Korea of the mind!

When Chloe came on her own she slept in the study on the sofa bed, but François wasn't put out. After all they'd been through, he'd been through, he tried not to fuss over small disruptions. He could sit to read at the dining table when Chloe was in his room; and it seemed that when she was there, an actual guest, Barb didn't hear the voices in the bedroom: as if her brain had decided they needed company, that they were too much alone, which was true; and when they had company, her mind relaxed, for a while. To be a good hostess, to be a loving mother, she didn't need to think about these things—they just *were* her. The neurologist had expressed surprise at the last visit—Chloe had come along—when they told him all that Barb still did around the house. For heaven's sake, he was impressed that she dressed herself without help.

"He just doesn't know how remarkable you are," Chloe had said to her mother in the car on the way home, and Barb had smiled, vaguely. The bitterness was all gone, the way the alcohol in *bananes flambées* burned off with the flame. She was all sweetness now, with occasional rue to be sure, but always sweet.

WHEN THE MAN fell in the bathroom in the night, he cried out for help. He fell with a loud thump, followed by several other smaller thumps, in the dark, in the bathroom off the bedroom. She knew how small that bathroom was—she wouldn't use it herself; she used the other bathroom, with the bathtub, on the other side of the living room; this bathroom had a tiny shower stall with a faucet handle as old as she was, and the same kind of tile on the floor that Daddy used to have in the washroom at his office down on King Street, back when he shared with Uncle Edward— and when the man fell he made a good bit of noise, a sort of shriek first, and then moaning—*"Ayayayayay"* and then a pause and then again *"Ayayayayay,"* and a pause, and again, and then also, early on, "Help, Barb, help me!"—which was what struck terror, breathless icy terror, in her body, because how did the man know her name?

If only François were there, but he was always traveling, leaving her alone with the girls—Where *were* the girls? Were they safe? But she was too frightened to get out of bed to go see—and what was *this* man doing in her bedroom in the middle of the night? Sitting up, her knees to her chest, her blankets pulled up—it was cold; the window was open a little and the air coming through blew dark and cold; that must be how the man had got in? Unless he was one of François's guests, the hooded ones she glimpsed only when she rounded the corners in the daytime, or more particularly at dusk, those guests who hid from her the way millipedes hide from the light, muttering just out of sight, but she knew he invited them in, though he always denied it. And maybe the man in the bathroom—on the bathroom floor, if she gauged properly from the sounds—was one of his many guests? She put her hands over her ears and closed her eyes and hummed as loudly as she could, so she wouldn't hear him moaning. Because maybe he was innocent, but just as easily it could be a trap, and if she went to help him, they might grab her by the ankle, and who knew, then? She kept her eyes as tightly shut as she possibly could but even behind her eyes she could see the hooded figures, men most likely, clustered in their dark robes in the corners of the room: they kept their faces hidden. Why? It must be for a reason. You can't trust someone you cannot see. Look people frankly in the eye, Daddy always told her, and shake hands firmly. Everyone trusts a firm handshake. But even behind the humming she could hear the man moaning—it broke her heart and terrified her in equal measure, and yes, without taking her hands from her ears to touch her face, she could feel her cheeks wet with tears, she sobbed silently, her breath and so her humming in hiccups, because she was as scared as she had ever been, all alone— What about the girls? Where were the girls? She should save them; but how?

When the terrifying doorbell rang—the doorbell of their apartment, as old as the bathroom tile, sounded a formidable alarm; they don't make things like they used to—light was creeping in the windows: dawn. Her alarm clock, its luminous face, said six a.m. The bathroom was quiet now. Had it all been a dream? Her doorbell or the alarm? But no, again, the piercing sound, like a fire alarm, but brief—certainly the doorbell. And a third time. Her bathrobe lay across the bottom of her bed and she slipped it on and tied the belt as she scurried to the door. Whose jacket hung on the back of the dining chair? Whose were those galumphing shoes? She was suddenly aware of being herself barefoot—should she go back for slippers? But the bell again, and now she could hear: "Barbara? Barbara!" A woman's voice, cracked and dry like an old leaf. Did she know the voice? Was it a trick? What if on the threshold stood one of them, with his hood, and he had come for her?

But Barbara was brave. Mother, always critical, said she wasn't really, but Daddy would remind her of the time on the Chris-Craft out on Lake of Bays when the motor gave out and the wind was up, and she never lost her cool though they had a long hard paddle of it, as day was failing, to get to Mrs. Schmoll's dock. Five miles by road from the cottage, and Mother had to drive over to pick them up. Old Mrs. Schmoll had poured them both a scotch while they waited, apparently unaware that Barb was only sixteen.

This wasn't old Mrs. Schmoll behind the door, it was Bernadine Murphy, of course it was, eighty-five if she was a day, a true senior, wee wiry white wisp of a thing, not as tall as Barb's shoulder.

"I know it's early," said Mrs. Murphy, dressed as if to go shopping, "but I waited till daybreak and I couldn't wait any longer. May I come in?"

Barbara felt self-conscious suddenly in her dressing gown. "I haven't made any coffee yet," she said.

"Don't bother about that," said Mrs. Murphy. "I just want to be sure everyone's all right. Are you all right?"

"I'm okay."

"I heard a loud noise in the night, and then your husband's voice—it comes up through the pipes, I couldn't help but hear it."

Barbara remembered the strange man. "Oh, he's not here, my husband. But there was—there is—"

"Can I just come see? We'll go together. I know the way. My place is exactly the same layout as yours."

Mrs. Murphy, small but purposeful, all but pushed past Barbara, who felt like a daddy longlegs in her nightclothes, an ineffectual flutterer. She hadn't even combed her hair! The bed wasn't made!

But Mrs. Murphy stood already in the doorway of the tiny bathroom, bending down, her blue-skirted bottom in the air, her voice sharp and authoritative. "Where's the telephone, Barbara? Where's the phone? We're going to call 911. That's all we have to do, they'll be here in a jiffy. Don't worry, he's breathing okay; his pulse is—well, I don't know. But he's breathing okay. We'd better not try to move him. He's a big fellow really, isn't he?"

"I don't know who he is or how he got there," Barbara said. "I don't know anything about any of it."

Mrs. Murphy stood straight and turned. She said very firmly, as though Barbara were a fool, "Don't be silly now. He's Mr. Cassar, and you're Mrs. Cassar, and he's your husband of over fifty years. I remember because we share a wedding anniversary—isn't that a coincidence?— though with my Brendan it would have been sixty. You've had a nasty shock and you're a bit confused, but we'll get it sorted out. Just pass me the phone there? Just hand it to me? Now."

IN THE HOSPITAL on the Saturday afternoon, exactly two years after the life-saving operation that almost killed him, François sat up in some confusion in his bed. Barbara tiptoed around him, stooped and bony as a Hogarth drawing, adjusting his pillows, bringing him ribbed plastic cups of water, laboriously cleaning his eyeglasses for him with her breath and the hem of her linen shirt. It was mid-April: outside the window, as they had two years before, cherries bloomed in vulgar, fecund profusion. Chloe sat in an armchair in the corner, reading or pretending to—what was the book? He wanted to ask, but the wrong words came out of his mouth. He knew they were wrong from the look on her face. She said something to him but her words melted together in his ears and he could not disentangle them, could not understand. He could tell he was frowning, furrowing, and her voice, a babble that made no sense, nonetheless soothed: this was what it must be like to be a baby, or an animal, to comprehend only the tone, the music, and not the import. . . . She was rummaging, suddenly, in the backpack at her feet, saying something swift and excitable to Barb, whose aspect was baffled, dear woman, so much of the time now that gentle vagueness about her—where had she gone? As if someone with an eraser had smudged her edges little by little, removing her outline, but had left her smile, her beautiful eyes—where did a person go, in this strange neurological decline? She wasn't alone at least, always imagining—hallucinating—people who weren't there; the doctor had said this was the defining symptom of her condition, the hallucinations. What distinguished it from other dementias. What had she said, herself? "Shards of memory and new worlds discovered"—as though she were Captain Cook embarked on a great voyage, sending back limited, cryptic dispatches: Australia—Tasmania—New Guinea—Tahiti!

What about him? Was he too now destined to drift across a vast sea in isolation unspeakable, like a man alone in a rowboat? What ailed him? What had befallen him? He could almost remember the bathroom's cold tile against his cheek, the pain a live filament down his side, twisted as he was between the toilet and the wall, in the dark, the porcelain pressing his thigh. It had felt an eternity, as though he would never resurface, a mountaineer trapped in a crevasse. Where had she been? Why did she not come when he called? You live alone and you die alone, he had reminded himself, blurrily in recollection, but he remembered thinking how precisely his mind had worked even in that grim, perhaps fatal extremis, how clear everything had felt, as if etched . . .

Now Chloe, who had been busily writing on the back of a large white envelope in black ink in capital letters, her copperplate penmanship, held up her handiwork for him to see, not before handing him the reading glasses Barb had so meticulously cleaned.

YOU HAVE HAD A SMALL STROKE. YOU ARE SUFFERING FROM APHASIA. HOPEFULLY IT WILL IMPROVE SOON. ARE YOU HUNGRY? YOU CAN CHOOSE BETWEEN PASTA AND TUNA SALAD ON THE MENU. DON'T TRY TO TALK— JUST POINT AT ONE IF YOU UNDERSTAND.

"Of course I understand," François said aloud. "I would like the tuna salad."

LANGUAGE RETURNED. He agreed with his daughter and his doctor that the brain, in its resilience, was a remarkable thing, more remarkable than any human invention. Which stood to reason. That it could encompass the world, all life, everything from the smell of the schoolroom at the French primary in Salonica—of chalk, sandwiches, and dirty feet—to the name of the Labrador—Laddie!—that had lived next door twenty years ago and rooted so obnoxiously through their garden, to the sensation of each of his four grandchildren's newborn scalps beneath his palm, each similarly warm and soft but distinct in the abundance and texture of its carpet of hair, to the pullulating emotion, a frothing fountain, that he had felt in his body at each birth—a miracle! A miracle! All this in a single floating mass within his skull, each moment of each day tucked somewhere in the brain's cauliflower folds—and then presumably also each thought as well, this thought too, though it might well be forgotten—and more than that, the imaginary, realms of dreams and wonders, inventions and possibility, and, in Barbara's strange case, the new departures, voyages that she could not share, words for which she could not find, would never again find—words themselves slipping from her grasp, disintegrating—but still, she'd said herself, new worlds discovered. Just a world she could not share.

All this, the brain, the brain and the body together a person, each of us one, just one, fully one, unlike any other—he, look, he, himself, François, once that plump, naked baby with a basilisk stare, photographed with only his Saint Christopher's medal around his neck, propped on a white fur rug in a photographer's studio in a narrow street near the Opéra in Toulon, his mother's dear, square hand hovering just outside the picture frame to catch him if he toppled—how many miles had he traveled (an American Airlines million-miler) in the more than three-quarters of a century since? Not for nothing had his parents put Saint Christopher, patron saint of travelers, around his infant neck; not for nothing had they named him François: François the Frenchman, the free. They had wanted so much for him, and he had surely disappointed. But his life had been unlike any other life, a wanderer's life—the Wandering Jew, he used to joke, though he wasn't Jewish. One of those jokes, like "You'll miss me when I'm gone," that he meant, in his heart. And still, he hoped against hope, already once returned from the dead two years before—not fully over yet.

THERE WAS TO BE no return home, not even to the apartment they'd inhabited for a decade with impatience and misgiving, looking out its windows upon nothing, brick walls and dingy roofs, hoping for a next station, a better final berth. On account of Barbara's illness, not even that modest respite was to be granted him. Itinerant to the last.

The stroke, after all, was not the thing: his brain's resilience was remarkable; his body's less so. The cancer in his esophagus had returned. The doctors took several days to tell him. Chloe blurted it out when he spoke impatiently of going home—"But it's come back, Daddy, the cancer has come back!" she wailed like a Greek chorus—but it was from the doctors' silence that he knew the news was bad. Still, in doubt, he hoped: doubt and hope were the same. Until they said it to his face—the smug mustachioed oncologist with his polka-dot bow tie, in his sunny office, two weeks later. And then he took it on the chin.

They sent him back to Elm Street, to the rehab hospital that two years before had been the site of his triumph over death, the place where he, who had never been expected to eat or walk or think again, had proven himself a phoenix. So briefly a phoenix, two short years, from the cancer diagnosis, but what he wouldn't have given to drive the Mazda one more time to the Food Emporium and wait in the parking lot with the AC on, and WQXR, while Barbara disappeared into the supermarket for twice as long as she'd promised and returned with enough food for a family of eight. How swiftly life vanished. What he wouldn't give to take the kids to the Beach House restaurant and sit in one of the booths near the door, not so comfortable but cheery, the black-and-white tile and the pretty green-eyed waitress, and he'd hold Barb's hand under the table like high school sweethearts—the American high school fantasy he knew only from the movies—while the grandchildren, beauteous in their youth without knowing it, Ines, newly silent, long-legged like a foal, arms crossed over her tiny breast buds, watching everything with those Byzantine blue eyes; chubby Lev with his blond curls and porcelain-white skin, his high giggle, in whose face François saw his own, only fairer; Aude, sparkles on her little fingernails, her spindly waving hands like seaweed in the current, singing pop songs under her breath; and her solid little brother, named after François's beloved long-vanished mother, a different mirror of his youthful self, always the clown . . . what he would have given to pay their absurd prices one more time, to order the ceviche—not very good—which slithered cold down his throat and snap the bland breadsticks, their sprinkled sesame seeds their only source of flavor. . . . All that was most banal was revealed to him, again, as beautiful, each physical sensation a tiny explosion of life, a burst of love . . . but it was better, perhaps, not to have known which visit was the last. What was the saying? It's always later than you think. He'd hoped—he'd always been an optimist, in spite of everything—for more.

Elm Street, which had seemed the first time an idyllic rehab stint, luxurious even, with its wicker furniture and glossy white hallways, the jolly preening parrot discreetly chained to his perch next to the cistern of iced cucumber water in the front lobby, as though this were a spa vacation in Florida rather than an anteroom to Death. . . . (What was the difference? his joker-self could still ask.) Last time, he'd bought the recovery crap, it had worked for him: a month of their tuna melts and paper bowls of sweet ice cream (alas no chips, on account of the gaggers) and he'd been back on his feet, good as new, the miracle man, he who'd been given up for dead. There'd been cheers and applause, even a red balloon when he walked, upright, if with a cane, past the squawking parrot and Jocelyn at the front desk to the trusty blue Mazda waiting under the porte cochere that blazing June afternoon, and the Buddha statue over by the shrubbery had seemed to be grinning and winking *for him*, for François, as a silver jet streaked overhead and glintingly caught the sun. He recalled it all so vividly, the surge of triumph, the win of it, his certainty that he would not any longer allow even a day to slip unnoticed from him, even a bad day. And he hadn't.

All of it that had seemed triumphal now loomed before him tinged with bitterness: yes, he knew these quilted polyester bedspreads, patterned either in peach and mint or terra-cotta and lapis, depending on the week; the vase of silk flowers, odorless, eternal, unsexed white lilies with garishly painted pistils, in their ugly pink bisque vase; the bathroom in the corner with its wheelchair-wide door—yes, he knew that smiling nurse in her pressed navy scrubs, the sound of her rubber clogs squeaking on the lino, her fat gold cross winking at her throat—Vicky, wasn't it? Amodeo. The love of God. His parents would have been pleased. But now she seemed Charon incarnate, her smile lugubrious and grasping, as he both feared and coveted her little paper cup of pills. This, now, was his waiting room: the hummingbird garden outside the window, the twin beds with their metal frames, the double rattan dressers, three drawers each side, containing a mere wheelie suitcase of their clothes, Barbara's and his (Because where else would she go? She couldn't stay at home alone. And even here, even in these circumstances, he could—he would—take care of her), as if they'd arrived for a brief holiday instead of for The End. He remembered their holiday to Florida, twenty years now—the awful hotel, the failure of that trip, in which he'd hoped to show her how he'd fallen in love, so long ago, with America. Even now, this would have been a nicer hotel room, if that's what it had been.

He was cold all the time. The children brought for his shoulders a chocolate-colored fine pashmina that he'd given to Barbara on their India trip, ages ago, and that she'd kept all these years, unworn, in its original wrapping in her bottom drawer—and when he draped it over himself he saw, in the mirror, his father, who'd worn a shawl—camel-colored, fringed—much of the time in his later years, and whom he now so resembled. But his father, who'd lived well past ninety—ninety-three and a couple of months—seemed only just a moment ago to have left the room, and how could it already be his turn? He wasn't old—almost seventy-nine, in these times a mere stripling. Could it really be that he would have to leave all this, even this? Even this bedspread, I'll accept—even this braying night nurse—even this farce of physical therapy every other morning—

He wasn't insensible to the ironies, to the strange serendipities of fate. Death had come for him two years ago, and he had cheated Death. *They* had cheated Death, his family, these women—Barbara, Denise, Loulou, Chloe, their constant vigils, their battles for his life. If he'd lived these two years it was because of their presences—prayers, Denise said, but the truth was more practical, more bodily, than that. They'd held to his lips the wetted green sponges for him to suck against his thirst, when he could not swallow; they'd helped the nurses turn his naked body in his bed to avoid bedsores; they'd sat up all night to ensure that in his delusions he did not tear the oxygen canula from his nostrils or attempt to leap from his bed; they'd pressed the doctors, the nurses, they'd stood by when the physios came for his swallow tests, they'd rallied in the waiting room to bolster one another in the times of lowest morale, for weeks Loulou had worked remotely, on calls with her colleagues in Europe at four in the morning, Chloe had sped up and down the highway in the night, shuttling between children and his bedside. They had all cheered on that Sunday afternoon of Memorial Day weekend when, after over a month not compos mentis, nil by mouth, twice intubated in the ICU for days, felled by MRSA, after thirty-six hours hyperventilating and tachycardic, fat old sot with ruined lungs that he was, but a bull of a man, a bull, he had returned to himself, to life—and they'd surrounded him, and his very arrival at Elm Street had been like that of a jubilant old general after battle . . .

Two years he'd been granted, two years to the day till he was back in the hospital, seven hundred and thirty days of life—he'd *lived* each one, but they had seen, too, the diminution of his wife, her spirit a fading light, and his sister, bent and broken, pickled in her Label 5. Life went on, was the point, when you cheated Death: no such thing as happily ever after. And two years on, as if in a loop, here he was, Barbara at his side barely knowing who he was—fifty-five years, very nearly fifty-three of them married, and half the time she took him for a stranger. And more bizarre still, in Ottawa, even now, his old friend Larry Riley bedridden and mute—that man with whom he'd railed and conversed and guffawed and wept—when Larry's boy David died, they'd wept in each other's arms—now silenced, comatose, in the later stages of exactly the illness that afflicted Barb, his body a mere shell, tended by sweet Babs, who was indeed a nurse, had been a real nurse before all those kids. And he and his old friend, his best friend of almost fifty years, though they couldn't embrace, couldn't speak to each other, physically so far apart, here they were, facing the end together, as close as they had ever been, brothers in the happiest days, and in the grief, and in this journey, whatever it would be, for which there were no words and from which there would be no return.

IN SPITE OF the stent, it became harder and harder to swallow. And the pain. The ineffable pain—Vicky with her cups of pills a godsend. Sometimes he would send Barbara to find her or her replacement, to ask, "Is it time yet? Is it? Yet?" Because the pills came every four hours, and of those, the middle two were pretty good—two hours of four, fifty percent, maybe he shouldn't complain, it could be worse—but the first and the last hour each time a battle, fighting to swim in the sea of pain, the first with the tide at least outgoing and the promise of relief, but the last hour a grappling not only with agony but with existential despair, as the pain became him, became all he was. In the second half of that last hour, he could do nothing but sit—he preferred, always, to be dressed and shaven, in his Brooks Brothers shirts, no excuse for slovenliness, and to sit in the wheelchair, in the garden first thing in the morning or at dusk, but inside in the controlled climate, by the window, in the day—with his eyes closed, breathing, breathing, trying to remember a life, a moment, outside, before the pain.

In those two good hours, though, of what was he not capable? He tousled his grandsons' hair, he admired the girls' drawings, he urged Barbara to eat ice cream along with him at the picnic table on the patio off their room, he allowed his sister, who had traveled, despite every terror, all the way from France, to pray over him, and he attempted to eat the chocolate-covered ginger she had brought. He tried hard not to be irascible; he wanted them to remember his best self. He read the *TLS*, *Le Nouvel Observateur*, Mazower's book on Salonica that he'd bought when it came out in 2004 but had put off, and off. He held his wife's hand. He let the girls push his wheelchair around the beautifully landscaped grounds, though when they encountered bumps or divots, the pain burst even through the muffling of the medicine. He held his wife's hand, and inhaled her beloved scent. He told them how he loved them, that there were not words for how he loved them—he'd long considered himself monstrous, the child of unspeakable error, doomed to punishment; but in these last years had at last known himself to be truly loved, cherished even, as he loved them all, all life—there, a hummingbird alighting; there, the sound of his granddaughter's laughter like a tinkling rivulet; there, Barbara's wide smile, her mouth always a little lopsided. In those good hours, dwindling by a couple of minutes daily like the sunlight in late autumn, he exhorted his great, resilient brain, at every moment (It had been a brain made for great things; had he let them all down? Too late to worry about that now—): Remember this—remember this—remember this—

WHEN HER GIRL CALLED—Which one? They sounded the same on the phone—she asked to speak to her father, and Barbara had to say he wasn't there. But then the girl said, Is there a bald man in a wheelchair in the room, and there was, over by the window, and the girl asked to speak to the man, so she brought him the phone. How sweetly, how sadly, he smiled as he took the receiver from her.

Often the man was asleep, though, or seemed to be. Then she would go walking. This was a strange dream, this honeycomb of long white corridors, along which clicked various women of different ages, sizes, races, always women, dressed in brightly colored medical scrubs, sometimes pushing carts. They all looked up and smiled when she greeted them, but when she asked for the way out, they didn't answer. Obviously a secret. Someone was keeping her here; the hooded men might be responsible. Behind any of the closed doors along the corridors she might have found a cluster of them, hiding. You had to be careful of the men. You had to be wary of opening doors. Anything might be a trap.

Walking, she sometimes worried about where she should be going. She was expected to be there, she had a feeling she was late, but she couldn't recall in the moment how she was to go. Anyone who might have helped her seemed to have vanished. Mother would be cross with her, certainly. Did she need her passport? Always best to have it, just in case; but she didn't even have her handbag—where might she have left it? How to find the way back to the start of this maze?

A parrot, yes, like a drawing of a parrot, in his bright colors—maybe her messenger in disguise? Because he could talk, the parrot—"Hello, pretty!" he was saying, a sort of code; if she only knew what to reply, he would help her escape. . . . He nodded, writhed and bobbed, sticking out that deathlike thick black tongue between the halves of his horned beak. Of course, she could be mistaken, and he an enemy envoy. Either way, she suddenly saw, he writhed, chained to his perch, a fat gold ring clamped around his ankle and a loose shackle to the wooden pole. He nodded at his foot, tilting his head, eyeing her with his bald, accusing eye, clucking the death tongue and emitting sounds: "Oh no, oh no," he seemed to say. "What now? Oh no!"

"It's not my fault," she insisted to the agent disguised as a parrot. "It's not my fault! I'm just trying to get out of here. I'm very late. My mother is waiting for me."

"Of course she is, dear," came a soothing voice at her elbow, a gentle but firm hand upon that elbow. Barbara turned to see the elegant older lady with the tanned wrinkles and the gold-rimmed pearl earrings— she'd seen her before, she knew who she was, but she couldn't quite—

"I'm Jocelyn, dear," the woman said in her deep, soft voice. "And you know me, we know each other well." She smiled sweetly and handed Barbara a perspiring plastic cup of cool water. Barbara sipped, dutifully. It tasted vaguely of cucumber. "Drink this, you'll feel better—"

Only when it was half gone—so refreshing—did Barbara realize it might have been a poison.

"Oh no! What now? Oh no! Hello, pretty!"

But Jocelyn was walking alongside her, guiding her back into the white honeycomb, past doors and doors, past carts and smiling women, speaking soothingly ("Oh no! What now?" But that voice faraway now), saying, "Mr. Cassar will be worrying about you. Let's just get you back to your room, and reassure him—"

"But Mother is waiting for me—I have to take the car—"

"Absolutely. In just a minute." Jocelyn's smile was radiant, her teeth pristinely white. Perhaps she wasn't as old as she appeared? "But first, let's pop by and see your husband—" Jocelyn slowed in the middle of a corridor, indistinguishable from the others, and without lifting her hand from Barbara's elbow, turned, with the other, the knob of a door on the left, a white door in the white corridor of many such doors, and she opened it and guided Barbara gently, yes, but firmly too, into the cool, shadowy room, so tidy, two carefully made single beds with their quilted peach-and-mint spreads, and the double-wide white wicker dresser, a few colorful children's drawings taped to the wall, the light soft and green, as the big plate-glass window was filled with sun-infused green-ery, a lawn, a hedge, a flowering border, all of it glowing green. And before the reflecting window, in the gloom, the bald man with his shawl in the wheelchair—she knew him at once, she'd know him anywhere. He was in charge of the hooded men, and of the horsemen who passed at dusk along the perimeter of the property; he was in charge of the smiling women in their pressed scrubs, of course he was; the scheme was his, he made everything as it was; he was responsible; he was her captor.

And the look upon his worn face, those sad green-and-amber eyes, when he turned toward her—of infinite tenderness, sorrow, love, a look that encompassed everything, that knew and accepted her absolutely; that knew, also, Death; that was, also, Death—nothing had ever frightened her more. Barbara grabbed Jocelyn's hand from her elbow and clutched it with both of her own. "But you must understand," she said with great urgency, "I can't possibly stop here. I am late, and Mother is waiting."

TOULON, FRANCE

Denise prepared everything as nicely as she could for Magi's visit. Magi was to come by at six-thirty, when she got off work, and they would have what they cheerfully called "a session," a gossipy couple of hours with a few cocktails and some snacks, before Magi went out to the boulevard and caught the bus home.

It seemed in some way wrong to do this, to have even a single happy hour, or a less than tragic hour, when she'd just returned from her brother's deathbed—nobody said this word, but when, after six weeks, she realized she had to return to her life and she said good-bye to him, everyone in the room (except perhaps Barbara) knew that it was their final farewell. She had made him promise that he would receive the last rites, and Chloe had told her yesterday that the priest had come by for this purpose—it had all sounded rather strange, the priest in a short-sleeved shirt with the host wrapped in a hankie in his breast pocket—but it was done, his soul was safe now, even though his mortal body breathed and suffered yet, fully conscious and present at last report, though they'd moved him today to the hospital for an IV port, and would move him tomorrow to the residential hospice, where he could at last be given morphine and be relieved of the terrible pain.

So he was with her, but not with her. She didn't want to speak to him on the telephone—he could have, still, on this day, though with great effort, but they'd said their farewells, and he was surely entitled to rest. As she was entitled to rest. What it had cost her, physically, emotionally, these last weeks in America, far from home—she could hardly bear it. She wasn't sure how much to say to Magi—her friend had rather a loose tongue, was known for it—but really, she knew she'd say something, because she was bursting with it.

It didn't seem possible that she'd said good-bye for the last time to François. That accursed ocean. When he'd first gone to America, a life-time ago, she'd wept for three days. He'd departed by boat, from Le Havre, in mid-August; the whole family had taken the ferry to Marseille and then rented a car for the long drive north. They'd stayed a night in Marseille, had driven the distance in a straight shot, almost nine hours, and had stopped the night together in a small hotel off the Avenue Foch near St. Joseph's in the port city, then still being rebuilt. The next day had had about it a curious loose-end aura, the four of them dawdling over lunch in the bistro across from the hotel, Maman sentimental already, Papa filled with last-minute advice. François's trunk had been delivered early, and they all boarded the ship with him in the late afternoon to see his tiny cabin—he'd been assigned the lower bunk, and another Ful-bright boy, named Broussard, headed for a different university, had got the top—and then they'd left him there, on board, with Broussard, to begin his adventure, while they returned to shore, and to their first eve-ning of being three, without him. But the ship did not set sail until the middle of the night, a terrible, stormy night, and what a strange evening it had been, Papa and Maman and she, with a single borrowed umbrella between them, eating supper in the same place they'd lunched a few hours earlier, only without François the restaurant had seemed sadder, the food less appetizing.

She, Denise, had kept up a bright patter—"The cabin wasn't too bad, was it? And that Broussard fellow seems okay . . ."—to which Papa responded with equal determined cheer, as if they were doggedly playing tennis in a high wind, while Maman, seeming almost not to hear them, gazed pensively at the rain spattering the darkened restaurant window, and the water-hazy streetlights beyond. That night they were all thinking, although they did not say it, that if only they hurried down to the seafront, they could still, surely, clamber onto the boat, they could still find him and throw their arms around him and urge him not to go. He was there but not there, not quite but imminently irretrievable. They knew it but didn't discuss it, because what would have been the point? He had to go—he wanted to go. And they had to make their peace with his departure.

So, too, now: her beloved brother, adored and impossible, her rock and, since their father's death, her life's purpose—she'd spoken to him very nearly every day all these years since Papa left them—was now not quite, but imminently, irretrievable. She knew loss too well, knew that your dear ones never left, that they stayed with you, spoke to you, attempted to console you, but that these ghosts had no arms to hold you, that no one else could hear their jokes. That their love was not enough. And that as more and more of these familiars passed away, the world around you became less and less interesting, less and less real. Much of the time, when alone, Denise conversed with her dead, and for several years she'd talked that way to François, not on the phone but in her apartment, recalling adventures, or worries, or silly things the girls had done when they were small . . .

Alive, not alive—at some point it made little difference. Magi would be there any minute. Denise emptied the box of Belin pretzels into the blue cloisonné bowl; she took the ice bucket—into which she'd already emptied two trays of cubes—from the freezer and put it on the lacquer tray on the coffee table, next to the two cut-glass tumblers (her favorites, taken from the big apartment up the hill, which sat empty and reproachful, a museum to her parents' lives, unvisited, certainly insufficiently visited, by those thoughtless nieces and their families) and the bottle of whiskey, ready to crack, its seal not yet broken.

She knew that the neighbors thought it peculiar that she pulled out the stops for Magi. Probably Solange, the concierge, gossiped about it—though Lord knew she'd had Solange around for cocktails enough times. But the fact that Magi was a cleaning lady in the compound, that she cleaned for two families Denise had known for forty years—that was somehow shameful or embarrassing. Or was it that Magi was a Muslim, Moroccan, an immigrant, and twenty years younger than Denise in the bargain—was that what made them all whisper? Her false teeth—she'd had them all pulled across the front, and wore a set of brilliant gnashers of suspicious evenness—probably didn't help the overall effect. The teeth looked false, and whereas Magi thought them an improvement, classy, as she'd put it, Denise knew that among the BCBG of the apartment complex, they marked her out unsalvageably as working-class. But so what? They all thought it was great to be working-class if you were mopping marble floors in Bâtiment F, but not to be allowed when you sat down for a drink and a smoke in Bâtiment H at day's end? The hypocrisy of it. Half of them probably thought they were lovers, two old lesbians—what other reason would they have to spend time together?—or else they thought Magi was a gold digger. They'd had a laugh about that, the two of them—a gold digger in a sand dune, they'd joked—she, Denise, had barely the shirt on her back, after all, a church mouse—would she drink Label 5 if she could afford better?

Denise consulted her watch (the gold watch her parents had given her for her fortieth; one of the girls probably imagined she'd get it, but she'd promised it to Magi—she wouldn't forget): Magi was late, doubtless detained by some additional last-minute task ("Could you just make sure the table's set? Could you be sure to finish ironing those shirts? He's leaving on a business trip; he'll need them all")—would it be inappropriate to start without her? One little one, surely, would be fine. And a quick cigarette, on the balcony, the ice clinking against the side of the glass, the cicadas in full song, the July air hot and still around her. She could see Simone Bléhaut walking the path to her garden, briefcase in hand, and, in the other direction, Docteur Bertrand, in his whites, holding his racket and a can of tennis balls. She used to like them. Simone and she were great friends, for years. Hard to imagine it now. So many had disappointed her—all of it, years of it, smiling at people who pretended to give a shit, pretending, herself, to give a shit. . . . No, that wasn't right, she had cared, God how she'd cared; and who, in their turn, had reciprocated? Who'd cared about her?

Over these past years, one by one the old friends had slipped away. Sometimes there'd been words—she'd had a shouting match with Sophie Blondeau, her former neighbor who now lived on the other side of the city, after the third time Sophie had canceled their plans at the last minute—"I think you have no idea how hard my life is," Sophie had said, and Denise had replied, "And mine? What about mine? Do you have any idea at all?" But that had been that. Mostly, though, she hadn't expressed her outrage—she'd simply stopped returning phone calls, and that had proven enough. Lifelong friends like Aurore, whom she'd held in her arms as a baby when she was herself ten years old, and friends of fifty years, Antoinette for example, fallen away like dry leaves in autumn. They all used the computer now, sent emails, which she didn't. So simply to let the phone ring unanswered was enough. It turned out that none of them cared enough to write a letter—though she'd likely not have answered that either—or to come to her door. Only young Maït, her goddaughter, forty-four now and single like herself, a "career woman"— which seemed at last acceptable, or largely, seemed at last to count in the eyes of the world as a life lived, rather than a life in abeyance—only Maït she saw regularly, over lunch so that she was fully alert; and of course, in the evenings, dear Magi.

Here she was, the doorbell's special three-times ring, and she stood on the threshold with her arms open wide, her big too-white porcelain smile.

"*Ma chérie*," exclaimed Denise, taking care not to set fire to Magi's hair with her cigarette when she embraced her. "Come in, drop your things, have a seat." Then, with a coy wave of her tumbler: "I couldn't wait, I started without you."

"Glad to hear it." Magi, having discarded her heels by the door, settled on the sofa with her feet tucked beneath her, appropriately *à l'orientale*, as Denise thought of it, and waited, beatific, for Denise to pour her a drink. "We have so much to catch up on—your trip. I'd hate to think my lateness spoiled your evening." She rolled her eyes. "But you know how Madame Améry can be—she shrieked as though she might faint when she realized her blue flowered tablecloth was still in the drying cupboard and I'd put the ironing board away. I'd taken off my smock already—can you believe it?"

"As if she couldn't have used a different tablecloth," Denise said sympathetically, pouring herself a second scotch to accompany Magi's first. The sun cast long shadows across the wall. She knew she'd often been like Madame Améry; she rued it now. By way of atonement, she called Odet in Cascais every other week. Francisco had dementia. Odet had wept to hear that Barbara did also, and wept each time when they spoke of François. She might even wail when she heard of his death; she was very sentimental. But yes, Denise understood what it was like to be Magi, put upon by others . . .

Magi, though, had such humor about it all. Denise loved being in her presence. Magi was laughing as she told the story of the Améry grandson shooting his grandfather in the back of his bald head with a Nerf bullet. "Monsieur was at his writing desk, his back to the room, and out of the blue, blam! It wasn't so much that it was painful as that he was terrified—he didn't know what had hit him! And you know how he is, old-school, such a temper, but Madame kept shushing him, saying, 'But, darling, it's so much better that Jules is running around with the gun because otherwise he'd be all the time on his computer, playing video games . . .' "

"Another?" Magi's second, Denise's third. How they laughed. As if floating. All the troubles drifted from view. They'd be there in the morning, but for now . . .

Until Magi asked about Denise's time in America. Magi had composed her face into an expression of solemn compassion: she knew François was dying now. She hid away her mischief along with her white teeth.

"But the family," Denise had to tell her. "My own family!"

"Tell me," Magi invited, all compassion now. She even reached a hand across the coffee table. Denise did not take it, but she appreciated the gesture. She felt cherished.

"First of all, I was told I couldn't smoke in the apartment. Not by Barbara—she's out to lunch, you know. It's worse with every week. I wasn't sure she knew me, half the time. No, by the girls, can you believe it? As if it were *their* apartment! They were guests just like me, but you wouldn't have known it. 'But there's a balcony right there,' they say, 'And it's summer!' As if that made it any less inconvenient—"

"At least it's not cold," Magi offered. "Because in winter it gets very cold over there, so I'm told."

Denise shrugged. "The line is that nobody has smoked in the apartment for years, that François and Barbara both quit—so what, I'm supposed to? When my brother is dying?"

"Inhumane," Magi agreed.

"And then, just once, one time, I had a little cigarette at bedtime in my room—I was sleeping on the sofa bed in François's study, with the door closed, mind you—and I'd barely started to enjoy it when Loulou—she was sleeping in the living room, on one of those inflatable beds, because her sister was in the bedroom with their mother—anyway, Loulou bursts in with only the barest knock—I was in my nightgown, but I could have been naked for all she knew, can you imagine?—and she tells me the whole apartment stinks of it, and could I please put it out! After maybe two puffs—I felt like a scolded schoolgirl!"

"Terrible," Magi agreed. "Not respectful."

"That's the thing, isn't it? Respect. I'm their aunt. I'm of an older generation. Honor thy father and thy mother—in our religion, maybe in yours too, that's a commandment. From the time of Moses. And I've been like a second mother to them. But do they treat me with dignity? Do they have the first idea?"

Denise hadn't really meant to launch into a litany of complaint, but she found Magi a very sympathetic listener. Almost a rapt listener. And when Magi left, the apartment would fall quiet, and she would be alone. She would remember.

So instead she told Magi about all her complaints, weeks of them. How they had resisted, had seemed almost amused by, her religious interventions, saying, "But Mama wouldn't like that," as if Barbara, always half-smiling, oblivious in the background, had any thoughts whatsoever. Frankly, Barbara needed to be prayed for too. And the girls. And then Loulou, with her endless work calls, from four in the morning you could hear her through the wall, and if you walked into the living room and tried to catch her attention, she'd turn her back to you, or step out onto the balcony, or frankly leave the flat to pace around on the sidewalk below with those wires in her ears, speaking and gesticulating apparently into the void like a mad person. Did any of them care how she, Denise, was feeling? But then they kept urging her to stay longer, saying, "But don't you want to be here with us? With him? What would you have to go back for? There's no rush, surely?"—as though her life, her whole world, her habits, her existence in Toulon, counted for nothing at all: her mail, her books, her plants, her friendships, her volunteer work at the parish, her monthly lunches with her goddaughter, the watercolor she'd been working on that she'd left, half-painted, on the dining table when she'd packed her bag and raced to her brother's bedside—not for the first time, mind you—never imagining she would stay so long, that she would have to purchase two summer outfits she could ill afford simply so as not to roast in the thirty-year-old tweed suit she'd brought with her—but she digressed. The point was that her existence had no reality for her nieces, bound up as they were in their own lives—they obviously thought she had nothing else to do but hold their hands through this crisis, as if she weren't suffering enough, to lose her brother and his wife at the same time, one physically, the other mentally, all gone at once, her dearest ones. . . . But this younger generation, so American, with their godlessness and lack of respect, their self-involvement, their failure— yes, their failure for one second to put themselves in her shoes—because yes, they were losing their parents, and Lord knows she understood the pain of that, but they had husbands and children, families of their own, and in that sense they were losing what was right and proper, the older generation, and they would live on and look to the future, as they should; but they could not seem to see, or to understand, that she, Denise, was losing everything. Everything.

She did not intend to say all this, quite, to vent her spleen so openly. Magi, dear woman, was not discreet. And yet. Where, now, was her real life? What was her real life? She was not about to say to Magi that once her brother died, she'd have none, that all her past and everyone she loved and trusted would have vanished from this earth—that would be an insult to Magi, whose good nature sustained her, whose forearms loaded with bangles jangled cheerfully when she moved, who licked the pretzel salt from her rose-painted brown fingers with the delicacy and attention of a grooming cat—beautiful, kind Magi.

As the sunlight faded from the room and Denise stood to turn on the lamps (the bottle of Label 5 ravaged now; the remainder of the ice a mere puddle at the bottom of the ice bucket), Magi, too, stood, straightened her skirt—a flippy little mustard-colored paisley wrap from the market in the Mourillon; Denise had seen them on the rack in the corner of the parking lot—and her lacy camisole—she might be approaching sixty but she kept herself in good shape, and the tops of her brown breasts looked as firm as those of a young woman—and patted at her frizzy cloud of hennaed hair, Denise thought once again how beautiful Magi was, how elegant she looked as long as she didn't smile and show those cheap teeth. If Denise had the money, she'd have paid for a new set.

"Thank you, darling friend." Magi wavered a little at the door, straightening after she put on her wedge sandals. She was suddenly taller than Denise, and bent to kiss her cheeks, in a gust of whiskey, tobacco, and her sweet lemon perfume. She bought that in the market, too, from the Provençal soap seller.

"Good night, my beauty." Denise pressed the *minuterie* on the landing and waited with Magi for the lift. Then she stood there listening to the elevator descend, to the ticking of the *minuterie*, and then the sound of Magi's footsteps in the lobby three floors below. The banging of the glass door. The hall light went out. Denise stood a few moments longer in the dark, then went back into her flat and bolted the door.

She consulted her watch, the watch that would in time be Magi's. Barely after eight-thirty. Up at the big apartment, at the top of the hill, there would still be the last sunlight, the beautiful late glow at the horizon, over the ocean. But the big apartment was locked and empty. For François in America it was barely afternoon, the siesta hour, two-thirty. Hopefully he was resting. In her mind, she could see him, not as he was now but in all his ages. If nothing else, on this planet, they had borne loving witness to each other's lives, to the days and journeys, the freight of emotions, to the blossoming and dwindling of their animal selves. Much sorrow and rage, but more than that, laughter, joy, and wonder. How, now, as the shadows had grown so long, to cleave to the light? To be a witness, to stand alongside, simply to have lived through these strange, beautiful, appalling times, to have been a night-light, a mirror, a support—that, too, was God's work, though the ambitious American nieces, faithless and perhaps soulless, might disdain it. That wasn't nothing.

This strange eventful history that made a life. Not good or bad—rather, both good and bad—but that was not the point. Above all, they had been, for so long, wildly curious. Just to see, to experience all that they could, to set foot anywhere, to speak to anyone, taste anything, to learn, to know.

She emptied the ice bucket, placed the tumblers in the sink. She eyed the whiskey bottle—there was so little left. But she would refrain, tonight. Her brother was dying. She wasn't curious any longer: much that she now knew caused her pain, and she strove, chiefly, to numb that pain when she could.

She opened the fridge. Almost nothing: a few eggs; one zucchini, bruised. A third of a jar of plum jam. Butter. In the cupboard, half a bag of macaroni, a sleeve of rusks. She wasn't hungry for supper. She would just go to bed, lie beneath her crucifix with her eyes closed. Where was God when you most needed Him? With François, inshallah, by his side, accompanying him.

All her life she had felt François beside her. He had carried her when she'd needed him to. She would have wished to do the same for him now, but she hadn't the strength. I am sorry, she told him. It doesn't mean I don't love you. But I am weak, you've always known that about me. Pray God He was with him, her brother, in these hours. She needed to sleep— she needed, now, to forget, to dream instead about Magi's pretty fingers, about the trip to the mountains they might take together in September when the heat had passed, a little weekend away, some fun, she'd drive and pay for the hotel—Magi was game, she'd said so.

Would she be able to sleep, without worrying, now? Perhaps if she finished the bottle, after all. Which of the glasses in the sink had been hers? Did it matter? If the glass was Magi's, was it not, in a way, like a kiss, a connection? If by chance she drank from Magi's glass, was she not then less alone?

CONNECTICUT, UNITED STATES

In the car on the way to the Beach House restaurant—at the wheel of my father's precious Mazda sedan, over a decade old and perfectly maintained—I reminded my mother that we were headed for a birthday party. Ironic as it seemed. She half-turned to me, her face unreadable. If asked to explain her expression, I'd have said, "She's taking it all in." Though equally, I might have thought that she was letting it all go.

Mostly I focused on the road, the narrow lanes on I-95 and the traffic swishing past close enough to buffet the old car; and then the exit, not our usual one, and which way to turn, off the ramp; then finding a parking place on the side street down the block from the restaurant. The muggy gray day had given over in early evening to light rain, not enough to merit running from the car, but I didn't want her to have to walk too far. Still, I was glad of the droplets on my bare arms: I could feel each one. And I could see everybody through the big front window, gathered at the first booth against the wall where we often sat, extended by an extra table, the bright seagull mural swirling behind them, Oliver and our friend Becca and our two kids and her two kids, each family set an older girl and younger boy.

As I peered in, the waitress delivered milkshakes in tall glasses, along with the extra in a beaker, like when I was a kid, a round tray full of them. Chocolate for the birthday girl, our Aude: nine today. They'd spent the afternoon at the multiplex in Port Chester, seeing *Despicable Me*. Becca and her kids had come out from the city on Metro-North as a kindness, to try to make the day festive.

"Are you ready?"

My mother smiled warily. Maybe she'd already forgotten.

"It's Aude's ninth birthday, right? This is your granddaughter's birthday party."

"Of course it is," my mother said cheerily, but I wasn't sure whether she fully understood. We would get through this. We had to. I held the door open and had her walk in front of me. I broke out in goose bumps at the blast of cold air on my rain-spattered arms.

"Welcome! Hello!" Jolly exclamations. Oliver and Becca stood up from their seats, a gesture of respect for my mother. "Sit, sit! We've only ordered drinks so far—"

"Happy birthday, darling," I leaned past my husband to kiss the top of our daughter's silken head, avoiding her pink plastic tiara with sparkles and the words BIRTHDAY GIRL.

"We haven't had presents yet, Mommy," she said in a faux-serious tone, as if scolding me. "Daddy said we had to wait for you."

"When we get home, darling, to the apartment." I turned to Oliver. "You picked up the cake, right?"

"Of course I did. Now sit, and order yourselves a glass of wine."

"I'm driving."

"You can have *one*."

I sat beside him, my mother, next to Becca, opposite me. Sticking out into the room at the end of the added table, we felt far from the kids' gay chatter. I was suddenly exhausted.

"Everything okay? Afternoon all right?"

Perhaps I shouldn't tell him now? Certainly I didn't want the kids to know. I didn't want to spoil the party. I was aware that if, as I suspected, my mother had forgotten, then I was the only one who knew, the only one for whom it was a reality, which seemed suddenly too much to bear alone.

"Keep smiling," I whispered, "but he died."

"What? When?"

"A few hours ago. When we came back from lunch, he was gone. They said he'd just died, but I don't think the aides were paying attention. It could have been anytime in that hour between twelve and one."

"I'm so sorry." He kept smiling, though more tightly now, and nodded slightly toward my mother. "How are you feeling, Barbara? Long day?"

"I'm a little tired, to be honest," she replied politely. "But I'm certainly happy to be here."

"I don't think she remembers," I said, then corrected myself: "I don't know that her brain could really take it in. It was a lot."

Oliver sighed. Becca, talking excitedly to the kids about the film, hadn't noticed. "And we were at *Despicable Me*," he said.

"That's all good. It's Aude's birthday. We've got to turn toward life, toward the light."

"And what will you guys have, at this end of the table?" Our waitress leaned in, pen and pad in hand. Probably a college kid doing a summer job, a young woman wrapped in the careless beauty of youth, her dirty-blond hair twisted in a messy bun, a tiny gold chain at her throat, her skin against her white button-down golden like honey. The restaurant smelled powerfully of grilled meat, the air filled with eager human noise, people laughing, talking, snippets of chatter floating to me out of the cacophony. I could almost hear the strident caws of the painted seagulls in the mural behind the kids' heads. Alive—everything around us was alive.

IT HAD BEEN a long day. I'd woken in the gray dawn of Monday, on the lumpy sofa bed in my father's study. Nobody else stirred. Oliver slept beside me, his legs tangled in the sheet. I tiptoed out to the main room, where the kids lay sprawled on the air mattress next to the sofa, our aging dachshund curled between them. The dog opened an eye, looked balefully at me, then shifted slightly, crescenting more tightly, and returned to sleep. My mother's bedroom door was closed.

I took the car keys from the hook by the kitchen phone, left the front door unlocked, and slipped down the fire stairs. I'd told Oliver the night before I'd get a Seven Sisters, a favorite Danish pastry from the local bakery, the kind Aude loved best, and I'd also always loved best. It had been, five years before, the first indication of my mother's incipient illness: she'd bought it in readiness for our visit, and at breakfast time had put it out on the table.

"Aren't you going to heat it up?" I asked.

"Heat it up? Do we heat it up?"

"Always," I said, "for twenty-five years."

Then, I was Cassandra; nobody believed me. But ever since, I could not consider the Seven Sisters without sorrow. It was barely six; the bakery wouldn't open for an hour and a half. Instead I drove in the other direction, up the highway to Stamford, along the winding road past the housing developments to the hospice. Only a few cars in the lot—presumably still the night staff—and when I stepped inside, into the great room, the quiet was absolute.

The hospice, of recent construction, was supposed to feel like home. Instead, it felt like an institutional lodge retreat, a bland confection where conferences or religious gatherings or writers might convene. Vaulted, beamed ceilings, yards of reddish wood, large sofas and armchairs upholstered in a sturdy nubby brown material, arranged around a large, presumably unusable stone hearth. A spartan open-plan kitchen with reddish wood cabinets, mottled vinyl countertops, a small soda fountain, a Keurig machine, an invisibly replenished bowl of green apples and bananas—an ersatz, utterly impersonal rendition of "home." Better than the hospital, though. And after all, only a few of the residents were mobile, and of those only one or two, to my knowledge, ventured, gaunt and trepidatious, into the common areas. Most, like my father, were bedridden; many, like my father, were on morphine and only very occasionally, and briefly, awake.

I passed no one on my way to him. The hallway was dark. His room, its window abutting a gray fence, was gloomy like the day. The night before he had been restless, his breathing noisy; but now he slept calmly on his side, curled like a child. As he neared death his skin had grown smoother, almost luminous, as if he were being purified. I could see the child in him, a spirit surfacing through his body, preparing to take flight. I held his hand—his fat fingers so warm, the feel of them so familiar, and it seemed he held my hand as he had always done, my father. I held his hand and spoke to him, because they said hearing was the last to go. I told him we'd take care of her, of our mother, that he didn't need to worry. I told him how we loved him, and always would, that he was free now, he could let go. Good night, sweet prince, I said. And flights of angels sing thee to thy rest.

We stayed awhile with our hands conjoined in silence. I heard an aide at the door but didn't turn around and the person slipped away without a word. Eventually I stood and kissed his forehead and drove to the bakery for the pastry and then back to the apartment, before anyone else woke up.

AFTER A FESTIVE birthday breakfast—Wasn't it fun to be nine? The best age!—my mother and I returned to the hospice while Oliver and the kids drove to retrieve Becca and her kids from the train station. *Despicable Me* had already been chosen, the matinée tickets purchased online. The table at the Beach House had been booked.

He was alone, my itinerant father, when he died; but by choice. Always private, to the last. We stepped out for deli sandwiches, tuna on rye in waxed paper, which we ate in the car, in the hospice parking lot, reluctant to make a spectacle of ourselves in the church-quiet common room. When we walked back through the double doors, one of two aides gossiping on the sofa leaped up and darted down the corridor, crying, "Wait a second." She returned heavily, breathless, moments later, to say, "He's gone. Just now. He's gone."

And he was indeed so still, though in the room his chest appeared still to rise and fall. Realizing that my mother hadn't followed me there, I went back into the corridor, where the aide was speaking softly: "You don't have to, if it frightens you. Come with me—we have a quiet sitting room just here"—she led her to an open door, to a room like the others but painted light brown, the color of American tan panty hose in my youth, with, instead of a hospital bed, one of the fat brown sofas, and a childlike painting of a rainbow on the wall.

The aide—her name tag said Kara—sat next to my mother and rubbed her back in large, even circles. My mother looked at her, wide-eyed, as if I weren't there.

"Kara," I said, "I'm just going to be with my dad for a few minutes."

"Mm-hm, that's good. I'm here." Her focus remained on my mother, a calm half-smile on her face. "We've called the doctor, who'll come certify—he's just driving over from the hospital—and we called the undertakers you put on file when he arrived. They'll be here in an hour or so. You've got a little time to say good-bye."

My mother let out something between a sob and a yelp, but her eyes were dry. Kara redoubled her circular strokes.

"Do you want to come say good-bye to Daddy, Mama?"

"Not just now, thank you." As if I'd offered her a cognac after her meal.

"And the pastor's on her way," Kara added. "I don't know whether you all practice any religion, but folks often find it helpful, some spiritual counsel."

"Thank you," I said. My mother said nothing.

I called my sister on my cellphone, standing next to my father's feet. They stood up still, two hillocks beneath the white sheet. She'd had, finally, to return to work in person, and had flown back to Paris on Friday, just three days before. Her husband and kids had returned to England, to the family home. It seemed hard to hear the news, expected though it was, alone in a hotel room. I told her I was standing beside him, that he looked as though he were asleep, that his expression was peaceful, which was true. She bravely said she'd call our aunt. I checked the time. It was getting on toward eight at night in Toulon. "You're sure you don't want to wait till the morning, now?"

"Won't she be upset if we don't tell her straightaway?"

"Maybe," I said. "But if she's alone, and already in her cups—it seems like a kindness."

"She won't come back for the funeral, you know."

"I know." I paused. "I'm sorry you guys have to make the journey again so soon."

"We knew we'd have to. Have you told Oliver?"

"He's with the kids at the movies. As close as we could come to a birthday party."

"Of course. I forgot. I said I'd call after, to wish her happy birthday."

"Birth day, death day. They're joined forever now."

"They're both Cancers," she said. "They were already joined."

After I ended the call I reached one final time for his dear hand, which had held mine, solid and warm, so few hours before. It was now marmoreal, smooth and cool, bereft of life.

My mother came into the room on the arm of an elegant ebony-skinned woman wearing a vibrantly embroidered stole—appropriately referred to, I later learned, as the stole of immortality: "Lord, restore the stole of immortality, which I lost through the collusion of our first parents, and, unworthy as I am to approach Thy sacred mysteries, may I yet gain eternal joy."

Indeed, Pastor Wright seemed joyous. With her arm firmly around my mother's bony shoulders, she wore a broad smile, her voice when she spoke high and clear: "There is nothing to fear, Barbara. This man is still your husband, and he still loves you, just as the Lord loves you. He has left his mortal body—it was old and tired, he'd been so ill—but we rejoice because his spirit is alive, alive in Christ, and immortal. We are all God's children," she asserted enthusiastically, "and you must know that your husband is *always* with you, for the rest of your earthly days and beyond. Have no fear! Just because after today you cannot see him in his familiar bodily form does not mean that he is not with you. Quite the opposite! He is more with you than ever. You will never be alone, because you carry him in your heart."

My mother appeared stunned.

"Would you like to hold his hand one last time, or to kiss his cheek? It's not the same, because his spirit has already departed his body, but he is with us in the room."

My mother hesitated.

"Some people," Pastor Wright offered, more gently, "like to say good-bye in this way—but others prefer not to."

"Thank you," my mother said politely, terror in her eyes. "I prefer not to."

Pastor Wright ushered my mother from the room. "Take your time," she said to me. "The doctor's here, but he'll wait."

"I'm just coming," I said. I had nothing more to say to him—all that needed to be said had been said—but I did not want Pastor Wright's, even with her goodwill and spiritual vim, to be the last energy in the room. He, who had wandered all his life unseen, so little known, so often feeling alone and unloved—I wanted him, his departing spirit, to know that we were with him, that we accompanied him, filled with love, to the gate. There is not more, as humans, that we can do.

I stood in silence, momentarily relieved by the illusory rise and fall of his chest. "What did you think of what she said?" I asked. "Don't tell me. I know."

Oh, he would have laughed and railed both. They'd made a pact when they married to leave religion out of it. He, who had escaped his family's stifling Catholicism, had never spoken to us about faith until the end, when, in the shade garden of Elm Street, in his wheelchair, his hands and feet puffy in the heat, he'd called himself agnostic, had said he did not hold with organized religion, which seemed to him so often false, but that he felt God's presence, that at various times over the years, when he most needed it, he'd felt God's presence. Perhaps that was all the pastor was saying to my mother and, by extension, to me—that we would feel my father's presence when we most needed it.

My father was alone when he died, yet not alone. On the last journey, angels appeared at his side to escort him home. In the last ambulance ride to the hospice, he and the paramedic chatted about Toulon, where the medic had stopped for a time while doing his military service. Yes, the medic knew Cap Brun, the fort built by Napoleon; yes, he knew the little chapel below, on the headland, the brilliant white figure of Notre Dame du Cap Falcon turned forever, hands out, to the infinite sea. When he was settled in his room at the hospice, the head nurse came to see him, a man from Belleville, Ontario, thirty minutes' drive from the house in the country my parents had bought in Canada for their retirement, where they'd spent the happiest times of their last twenty-five years. Yes, he knew the rural route along Hay Bay, he'd known it all his life, and sure, he knew which house it was, that old brick Victorian bang up against the road—they'd done a lot of work on that house, in the early '90s—and planted that wild, glorious stand of lilacs—was that his family? Imagine that. And over his last weekend, when my father was already deep in the arms of Morpheus, surfacing for only a few moments at a time sleepily to blow us kisses, through those last hours, the nurse who tended him, a gentle, generous woman originally from Haiti, shared his very name— hers was Françoise—and spoke to him, at the last, in his mother tongue, the language of his lost life, in French.

EPILOGUE

TLEMCEN, ALGERIA

Tlemcen, pearl of the Maghreb, site of holy sites, home over the centuries to the Sufi mystic Abu Madyan, to the historian and scholar Ibn Khaldun, to the great freedom fighter Abd el-Kader; founded as Pomaria by the Romans, capital to the sultans of the Zayyanid dynasty, where they built their magnificent El Mechouar Palace, a town tucked in the lee of the Tlemcen Mountains with the fecund plains of Hennaya and Maghnia spreading out before it. The ornate square red minaret of Sidi Bou Medine, dedicated to Abu Madyan, dominates the immediate vista; the town's casbah is a warren of narrow, whitewashed alleys, its European quarter laid out around generous plazas. The substantial, relatively comfortable Hotel de France—a provincial hostelry with a restaurant and with running water in almost all the bedrooms—gives onto such a square, in which an iron-laced kiosk awaits a band, the plaza shaded by trees and lit, in the evenings, by flickering gas globe lanterns, their pedestals of art deco design.

This third weekend of February in 1927, spring approaches the town in a thrilled whisper, awakening the arid winter landscape. The plains are greening, an emerald mist over the brown earth. The almond trees are in bloom, each tree a snowy cloud of white flowers, their hearts tinged with rose, and alongside them burgeons the occasional early peach, pink and kindly, the promise of summer's blushing heat.

Along the avenues, up the hillside to the clifftop vista, a young couple walks hand in hand. They talk only rarely, but the sway of their bodies, the dance of small distances, speaks for them—of hope, anticipation, of barely contained desire. Among the crowds—French and Algerian both—enjoying a Saturday morning promenade, the couple doesn't stand out. They may appear recently married, perhaps, in the childless, honeymoon flush before family life truly begins . . .

In fact, they are not quite a couple, not yet, and the closing space between them signifies, momentously. Gaston, home from Paris for the February holidays (iron-gray Paris, where he dreams of the light, the great sky, the bleached and salted coastline), is in his second year at Polytechnique, known as l'X, which he entered in the autumn of '25 with the respectable rank of twenty-seventh, an achievement still more impressive given his humble background. Twenty-one and a half years old, by his own definition a fine-looking fellow, with his strong nose and fine head of black hair, and by that of the *Écho d'Alger* a local celebrity—his national physics prize at seventeen was covered on the newspaper's front page, alongside Ismet Pacha's presence at the Conference of Lausanne; the theft, in Italy, of the jewels of Prince Giustiniani; and the heroism of a professor from the American University of Beirut who attempted to save a French count from drowning. Gaston, the youngest son of a single mother (his father abandoned the family when he was eight), an elementary school teacher who begged and borrowed for his board at the lycée, rewarded her by flourishing.

Despite his modest origins, the glamor of Paris has not dented his confidence: far from it. He considers himself no less than the others, destined for a great naval career; he will brook no impediment. He dreams, too, of being a man of letters, perhaps a novelist, like Proust. In Paris, he's learned to drink with the best of them, to fence, to gamble (a little), and to win. But until this past Christmas, he had not fallen in love.

Now, acting in secret—he has told his mother this is a scholarly junket to research Abd el-Kader, the late military and spiritual leader for the

Algerian people—he boarded the train to meet his beloved. He swept her from the platform at Sidi bel Abbès, and together they proceeded to Tlemcen, where he had, by letter, booked two rooms at the Hotel de France, one (hers) with private bath.

Lucienne, chaste almost to a fault, has as yet no formal indication of his intentions. Officially, they are visiting together the fourteenth-century mosque of Sidi Bou Medine, spiritual home of the Sufi mystic Abu Madyan, and the ruins of the thirteenth-century palace of El Mechouar. She teaches at the girls' high school in Sidi bel Abbès, less than a hundred kilometers from Tlemcen, but she has never before been here. It isn't easy for a woman to travel without an escort; Gaston, whom she knows and trusts, offered his services. In Sidi bel Abbès, she has lodged for almost three years with the Sultana family in an apartment building near the school. The youngest of four sisters, of whom two are long married, she considers herself (has considered herself!), at almost thirty-five, destined for a spinster's life: her older sister Jeanne, already in her mid-forties, of fragile health, lives with their eldest sister, Fée, and her husband in Constantine, and helps to manage their household. This is not what Lucienne wants for herself, yet she has grown, since turning thirty, increasingly resigned.

But now, but suddenly, this—the possibility of bliss unimaginable, unforeseen and unforeseeable. Is she imagining this? Is he? No suggestive word has been spoken between them. But they are animals; their bodies speak.

Who could deny them a happiness that feels ordained by God? That it will displease, even shock—they are prepared for this. Explaining their situation to the Church, they will seek and be granted the Vatican's blessing, after which there'll be nothing more to be said. That they are joyous together, that they belong together, that this is the world as it should be, two eternal, mythic lovers in the country of their conjoined future—the certainty that this love is their life's masterpiece—of this memory Gaston will write, years later, "Since then, the spring for me is a landscape of flowers, in the middle of which rises a minaret, and happiness is to walk in this landscape, or anonymously in a crowd, a crowd clad in burnous, with Lucienne on my arm, as she was that day, when everyone took her for my wife."

Bliss is anonymous in the crowd; bliss is blessed by God. Where they are known, their noble purity appears less sure. Because Lucienne is more than a decade older, certainly, though not quite old enough to be his mother. But not chiefly for this reason. Rather, because she is almost his mother, might have been his mother: because she is his mother's youngest sister, the cosseted baby of the family, the prettiest one, mysteriously unmarried in her thirties. (Lest anyone be inclined here to elide the facts: she was his aunt, theirs an incestuous relationship.) And while the two of them will never question their union—they consider it divine, all the more so once the Vatican issues, in their names, a written dispensation, licensing their love—they come to understand that their familial relationship is best left unmentioned. "We are cousins," they will say vaguely, upon occasion; but Lucienne will never tell anyone, not even her children, that she, as a girl, dandled infant Gaston upon her knee.

They believe as much in their country as in their love. Their faith is passionate, and they dream not simply of building a life but of building it *in this place*, in Algeria, specifically in Algiers, their beautiful city by the sea, where they are at home—in Bab el Oued, in Frais-Vallon, in Bouzareah, in Mustapha, in El Biar, on the Chemin des Sept Merveilles in Telemly, where Lucienne's parents ran the restaurant . . . as far as Blida, where he was born, or L'Arba, where Tata Baudry, aunt to them both, is midwife to all. As far as Constantine, home to her sisters Fée and Jeanne; as far as Oran, home to his sister Yvonne and her husband, Léon; as far as Tlemcen, beautiful Tlemcen. They call each other, tenderly, "Aïni"—"my eye," "my source," "my flower," "my choice"—and with that name evoke not only their feelings for each other but the very place these feelings are first expressed, beneath the almond blossoms on the hillside above Tlemcen. For them, as for Abu Madyan, Exemplar of the Seekers, all is God and God is all: themselves, their love, their land, the light.

Ultimately, though: the holy city does not belong to them, nor they to it; it never has. Just as their love is in the eyes of others an abomination, so too the country does not belong to them, has never belonged to them—though they will fail, for so long, to understand this. History unfolds beyond their small lives, before, around, and after them, implacable, enduring. And the cost of their illicit love, and the cost of their forefathers' sins, will be for them and their children to be cast from that illusory paradise, to wander the earth, belonging nowhere.

"We would surely die from grieving and yearning out of separation from You, / Yet in reality Your essence is within us," hymned Abu Madyan, almost a thousand years ago. They, too, carry the source within them. But for their children, cast into a windblown century without God, where is there to be but alone and unseen, anonymous in the crowd? Who will carry us back to a place that lives only in the vast imaginary? "Do you not see how a caged bird, oh youth, / Breaks into song when it recalls its ancestral home?"

As noted in the front of this book, this is a work of fiction. But the Cassar family's movements hew closely to those of my own family. My father's parents were born and raised in Algeria, which was a French colony from 1830 to 1962, when the country gained its independence following an undeclared but brutal war (1954–62). The *harkis* were the indigenous Algerians who fought on the side of the French in that war, and who were forced to leave their homeland for France, along with the colonizers, known as *pieds-noirs*.

TUNISIA (1881–1956) AND Morocco (1912–56) were French protectorates; and from 1923 to 1946, Lebanon and Syria were under French mandate. (In addition, French West Africa was a federation of eight states that included Senegal and Mauritania, and French Equatorial Africa was made up of four states, including Chad and Congo.)

IN JUNE 1940, the Germans invaded France. An armistice was signed and Maréchal Pétain, eighty-four at the time and a celebrated veteran of World War I, was made the leader of the collaborationist government based in Vichy. General Charles de Gaulle made a famous speech on BBC Radio on June 18, 1940, inviting his compatriots to join him in England and form the Free French government.

FROM JUNE 1940 to December 1942, the French navy was out of combat. In November 1942, Admiral François Darlan of the Vichy government signed a pact with U.S. general Dwight Eisenhower in Algiers that brought the French navy and all of the French overseas territories (including in Africa and Indochina) over to the Allies. Thereafter, Algiers became the capital of de Gaulle's Free French government.

GASTON CASSAR, a naval officer before and during World War II, was an alumnus of the École Polytechnique, an elite French engineering school whose graduates are referred to as "X."

SALONICA, NOW THESSALONIKI, is a port in Greek Macedonia, important for Mediterranean trade since its founding in the fourth century B.C. It was, from 1492 until World War II, one of the most important centers of Jewish life in Europe. In 1943 the Germans deported forty thousand of Salonica's forty-three thousand Jews to Auschwitz, where almost all of them died.

ACKNOWLEDGMENTS

Some books take a lifetime to write and could not be completed without support and assistance from many quarters, including from other books. In his retirement in the 1970s, my grandfather Gaston Messud wrote, for my sister and me, a memoir of his and our grandmother's life between 1927 and 1946. Reading parts of that memoir twenty years ago, was, for me, the beginning of this project. (I read all of it, well over a thousand handwritten pages, only in 2017.)

From 2009 to 2015, I had the great good fortune to teach in the MFA Program at Hunter College CUNY—thanks to Peter Carey—and had over the years generous help from some of the program's remarkable writers (in their capacity as Hertog Research Fellows), among them Fatin Abbas, Rebekah Barnett, Nora Lewontin-Rojas, and Alex Richardson. At Harvard, the amazing Marie Emmanuelle Thomas Hartness offered invaluable assistance with historical research, along with kindness, wisdom, and precious friendship. (I haven't stuck strictly to the historical record; any historical lacunae or errors are my own.)

Professor James Engell and Dean Robin Kelsey at Harvard enabled me to take an unpaid leave to work on the book in 2022 when I despaired of ever finishing it. Particular thanks to Jorie Graham and colleagues in Creative Writing, past and present, to Lauren Bimmler and Case Kearns, and to my students over the past decade, as well as to the staff of the Harvard Libraries. Special thanks also to Daphna Shohamy and the Zuckerman Institute at Columbia University, where I was writer in residence in 2022.

I'm enormously grateful to my publishers in the USA and the UK—I feel very lucky to work with Jill Bialosky, Drew Weitman, Louise Brockett, and the team at Norton; and with Ursula Doyle, Zoe Hood, and the team at Fleet. Special thanks to Michael Taeckens. There aren't words for my gratitude to Sarah Chalfant, Andrew Wylie, Rebecca Nagel, and Luke Ingram of the Wylie Agency.

Heartfelt thanks to many friends for immeasurable gifts, including holding long conversations, making thrilling art, writing letters, reading drafts, spurring laughter, and offering respite and light in dark times— among them Shefali Malhoutra, Sheila Gallagher, Mark Gevisser, Ira Sachs, Homi Bhabha, Mary Bing, Itamar Kubovy, Melissa Franklin, Susanna Kaysen, John Daniels, Jill Abramson, Diana Weymar, Sylvia Brownrigg, Susan Dackerman, the late and much missed Louise Glück, Barbara Hoogeweegen Prideaux and Charles Prideaux, Bob and Peg Boyers, Leah Stewart, and Amitava Kumar.

I owe my family everything—those who've gone before and yet accompany me on the journey, and those whose lives daily make mine worth living: Elizabeth, Vasya, Beatrice, Sasha, Max—and Livia, Lucian, and James, always. *You are not alone, the poem said, in the dark tunnel.*[*]

[*] From "October" by Louise Glück.